His feverish lips
whispered his desire. . . .

Brandon's arms tightened around her, not gentle now, but harsh, demanding, staking the claim they both knew she would not deny. One last quiver of alarm ran through Celia's body. Could she let this happen again with a man who had never offered a single promise . . . a single sweet word of love?

Then his mouth was hard on hers. His tongue became a weapon of assault, driving away even the will to reason. She felt his hands run down her back, bold and insolent, undoing the little buttons on her blouse; felt the searing warmth of probing fingers, burning through the sheer fabric of her chemise; felt the sinewy strength of his body, taut and relentless as he drew her to her knees beside him on the sand. . . .

*Introducing a new
historical romance by Joan Wolf*

DESIRE'S INSISTENT SONG CARRIED THEIR PASSION THROUGH THE FLAMES OF LOVE AND WAR . . .

The handsome Virginian made Lady Barbara Carr shiver with fear and desire. He was her new husband, a stranger, wed to her so his wealth could pay her father's debts, an American patriot, sworn to fight Britain's king. But Alan Maxwell had never wanted any woman the way he wanted this delicate English lady. And a hot need ignited within him as he carried Barbara to the canopied bed, defying the danger of making her his bride tonight . . . when war could make her his enemy tomorrow. . . .

Coming in July from Signet!

MOONWIND

Susannah Leigh

A SIGNET BOOK

NEW AMERICAN LIBRARY

NAL BOOKS ARE AVAILABLE AT QUANTITY DISCOUNTS
WHEN USED TO PROMOTE PRODUCTS OR SERVICES.
FOR INFORMATION PLEASE WRITE TO PREMIUM MARKETING DIVISION,
NEW AMERICAN LIBRARY, 1633 BROADWAY,
NEW YORK, NEW YORK 10019.

SIGNET TRADEMARK REG. U.S. PAT. OFF. AND FOREIGN COUNTRIES
REGISTERED TRADEMARK—MARCA REGISTRADA
HECHO EN CHICAGO, U.S.A.

SIGNET, SIGNET CLASSIC, MENTOR, PLUME, MERIDIAN AND NAL BOOKS
are published by New American Library,
1633 Broadway, New York, New York 10019

First Printing, May, 1986

1 2 3 4 5 6 7 8 9

PRINTED IN THE UNITED STATES OF AMERICA

Burma, April 1889

Sixteen was definitely more interesting than fifteen.

Celia St. Clair stretched out the pointed toes of her new white kid slippers, delighting in a froth of snowy dimity that flared up around her ankles. It was barely nine o'clock, but already the day had turned warm, and she could feel little prickles of moisture forming on her forehead. Yes, it was much more fun to be a day older than yesterday—just a single day!—and draw up her hair for the first time in a Psyche knot on top of her head and wear her skirts to the floor.

Well . . . *almost* to the floor.

Celia laughed, a light sound that echoed the silvery tinkle of pagoda bells on the hillside across the river. Here in the semitropics of Burma, where sharp seeds from the grasses on the *maidan* had a nasty way of catching at trailing hems, skirts were an inch shorter than those in the fashion magazines from Paris, and the elegant moirés and silk-backed satins her heart hungered for were rarely seen except on occasional cold, misty nights in winter. Still, it was better than being stuck in little-girl dresses with her booted ankles fully exposed—or worse yet, she thought with a grimace, in opaque white stockings and round-toed black slippers with black straps across her ankles!

If only she were a little more . . . well, more *rounded* in the chest.

Sighing, Celia glanced down at the heart-shaped neck of

her new dress, prettily trimmed in pale blue ruffles to bring out the highlights in her soft gray eyes. If only she were more like Mama. Mama had such a splendid figure, with a tiny waist swelling into a bosom that was almost, but not quite, formidable, and slender hips that gave way to a fashionably small bustle in back.

"Don't worry, mouse," Serena St. Clair would tell her daughter with a laugh whenever Celia became too impatient. "You'll grow up soon enough. You're just a late bloomer—like I was. Enjoy being a child while you can."

Enjoy being a child? Celia wrinkled her nose at the very idea, though she knew it was unfair to blame Mama too much. After all, Mama must be forty, well past the age when such things mattered anymore. She could hardly be expected to remember how anxious a young girl was to become a woman. In the meantime, fortunately, Sin-Sin had turned out to be an excellent seamstress, and the ruffles she sewed on her young mistress's bodice, inside as well as out, gave the impression of ripening curves that were not yet there. Any woman looking at her would know, of course—women had a way of sensing such things, especially in an attractive rival—but the unwary male eye would be deceived.

Celia smiled as she leaned back and propped her feet up on an overstuffed wicker footstool, newly recovered in blue chintz after the long, damp winter that had left everything smelling of mildew. The stagnant heat was already making itself felt, and the punkah, flapping halfheartedly in the center of the ceiling, barely stirred the dusty air. Soon, green bamboo screening would be lowered around the veranda, shutting out the sunlight, but for now the room was open to the outside and she could see the Irrawaddy drifting by at the edge of long sloping gardens.

A clumsy Indian barge floated on the muddy current, its rowers with their large, crudely carved oars already lethargic in the heat. Nearer by, sampans crawled along the shore, and a pair of white-sailed yachts skimmed past, showing the superiority of Her Majesty's officers over the half-primitive people they had conquered and ruled. In the foreground, the vivid colors of an English garden, not yet parched by summer sun, were so intense they almost seemed to clash. Enormous crimson hollyhocks looked even brighter against the dazzling yellow of phlox, and long dirt paths were edged with larkspur and sweet-scented petunias in shades of red and pink. As the season advanced, the flowers would wither, and the *mali*, with timeless patience, would dig them up, replacing them with balsams and cockscombs and zinnias, which in turn would die and be replaced by more of the same.

Celia stared idly at the garden for a moment, caught up in thoughts far more intriguing than the exotic beauty of the landscape. Deceive the male eye, indeed! There was only *one* male eye she was interested in deceiving—and she had made a good start that morning.

They had had an early visitor, young Schuyler Maarten, the son of Willem Maarten, a wealthy planter who had been their nearest neighbor for as long as Celia could remember. She had been surprised, an hour earlier, to spot his tall, lean form strolling up from the stables, though even at that distance she had recognized him instantly. There was a confidence in his step that was almost a swagger—a buoyancy that would have seemed arrogant in anyone less gay and charming. He had paused at the base of the veranda steps, glancing up, expecting, Celia knew, nothing more than the little girl he had always seen there before.

That he saw something quite different this time was satisfyingly apparent from the look that widened his blue eyes.

"Why, Celia." Surprise dissolved into a slow, easy smile. "What a charming dress. And a new hairdo, too. Can it be you're all grown up?"

I've been "all grown up" for a long time, Celia thought rebelliously—only you never noticed! But young as she was, she had already learned that men were rarely attracted to women who spoke their minds.

"How good to see you, Skye," she said, keeping her voice appropriately playful. "Especially today. It's my birthday—or did you know? Perhaps that's why you came over so early. To bring me your best wishes."

"And you think I didn't?" His eyes brightened with amusement. "Ah, Celia, what a heartless little creature you're turning out to be. Have you so little faith in men? Already? At your age? Of course I came to bring you my best wishes—and to give you these." He drew a bouquet of scarlet hibiscus out from behind his back and extended it toward her. "An unworthy gift, I'm afraid. Lovely as they are, these blossoms do not begin to match the loveliness of the grown-up young lady I see before me."

He was laughing as he spoke, but there was something curious in his voice, a kind of vibrating softness Celia had never heard there before, and for an instant she was too confused to respond. Then, delighted, she reached out and caught up the bouquet, burying her face in it to hide the beginnings of a very un-grown-up blush.

"Skye, how thoughtful! Did you really bring these for me?" The dark green leaves tickled her nose, and to her embarrassment, Celia felt her heart begin to beat outrageously fast. As long as she could remember, she had been afraid of old Willem Maarten, a bushy-browed, harsh-mannered man, but Skye with his golden hair and lithe figure had always seemed a young god to her. A god who, with the advantage of six years in age—and dozens in sophistication!—had never seemed to notice her . . . until today.

She looked up to see that he was smiling.

"Why, Celia," he said lightly, "can it be you doubt me?"

Celia caught the teasing in his voice and laughed. "I do indeed, Skye Maarten. For all your pretty words, these flowers look suspiciously like the ones that grow in our own garden. Besides, you could hardly have ridden all the way over here in this heat without their wilting. I think you picked them just a minute ago, on your way up the path."

"Caught, am I?" He grinned infectiously. "Well, then, I confess—I left my horse at the stable and was walking up to the house when I saw the *mali* with his watering can, nursing those English flowers your mother struggles to keep every summer. 'It is the missy-sahib's birthday,' he told me—and very excited he was about it, too. I think he has a soft spot in his heart for you, pretty Celia. 'She is sixteen today.' I could hardly let an occasion like that go by without some gesture"—he nodded toward the flowers— "however inadequate."

Celia tried to laugh, but that strange, disturbing undercurrent had crept into his voice again, and she did not quite succeed.

"Then you were just pretending. You didn't remember at all."

"I didn't," he admitted. "But I will remember next time. April 11—a date that will be engraved forever on my heart."

"The seventh," Celia snapped back. "Today is April 7." Then, catching the sparkling highlights in his eyes, she was at last able to laugh the way she had wanted to before.

"The seventh—I *will* remember, Celia." Skye lounged casually against the veranda post, finding himself unexpectedly absorbed in the charming vision he saw in front of him. He had always been fascinated by young girls just on the verge of womanhood, especially when they were good-looking.

On impulse, he leaned forward, his voice a deliberate caress. "I chose the hibiscus because I remembered what a tomboy you used to be, and I thought the flaming scarlet would suit your spirit. If I had known how lovely—and how soft—you were going to look, I would have selected something more feminine. Creamy frangipani perhaps, with its sweet perfume . . . or dainty wild orchids from the branches of a tree."

His eyes darkened challengingly, toying with Celia's innocence, and she felt the warmth rise to her cheeks again. Then, as if sensing her confusion, he turned back into the casual friend of the family come to pay a call. His behavior was scrupulously proper—still, there was something in the way he looked at her, something distinctly unsettling, and Celia was not sure whether she was disappointed or relieved when he finally took his leave to join her father in the study.

The wide double doors were open, as always in the hot season, and the voices of the two men drifted back to Celia where she sat in her wicker chair on the veranda. She was aware of what they were talking about, aware too that in a way it affected her, yet she could not coax her mind to dwell on it as she ran over every look, every smile, every inflection in her memory, replaying them again and again, even after Skye was gone. She had placed the flowers on a low table beside her, not wanting to stain her new dress, but she could not resist reaching out every now and then to run her fingers over the edges of the fragile petals.

Skye Maarten. Handsome, golden, wonderfully dazzling Skye Maarten. It seemed to her at that moment that she had loved him all her life. She let her eyelids close, as they often did when she thought of him, and imagined what it would be like dancing with him for the first time at an elegant ball, with all the other couples pulling a little aside to give them room. How perfectly Skye's tallness would set off her petite grace; how ethereal her silvery-blond tresses would seem against his vibrant coloring; how achingly soft the wide bluish-gray eyes that gazed up into deep, almost violet blue.

"What a striking couple," everyone would say—and, oh, they would be right.

Celia kicked the footstool away and flipped her skirt with one hand, trying to show just the edges of a knife-pleated taffeta drop-skirt. She revealed a flash of ankle as she did, not at all modest, but it was a pretty gesture all the same, and she could not help liking the way it looked.

A slow, secret smile played with the corners of her lips as she thought about the time when she would see Skye Maarten again . . . and how accomplished she would be at flirting then.

Ian St. Clair paused in the shadowy doorway that led to the interior of the house. His daughter, engrossed in her own thoughts, had not yet noticed him, but he had spotted her the instant he stepped out of the study. And he had not failed to see the subtle way her lips were curling at the corners.

A faint scowl crossed his features as he glanced out at the sun-baked path dividing the garden symmetrically in two. A line of black ants, drawn out by the heat, threaded a twisting course along it. Behind, on the hills and fields surrounding the house, acres of rubber trees stretched out in even rows, shimmering in the sunlight. Soon it would be so scorching that the ground would burn, even through the thick soles of his boots, and metal tools would be too hot to touch. If he was going to get any work done, he had to get started now. But . . .

The scowl intensified, etching deep furrows in his brow. So young, he thought helplessly. This girl of his was still so young—yet not young enough for him to protect, the way he had when she was a little child. What was there about the business of being a father that made it harder instead of easier with each passing year?

Even as a toddler, Celia had had a crush on young Schuyler Maarten, following him around with flattering hero worship whenever he rode over on his pony. And even then, though Ian would not have shown his feelings by confessing it aloud, he had found the fact unsettling. Not that the boy wasn't handsome enough to turn any young girl's head, and graceful too—and not that he couldn't be charming when he wanted. But there had always been a sort of insolence about him, an arrogant high-handedness in his manner toward others, as if the expectation of

inheriting a title one day from his maternal grandfather
made him different from everyone else.

Still, Ian had not been unduly alarmed. For all that he
disliked the lad, and for all that he fretted over the attach-
ment that grew rather than diminished as Celia entered her
teens, he never worried that Skye would be flattered by her
crush and come courting. Old Willem Maarten might have
been a shifty rascal, but no one had ever called him stupid.
He had already been the largest landowner in the area
before his marriage, and his wife brought with her not only
the mystique of aristocracy but also a considerable fortune.
He knew his son could make a better match than Celia St.
Clair, the daughter of a Scotsman who had pulled himself
up by his bootstraps and did not possess a thing beyond the
land on which his trees were rooted.

Nor had Ian truly worried about an illicit dalliance.
Running his finger along the inside of his collar, Ian felt
the sweat that had begun to trickle down from a thatch of
sandy-gray hair. Give credit where credit was due, it
didn't look like the boy was trying to take advantage of his
neighbors' daughters. There had been rumors about native
girls, of course, and even—though it might be no more
than malicious gossip—sly insinuations about a fling or
two with one of the slender brown-skinned boys who
enjoyed a certain popularity in the area. That practice,
shocking as it might be in other places, was winked at
here, in a predominantly male society, and many of the
men, not wanting the complications of a mixed-blood
baby, openly bragged that they kept their "activities" to
their own sex, even after they were married. Unlike the
others, however, Ian had never managed to stomach the
idea. That a youth might want to test out his newfound
virility was one thing. Hadn't he felt the same way when
he was young and hot of blood? But the other . . . ?

He broke off the thought, turning his eyes from slender
rubber trees to the tepid brown water, placid now that the
breezes were dying. Burma had been home for so long, he
did not think he would be comfortable anywhere else. A

water buffalo waded through the spongy yellowish foam at the river's edge, letting the lazy current play against its legs and chest. A naked boy, about nine or ten, dived in after it, laughing and shouting as he bullied it back to the shore.

Dammit, there was no point worrying about what might or might not have been had things remained the same. The point was, they hadn't. Everything had changed two months ago when old Willem Maarten, with a bank loan just taken out and the money heavy in his pocket, had sat down for "a friendly game of poker." Gambling had always been his weakness, and that night was no exception. With little head for cards—and even less for liquor—he had lost everything within a few hours. In desperation, he threw the deed to his plantation on the table . . . and lost that too.

The next morning, unable to face what he had done, he shot himself. When his wife's embarrassed lawyers arrived a week later from Rangoon, they had been forced to tell her that he had run through not only his own inheritance but also hers. Nothing was left but debts.

Suddenly, Ian thought grimly, Celia St. Clair, with her modest expectations, was not such a bad catch after all.

He squinted into the glare, setting his shoulders in an unconsciously military posture. Celia, of course, would not see it that way. Celia would think that Skye had begun to notice her because she was growing up and getting prettier every day. And Serena would support her.

Serena . . .

Ripples of hot sunlight gave the garden an illusion of motion, almost as if the bright-hued flowers were laughing at him, just as *she* would laugh if she could hear the way he was fretting now. The garden was Serena's special pride, and because he loved her, Ian took pride in it too. In truth, it was a pretty place, full of color and studied grace, and it did his heart good to walk along the paths in the early-morning hours before the heat was up. He took great pains to hide his fondness, however, sensing in that soft-

ness something not quite masculine, not suited to his
sturdy pragmatism and dour Scottish background. It was
more seemly for a man to rejoice in the feel of the soil
after the monsoons, moist and rich as it trickled through
his fingers. Or the smell of rubber trees, ripe, pungent,
always there—a subtle undertone to the scent of flowers
and dry dust.

He turned his gaze back to his daughter, still seated on
her wicker throne, golden sunlight setting off the abundant
silvery crown of her hair. She made a guilelessly pretty
picture, framed by dark potted ferns and spidery orchids
dangling from the eaves. The frothy white of her dress was
reflected in the landscape: in the graceful pagoda on the
hillside across the river; in an egret poised motionless
against the muddy water; in that pair of sails, limp now,
barely flapping in the stagnant air. How like Serena she
looked. How very like the girl he had married . . . the
woman he loved with a quiet distraction he could never put
into words.

Ian could still remember that moment he had first seen
her, an image as sharp and poignant in his mind as if it had
happened yesterday. She had been standing on a northern
English hillside, up to her knees in blowing grasses and
wildflowers, and white-blond hair had whipped around her
fragile face, giving her a fey quality that had taken his
breath away and captured his heart forever. For the first
time in his well-ordered life, Ian St. Clair had forgotten to
be cautious, and all thoughts of the sturdy, sensible wife
he had journeyed from the eastern reaches of the Indian
Empire in hopes of finding had vanished from his mind.
He had known then, without understanding, that he wanted
this lovely elfin creature—wanted her more than he had
ever wanted anything, or anyone, in his life—and if he
could not have her, he would accept no one else.

That she was already pregnant with another man's child
had not distressed him overmuch. Ian had never had any
illusions about himself. He was a short man, stocky, but
powerful of build, with thick sandy hair that curled too

much to be fashionable and features that were rigid rather
than strong. No one had ever called him handsome. Certainly no one could call him rich. Had Serena not been
frightened and alone, abandoned by the lover whose promises had come to naught, she would never have looked at
him, much less considered marrying him, and he knew it.
He was not too stubborn—or too proud—to take her however he could get her.

Even now, more than twenty years later, it still made
him bristle to think of the scoundrel who had used her so
badly. A distant cousin, gossip said at the time, with
enough wealth to do what he wanted—but not enough
backbone to stand up to his family and marry the girl he
claimed to love. And all because she had been born on the
"wrong side of the blanket."

Well, be that as it may. Ian shrugged off the thought.
The boy had been a cad, but he had been a fool too, and
his loss was Ian's gain. Ian had married Serena three
weeks after he met her, just time to post the banns, and
taken her away on the first ship to the Orient. When she
had lost the child she was carrying, he had grieved, truly
and deeply, not only for her pain but also for the stillborn
boy who would have been his son. They had waited many
years for another, a girl who was to be their only heir.
When she came, Ian doted on her shamelessly—and quite
characteristically, though he would have died before he
admitted it—pampering her the way he pampered her delicate, beautiful mother.

They had had a good life, he and Serena. At least it had
been good for him, and he thought good for her too. He
had made a modest success of the plantation, giving her
every necessity and more than a handful of luxuries, and if
she did not truly love him in a romantic way, he knew she
cared deeply and was grateful for the life he had given her.

But he knew, too, in that secret part of his heart he
rarely explored, that it was not the life she would have
chosen for herself. And it was not what she wanted for her
daughter.

The light had begun to change, whitening subtly as midday approached, and the shadows on the veranda seemed to grow darker, half-hiding Celia as she curled up in the chair, her legs tucked under her like a little girl. She had pulled a blossom out of the bouquet and was holding it up to her face, the brightness of the petals bringing out a pink flush in her lips and cheeks.

So like Serena, he thought again. And yet so different too.

He studied her face in the shifting light, intrigued that such a thoroughly unique creature could be a part of Serena and himself. There was an earthiness about the girl that her mother had never had, a kind of strength that made her porcelain-doll prettiness more provocative than delicate. Too much of Ian's Scottish blood flowed through her veins for her features to be called dainty. Her brow was wider than Serena's, her gray eyes the same color but larger, her nose straighter, her chin squarer, with a hint of a cleft at the center and a decided inclination to tilt upward, especially when she wanted her own way. As for those lips . . .

Ian frowned as he wondered what trick of nature had painted them so round and red. Certainly Serena had never looked like that. The child was barely sixteen, yet already her mouth was full and expectant, her lips half-parted, as if to smile or pout or . . .

No, she was not like Serena at all. Serena had loved even her cousin with a young, romantic heart. When Celia loved, it would be with her body as well. Ian had not missed that coquettish little trick she played with her skirts, flicking them up so they would billow around her ankles. She had not done it well, not this time—but how long would it be before she learned? And when she did, men were certain to notice.

Men like Schuyler Maarten.

Well, at least he would not have to worry about that for a while. Ian stiffened his spine, Scottish practicality reminding him that half the workday was gone and he had accomplished nothing. Young Skye, to his surprise, was showing himself to be made of sterner stuff than his father. In fact, he had stopped by that morning only to inform Ian, along with the rest of the neighbors, that he was off to see the world. He would not be back, he said, until he had at least made a stab at recouping the family fortune.

Not that he would succeed, of course. The boy didn't have it in him to do anything big, not on his own, though Ian had to admit it was game of him to try. But whatever happened—win, lose, or draw—he had to be gone at least a year. More likely two or three.

And that was a year or two in which Ian St. Clair did not have to worry about keeping him away from an impressionable—and increasingly marriageable—young daughter.

Celia raised a quizzical brow as she turned to see her father standing in the doorway. Just as Ian had with her a moment before, she read the expression on his face, and she knew what he was thinking. "Why, Papa," she teased. "What on earth has made you so grumpy? You look like a bear who had his pot of honey taken away from him."

"Humph!" Ian kept his features stern, determined not to let her get around him as she usually did. He did indeed look like a bear, and he knew it. "I suppose you've been listening at keyholes again and heard everything that's going on. Yes, and judging by that smug look on your face, you think young Maarten is going to come back covered with glory after his daring exploits. And be so smitten with you that he'll ask for your hand when he does!"

Celia ignored his gruffness. "Why should I listen at keyholes when the door was open and you took no pains to lower your voice? Besides, you're being unreasonable about Skye, and you know it. It *is* reckless of him to go off like this with no definite plans. I admit that. But anyone else would be sitting around crying and saying what a rotten trick fate had played on him. At least Skye is doing something about it!''

"The boy *is* showing more gumption than I expected," Ian conceded grudgingly.

"And more interest in me?" Celia looked up through thick golden-brown lashes. "Face it, Papa, Skye is beginning to notice me—even if you don't want him to. He came here first, you know, before going to talk to any of the other neighbors. And he brought me these for my birthday." She picked up the flowers, drawing them briefly against her breast. "Wasn't that sweet of him?"

"Clever, too," Ian grumbled, "to get them over here in such good condition. He must have ridden like the wind to keep them from wilting."

Celia laughed. "Of course he didn't, Papa. You're looking like a bear again! You know as well as I that he stole them from our flowerbeds. Well, not 'stole' exactly—the *mali* gave them to him. But don't worry. It didn't ruin your precious garden to have a few blossoms cut out of it."

"Not my garden. Your mother's. It's a lot of nonsense as far as I'm concerned, trying to keep English flowers growing a few months out of the year. But she was raised on a fancy estate, you know, with gardens all around, and it makes her happy. I put up with it for her sake."

Celia wrinkled her nose speculatively. She did *not* know, in fact, for her mother's past had never been discussed in front of her. She had heard vague allusions about it from time to time, but the subject always seemed to change, sometimes quite abruptly, when she came into the room.

Still, this hardly seemed the time to press questions that had never been answered before.

"There you go, being grumpy again. And silly, too! Do you think I can't see you from my window, walking through the gardens at dawn, before anyone else is out? Come now, Papa—confess! You love the flowers as much as Mama. Only you're afraid to admit it, for fear it will spoil your image."

"Don't be impertinent, mouse! That's no way to talk to your elders."

"Mouse, indeed!" Celia straightened up in mock indignation. "It was all very well to call me that when I was a baby, but I'm too grown-up for childish nicknames."

"Ah, so you don't like it when I call you 'mouse.' Is that it?"

His eyes glowed, and Celia knew he was remembering the way he used to tease her when she was a little girl, pinching her nose and making funny squeaking noises when she started to giggle. She had always been aware that she was the only one, even including Mama, who could get him to let down his guard and laugh as if he were a boy again. It was one of the strongest bonds between them.

"No, I don't like it—just as you don't like the flowers!" she challenged, and was rewarded with a hint of pink in his cheeks. Poor darling Papa. How funny he was when he tried to hide his affection behind that stuffy manner.

She laughed as she set the flowers back on the table and stretched out her hands.

"I'm not a little girl anymore. I know you'd like to keep me that way, and I love you for it, for you are very dear—and very good—to little girls. But it won't work. I *am* growing up. There's nothing you can do to stop me."

Ian threw her a gruff look, more sheepish than he realized. "You know me too well, daughter."

Celia laughed as she squeezed his hand. She *did* know her father. Better than he knew himself. As long as she could remember, she had been able to twist him around her little finger, teasing and coaxing, wheedling, crying if she had to, until she got what she wanted. This would be no exception. Oh, he might rant and rave—he might throw out all sorts of terrible, dire predictions—but she was going to have her way in the end.

When Skye Maarten came back, she was going to be his bride.

Shanghai, January 1890

It was the first day of the new year, but that fact meant little in a city that reckoned time by the ancient Chinese calendar. It meant even less in the dingy room in which Brandon Christopher found himself.

An opium den.

Brandon's nostrils flared with distaste at the faintly sweetish odor that came from somewhere in the back. He had paused briefly at the base of a short flight of steps leading down from outside and was squinting into the dimness.

The place appeared to be a small antechamber, perhaps eight or ten feet wide, with an unpainted wooden table and three-legged stool on one side, and a small iron stove on the other. In the center of the rear wall, a low narrow door was flanked by a pair of casementless windows, half-screened with grimy beaded curtains that partially obscured the rooms beyond.

Behind one of them, the lanterns had been turned up, and Brandon could see a group of Chinese men crowded excitedly around a high table covered with straw matting. The brittle clatter that punctuated their low murmurs told him they were playing fan-tan, and he knew without venturing closer that the keeper of the table had just taken a handful of ivory markers out of a pile in the center and covered them with a bowl while the bets were being placed. When the bowl was lifted, nimble fingers would count them out in groups of four, leaving a remainder of one, two, three—or none at all. Those who had wagered on the correct number would collect their winnings, the markers would be placed back in the center of the table, and the spirited action would begin again.

Behind the other beaded curtain, however, the room was dark and still. Brandon hesitated, staring for a moment in that direction, then headed toward it.

As he approached, he could see that there were two men in the room. One of them, an elderly Chinese with a long gray beard, was lounging on a narrow wooden bunk, an unlighted opium pipe dangling from his fingers as he stared up at spidery cracks that crisscrossed the dingy ceiling. The second man busied himself with a large brass pan from which he had just begun to pour a dark pastelike substance through rag filters into a woven basket lined with bamboo paper.

In spite of himself, Brandon could not resist watching. The process of preparing opium for sale, he knew, was a time-consuming operation. First the spherical ball of raw opium, about six inches in diameter, was cut in half and the interior removed from its casing of dried leaves and poppy trash. Next it was boiled in pure spring water, after which it was allowed to soak overnight, then strained and boiled again. The scum, which formed continually on the surface, was removed with a feather and placed in another pan at the side. When the entire process was finished, the ball might yield three or four pints of high-quality opium. The dregs and scum were not wasted, for they would be boiled later with the washings of the pan and sold in that inferior state to the poor.

The man had nearly finished straining the opium when a slight sound drew his attention toward the beaded ropes. His eyes narrowed just slightly as he caught sight of Brandon, but he recovered quickly.

"You likee—" he began, a sly, greedy look coming into his eyes.

Brandon cut him off before he could go on, telling him

in fluent if heavily accented Mandarin what he had come
for.

This time the man showed no change of expression.
Moving slowly, he removed the rag filter from the basket
and set it on top of a large brass pot so the valuable
drippings would not be lost. Then, without comment, he
led the way out of the room.

Brandon followed as the man guided him down a long,
narrow hallway. The sharp click-click of his leather boots
contrasted with the softer padding of felt-soled slippers.
When they reached the end, the man paused, gesturing
toward an open doorway.

Brandon had never been in an opium den before, but the
place seemed hauntingly familiar, as if he had seen it long
ago . . . or experienced it in the dim reaches of a half-
forgotten nightmare. It was a low-ceilinged room, uncar-
peted like the hall outside, with no door other than the one
through which he had entered, and only a few boarded-up
slits of windows high in the walls. A solitary lantern
dangled from the ceiling, but it was so caked with soot it
gave almost no illumination. What little light there was
came from the flames of opium lamps glowing eerily in the
darkness.

The smoke was denser than he had expected, a gray-
white fog that floated through the room, and his eyes took
a moment to adjust. Wooden bunks, four feet wide, were
arranged in double tiers along the walls on three sides, and
on these, figures slowly came into focus, groups of men
lounging together in twos and threes. Some reclined on
their sides, placidly puffing at long pipes; others lay back
motionless, their bodies sprawled out in grotesque pos-
tures, their heads propped up on hard wooden pillows. An
assortment of unmatched couches, also constructed of wood
with the same awkward headrests, were lined up on the
fourth wall and scattered at other places throughout the
room. The quiet was broken only by the rhythmic rasping
of men asleep and the hissing and bubbling of burning
opium.

The attendant had slipped out of the room when Brandon entered, ducking into the hall. Now he returned and sidled up to him as if to be of service, but Brandon waved him back. He had already spotted what he was looking for.

The boy they had told him about at the hotel, the one the desk clerk described with such ghoulish detail, was lying by himself on a couch at the far end of one of the side walls. Brandon felt his body stiffen, and for a moment he considered turning around and walking out of there. Then, thinking better of the impulse, he went over and forced himself to look down.

The waxen pallor of the boy's skin was startling in the yellowish glow of the lamp beside his bed. The hair that spilled around his face, longish, slightly curling like a girl's, must once have been a shiny strawberry blond; now it was dulled to the color and texture of old straw. That he was white hardly came as a surprise. Nationality meant little in a place like this, and even the innate suspicion of the Chinese for the foreigner was muted by drugs. That he was known only by his first name was also not surprising. Identities were frequently lost in opium dens.

If he had had to guess the boy's age, Brandon thought grimly, he would not have succeeded. A soiled Chinese shirt, unfastened in front, fell away to reveal a painfully emaciated chest in which every rib could be counted, and the veins on his neck stood out like an old man's. His skin, though unlined, was drawn tautly across his face, giving his head the look of a whitened skull. Yellow-green eyes stared out of it, not dull, as he had expected, but unnaturally bright and glassy.

Brandon leaned forward, drawn by some macabre impulse to gaze deeper into those haunting eyes. As he did, a slow shudder ran through him, and he drew back, feeling for an instant as if he had gazed into the eyes of Death itself.

The motion, subtle as it was, seemed to rouse the boy, and he stirred slightly, though it was clear he still had not seen Brandon standing in front of him. Turning his head, he raised a pale hand and beckoned limply to the attendant, who hurried over.

Brandon watched, sickened but unable to look away as the attendant began the elaborate preparations for smoking. He picked up the pipe, a two-foot length of bamboo blackened with age and use, and with a twisted length of wire he scraped away the residue from the red-clay bowl. This he collected in a special receptacle so it could later be mixed with the dregs and pan washings that were peddled to the poor.

When he had finished, the man turned his attention to cooking the opium. Taking up a small portion of the sticky black substance on the end of a long needle, he held it with a steady hand over the flame. After a minute or two, Brandon saw it begin to bubble, expanding until it was several times its original size. The dark color eased slowly into a bright golden brown, and the aroma grew noticeably sweeter.

Brandon felt suddenly nauseous, as much from the sight as the smell, and he took a clumsy step backward, detaching himself from that ugly scene. The shadows seemed to close in around him, and he had a sudden uncanny sense that eyes were on him, watching from all directions.

Not exactly rational, he reminded himself. Any other place in the Orient, he would have stood out boldly. Although no more than average height, he appeared taller than he was, and his shoulders were broad and powerfully built, giving him an aura of power. Dark auburn-red hair, worn carelessly long, was brushed back from his brow, and deep green eyes and strong chiseled cheekbones lent his face a rakish, romantic look. But here, in a roomful of men lost in opium dreams, it seemed unlikely that anyone was aware of his presence.

In fact, only one pair of eyes *was* watching. These belonged to a newcomer who had entered the room a few minutes after Brandon and was hovering just inside the door. He was almost painfully nondescript, easy not to notice, especially in that setting. His hair, while thinning, was still black, his skin sallow enough not to be noticeably Caucasian.

But his dark eyes were alert as he took in the scene.

So Brandon Christopher was here . . . in an opium den. His lips twisted into a thin smile as he mulled over what he knew about the man standing across the room from him.

Brandon Christopher. The grandson of old Levi Christopher, a scoundrel if there ever was one, but a man of courage and vision who had risen from poverty to a position of power on the eastern American seaboard. He had built his vast shipping empire on whaling and slaving, with no apologies for either, then sat white-haired and erect in his own pew in a Boston church for the last twenty years of his life, daring anyone, including the fire-tongued preacher, to call him to account for his sins.

Those final years, however, were reputed to be unhappy, for the old man was bitterly disappointed in his three sons and even more contemptuous of the men his daughters married. At his death, he shocked the world one last time by cutting them off entirely and dividing his fortune among his several grandsons. Brandon, always the favorite, had inherited the lion's share of not only the old fox's wealth but also his shrewdness.

Brandon had done his grandfather proud. In less than a decade he tripled and quadrupled his original stake, setting the groundwork for an empire of his own that rivaled anything the old man could have imagined. Then, bored with the rigid confines of his native Boston, he left everything in the hands of competent managers and set off to explore what his family referred to, with slightly pinched nostrils, as the "seamier" side of the world.

Now, so it was rumored, he was beginning to grow restless again. The challenges were fewer every year, more limited. Life was less exciting than before.

The attendant had just finished the tedious process of cooking the opium and was beginning to fill the pipe. Brandon, unaware of the watcher in the shadows, found that, for all his qualms, he still could not tear his eyes away. The man rolled the warmed drug several times around the red-clay bowl, then flattened it in the center and punctured it with the needle, just above the perforation that led into the stem. The boy turned over on his side, and the attendant placed the pipe in his fingers, helping him guide it over the flame, tilting it until the opium caught fire.

As Brandon watched tight-lipped, the boy took a single deep draft and released it slowly through his mouth and nostrils.

"Nasty stuff, that smoke," a voice said amiably in his ear. "I warn you, you'll be smelling it for days. It clings to the inside of your nose and throat, especially when you're not used to it. Makes your eyes tear too."

Brandon turned to see the stranger standing beside him. He was an inch or two taller, perhaps more, but he did not look it. There was a decided stoop to his shoulders, and his belly hung over his belt, giving him a middle-aged sag.

"It doesn't seem to have affected you," he remarked dryly. "Your eyes are clear enough."

If the man was offended, he did not show it. "It's even harder on the smokers, you know. At least at first. The stuff is damned strong. Acrid, too. You can tell the novices, most of them anyway. They cough like hell when they take a drag."

Brandon's eyes had slipped back to the boy, and the man, watching closely, sensed what was going through his mind. Clearly it was a long time since that one had been a novice. For an instant he was almost sorry he had chosen this method of approach. It had been so long, he had forgotten what it felt like, seeing something like this for the first time.

"I met him once," he said, keeping his voice casual. "About six months ago. A nice kid, clean-cut—kind of happy-go-lucky, if you know what I mean."

Brandon winced visibly. "Six months? My God! Does it always work that fast?"

The man laughed hoarsely. "I can see you don't know

much about opium. No, it rarely works like that. As a matter of fact, it *never* does—by itself. Usually it takes a few months, even a year, before the initial stage of euphoria wears off and addiction sets in. After that, it's a long way to something like this, which, by the way, doesn't always happen. I've known some addicts who've been hooked on the stuff for ten or twenty years and still manage to get to work every day. Lead relatively productive lives.''

"Then . . . ?'' Brandon glanced at the boy.

"Must have been sick already. Tuberculosis—that's my guess. It's not uncommon in the dens. Actually, the stuff seems to do some good. Many of 'em start taking it in the first place to relieve the cough.''

"And that makes it all right?'' Brandon looked at him with disgust. "You justify the whole thing that way? Because it's some kind of . . . medicine?''

The man made no effort to reply. He pulled out a pack of cigarettes, flicking the end against his hand, and held it out to Brandon. "Care for one? No? Well, you're wiser than I. Nasty habit. Wouldn't be surprised if the doctors told us one day it's as bad as the stuff those poor devils have in their pipes.''

He followed Brandon's gaze as it strayed back to the boy. There was a pack of cigarettes beside him, too, lying on the tray with the rest of his paraphernalia. Sometimes they smoked between bouts with the pipe, or refreshed themselves with a cup of tea to relieve the occasional nausea. But this one didn't seem to have the energy even for that.

"It's a pity,'' he drawled slowly, "the way they did it.''

Brandon stiffened slightly. "The way they *did* it?'' He stared down at the boy, sensing things he could not quite see; seeing them too, perhaps, but not acknowledging them. More than ever he wanted to turn around and walk away, but he knew he would not.

"They had to do something to make him want the drug.

He had quite a tidy sum of money with him. More at home, rumor has it, though he couldn't seem to get his hands on it. Probably in trust. At any rate, he had a decent amount of traveling money. To get him to part with it, they had to make sure he was hooked. The physical sensations aren't enough, not at first. What's important is the whole . . . uh . . . social milieu."

He hesitated, looking away briefly. When he turned back, his eyes had hardened.

"One of the effects of opium, they say—in the earlier stages—is an increase in sexual appetite. They made it all fun and games for him, capitalizing on the breakdown of natural inhibitions that occurs during smoking. Only their idea of fun, you see, was a little warped. They used him in more ways than one. When they were finished, he was . . . not quite a man, if you get what I mean."

Brandon had turned so pale his face was almost an echo of the boy's. The fleeting resemblance was uncanny, for their features were not dissimilar, though Brandon's hair was a darker, more intense red, his eyes deeper and greener.

"You bastard," he muttered through clenched teeth. "Doesn't he have trouble enough as it is? Do you have to go around spreading vicious stories—?"

"They aren't stories," the man replied coolly. "They are the truth." He took a deep puff of his cigarette, exhaling evenly through his nostrils, the way the boy had with the opium. Only when Brandon had calmed down did he go on.

"I do know how you feel, but there's nothing that can be done. His body is beyond help; he will be dead in a few days, if not sooner. And, God knows, you cannot ease his tortured soul. The kindest thing now is to let him die in peace." He saw Brandon's eyes flick hastily toward the still figure on the couch. "Don't worry that I talk so freely in front of him. He is beyond hearing. He is beyond even seeing that we are here."

Brandon sensed he was telling the truth, but something in those cold, even tones turned his stomach. How could any man stand there, seeing what he was seeing, and not react?

"Who are you?" he asked suddenly. "Who are you, and what the hell are you doing here?"

"Colonel Robert Quarrie, U.S. Army, retired." The man nodded brusquely as he snuffed out his cigarette in a receptacle on the tray. "And I am here because I followed you. I need your help."

"The devil you say!"

"An apt choice of words." Quarrie chuckled softly at the shocked surprise in Brandon's tone. "I'm never quite sure myself whether I'm fighting the devil or have made a pact with him. I wasn't lying before. You can't do anything to help that boy. He wouldn't have the strength to take a cure, even if he wanted it, which, incidentally, I doubt. But you *can* make sure that the men who brought him to this pay for what they did. And that they never have a chance to do it to anyone else."

He paused briefly, fixing Brandon with a penetrating gaze.

"You see, I'm a member of a well-organized effort to wipe opium growing, shipping, and trading off the face of the earth. We are looking for recruits, so to speak."

Brandon stared at him, frankly incredulous. "Do you seriously expect me to believe the United States Army is involved in an antiopium operation?"

"Hardly." Quarrie laughed. "At least not here in the Orient, where opium is legal. As a matter of fact, some of my fellow officers have managed to bulk up their purses quite nicely, investing in the trade themselves. That's one of the reasons I left. I'm still working for the government, but I'm involved in a special top-secret project—and if you decide not to join us, I'll expect you to give me your word you won't speak of this to anyone. The authorities have finally begun to worry about the amount of opium hitting the West Coast; it increases every year. The time to strike at the source is now, *before* it can become a major problem."

Brandon eyed the man warily. He had been too stunned at first to take in what he was saying; now his keen mind began to sort it out, and he had to admit it made sense. *If* Quarrie was telling the truth.

"But why would you want me?"

"We want someone who can work for us without appearing to do so. *Sub rosa*, so to speak. A man who can pass himself off as a drug smuggler, or better yet a pirate, and make the image stick. I'd do it myself, but I'm too well known in these parts. Besides . . ." He threw up his hands self-deprecatingly. "Look at me. Would anyone take me for a pirate? A man at the peak of his fighting form? You, on the other hand—"

Brandon laughed sharply. "That story has holes all the way through it, Quarrie. If you knew the first thing about me, as you claim, you'd know I'm as recognizable in certain circles as you are. I could never—"

"Ah, but you could . . . Mr. Christopher. You see, I do know all about you. That's precisely why I think you *would* be believable as a pirate."

"Really?" Brandon threw him a shrewd look. "Since you know so much, you must realize I have a considerable fortune at my disposal. Why would I risk my neck for the profits from a few opium deals?"

"Not a few—a great many. And rich men always want to be richer. That, I suspect, is a rule of nature. At least that's what everyone thinks, which, after all, is what counts in this case. Then, too, rich men have been known to grow bored for want of—how shall I put it?—a challenge."

"A challenge?" There was a sharp edge to Brandon's voice, and Quarrie sensed he had hit a nerve. He hastened to press his advantage.

"I can't guarantee you'll change the world if you take me up on this, but you might. Is that challenge enough? I can't even guarantee you'll be able to avenge that poor bastard lying there, half-dead already, but I'll give you a chance to try. I have to warn you, though . . ." A new light came into his eyes, a hot intensity that had not been there before. "This is going to be dangerous. The odds are better than fifty-fifty we'll both be dead before it's over. But if we're not—and by God, even if we are—chances are we'll leave the world better than we found it."

Brandon studied him for a long moment, gauging his sincerity and accepting it. The boy had stopped smoking now, lying still on his pallet, his eyes open, as if in death. Beyond help, as Quarrie had said. But what about the next boy—and the next?

"You want my answer now?"

"Of course not." Quarrie's voice was easy now, his manner relaxed. He had lit another cigarette, a red glow in the darkness. "Take a day or two to think it over, more if you want. I'll check back with you at your hotel. You're staying on the Bund, aren't you? At the Central."

He did not wait for an answer. Flicking his ashes on the tray, he turned up his collar against the outside chill and headed for the door. Just before he reached it, he turned.

"His name," he said, gesturing with the tip of his cigarette, "was Michael."

Brandon did not question his use of the word "was." The boy—the essence of him—already belonged to the past.

"I know."

"We have him."

Quarrie's eyes glittered as he beckoned to a shadowy figure skulking in a narrow doorway halfway down the street. The man who materialized was slight, with high Slavic cheekbones and a yellowish complexion that could have been almost any nationality.

"You seem very sure of yourself." His voice was raspy and lightly accented.

"I usually am," Quarrie replied complacently. He dropped the cigarette, grinding it out with his foot. "And this time, I know I'm right. I was there; you weren't. I saw the look on his face when I put the proposition to him."

"What makes you think we can . . . trust him?"

Quarrie chuckled. "What makes me think he won't decide to go into business for himself, you mean?"

"It is a temptation," the other man reminded him. "He'll be handling large quantities of opium. There's bound to be a certain . . . inclination to channel it in other directions. Great fortunes have been made on less than that."

"The man already *has* a great fortune. Have you forgotten?"

"Wealthy men can be tempted too. Have *you* forgotten? You said so yourself. That was why you thought he'd make a convincing pirate."

"Wealthy men *can* be tempted," Quarrie admitted. "But not this one. He doesn't need the money. Or want it. What he needs is . . . something else."

His eyes took on a faraway look as he stared down the long row of European buildings, all gray, lining each side of the street with a bleak sameness. *Something else*. The words amused him. An interesting way to put it.

He was smiling faintly as he turned back.

"I told you. I am sure of him. Brandon Christopher is ours."

The boy, Michael, died early the next morning. Brandon found his body outside in the alleyway shortly after sunrise when he went back to the opium den to check on him. The attendant had placed him there an hour before, while he was still breathing, so his restless spirit would haunt that narrow lane instead of the dim, stifling chamber in which he had spent the last weeks of his life.

A flash of rage shot through Brandon as he realized what they had done. But it passed quickly, replaced by a calm resignation he had not expected. Obviously they had given the boy enough opium to see him through—his face was placid and untroubled. What point was there railing at alien customs and superstitions, when it could not have mattered to young Michael where he died?

Brandon took the body for burial high on a nearby hillside. The act aroused no curiosity, for both men were white, and it was naturally assumed one would look after the other. And it had long been a Chinese custom to locate graves on the sloping banks of hills or mountains. "Our ancestors like being where they can keep an eye on us," a young Chinese once told Brandon with a grin. "Besides, the breezes there are cool. The view is pleasant. Why not?"

Why not, indeed? Brandon had agreed then, as he agreed now. He too would like his grave on a hillside when the time came. He would do as much for Michael.

He had hired bearers to carry the body up the rugged slopes, but he had not taken the time to have a wooden coffin made; the boy was wrapped instead in a bright silk banner, red, the color of good fortune. The air was unusually crisp, even for a winter's day, but the men were sweating profusely by the time they reached the site he had chosen. They laid down their load, expecting him to hand them a shovel and order them to get on with their work. Instead, he dismissed them, thanking each with an extra bonus of sycee, and turned to the task of burying the boy himself.

The earth was hard, but the exertion felt good, and Brandon dug the grave deeper than he had intended. The ring of the spade against the rocky soil had a sharp sound, and the air smelled clean, even with the sweet stench of opium still in his nostrils, as Quarrie had warned. Perspiration poured freely from his body, and he took off first his jacket, then his thin cambric shirt, letting an icy wind bite against his naked chest.

The sun was already well past its zenith when he finally finished mounding the dirt on the grave. He was aware, as he stood there one last moment, staring down at that freshly turned earth, of a sense of anger and helpless futility. He had done the best he could for the boy, but his best had been damn little. Cursing softly, he looked down, surprised to see blisters forming on his palms. How long had it been since he had done any manual labor? Since he had toiled with a pick and spade . . . or tugged at the sheets and halyards of a tall-masted clipper?

He arched his body, stretching the cramped muscles in his back and shoulders. He had intended to whittle a rough wooden cross out of a branch or piece of fallen wood, but looking around, he saw nothing suitable, and he gave up the idea with a shrug. It would have been an empty gesture anyway. Young Michael had died a most unchristian death. All the symbols in the world could not alter that.

Below him, the waters of the river, dark and serene now that they had left the town, meandered pleasantly through scattered fields and orchards. Brandon leaned on the handle of his shovel as he stared down at that timeless setting. The Chinese, so unfathomable in many ways, were right about one thing. If you had to leave someone behind, it was better to do it in a place like this.

He straightened, wincing slightly as he slung the shovel over his shoulder.

"Enjoy the view, Michael," he said softly. "Rest well."

The wind picked up as he made his way down the hill, but the cold was bracing, even though his jacket and shirt were still drenched with sweat. His hands felt raw against the rough handle of the spade. By God, it would be good to be on board ship again. Good to have his hands callused with honest work. Good to hoist a line and feel it creak and give beneath his strength.

Good to hoist a line . . .

Brandon paused, looking down at the town, now half an hour's walk away. The sun had just begun to set, and the first hints of pink shimmered along the horizon. He had not realized until that moment where his thoughts were taking him, yet he knew he should have. He had not dwelled on Quarrie all day, but obviously the man had been there, lingering just beyond the fringes of his consciousness.

What a sly dog! *Take as much time as you want*, he had

said. *Think it over*—and why not? He had known all along
what Brandon was going to decide.

But did he know *why*?

Brandon shifted the shovel to his other shoulder as he
continued down the dirt path. Had he guessed why a man
might be willing to do what he asked? Did he care? Or was
it enough to be sure he was going to have his way?

And have it he would. Brandon knew that now, as he
would have known before had he stopped to think it over.
Tomorrow, or the next day, when Quarrie dropped by his
hotel, he would hear the man's terms . . . and he would
agree to them.

By this time next week, he would be well on his way to
becoming a pirate.

Dusk had turned everything to a soft gray as he made
his way through the crowded back lanes of Shanghai,
heading for the Bund. The Chinese New Year was still
weeks away, but to his surprise, preparations for the festivities were well under way. Shop doors were open,
despite a distinct evening chill, and men and women hun-
kered just inside, chatting noisily with each other or calling out shrill greetings to friends across the way. Craftsmen,
their tools spread out on the pavement or on rickety wooden
tables along the walls, were still busy with their work,
taking advantage of the last rays of daylight.

Brandon caught an occasional glimpse of shop interiors
as he hurried past. Lanterns had been lit against the deepening shadows, and vivid red wall hangings glittered with
gold Chinese characters. The smell of bean paste and
ginger drifted out, of incense and jasmine tea, forming an
accent to the musky odor of the street. A pair of workmen
had stretched a red banner along the narrow lane, imped-
ing traffic as they painted out the good-luck messages that
were a part of every New Year's celebration.

In a small open courtyard just off the street, an old man
was putting the finishing touches on an elaborate large
tiger constructed entirely out of paper. Fascinated, as much
by the form as the skillful craftsmanship, Brandon stopped

to watch. It was an uncanny representation, not at all lifelike, yet somehow frighteningly real, with huge jaws open . . . ready to devour.

The Year of the Tiger.

Brandon's lips turned up grimly at the corners. The tiger with its timeless sense of mystery, its superhuman strength . . . its legendary ferocity in a fight. Exactly the image he himself was going to have to convey in the months—and years—to come.

The Tiger.

Impulsively he seized on the symbol, taking it for his own. It was, after all, exactly what he had in mind. An illusion of invulnerability—the threat of vengeance—a scourge to brave men and cowards alike. What more could he ask?

Taking a long, deep breath, he studied the paper image again, feeling the strength that seemed to flow out of it into his own body. Yes, the Tiger—it was perfect. When men spoke of him in days to come, they would not speak of Brandon Christopher, though there would be many who knew, or guessed, his real identity. They would speak of the Tiger.

And they would know what they were up against.

Macao, Some Weeks Later

Flashes of color exploded across the night sky as the Chinese of Macao ushered in their new year with a display of fireworks. A young girl with creamy golden skin and hair as black as jet paused briefly on the esplanade that curved around the tip of the Portuguese peninsula. High above her, a sudden burst of sound echoed like thunder, sending shivers up and down her spine.

Teresa Valdes was a product of the Orient. In her blood she carried the strengths—and weaknesses—of that part of the world. Her father, Sebastião Valdes, was a minor Portuguese trader, born and reared in the colony; her mother, a beautiful Eurasian of French and Chinese descent, had been one of his many mistresses. For the first seven years of her life, Teresa had known her father only by name, for Sebastião, disliking complications from his various unions, had dismissed his paramour the instant he discovered she was pregnant, shipping her off with a minimum of regret to nearby Hong Kong. After that, he made no effort to maintain contact, neither knowing nor caring what had happened to them. But Teresa, through her mother, had always been aware of where he was and what he was doing; aware, too, in some vague way, that he owed her something, though he was unwilling to acknowledge his debt.

Those early years, spent in crowded, rat-infested slums, were hard ones for both mother and daughter. The money

Sebastião had given his discarded mistress, though frugally managed, lasted barely until the child was born. After that, the woman struggled as best she could, earning loose change the only way she knew how, but her health had been broken by childbirth, and as it continued to deteriorate, things grew increasingly difficult. Even before she learned to walk, Teresa had already learned that life was not pretty, and begging and thievery—grasping and hanging on with both hands—were the only ways to survive in a world that knew neither gentleness nor pity.

A searing flash of white, intense but aborted, burst with a loud pop over the dark waters. Teresa's hand slipped up to her breast, resting for a moment on a heart that was beating much too fast. Ever since she was a little girl, she had always hated that night of the new year, with its jolts of light and noise. She was older now, she knew she was being foolish, but she could not forget the feeling that made her want to crawl under a narrow cot and clap her hands over her ears.

A hint of movement showed in the shadows behind her, and Teresa jerked her head back, searching the darkness. Was someone there? she asked herself nervously. A man? *The* man?

But that was ridiculous! Teresa forced a laugh as she started forward again. Of course there was someone there! People were always out on a night like this. It was just the darkness that was making her imagination run away with her. The darkness and the fireworks.

Ahead of her, on the ocean side of the road, tall banyans loomed, black, hulking shapes, their twisted branches stretching out over the sand and water. Teresa paused to look up, intrigued as always by the brooding aura they exuded at night. They had looked so different that first afternoon, so beautiful, all splashed with bright spring sunshine.

She had been no more than a small child, but the scene was still indelibly stamped on her memory. She had just celebrated her ninth birthday, Chinese style, at New Year's, making her, by the white man's count, somewhat more than seven years old. Her mother had been brought to the house of the dying the week before, and although she was not sure, for no one had seen fit to inform her, she sensed the woman was already dead.

The knowledge brought with it no grief. Teresa had had little more awareness of the woman who had borne her than of the man who was her father. Long and increasingly debilitating illness had made her a vague figure, shadowy and insubstantial to her young daughter. Only one thing of the mother remained in her heart, one tangible quality, and that was a deep and abiding hunger to be accepted in the world that was three-quarters hers by birth.

The sense of herself as a Westerner, a "European," was subtle, but deeply ingrained, coming as much from her surroundings—from the consciousness that she was different from the Chinese among whom she mingled—as it did from her mother's unrealistic ambitions. She had been given the Portuguese name Teresa in the hopes that her father would accept her, but Sebastião had not even acknowledged the message informing him of her birth. Nor had he acknowledged her mother's naive efforts to enroll her in a Portuguese school run by the Christian Brothers, a double folly, for not only was she tainted by the yellowish cast to her skin, she was a girl as well. Without money or influence, she could hope for nothing more than the life her mother had led.

Had Teresa been older at the time, she would have realized that the odds against her were insurmountable. But at seven she was aware only of three things. Her mother was dead, there was no one to take care of her, and Sebastião Valdes of Macao was her father. With the singlemindedness of a high-spirited child who had always had to fend for herself, she stowed away on one of the ferries that plied between Hong Kong and the Portuguese colony. Her first view of Macao was the banyans on the esplanade, and the sun seemed to nestle in their leafy branches as she slipped over the rail and swam to shore. Soaking with seawater, she made her way up and down narrow side streets, one after the other, until she recognized the sign that identified her father's store.

Sebastião had been in the back, enjoying a cup of strong sweet coffee with business associates, when that little whirlwind of black and gold startled them all by bursting into the room. His first reaction had been one of anger; his second, amusement and a quite unexpected sense of admiration. Two things had impressed him at that initial meeting: the child's uncommon spunk, and the luminous beauty that showed through tattered clothes and blackened smudges on her cheeks.

Teresa could not have chosen a better time to confront her father. With the birth of yet another stillborn child a few months before, Sebastião had at last given up hopes of a legitimate heir, and sensing age pressing upon him, he had begun the unrewarding task of culling through an unlikely lot of bastard sons. Now, suddenly, with no effort on his part, he had found exactly what he was looking for! A child with unquenchable spirit and a quick wit. She was not a boy, of course—he could not groom her to take over the business when he died—but she was something even better. She was a mirror of everything he wanted to see in himself, a last chance at immortality, and he seized on it impulsively.

It was a decision he was not to regret. Teresa, with food in her stomach and a roof over her head, turned out to be a winsomely feminine little creature, and Sebastião doted on her, enjoying her laughter and coy ways as he had once enjoyed her mother's, but with an innocence of heart he had not known before. It was his special delight, as she grew, to dress her in expensive silk and Canton crepe, emphasizing the exotic aspects of her beauty with traditional Chinese robes; and because Teresa had come to adore him unquestioningly, she did not object, as she might have otherwise, though she treated each new piece of finery as a pretty costume, not the garb that was her birthright. In all that time, she asked for only one thing, a chance to have the education her mother had taught her to crave. Sebastião, surprised but not displeased, agreed readily, hiring the finest tutors to introduce her to a level of learning the good Christian Brothers could never have offered.

It sometimes seemed to him, as he watched her pore over her books and scrolls, learning Western letters and Chinese characters with equal ease, that he must be grooming her for something.

It was not until one afternoon when she was nearly fourteen, and Lin Ch'ung came into the shop, that he realized what it was.

"Lin Ch'ung" was almost certainly an alias, defiantly chosen, with no pretense at reality, but no one, least of all Sebastião Valdes, had the audacity to question him about it. He had probably taken it in his youth, no doubt even then tongue-in-cheek, for the "Leopard-headed" character of *The Water Margin*, from whom he had lifted the name, was a master of the martial arts, and Lin had always been more renowned for brains than the sinewy strength of his limbs. He was reputed to be the head of one of the more powerful secret societies, though there were a mean-spirited few who whispered that he was nothing but a common gangster. One thing, however, was undisputed. There was no important trade in the colony, be it precious gems or opium smuggling, in which he did not have a stake.

Teresa had been in the back, putting the books in order, when Lin arrived. Sebastião, flattered at the idea of having such a distinguished caller, had clapped his hands together, signaling for her to bring a pot of tea and two cups. She came out a few minutes later, her eyes modestly lowered, as befitted the daughter of a merchant waiting on an important client. But as she had placed the lacquered tray on a low table between the two men, she looked up with the bold, curious gaze that was so characteristic of her.

And Lin had looked back.

A dull knot had tightened in the pit of Sebastião's stomach, and conflicting emotions had swept over him.

His natural feelings as a father made him rebel against what he knew Lin was going to offer. The man was much older than Teresa—*por Dios,* he was older than Sebastião himself!—and he had a reputation for extreme cruelty. How could he give his daughter, his little flower, to a man like that?

But Lin Ch'ung was rich.

The thought nagged at the back of his mind, chipping away his conscience. Lin was richer than anyone Sebastião had ever known—and he was powerful. He could do a great deal for a girl like Teresa, whose legitimate prospects would be few. Was it fair to deny her the prestige and luxury that would be hers as Lin's mistress?

And of course Lin could do a great deal for Sebastião in return.

So at fourteen, Teresa Valdes had been sold, traded for patronage and a place in her new lover's powerful organization. The day on which the transfer was made—for that was how she regarded it even then, a transfer of valuable commodities between two men of business—was as sunny and tempting as the day she had first come to Macao. She stepped out of her father's house and into the carriage that was to take her away, an outwardly calm figure, dry-eyed, with her head held high . . . and an empty place inside her that knew no one could ever be trusted again.

The wind whistled across the esplanade, cutting into Teresa's thoughts as it whipped her skirt above her ankles. Shivering, she tugged at the silk crepe shawl she had wrapped around her shoulders, wishing now she had had the good sense to bring the Russian sable cape Lin bought her last winter. Almost without thinking, her eyes darted back, scanning the shadows for the man she thought she had seen before.

To her surprise, he seemed to be there.

Teresa stopped abruptly, her heart fluttering irrationally, though she tried to still it. Yes, surely there *was* a man there, leaning casually against the sea wall, as if he were waiting for her to go on.

It could be he, she thought helplessly. It *could* be, but he was so lost in shadow it was hard to tell.

She had first seen the man a week before, in the marketplace. It was early afternoon, and she had just stopped at an open-fronted shop to browse through a new shipment of silk from Canton when she became aware that someone was standing nearby. Glancing up, she found herself gazing into the darkest green eyes she had ever seen.

Something about those rugged masculine features was hypnotically compelling, and in spite of herself, Teresa could not keep from staring. Perhaps it was the man's coloring, she thought, trying to justify her unseemly behavior, for auburn hair was unusual in that part of the world. Or perhaps it was the way his wide, sensuous lips parted, making him look as if he were deliberately mocking.

The man did not look away, as anyone else would have done, but appraised her with insolent eyes, cool and hot all at the same time, and Teresa gasped with shock as she recognized the bold message he was sending. Horrified, she turned away, a minute too late. Murmuring a hasty excuse to the shopkeeper, she hurried out into the street, searching for the carriage that always followed her when she went shopping. All the way home she told herself that she would forget what had happened, that it was of no consequence, that she was just being silly, making a fuss over nothing.

But somehow she could not get those eyes out of her mind. Those eyes, and the way she felt, soft and melting inside, when he looked at her.

She had not expected to see the man again, but he had been there, where she could not fail to notice him, the next morning when she went for a promenade along the sea wall. He was there again in the afternoon as she took one of the spirited China ponies out for a ride. After that, she saw him at least twice a day, and while he never so much as glanced her way again, she was always intensely aware of him, sensing, though she could not see, the magnetic power of those deep green eyes. Somehow, inexplicably, she knew he was aware of her too.

Now, if he was here, behind her in the darkness . . .

Teresa cut across the road, heading impetuously for the dirt path that zigzagged up the steep hillside. Of course he was not here! It was just someone—*anyone*—standing by the wall, watching the fireworks cascade across the sky. Still, the night *was* cold, and she did hate those jarring bursts of light and sound that came every few minutes. It would be more rugged, crossing the hill, but it would be faster too, and she would reach the other shore of the narrow peninsula much sooner.

It took her several minutes to scramble up the rocky path. As she paused at the top to catch her breath, she found herself straining for hints of motion below. There was something distinctly menacing about the man—she had sensed that the first time she saw him—something that warned her he could be dangerous. Yet there was something exciting too, a challenge she could feel but not understand, and she was almost disappointed when the darkness proved empty and she could hear nothing.

Teresa had not been unhappy during the six years she had been with Lin. He *was* a cruel man, vicious and sadistic in his treatment of others, but that was a part of his nature he never showed his young mistress. In her eyes, he always appeared generous and patient, considerate even when it came time to approach her bed, and a part of her truly cared for him. But another part—the part that was young and bursting with passion, the part as yet untried—hungered for something more. It was that unnamed yearning that was aroused now by the sense of a man, a darkly handsome stranger, behind her on the path.

She began to move forward, aware for the first time of how dense the vegetation was on the hilltop. The darkness seemed more intense here; the moonlight barely shivered through thick branches arching overhead. Only the fire-

works maintained their clarity, showing in sporadic bursts
when she least expected them.

A faint rustling sounded somewhere nearby, and Teresa
halted abruptly. A branch snapping in the wind? A little
animal foraging for food?

Or a footstep on the path behind her?

She listened tensely, every muscle in her body alert. But
whatever the sound was, it stopped when she did, and she
could detect nothing. Once again she started forward,
slowly this time. Cautiously.

As she did, the sound started too.

This time there was no mistaking it. Teresa's blood
turned to ice water. The footfalls were too clear now, too
blatant to take for anything else.

He was there. The man she had sensed below was
somewhere in the darkness, only steps away.

Apprehension turned to fear, chilling her heart. He was
there—and he had come onto that lonely path to follow
her! What had seemed exciting, almost tantalizing a moment before, was terrifying now, and she felt as if her
heart had stopped beating. This was not a fantasy anymore, not some game she had conjured up in her imagination. This was real, and she was in danger!

Quickening her pace, she began to race along the path,
trying to get away. But the sounds behind her quickened
too, and she knew she was not going to make it to the
other side.

Slipping off the path, she stopped for an instant, gauging the footsteps. A surge of hope coursed through her as
she realized he was farther away than she had thought. The
shadowy trees provided a screen as her agile mind whirled
frantically, trying to figure out what to do.

The grotto? Yes, of course—that was it! Surely she
would be safe if she could just make it to the grotto! It was
a smallish place, not at all like the cavern the tourists
frequented, but it was cool and mossy, a great favorite
with children on a hot summer's day, and she could remember how to find it, even in the darkness.

It was all she could do to keep from running, but common sense warned her to move stealthily. One rock kicked clumsily to the side, one twig that cracked beneath her feet, and it would all be over. The man was a stranger here; she was sure of that. If he had been on the peninsula only a week or two, if he had not had a chance to explore this part of it, then she would be safe. He would have no idea where to look for her.

By the time she reached the grotto, she was too frightened to think rationally, and forgetting caution, she hurled herself through the narrow opening, slipping treacherously on slick, mossy ground. The sheer rock wall felt cold as she pressed her back against it. Her heart was beating so wildly she could almost hear it echo in that great empty cavern.

Oh, please, don't let him be here, she prayed desperately. Please, *please*, let me have eluded him.

But just at that moment, as she dared to hope, a brilliant flash of light seared through the night, illuminating the entrance to the grotto. There, silhouetted against a backdrop of inky blue, was a rugged masculine form!

He had found her.

A strangled gasp burst out of Teresa's mouth. She could not see his face in the shadows, but she did not need to. Even without seeing, she knew it was he. And she was in his power.

She longed to run to the back of the grotto, cowering childlike in the shadows, but she knew it would do no good. There was something almost animal in that presence in the doorway, something inherently primitive—and animals had a way of scenting out fear.

Steeling herself to a boldness she did not feel, she stepped forward. "Who . . . who are you?"

She still could not see him clearly, but white teeth seemed to flash in the darkness, and she sensed he was laughing.

"My name does not matter." His voice was sharp-edged, but deep and resonant. "Men call me . . . the Tiger."

"The Tiger?" The words sent a shiver through her. She had not heard the name before, she still had no idea who he was—but the very thought somehow made him more ominous than before. "Why are you here? Why did you follow me into this place?"

His laughter was audible now, a muffled sound low in his throat. He started toward her, then stopped, caught in a ray of moonlight that seeped into the darkness. Tanned skin looked almost eerily white, but his hair had turned to jet, and dark eyes blazed with secrets they had only hinted at before.

"Why?" he drawled. "I should think that was obvious."

"If you . . . if you think you can . . . can force yourself on me, you're crazy! I'll scream if you try! Someone will hear, and they'll come and—"

"No one will hear." His voice was soft, almost soothing. "No one will come. You know that as well as I. And you are not going to scream . . . any more than I am going to *force* myself on you. We have looked at each other, Teresa Valdes. There is unfinished business between us."

"Oh, no . . ." Teresa felt her fear mount, mixed with other emotions she could not control. "No, that's not true." She *had* looked at him, and she had thought what he was thinking now. Only she hadn't realized it at the time. And she hadn't meant the look to be an invitation—at least she didn't think she had.

She hadn't *wanted* it to be an invitation.

Terrified, she fixed her eyes on the opening behind him. It was so narrow—so very narrow!—but somehow she had to get past him and through it. He was fully capable of doing what he had suggested. And she was not at all sure she was capable of stopping him.

With a cry of desperation, she rushed at him. If only she could startle him enough to let down his guard, if she could just shove him aside on the slippery stones . . .

But he was ready for her. Strong hands caught her

wrists in a viselike grip as she surged forward, pinning
them behind her back. Strong masculine arms forced her
full length against his body, tightening his hold until she
could feel every strained muscle in his chest, feel the
pressure of his thighs, lean and taut . . . feel even that
hard thrust of his erection against her belly.

She tried to scream, but the sound choked in her throat.
She squirmed desperately, struggling to work loose. She
had just opened her mouth, teeth bared, ready to sink into
his shoulder, when a loud explosion shook the earth, the
last final burst of a dozen firecrackers all at once. Crying
out in fright, she threw herself against him, not thinking
what she was doing, wanting only to get away from that
terrible vibrating crash.

Her arms, freed now, locked suddenly around his neck,
clutching, not pushing him away. Her head arched back,
her lips parted, surrendering instinctively to a force more
potent than her will. All thoughts of resistance vanished as
she felt him draw her down to the earth, tugging at her
skirt, pulling it up around her hips, thrusting himself deeply,
urgently, penetratingly into her.

It was only afterward, as she lay on the cold ground
where he had left her, that reason returned, and she realized with sickening shame how easily she had given in to
his savage male demands. Her whole body began to tremble, lightly at first, then violently, and she squeezed her
eyes shut, fighting the urge to weep anguished, frustrated
tears for the first time in her life.

"Shhhhh . . ."

Gentle fingers touched her brow, brushing back dark
curls damp with sweat. Opening her eyes, Teresa was
surprised to see that he had lit a candle and was crouching
a few inches away. He had made no effort to remove his
clothes, but they were, like hers, in disarray, and she was
more aware than ever of his lean, hard body.

He drew his hand back, but his eyes were still touching
her, an intensely sensual feeling, as if he were wooing her.

In spite of herself, she felt something deep inside begin to respond.

Horrified, she pulled herself to a sitting position. Her skirt was badly rumpled, but she did what she could with it, tugging it over her legs again. She could do nothing to change what had happened, but at least she could salvage what was left of her dignity.

"Do you always carry a candle with you?" she asked tartly. "So you can watch your conquests squirm?"

He rocked back on his heels, studying her with a distinctly unsettling look.

"I wasn't aware you were a 'conquest.' In fact, I thought it was *your* beauty that had conquered *me*. But I'm glad to see you've recovered your spirit." He grinned wickedly. "As for the candle, it was a lucky coincidence. I just picked it up in the market. All the hotels seem to be electrified nowadays, but lights have a way of going out at the damnedest times."

"Lucky indeed." Teresa struggled to regain her composure. If he was going to chat casually about nothing at all, then so was she! "It will make it all the easier for me to get out of here without stumbling." She drew herself to her knees, adding icily, "Now that you have had your way with me, would you be good enough to step aside and let me pass? That should be no hardship, since you've finished what you had in mind when you came here."

He stood up but made no other move.

"We had our way with each other, Teresa. You were not exactly unwilling in this little encounter. As a matter of fact, you turned out to be surprisingly . . . hot-blooded." He wedged the candle in a narrow crevice, freeing his hands as he turned back. "And what makes you think I'm finished with you?"

"But . . . but surely after . . ."

Her voice caught in her throat as she saw him reach up and unfasten his shirt. In one fluid motion he removed it, together with his jacket, tossing them both on the ground. He looked even more virile now, and she was mesmerized by the taut, powerful muscles that rippled across his chest. In spite of herself, her eyes followed his hands downward, watching him slide tight-fitting pants away from his body. The light was frighteningly clear now, the shadows emphasizing, not diminishing the proof of his masculinity, and she saw with shocked surprise that he was ready for her again.

He laughed hoarsely. "You've been with an old man too long. It's time you found someone the right age. You need a man who's young and strong." He let his eyes play frankly with her body. "I'm not likely to be satisfied with one rough tumble on the ground . . . and neither are you."

Teresa tried to protest, but the words would not come. He was too much in comand now. Too sure of himself. Kneeling beside her, he rested his hands lightly on her shoulders, caressing the base of her throat, gently—oh, so gently—sliding elegant Chinese silk away from her quivering flesh.

"Hush, sweet Teresa, why do you tremble so? Do you still think you have to struggle?" His fingers seemed to be playing with her, soft against the softer skin of her breast. His lips followed, teasing with intimacies she could not resist. "You are fighting yourself, not me, don't you know that? There is nothing wrong with being a woman. Nothing wrong with being full of passion and excitement."

Her sobs were stifled as she felt him enter her—a last token of protest, for already her blood had begun to warm again, and there was no room in her heart for thought or reason. They remained together well into the evening, making love again and again with such ardent passion she no longer even tried to deny what she was doing.

It was he who finally ended that long, delirious session of lovemaking. Pulling away, he drew her up beside him, moving gently, with an easy nonchalance that was almost as disconcerting as his initial roughness. Teresa could not help thinking, as he slipped the dress over her head and fastened it with expert fingers, that he was extremely adept at such matters. When he finished with her, he pulled on his own clothes, scowling ruefully at the disheveled condition of his coat, which he had thrown on the ground some time before to cushion their passion.

"Next time we will have to find a better place for our rendezvous."

"Next time?" Teresa gaped at him in horror. "You must be mad! There isn't going to be a 'next time.' I've already been foolish enough, staying with you like this. I don't know what excuse I'll give for coming back so late. I wouldn't dare—"

"Of course you would." His face contorted with amusement. "I have no doubt you'll come up with something good for tonight. I'd be willing to wager you have a devious little brain behind that pretty face. As for 'next time,' rest assured there *will* be one. I promise you that."

Hot retorts rose to Teresa's lips, but she bit them back, seeing no point in arguing. Her body, satiated from his skillful lovemaking, gave no hint of the renewed longings that would plague her all too soon, and she was certain she would be able to resist his advances. She had to! It would be much too dangerous, seeing him again. And too degrading. One such encounter could be called exciting, a part of growing up, of proving to herself that she dared to be a woman. But to do it again? That would be the worst kind of folly.

It was not until she was back on the path, alone but keenly aware of *his* presence somewhere in the darkness behind her, that Teresa at last dwelled on the magnitude of what she had done. Horrified, she realized she had risked not only her won safety but also her father's. If Lin were to discover what she had done, both their lives would be forfeit. Sebastião might have been a weakling, selling his daughter for a rich man's influence, but he was the only person who had ever made her truly happy, and she could not bear to think she might be the instrument of his destruction.

No, there would not be a "next time." She would absolutely—*absolutely*—never see that man again.

* * *

Teresa meant her rash vow when she made it. But the next morning, awakening alone in a satin-sheeted bed, her body stirred to the sweet yearnings he had awakened, and she felt her resolve begin to weaken. As she went out for an early ride, she promised herself—*swore* to herself—that she was going to cut him dead the instant she saw him. Instead she found her eyes searching every twist in the road, vainly as it turned out, for any trace of him. When she returned, she was cross and irritable, hating herself for the way she snapped at anyone who ventured near, but unable to do a thing about it.

Three days later, when she still had not seen him, she began to be frantic. What if he was only toying with her? What if he had no plans to see her again? What if he had never intended any more than that one night of ecstasy?

When at last the message arrived, carried by a ragged little urchin from the docks, Teresa was too relieved even to remember her vows of caution. No risk seemed too great, not her safety, not her life—not even her father's —to be with him again. She was trembling once more, this time with expectation, as she felt him draw her at last into his arms. He did not disappoint her.

Their affair continued throughout the spring and well into the summer, always on the terms he set. They met when he said and *if* he said, sometimes twice a day, sometimes not for an agonizing week or two. And always it was at the place he specified. When she thought about the cavalier way he disregarded her feelings, Teresa hated him thoroughly, and she would swear never to see him again. But then the message would come—a few words on a torn sheet of paper—and something in her could not say no.

Sometimes it seemed to her he was almost insanely foolhardy, bringing her to his hotel room or taking her by open boat to a rented villa on one of the neighboring islands. But there was a kind of wariness about him too, a subtle instinct that always made him stop just this side of total recklessness, and she sensed that he, like her, was not particularly anxious to get caught.

"You are impossible, do you know that?" she railed at him. "You don't care how I feel! Everything has to be your way. I see you when you want and where you want. I don't have a thing to say in the matter."

"Oh?" He lay back on the bed, his tanned naked body looking exceptionally dark against the white sheets. "And where would you have us meet, pray tell? Do you have a place in mind for our little trysts?"

"You know I don't. It's just that you always have to . . . to be in control! I have no control at all."

"Ah, so that's the problem." He pulled her down beside him, running his hands impudently over the slender curves of her thighs. "You're a lady who likes to be in control, is that it? You can't stand the idea of someone else calling the shots."

"That's not fair." Teresa squirmed, trying to pull away, even as she felt her body begin to succumb. "It's just that you won't tell me anything about yourself. Even your name."

He drew back, his eyes chilling. "I have told you. I am the Tiger. That is all you need to know—and all you ever will."

Teresa started to persist, but he stopped her with the hard, demanding pressure of his mouth, and because passion left no choice, she gave in. But later, when she was alone again, the idea gnawed away at her, and she determined to find out more about him. It took her several weeks, but at last a few cautious inquiries brought the information she wanted.

"Your name is Brandon Christopher," she flung at him the next time they were together. "Don't try to deny it because I know I'm right."

She was surprised to see his lips form into an ironic smile.

"Why should I deny it when it's true?"

The calmness in his tone was infuriating. He had made

such a secret of the whole thing before—now he did not seem to care! Was he only playing with her?

"They say you are very rich." She pouted. "They say you have a huge fortune at home in America."

"As huge as the fortune your lover possesses?"

Teresa stiffened, pulling away to sit by herself at the end of the bed.

"I don't like it when you talk about Lin. It . . . it reminds me . . ." She faltered, flushing with embarrassment at the unwelcome sound of rough male laughter.

"It reminds you that you're betraying him every time you let me make love to you? Your solicitude touches me, my dear. You show great concern for a man everyone knows is a monster."

"He is not! At least not with me. Oh, I know what everyone says about him, and I suppose it must be true. But with me he's never been anything but kind. I will not stay here and listen—"

"All right, all right." Brandon sat up beside her, drawing her soothingly into his arms, an uncharacteristically conciliatory gesture for him. "I won't talk of Lin anymore if it upsets you. Why the hell would I want to? I'd rather talk about you—and me." And he kissed her, making her forget everything else, even those sporadic bouts of guilt.

Brandon Christopher could be the most aggravating man in the world, as Teresa was to discover often enough in the weeks to come, and there were times when she despised him so much she almost managed to keep her vow and have nothing more to do with him. But he could be tender, too, and teasing—and there were other times when she relaxed so much in his arms, nothing else seemed to exist.

True to his word, he never spoke of Lin again, not directly, although he did manage to draw her out of herself, coaxing her to talk about various aspects of their life together. Flattered by his attentiveness, Teresa found herself chattering on about the most trivial subjects, like the trees Lin had planted for her on that other island, where only a few were allowed to go. She knew the place was a secret, of course—she would never have said anything to give it away—but surely it couldn't hurt to talk about the landscape. Besides, it would do Brandon good to hear about all the money her lover was spending to please her.

"They are the most beautiful flowering trees. I forget what they are called, but they come all the way from . . . Oh, what is that place again? Ceylon!"

"They must be very delicate then," Brandon teased. "Are you sure it won't hurt them, being so close to the sea?"

Teresa tilted her chin up. She knew nothing about gardening, and she was never sure when he was making fun of her. "They are very strong, and anyway, they aren't *that* close to the sea. The villa is two or three miles from the shore, and that's after you sail into the cove. It's at the top of the highest hill on the island. You can see all the way to Lantao."

"It must be a pretty sight at sunrise. Or are you too lazy to get up that early?"

She giggled. "I'm not lazy at all. Besides, you don't know the first thing about it. That's exactly the wrong direction to see the sun rise over Lantao. You'd go there if you wanted to watch it *set*."

It did not even occur to her, as she snuggled back into the warmth of his arms, that she had just given Brandon Christopher the approximate location of her lover's secret hideout, from which his opium operations were carried out. Nor did it occur to her in the days that followed that there might be a reason for all those other seemingly innocent questions. What is it like there? What direction does the wind blow in the morning? How far do you have to go to get to a freshwater stream? She knew only that he was paying attention to her, as no one had since she was a little girl and Sebastião had doted on her, and she was ready to answer anything if it would keep his mind from straying to thoughts other than her.

She did not even realize what she had done, a month later, when Lin's most trusted lieutenant, a middle-aged

Chinese named Soong, came to her, his face stricken with fear and horror.

"They are dead," he blurted out. "My master, your father—everyone. We were certain no one could find our hideout, but somehow they managed. I don't know how, but they did. All is lost. There was only one survivor . . . and he was so badly hurt he died after he got to us."

Numb with shock, Teresa listened as he recounted the brutal details of a surprise dawn attack. Lin and his men had been so sure they were safe, they had not posted adequate sentries. Now they had paid for their carelessness.

"I was spared myself," Soong told her, his voice shaking so badly it was barely audible, "only because Lin wanted me to wait for the two ships that were due today from Canton. I was to act as pilot and guide them into the cove where the others are." He paused, the color draining out of his face. "Where the others *were*."

Teresa began to shake almost uncontrollably. The cup she had been holding slipped from her fingers and clattered to the floor. "But who . . . *who* could have done such a thing?"

Soong stared at her dully. "The American, of course."

"The . . . American?" Something turned to ice inside her, and she tried not to think about it. "What American?"

"The red-haired one. The man they call the Tiger. He's been trying to cut in on our territory for months. We knew about it, but we didn't think he was a threat."

The Tiger.

The man continued to talk, but Teresa barely heard a word he said. As soon as he was gone, she brushed aside the maids who hovered solicitously around her and ran up to her room, bolting the door behind her.

The Tiger, he had said. But the Tiger was Brandon Christopher.

And Brandon Christopher was her lover!

She flung herself on the bed, trying bitterly to force the tears that would not come. Gone, everything was gone—the men, the villa, the tall ships in the cove. Soong might not know how the Tiger had learned their whereabouts, but she did.

She did—and she knew who was to blame!

Sitting up, she bunched the soft Western-style pillow against her breast, clutching at it with white knuckles. Waves of guilt alternated with anger, and because the latter was the more comfortable emotion, she clung to it, directing her pain outward. It was easier to hate Brandon than herself. Easier to remember how he had accosted her than to think how willing—how eager!—she had been to betray both father and lover in his arms.

He had used her!

She jumped up, pacing back and forth like a caged animal trying to get out. He had used and betrayed her. He never cared about her, never loved her the way she loved him, never *really* wanted her. He only wanted to get at her lover. And he had succeeded all too well!

She paused at the window, her fingertips running along rippled glass, chill now with the first touch of evening. Slowly her mind started to function again, and she forced herself to look at things with the cold objectivity that had eluded her before.

All is lost, Soong had said . . . but was that quite accurate? There were still the two ships, and the men on them, and the men who had been in town for one reason or another. Then there was that Englishman, the one who had been so useful to Lin of late. They might yet be able to reorganize if . . .

If they found someone bold enough to be their leader.

Teresa turned slowly into the room, excitement painting a flush in cheeks that had been ashen before. What she was planning might have been impossible in a European environment, but here in the Orient, where secret societies were an ancient tradition and women had long been accepted as members, sometimes even in positions of authority . . .

For the first time she was grateful for the Chinese blood

that flowed through her veins. It would make her more convincing in the role she was about to assume.

She would put Lin's organization back together.

The idea was frightening, but it was exhilarating too, offering a kind of challenge she had never known in her young life. She would gather together the men and the ships—yes, and she would sell her jewels, too, if she had to. Anything to get started again.

She could not hope to recoup everything, of course. She had nowhere near her former lover's influence and connections. But she could at least salvage the opium-smuggling operations. And when she did . . .

She glanced back at the window, a golden mirror of reflected lamplight. For a fleeting moment she thought she caught a glimpse of red hair and taunting green eyes, and she knew that wherever he was, he was laughing at her.

When she did succeed—when the money and power were hers—she would use them to destroy Brandon Christopher.

She would avenge herself on him if it were the last thing she did.

Orchids in the Spring

1

Celia's eyes sparkled as she cast a last glance at her image in the long wardrobe mirror. Downstairs, the guests had already begun to arrive for the ball her parents were giving, and music drifted upward, setting her toes to tapping on the polished teakwood floor.

The nearly four years that had passed since Skye Maarten went off to seek his fortune had brought subtle and generally satisfying changes in her appearance. Not that anyone could call her truly beautiful, she thought as she tilted her head to one side, gauging the effect on wispy curls that strayed from her Psyche knot. Her brow was too wide, her chin too square to be the perfect oval fashion demanded, and her coloring was nowhere near as striking as ravishing raven-haired Lady Elizabeth Crofte-Johnston's, by far the most glamorous young woman in the neighborhood. Still, there *was* something decidedly winsome in that coronet of silvery blond hair, giving her features an elusive softness. And large gray eyes looked melting and sensuous, framed as they were by surprisingly dark lashes, deepened with just a hint of kohl.

"Do I look all right, Sin-Sin?" she asked needlessly.

Ma Sin slipped up from behind to share her reflection in the mirror. They made a striking picture, the one girl dark, the other fair and almost delicate in a lavender-and-silver gown. The servant had been dressed to complement her mistress, with a crisp white *ingyi* setting off the purple silk of her *longyi*, draped gracefully over boy-slender hips.

"The missy-sahib looks very pretty," she said with a light musical accent. "Like always."

"No prettier?" Celia teased.

Ma Sin smiled, knowing what the other girl was after. "Much prettier," she conceded, pausing just slightly before adding: "*He* will most certainly approve."

Celia, caught up in her own thoughts, failed to notice that brief flicker of hesitation. These past six months, since Skye Maarten suddenly reappeared, had not been quite the blissful heaven her daydreams led her to expect. Recently, however, things had begun to look up, and every hopeful instinct in her heart promised that tonight, at last, her dreams were going to come true.

"At least you don't have to sew ruffles in my dresses anymore," she said with an impish grin.

"No." Ma Sin laughed indulgently. She was slightly younger than Celia, but she had been married for two years and had borne her first child, so she regarded herself as the older of the two. "It is easier to sew the missy-sahib's dresses now. I do not have to make the fronts so round. You are round enough all by yourself."

"You don't think I'm *too* round?" Celia studied her image with a faint frown. As Mama promised, her figure was finally conforming to heredity. But Serena St. Clair was fully two inches taller than her daughter, and Celia sometimes had the feeling that Mama carried her voluptuousness a little less conspicuously.

"For a Burmese girl, yes," Ma Sin replied, amused. "We have slim hips, almost like a man's. And we are straighter on the top, too. But English girls are supposed to have—what do you call them?—'curves.' I have noticed that your men like it that way."

Celia, who had noticed the same thing, felt considerably better. Any man looking for perfect features and a stunning sense of style was sure to settle on Lady Elizabeth Crofte-Johnston. But if he preferred softly feminine figures—

and quite a number of them seemed to—then *she* would be his choice.

She could not help remembering how she had felt that afternoon Skye finally came home. She had been so excited and full of anticipation. Yes, and proud too, for he had succeeded far better than she dared to hope. Even Papa had had to admit grumpily that young Schuyler had not ''done too badly for himself.''

She had been certain then, with all the confidence of youth—and totally ignoring the fact that Skye's circumstances had once again changed, this time for the better—that he was going to come calling on her. Instead, to her chagrin, he had begun paying court to Elizabeth Crofte-Johnston, whose father, she noted cattily, owned twice as much land as Ian St. Clair. It had been small comfort, a few weeks later, when he turned his attentions from her to her plainer if wealthier cousin, Delilah.

''You must not let it hurt you so much, mouse,'' Mama told her gently. ''Skye's mother has been living for more than three years on the charity of neighbors. His first duty is to her. He has to make the most advantageous marriage he can, no matter where his heart might lead.''

''But that's not fair!'' Celia cried out rebelliously. ''I'm going to inherit Papa's plantation one day. Skye's mother can come and live with us. What more does she need?''

Serena, who knew only too well what it would be like living in close proximity with Skye's demanding mother, wisely held her tongue. ''Wait and see'' was all she said. ''Things have a way of changing when you least expect it.''

And in the end, Celia thought gleefully, Mama was right. Delilah's father, astonishingly, proved even more stubborn than Papa, positively refusing to allow his daughter to marry Skye. And Lady Elizabeth, after what seemed a promising courtship, turned him down flat.

At last he was free to follow his heart—and his heart led him to the girl he had wanted him all along! The day after Elizabeth refused him, he finally showed up, a sheepish grin on his handsome features and a bouquet of red hibiscus in his hand. He had been a fixture in her mother's parlor ever since, appearing every afternoon, a certain sign to Celia—and the entire neighborhood—that he had settled on her. He had been giving broader and broader hints these past few days that tonight was the night he was going to make it official.

Celia spun around excitedly, enjoying the filmy lightness of her skirt as it floated away from slender, shapely ankles.

"Mama was right, Sin-Sin. This dress is perfect. Don't you think so?"

"The memsahib is always right about dresses," Ma Sin agreed. "You are a foolish little girl to fight so much with her."

Celia, catching the affection in her voice, felt no urge to bristle. Besides, she could hardly deny what Sin-Sin was saying. She *had* argued quite bitterly with her mother over the dress. She had longed for something more sophisticated, sheer black grenadine perhaps, over changeable taffeta in brilliant peacock tones, but Mama had insisted on pale lavender silk. And as usual, Mama had been right. Soft pastel was the perfect accent for youthful innocence, especially with the way the sheer fabric clung to the ripening curves of Celia's high young breasts, flaring out just slightly over rounded hips to a small, becoming bustle in the back. Lady Elizabeth, no doubt, would appear dripping in diamonds—and Delilah too, though to lesser effect—but all eyes would be on Celia St. Clair, with no adornment save wild orchids in her hair and a heart-shaped gold locket at her throat.

The music swelled suddenly, flooding the empty upstairs, and Celia realized guiltily that the dancing had begun.

"You are late," Ma Sin chided. "Many of the guests are here, I think. The memsahib will be angry."

Celia's lips rounded into an unconscious pout. It was one of Mama's strictest rules that she be there to greet the

guests when they arrived, but she could not bear the
thought of going down. Not yet.

"Oh, Sin-Sin, if only I could make a really grand
entrance. Imagine how Skye would feel if he arrived just
then and looked up to see me standing at the top of the
stairs. What fun it would be to come floating down like a
fairy princess. Or Cinderella at the ball!"

Sin-Sin laughed, a light, distinctly Burmese sound, like
the bells on the pagodas that graced the hillsides. "You
think he would let you get away with that? No, it is Master
Schuyler who always makes the 'grand entrance.' Is it not
true that he never arrives anywhere on time?"

Celia had to laugh with her. "Skye does have a sense of
the dramatic," she admitted. "No matter how late I was,
he'd be certain to be later. Besides, Mama would be
furious—and that would spoil the effect." She started
toward the door, stopping only when the servant's voice
called her back.

"Missy-sahib . . . ?"

Celia turned to see Ma Sin looking uncharacteristically
awkward. Long dark lashes brushed her cheeks as she
stared pointedly at the floorboards.

"Yes, Sin-Sin? What is it?"

"They do say . . ." The girl looked up, eyes troubled.
"Well . . . they say there are reasons why the Lady
Elizabeth refused him."

Celia's stomach gave a slight turn, but she forced herself to ignore it.

"Of course they do," she replied sharply. "People are
always saying things like that. You know as well as I what
it's like here."

"I do. It is a small village, and in a small village people
have nothing to do but gossip. Still, I cannot help—"

"Still, nothing! Come, Sin-Sin, admit it! Elizabeth had
reason for saying no to Skye. Don't forget, she was his
second choice. He had already offered for Delilah, and
everyone knew he had been turned down. Besides . . ."

Celia paused, caught up in a thought that had not occurred to her before.

"Maybe it wasn't Elizabeth who refused Skye at all. Maybe he decided not to ask her, and she spread the story to save her pride. He wouldn't bother to refute it. Why should he? Skye doesn't care a whit what people say about him."

"No," Ma Sin conceded very softly. "No, he has never cared for things like that."

Once again Celia missed the hesitation in the other girl's voice. The conversation was already forgotten as she stood at the top of the stairs looking down at the festively decorated entry hall filled with people who had paused to speak to their host and hostess before proceeding into the ballroom. The wide double doors to the outside had been propped open, but Ko Taik, Ma Sin's young husband, stood at attention beside them, all puffed up, as if he thought his services as doorman might be needed at any second. He was splendidly garbed in a starched muslin *ingyi*, with a yellow *longyi* of Mandalay silk and a truly splendid yellow-pink *gaung baung* on his head.

The music paused, as if on cue, just at the moment Celia set her foot on the top step, then started up again. The sound was a sore temptation, and she dreaded the hour or so she was going to have to stand in the hall receiving guests. The orchestra consisted primarily of European instruments, with strings predominating, but Serena St. Clair had added a few Burmese touches, and the rhythm was underscored by a faintly primitive beat of castanets and local drums.

Celia's feet barely touched the stairs as she drifted down. Clouds of silk and lace swirled prettily around her, but all she could think was how much she wished it were Skye and not the youngest Claridge boy standing at the base of the steps looking up with adoration in his eyes.

Mama gave her a reproachful look as she slipped in beside her, but she was too much of a lady to say anything in front of the others, and Celia turned her attention to the

arriving guests. There was enough of her mother in her to
enjoy the idea of being a gracious hostess, although there
was enough of her practical, down-to-earth father, too, to
bristle at the fuss and feathers. Especially on a night like
tonight.

"I say, Celia, I don't think you've heard a word I've
said."

Celia was startled to see Roderick Claridge bending over
her hand with what was obviously intended to be a rakish
look on his face.

"I'm sorry, Roddie. I was rather late getting down. I
haven't had time to catch my breath. It's good to see you.
I'm glad you and your family could come."

The words were barely perfunctory, but the boy, as
usual, did not seem to catch on. Celia had liked Roddie
Claridge well enough when they were growing up—she
still liked him in a way—but he had outgrown neither his
awkwardness nor his baby fat, and she hated it when he
looked at her with huge calf's eyes.

"You will save a dance for me, won't you, Celia?"

"Of course, Roddie," she replied coolly. "You know I
always try to dance at least once with everyone when we
have a ball at our house. Mama says that's part of being a
good hostess."

This time Roddie caught on. As he headed toward the
ballroom with a sulky expression on his face, Celia was
aware of the disconcerting sound of laughter in her ear.
Glancing around, she saw that Ashton Claridge, Roddie's
older and considerably better-looking brother, had slipped
up beside her.

"What a heartless wench," he scolded, still laughing.
"You know perfectly well what the poor boy meant, yet
you insist on misunderstanding. How can you be so cruel?
Have you no sympathy for the fragile male ego?"

"Cruel, fie!" Celia quipped lightly. Next to Skye, Ash
Claridge was the handsomest young man in the territory,
and even a few months ago she would have been flattered
by his attentions. Tonight she had too much on her mind to

be more than mildly amused. "Don't you think it would be crueler to lead Roddie on when I can never care about him the way he wants me to?"

Ash's dark eyes turned solemn. "Yes," he agreed quietly. "*If* you really can't be interested in him—or anyone else. I wonder, are the rumors I've heard true?"

He was about to say more when the conversation was interrupted by a flurry at the door. The Crofte-Johnstons had arrived, Elizabeth, as always, entering a few paces ahead of her parents.

It was amazing, Celia thought irritably, the way one could always tell by that subtle break in the conversation when Elizabeth appeared. Almost against her will, she found herself looking toward the doorway, aware as she did that Ash Claridge, beside her, was doing the same thing.

Elizabeth would have been considered a beauty anywhere. Here, where only a handful of women had anything approaching *ton* and elegance, she was outstanding. Tall and almost excessively slender, she moved with regal grace, underscoring the aristocratic lines of perfect features and the creamy pallor of satin-smooth skin. Small, but fully faceted diamonds had been arranged in jet-black tresses, like stars against a cloudless sky, and an extravagance of diamonds and Siamese sapphires at throat and wrist accented the sophistication of her deep blue velvet gown, cut frankly flat in front, with no ruffles to detract from willowy elegance.

She posed for an instant in the doorway, smiling faintly as her eyes met Celia's. Then, moving forward, she held out her hands.

"Why, Celia . . . How very—charming you look."

A faint flush rose to Celia's cheeks. The way Elizabeth's voice lingered on *charming*, she might as well have purred—How *sweet* you look, Celia dear. Or—How very like a little girl!

"You, too, Eliza," she replied, holding her voice steady. "That dress is most becoming. How daring of you to choose velvet. Anyone else would think it was reserved for matrons.''

She had intended the words to be coolly gracious, an unruffled response to the other's cattiness. But to her consternation, they had came out just the opposite, and everyone within earshot had to have heard.

Elizabeth, sensing her victory, laughed.

''I really must be getting inside. That music sounds divine. I hope you aren't going to be stuck out here too long. It must be absolutely agonizing. How fortunate for me my mama is not as strict as yours.''

She timed her exit perfectly, just starting to leave, then turning, almost as an afterthought.

''Are you coming, Ash? It must be so . . . boring for you out here.''

Celia's eyes flashed with anger, but somehow she managed to bite her tongue as she watched that regal figure sweep into the ballroom. Why was it she always insisted on sparring with Elizabeth? She ought to know by now that for pure malice, no one was ever going to get the better of her.

''Quite the witch, isn't she?'' Ash remarked dryly. The amused look on his face was all the more unsettling because Celia was not sure whether he was laughing at Elizabeth or at her.

''You didn't seem to mind. You never once took your eyes off her.''

''Quite right,'' he agreed comfortably. ''Why should I? She's easy to look at. A very beautiful woman. Also— don't you think?—a little sad.''

''Sad?'' Celia eyed him skeptically. If there was one thing Lady Elizabeth Crofte-Johnston was not, it was sad. ''What an odd thing to say.''

''Is it? Think about it, Celia. When Liza was fourteen, she already looked twenty; now that she's nearly twenty, she could pass for a woman of the world. She's grown up too quickly—and too easily. She never had to do anything to make men seek her out, and it's never occurred to her that one day she might want a woman friend. What's going to happen, do you suppose, ten or fifteen years from now, when her looks begin to fade?''

Celia stared at him, puzzled. Why on earth would anyone worry about ''ten or fifteen years from now'' when the evening was just beginning and music beckoned?

Ash caught her look and grinned. ''I'd ask you to save a dance for me,'' he said, bowing with exaggerated courtesy over her hand, ''but I'm afraid my ego might prove as fragile as my brother's.'' With that, he was gone, strolling nonchalantly into the ballroom.

Celia stared after him with ill-concealed envy. More than ever, she hated the strict conventions that forced her to remain in the entry hall while the other young people were inside having fun. If she couldn't dazzle Skye Maarten with a grand entrance, then at least she wanted to be dancing with a handsome young man when he arrived! Perhaps Ash Claridge, for he had been looking at her just now in quite a flattering way.

She threw a pleading glance at her mother, not expecting a response, but to her surprise, Serena smiled indulgently. She had not failed to see the breathless eagerness on the girl's face, and even more than her daughter she understood what tonight meant. All too soon the tardy swain was going to show up, and when he did, Celia would have eyes for no one else. Until then, she had one last chance to enjoy being pretty—and popular.

''Go ahead. Have a good time. I wouldn't want the dancing to be half over before you got to it.''

Celia threw her arms around her mother, hugging her impulsively, then hurried off before she changed her mind. Her spirits soared as she lingered for an instant on the threshold, caught up in the bright lights and dazzling display of color that seemed even more enticing now that she was no longer on the outside looking in.

Serena had outdone herself with the decor. Sliding partitions into a number of smaller rooms had been removed, as had the bamboo curtains that screened off the veranda, and the dance floor seemed to extend out into the garden itself. Remembering the graceful splendor of castles of her youth, she had disdained the use of common lanterns, opting instead for shimmering candles set in ornate crystal chandeliers and brass sconces on the walls. A profusion of wild orchids spilled out of the shadows on all sides, turning the room into a bower of white wicker and pale purple blossoms.

No wonder Mama wanted me to wear lavender, Celia thought, laughing. She had planned the entire decor to set it off!

She had little time to admire her mother's handiwork, for no sooner had she shown herself in the doorway than a young man appeared at her elbow and she was swept into the swirling throng of dancers. Another willing partner claimed her as soon as the orchestra paused, then another, and she quickly found herself lost in the sweet, seductive spell of the music. She had always loved to dance, her youthful body responding to the ebb and flow of rhythms outside herself, and there were moments when she almost forgot to glance at the door and see if Skye had arrived.

He was still not there an hour later when it came time for the orchestra to take their first pause of the evening, and Celia, belatedly remembering her duties as hostess, excused herself from the group of young men who were clamoring for her attention. Mama might have been remarkably tolerant before, letting her join the dancing earlier than usual, but she would never forgive her if she did not take at least a few minutes to look around and make sure everyone was having a good time.

Her first stop was a small room just off the veranda, where a long bar had been set up, flanked by tin chests filled with ice and bottles of beer. Ordinarily, when ladies were present, Ian St. Clair doled out spirits in sparing measure, but tonight the liquor flowed freely, and Celia noted with amusement that several of the gentlemen were already more intoxicated than propriety allowed.

At the other end of the room, opposite the bar, small

tables covered with snowy damask held an impressive
array of light refreshments. The main feast would be later,
after the first round of dancing had ended and comfortable
wicker chairs had been set up on the veranda, but those
with an earlier appetite would find ample delicacies to
choose from. Tea sandwiches were always a favorite at
any St. Clair gathering, for the English-style bread was
topped with generous globs of real sweet cream, a welcome change from the rancid tinned stuff most of the
planters were used to. Various local and imported cheeses
had been arranged on china platters, together with an
attractive assortment of cold meats and thin slices of duck
and richly spiced chicken. Pungent, aromatic accents were
provided by native condiments, scattered in small bowls
around the table: hot chilis and salted peanuts; brittle twists
of dried squid and abalone; pickled tea leaves; Chinese
sweetmeats seasoned with garlic and sugar.

Everything seemed to be going smoothly, and she was
about to leave when she caught sight of a gawky dark-
haired figure at the edge of the veranda. A twinge of guilt
assailed her as she recognized the girl who was accepting a
glass of fruit juice from a tray held by one of the servants.
Poor Delilah—they said she had been genuinely fond of
her reluctant suitor. It must be dreadful for her tonight,
standing in the corner, watching as one young man after
another whirled Celia out onto the dance floor. And soon
Skye would arrive, making things even worse.

Celia eased back into the doorway, trying to slip away
unseen. But it was too late, for Delilah had already spotted
her.

"I'm afraid we arrived unfashionably early," she said
as she headed toward Celia. An apologetic smile lit up her
face, making her look, for a moment, almost appealing.
"You hadn't come down yet. You were still in your room,
your mother said, putting the finishing touches on your
coiffure. But I did want a chance to greet you properly."

"Oh, well . . . I'm glad." Celia squirmed at the genuine warmth in the other girl's voice. She couldn't help

wondering, had their positions been reversed, just how gracious *she* would be. "It really is good to see you, Delilah. It's been . . . it's been much too long."

"Yes, it has." Delilah's smile softened, giving Celia the unsettling feeling that she knew what was going on in her mind. "I wanted to tell you how lovely you look. What a clever idea, putting orchids in your hair. They look very natural. And so pretty."

If anyone else had uttered the words, they would have sounded stilted. But Delilah obviously meant them, and it did nothing for Celia's sense of guilt to realize that the girl felt no rancor, despite her personal disappointment.

"Thank you," she murmured hastily. "That's kind of you to say. You look very nice too." She flushed as she realized how insincere she must sound. "Those are such . . . such lovely jewels! I've never had anything half so beautiful. Rubies are a perfect choice for you. They go so well with dark hair."

Delilah laughed. "You really don't have to do this, you know. Why is it, I wonder, that people always think they have to say certain things, even when they're plainly untrue? I've always known I'm not pretty, and I've never minded, not really—though I daresay I'm supposed to. I sometimes think it's more painful for everyone else than it is for me."

"Why, what a thing to say." Celia found, rather to her surprise, that she was smiling back. There was something about Delilah that was hard not to like. "And I meant what I said. You *do* look nice. I know that's not the same thing as pretty . . ." She paused, Ash's words of a short time before coming back to her. "But then, prettiness doesn't last long, does it? Mama often says that the women of her age who are the handsomest weren't considered beauties when they were young."

"Perhaps you're right, though I don't think that always holds true. You, for instance, are probably going to be even more beautiful when you're older. You have the kind of face that ages well. There is character in it, I think."

The compliment was so unexpected that Celia, who still had not forgotten all those nasty things she thought about Delilah when Skye was courting *her*, was more embarrassed than ever. It was an acute relief when the music started again and Ashton Claridge materialized suddenly at her side.

Ash was a superb dancer, and any other time Celia would have felt as if she were floating on air as he spun her around, moving with a deftness most of the other young men lacked. But the conversation with Delilah had unnerved her more than she realized, and she was preoccupied, barely hearing what he said until he jolted her back to reality with a quizzical:

"Where on earth are you, Celia? Not with me, that's for sure. I've been flirting with you outrageously for the past several minutes, and you haven't so much as chided me once."

Celia looked up, a little embarrassed. "I . . . I was thinking."

"That," he replied, "was obvious."

"No, really, I was *thinking*. About what you said before. About Elizabeth."

"Elizabeth?" Ash stared at her, mildly surprised.

"You said she isn't going to be so 'easy to look at' in a few years. I didn't understand what you meant, but I think I do now. It isn't going to matter then, is it? That Delilah isn't beautiful."

Ash slowed, missing a beat of the music. "Delilah *is* beautiful," he said quietly. "Though not the way you mean it. She's beautiful inside, where it counts. The man who has the sense to marry her will be a lucky devil."

"If you think that"—Celia raised probing gray eyes to his face—"why are you dancing with me instead of her?"

Ash looked startled for an instant, then laughed. "Perhaps because I'm a fool, like all the others, and follow my eyes instead of my head."

He twirled her around suddenly, driving all other thoughts from her mind as he wove an intricate pattern in and out

among the other couples. It was all Celia could do to keep
up with him, and she did not even notice the moment they
pulled away, dancing toward a quiet corner on the veranda. Only when it was too late to protest did she realize
he had stopped and was holding her at arm's length.

"You're making a mistake, you know."

His voice was so husky she couldn't make it out for a
second.

"A mistake? I . . . I don't know what you mean."

"Oh, I think you do. I think you know very well what
I'm getting at."

Celia *did* know, and she felt a moment's queasiness, the
way she had before when she was talking with Sin-Sin.
What was there about Skye Maarten that made people feel
they had to warn her against him?

"But that's ridiculous!" No one knew Skye the way she
did. He was young, of course, he was wild, but he was
sensitive too, and he would make a good husband once he
settled down. "You can't call it a mistake to set my heart
on the man I love. Or are you saying I'm foolish because
the man I want isn't you?"

"Perhaps . . ." Ash grinned obligingly. "There's some
truth in that, I admit, though it's not the way I meant it.
What I meant . . ." He broke off, laughing. "But you
don't want to hear this, do you? If you did, you would
have figured it out for yourself long ago, without any help
from me."

He drew her back into his arms, guiding her expertly
onto the dance floor. Celia followed, a little bewildered as
she tried to sort things out in her mind. Had he been trying
to tell her something about Skye? Or was he only flirting?
Feeling safe because he knew she was practically promised
to someone else?

Ash made no mention of Skye Maarten again, or anything else even remotely personal, but Celia, remembering
how she had felt when he pinned her with those challenging eyes, was grateful when the music finally came to a
close. She didn't even mind too much that it was his

younger brother, Roderick, who claimed her for the next dance.

Roddie was even more awkward on the dance floor than off, and Celia managed to forget all about the uncomfortable feelings Ash had aroused in her as she tried, not always with success, to keep her toes from being trampled on.

The dance was just drawing to a close when Skye Maarten appeared in the doorway. One glimpse of him was enough to make Celia forget everything else. She knew she was hurting Roddie's feelings as she craned her neck to look at him, but she couldn't help herself. All her concern tonight, her thoughts, her eyes, were only for Skye.

There was a breathtaking elegance about him as he stood back-lighted in the wide double doorway. Never had he appeared handsomer or more dashing. Dark, tapering pants and an impeccably tailored black jacket emphasized his tall, slender frame, and Celia could not help noticing that he had acquired a new waistcoat, heavy white Chinese silk embellished with white embroidery. The same masculine shades that looked so drab and somber on other men suited his dynamic coloring: fair hair seemed even more golden, blue eyes more entrancingly echoed with violet.

Celia did not wait to thank Roddie for the dance, but deserted him the instant it was over, hurrying off in Skye's direction. She was halfway there before it occurred to her that men were supposed to come to women, not the other way around, and she stopped, her face a mirror of impatience as she watched him cover the distance between them.

"You are late." She pursed her lips into a flirtatious pout as he finally reached her. "I had begun to think you weren't coming."

"Had you?" Skye laughed as he looked down at that bright, confident, deceptively childlike face, knowing full well the idea had never crossed her mind—though it had his. "Perhaps I was lingering just outside. Listening to haunting strains of music . . . and staring up at a blue-velvet sky.''

"You were . . . stargazing?'' Celia was aware of a vague sense of unease. It wasn't like him, turning poetic this way. "Ah, you were thinking about coming inside. Quivering with anticipation, I hope.''

"Quivering,'' he admitted. "But not with anticipation. With fear.''

"Fear?'' The word caught her off guard, faintly ominous, though she was not sure why. "What would make you afraid?''

Skye caught the tremor in her voice, and for the first time since he had entered the room, he found himself enjoying the situation. When she was like this—when she was unsure of herself, timid—she reminded him of the young girl he had been attracted to long ago.

"It doesn't make you the least bit afraid? This thing you are about to do?''

Celia felt her heart skip a beat. Never before had he come so close to saying the words she longed to hear.

"And what . . .'' She hesitated, terrified of spoiling things by pushing too hard, but unable to stop herself. ". . . what am I about to do?''

Skye held out his arms.

"Why, dance with me, I hope.''

2

Serena St. Clair stood on the sidelines watching as gaily clad dancers flitted past like so many fireflies against the backdrop of a midnight sky. Each of those youthful faces seemed to glow with a secret excitement all its own, but she had eyes for only one, her daughter's, as Celia swept by in the arms of the man she had wanted since she was a little girl.

They had been dancing together since Serena came into the room. Three dances at least, perhaps four or five, and she knew as well as any mother what that meant. In a society governed by rigid dos and don'ts, every pattern of behavior had its meaning, and any young man who monopolized a girl's attention as thoroughly as Skye Maarten was doing now was making a declaration almost as telling as the formal words he would utter to her father the next day.

The music was sweet and liltingly sensuous, a romantic, old-fashioned melody, and Serena, listening, felt herself drawn back into the past. It was almost as if she were a little girl again, huddled with her cousins at the top of the broad, curving staircase, looking down at merrymakers arriving for a ball in her grandfather's house. It was the first time she had been allowed such a privilege, and though she did not know it then, the last, for most of her childhood was to be spent in the kitchen with Cook and her boisterous brood of sons. But that night, the old earl had been away, and the women of the house, kinder than their menfolk, had seen no harm in letting her enjoy herself, "just this once."

She had pressed her nose excitedly between the rails, feeling cold wood on both sides of her face as she peered down, fascinated, at the scene below. The ladies of that era were not as elegant as now: no sleek silhouettes accented natural feminine grace; no pencil-slim satin skirts arched over flattering bustles in the back. But to her childish eyes, those yards and yards of shimmering taffeta, spread over wide hoops and crinolines, seemed the epitome of style and beauty. One gown in particular took her breath away, a gleaming mauve silk, its ruffled sleeves and skirt trimmed with deep purple velvet ribbon and tiers of silver lace.

"Someday I'm going to have a dress just like that," she boasted, sensing even then that the gown would suit her silver-blond coloring. "And I'm going to have my hair done that way too, with—"

"No, you're not," her cousin Andrew broke in. He was two years older than Serena and had never liked the child who was livelier and more popular than he. "Dresses like that are too grand for you. What makes you think anyone is going to invite *you* to a ball? When you're old enough, they're going to stick you in the scullery with the maids, where you belong."

"They will not," Serena retorted hotly. "Why should they? I have nothing to do with the maids. The earl is *my* grandfather as well as yours. And why wouldn't I be invited to a ball?"

"Because you're a *bastard*, that's why!" Andrew's spiteful round face glowed with triumph. "I heard Grandfather say so. You're nothing but a filthy bastard—that's what he said. You don't belong with the rest of us."

The outburst ended quickly, for one of the older girls, overhearing, gave the boy a sharp cuff on the ear, telling him to mind his manners or "I'll send you straight to bed." But for Serena—who had not even known what the word "bastard" meant, except that it must be something terribly shaming because Andrew enjoyed it so much—all the sparkle and excitement seemed to go out of the evening.

It took her several days to work up the courage to ask Cook about it. But that good woman, horrified at the way the earl's family treated a child who was, after all, "one of their own," only made a hasty excuse and changed the subject, leaving her as much in the dark as ever.

It was a word she was to hear often enough in the years to come, though never with the same innocence, for one of the rougher servant girls had been all too ready to satisfy her curiosity, telling her in particularly graphic terms exactly what it meant. Her father, it seemed, had indeed been the earl's son, the old man's favorite until he had been banished, dying in exile in the colonies. But her mother was nothing more than a pretty little upstairs maid, a hapless serving girl who had died—rather to everyone's relief, Serena thought bitterly—a few weeks after giving birth to her. The family, conscious of their position, had acknowledged a certain responsibility toward the child, seeing that she was properly fed, clothed, and sheltered. But that sense of duty had not extended toward making her feel wanted or accepted, and with each passing year she became aware of a growing sense of loneliness and isolation.

Until Charles came to visit.

Serena sighed, trying not to let her mind drift back to the past, but unable to resist its lure. In Charles she had found everything she was looking for: warmth, generosity, liveliness, acceptance, and above all, laughter. Although he was a distant cousin, he was nothing like the rest of the family, and Serena, as taken with his free, open spirit as she was with his dashing good looks, had been more than ready to be swept off her feet.

The week of his arrival, Charles took her for a ride in the carriage, right down the main highway, past all the neighbors' houses, as if such behavior were not the least bit scandalous. It was a brisk autumn day—Serena could remember it still—and when they returned, her cheeks were flushed with pink. They had, of course, been severely reprimanded for their behavior, but far from deterring them, that rebuke only made them conspirators, and they found ways to see each other in secret. By spring they had become lovers, meeting as often as they dared in an abandoned caretaker's hut on the far side of the estate, where their comings and goings were less likely to attract notice.

Those summer months she spent with Charles were the happiest of Serena's life. Her body had not been truly stirred, as it would later be by the gently patient husband who took time to satisfy her yearnings as well as his own. But her love for him was a passion of the heart, and that had always been more important—and more rewarding—for Serena.

She had been a little frightened when she first realized she was pregnant, but only vaguely so, for she was still naive enough to believe in her lover . . . and Charles had not disappointed her. He was delighted with the idea, he told her excitedly, and more than ready to stand up to the tyrannical old earl. After all, he had a little money of his own. They did not need his family, not really. They would run away and live together . . . and be ecstatically happy for the rest of their lives.

Thus it came as a complete shock that afternoon the old earl called her into his study. Serena had not been afraid at first, not even when he leaned back and peered at her through his monocle, telling her in self-righteous tones that she was no better than her mother and he wanted her to pack her belongings and get out. Dimly she wondered why he was doing all this. Once she and Charles were married, they would not expect to live there anyway.

But when she tried to say as much, he laughed. "I have sent Charles away," he told her coldly. "You are never going to see him again."

With those words Serena's world was shattered.

She nursed her grief for weeks, wandering alone among the moors and meadows around the cottage of Cook's sister, where she had taken temporary refuge. At first, childishly, her heart regretted the pretty dresses she had expected to have, the gala parties she longed to attend, almost as much as the lover who had not had the courage to stand by her. Only as the child became more real, a tangible physical presence in her body, did Serena at last begin to think about her own precarious existence, and the fear that had been only a little thing before began to gnaw away inside her. It was that terror, as much as the white-blond hair whipping around her face, that gave her the fey quality which so captivated Ian St. Clair the first time he saw her.

Ian had seemed, in many ways, the answer to a prayer, and Serena, recognizing in him what might well be her last chance, was sorely tempted to withhold the truth about the child until it was too late and he was stuck with her. But because she genuinely liked the taciturn, clumsy Scot, and because she could not bear the thought of beginning a new life based on deceit, she choked back her fears and told him everything. To her amazement, it made no difference. Ian had married her anyway, as quickly as the law allowed, whisking her off to another continent, another *world*, without so much as a moment to look back.

The music changed, picking up the tempo of a more modern tune, and Serena, glad of the distraction, forced her mind back to the present. Thoughts of Charles were painful even now, and best left behind.

Glancing around, she caught sight of her husband, conscientiously making his rounds among their guests, hating every minute of it, she was sure, but going through the motions anyway because he knew how much the teas and balls and soirees meant to her. Ian was a good man, and with the passing years, she had come—in far deeper ways than she ever had with Charles—to love and respect him. He had been there for her, holding her hand, weeping with her, when she lost that first little stillborn boy she had wanted so much. He had been there again, strong and supportive, through all the agonizing miscarriages. And he had almost burst with pride when she finally presented him with a healthy baby girl.

Yes, he was a good man, and she was grateful every day of her life that he wanted her. But sometimes—just sometimes—when she looked at him, she wished he could have been not only good, but handsome as well, and charming . . . full of fun and laughter. It was at times like those that she was glad her daughter had found Skye Maarten.

"Mrs. St. Clair?" The voice belonged to a middle-aged timber merchant, down on holiday from one of the hill stations. "May I have the honor?"

Serena turned toward the man, smiling vaguely. Ordinarily she would have been pleased to accept—that was one of the few compensations of being isolated in the colonies, where men outnumbered women a dozen to one. Even matrons were not expected to dress in drab burgundies and grays and sit on the sidelines while young girls had all the fun. Tonight, however, she refused, pleading a sudden bout of faintness, for she knew she could never make her true feelings understood.

How could she explain to this man, a virtual stranger, that she was already on the dance floor floating in the same strong arms that held her daughter? That, through Celia, she was living her life over again, and just for tonight, all the hurts and disappointments of the past had been swept away?

Celia, absorbed in the exhilaration of dancing with Skye, was barely aware of her mother's eyes fastened on her graceful form. Only occasionally did she catch a sense of that proud, possessive gaze, and glancing over her shoulder, she would cast a conspiratorial smile in her direction. Dear Mama, she was so sad sometimes . . . it almost seemed she had lonely secrets hidden in her heart. It was good to see her smiling so youthful and happy, as if she—like her daughter—had not a care in the world.

Turning back to Skye, Celia tried the same radiant smile on him and was rewarded with a gentle if somewhat subdued response. Skye was not as good a dancer as Ash, but he was skillful enough, and she had the heady illusion that she was as light as a feather as he whirled her around and around in his arms.

Just like he had before, she thought giddily—in every daydream she had ever dreamed! Reality more than lived up to her expectations. Skye was as exciting now as he had been in fantasy, a tall, lithe figure, vibrantly handsome, the perfect foil for her own dainty grace. His hair shimmered golden in the candlelight; his dazzling blue eyes glowed almost violet, reflecting the lavender of Celia's dress as she arched her neck to gaze up at him.

And all the other dancers drew subtly to the side as they passed!

Celia laughed softly, thinking what a child she had been when she first started dreaming those dreams. What a naive little girl. And yet she had loved him even then.

"You seem very pleased with yourself." Skye's voice cut into her reverie. "Tell me, are you going to share the secret?"

Celia let long lashes flutter briefly against her cheeks. "If I shared it, it wouldn't be a secret anymore."

"And a good thing, too. Women have too many secrets, if you ask me. An annoying habit. I hope you aren't planning on keeping any from me."

"Ah, but I am." Celia looked up, still laughing. "It's a woman's right, you know—to keep little parts of her heart all her own."

"Indeed? Why is it women always claim as their 'right' those things calculated to torment a man? You are heartless minxes, the lot of you."

"And you can't stand the sight of us—is that it?"

"No . . ." He dropped his voice, deliberately low and teasing, partly because he knew it was expected, but partly because the repartee had begun to amuse him. "No . . . I enjoy the sight very much. Too much for my own good."

He had drawn her subtly closer. Now he tightened his hold, just a bit more than decorum permitted, and Celia felt almost giddy, though whether with the swirling rhythm of the dance or Skye's boldness, she could not tell. Confused, she looked away, just in time to see that Ash Claridge, who was standing with a group of friends at the side of the room, had turned his head and was watching her with quite a complimentary gaze.

The sense of flattery was heightened as she turned back to see a faint frown on Skye's face.

"Why, Skye Maarten, don't tell me you're jealous!" She was only half-joking, for his expression told her he was indeed displeased by Ash's attentions, though his lips were quick to deny it.

"Jealous? Of Claridge? Hardly that, my dear. Still, I hope you haven't been flirting with him all the time I've been away. I had visions of you sitting by yourself in the garden, a bouquet of red hibiscus clasped in your hands, sighing while you waited for my return."

Celia laughed. "The whole three and a half years you were gone? Not likely. What a dull existence that would have been. All daydreams and no substance! Besides, what makes you think my dreams were of you? Maybe I was hoping for someone more . . . romantic."

"Who could be more romantic than I?"

"Oh, I don't know. A tall, dark stranger perhaps—a daring young colonel in Her Majesty's service at the far reaches of the Indian Empire."

"Colonels are never young. They're scrawny middle-aged men with little clipped mustaches and almost no hair on top."

"Well, then, a pirate! That's more glamorous anyway. Someone like . . . the Tiger!" She started to laugh again, liking the turn the conversation was taking. "We've been hearing all sorts of exciting stories about him, even here. They say he's an American, and very bold and dashing! He's supposed to have red hair and the darkest green eyes in the world."

"In the *world*? My, my, how exotic!"

"Now you're being jealous again, and all because I

think he must be very handsome." She looked up, teasing. "Have you ever seen him? Is it true? Are his eyes really deep and green?"

She was surprised to feel him stiffen just for an instant. Then his expression relaxed again, and he began to shake his head. "Good God, how should I know? Where would I have gotten to know a man like that?"

"Nowhere, I suppose," Celia conceded, a little disappointed. "But you have been very mysterious, you know—about where you were and what you were doing those years you were gone."

"And where I got my money? Don't worry, your father quizzed me about it quite thoroughly—you can get the boring details from him if you really want them. No, my frivolous little darling, I wasn't sailing the seven seas with the Tiger and his crew, and from what I've heard of the man, it's just as well. He's dangerous and unscrupulous, and you'd better hope you never get close enough to make out the color of his eyes."

A faint shiver ran through Celia's body, not at all unpleasant, and she would have asked more about the man they called the Tiger if the music had not ended at just that moment. Skye paused but continued to hold her, and she sensed he was about to claim her again, as he had for the past hour. For an instant she was tempted to give in, but she could not forget that her mother had been watching all evening. She adored dancing with Skye—she would dance with him forever if it were up to her—but tonight of all nights, she didn't want even a shadow of disapproval to mar her happiness.

"Come." She caught hold of Skye's hand, pulling him after her. "You must help me be a good hostess and see that things are running smoothly. I can bear to miss a dance or two if you are with me. And besides . . ."

She caught herself just in time. *Someday this house will be yours too*, she had started to say, *and you and I will be host and hostess together*. But that would be presuming too much before the words had been spoken.

"Besides, we can't keep dancing like this. People are going to talk if we don't choose other partners. It's too . . . too scandalous!"

Skye laughed, knowing full well what she had been about to say and enjoying the sense of his mastery over her. He bent his fair head closer, ignoring her protests as he swept her back onto the dance floor with the opening strains of the music. This time, he did not steer her out into the center, as he had before, but wove a nimble course between the couples at the edge, past the open French windows and onto the veranda, down the steps that led to the garden.

Celia followed almost numbly, too unsure of her own reactions to protest until suddenly it was too late and the lights of the ballroom were gone, the moonlight almost day-bright in the silent garden around them. She adored Skye Maarten more than she could put into words, she could not believe this moment was finally happening, and yet it was frightening too. Everything was going so fast, she couldn't catch her breath.

"I . . . I oughtn't to let you do this." She looked up, half-hoping for reassurance, but his expression was un-readable. "Everyone knows a young girl isn't supposed to go walking with a man in the garden after dark. We . . . well, we shouldn't be here."

"Oh . . . and where *should* we be?" His lips twisted, a faint hint of teasing.

"I don't know, but not here! I mean, everyone must have seen us leave. And Mama . . . What will Mama be thinking?"

"Probably, 'Well, and it's about time!' if I'm any judge of mamas. If I *hadn't* taken you for a walk, I daresay she'd have sent someone to persuade me with a shotgun."

"A shotgun?" In spite of herself, Celia started to giggle.

"Why not? Mothers *have* been known to get anxious when young men dally with their pretty daughters. And fathers have occasionally used a shotgun to very good advantage."

."But Papa could never use a gun on anyone! Poor darling. He's too tenderhearted, though he'd die before he'd admit it. He'd make a great show of aiming, and squint his eyes and shoot . . . and miss by a mile."

Skye laughed. "I didn't mean your papa. He's a fine huntsman, the best in the area, but you're right, he'd be no good in a situation like this. No, I was thinking your mother might use her charms to coax someone else to do the job for her. Maybe that timber merchant from the hill stations who tried three times to get her to dance."

"*Three* times?" Celia cocked her head to the side. "You're very observant, Schuyler Maarten. Here I thought you had eyes only for me, and all the time we were dancing, you managed to see what my mother was doing."

"I managed to see *everything*, including the way Ashton Claridge was watching you while he pretended to chat with his chums in the corner."

There was an edge of sharpness to his voice, and Celia had all she could do to keep from smiling. "You don't have to worry about Ash Claridge—surely you know that."

"Don't I?" He had not failed to notice the way she craned her neck before, to look back at Claridge. Plainly she was more than a little flattered by his attentiveness. "I wonder . . . Well, there *is* one way to prove it."

"Ohhh . . ." Celia began to tremble as she saw the way he was looking at her. This was not the sweet proposal she had half-expected when he lured her out into the garden; instead it seemed that he did indeed expect her to prove her love—and with the kind of kiss no decent woman could give a man who had not yet made his declaration.

She half-tried to pull away, but he was much too fast. Although she could not know it, he had seen that brief flicker of hesitation, and it worried him more than he cared to admit. He had already made up his mind that the little St. Clair heiress with her modest expectations was the best he could hope for, and he had spent a long hour before, pacing back and forth in the garden, steeling himself for what he had to do. He was not about to ruin everything now by giving her time to think what she was doing. On impulse he lowered his mouth to hers, forcing it open, scavenging with his tongue.

He was rougher than he had intended, and Celia, awakening rudely from dreams of tender lovemaking, at last managed to resist. But his arms were so strong she could make no move against him; her own limbs turned weak and quivering, and she found herself engulfed suddenly in the first feverish stirrings of a passion more intense than anything she had even sensed before. In all those girlish daydreams, never once had she imagined that a man's body would feel so hard and muscular. That the smell of him in her nostrils, the taste on her parted lips, could be so compelling.

Sensing her acquiescence, Skye tightened his hold, curious to see how far he could go. Her tremors increased, surprising him with a hot-blooded ardor he had not suspected beneath that porcelain-pretty surface. Full breasts crushed against his chest, a none-too-pleasing reminder of the way her figure had ripened in recent months. He preferred his women slender and boyish of build.

He ran his hands down her back, a smooth, mechanical gesture. Fortunately he had a body that never failed to respond, even under adverse circumstances, and he knew he would be able to perform his marital duties with a minimum of difficulty. His hands rested briefly on the horsehair pad that puffed out her bustle, then slipped underneath, toying with round buttocks before passing on to the more welcome feel of her lean upper thighs. The touch excited him, kindling an unexpected warmth in his groin, and he made no effort to hide the fact that he had grown hard for her.

Once again her response surprised him. Instead of drawing back, she arched toward him, an instinctive gesture, as if her needs were as urgent as his. He slipped his fingers from behind and into the warm crevice between her thighs, intending only—so he told himself—to whet her appetite so she would not look at anyone else in the months to come. But the sensations in his own body, once aroused, were hard to quell, and he found himself chafing at the thought of letting her go.

And dammit, why should he? What harm would it do to take her down to the gazebo by the river and give her a taste of what would be hers as a bride? Harm, hell—it might actually do good. Ian St. Clair, that stubborn old bastard, was certain to insist on a long engagement . . . and long engagements gave flighty young daughters time to change their minds.

But if Celia already belonged to him, if she was his wife in everything but name, she would not be able to refuse him later. Even if she wanted to.

The throbbing in his groin intensified, but he forced himself to slow down, caressing her lightly, almost teasingly . . . not wanting to frighten her now that he was so close. Celia, sensing the new tenderness in his lovemaking and aching for it, melted into the smoldering passion of his embrace, and he dared hope for a moment he was going to succeed.

But to accomplish his objective, he had to ease his hold long enough to get her to the gazebo, and that was his undoing. The instant she felt cool night breezes blowing between them, reason returned, and she realized with horror what she had almost done.

"No!" she cried out, drawing back. "Oh, no—we can't do this."

"We *must* do it." He caught hold of her arm. "You can't deny me now. It's gone too far for that. Or yourself. You know you want this as much as I do."

"But I don't." She twisted away, knowing even as she did that she was lying. "I don't! Not really. Well, I *do*, but . . ." She broke off, searching for something to save herself from the rising flood of passion that threatened to sweep over her again. "We have to get back! Mama may have expected us to come out here, but she didn't expect us to stay all night! If she doesn't see us soon, she'll be worried. Then Papa *will* come after us."

Skye took a step backward, not liking it but having to admit she was right. He *didn't* dare press her now. The risk would be too great. But he didn't dare put the thing off too long either. He had to get her into bed before she could start having second thoughts about him.

"Meet me later, then. After the party is over—in the gazebo by the river. I'll be waiting, just before dawn, when the first color reddens the sky. I won't try to push you again, I promise. I wouldn't have done it now, only I wanted you so much I got carried away. But I have to see you one more time . . . before I talk to your father."

Celia recognized the emotional blackmail in those words, and she knew she should refuse, but she couldn't bear the thought of rejecting him, not twice in one evening. And after all, would it really be so foolish? The tryst was hours away. She had plenty of time to collect herself before then. It would be her choice—hers alone—whether anything happened between them.

"All right. I'll meet you then, but I have to get back now."

She was aware as she raced along the path and up the steps to the veranda that Skye was following with his eyes, but she didn't trust herself to turn and look back. The memory of those ardent caresses was still too potent, the sense of warmth that flooded through her veins as keen now as when he had drawn her, soft and trembling, into his arms.

Was she going to be strong enough to say no to him? Or did she love him so much she would surrender before her wedding night?

Her face was flushed with excitement as she returned alone to the ballroom.

Behind Celia, in the garden, Skye Maarten was following her retreat with not quite the expression she might have hoped for on his handsome features.

It was not that he didn't think she was pretty. Skye frowned as he caught hold of the branch of a young

tamarind. She was very pretty, and in a way that appealed
to him, for he enjoyed the idea of having a wife who
would excite envy and admiration. But his attraction was
hardly the sort a man wanted to feel for the woman with
whom, from time to time at least, he was going to share
his bed. Round-hipped, full-breasted blonds had never
caught his eye; he liked his ladies lean and willowy, with
an exotic sensuality that enticed rather than stifled.

Damn Eliza Crofte-Johnston!

Skye ripped off the slender branch, snapping it in half
and tossing it to the side. Now *there* was the woman he
should have had! Tall, elegant, snobbish Eliza—a perfect
mate for the life he had in mind.

A burst of raucous masculine laughter came from the
side of the house, and Skye looked up, surprised to see
lamplight spilling onto a darkened area of the veranda. He
had not noticed that particular room before, for it was shut
off by interior doors from the rest of the ground floor, but
he realized now that card tables had been set up for the
enjoyment of the men.

Funny, he thought, squinting as he stared at the doorway. Ian St. Clair was usually too much of a puritan to
allow gaming in his house. But then, Ian didn't usually
allow heavy drinking either. Obviously tonight was a night
for casting rules aside.

He glanced at the river, dark brown and glowing, a strip
of silk-velvet ribbon in the moonlight. The smell of Celia's
perfume clung to his nostrils, reminding him distractingly
of plump young breasts pressed insinuatingly against his
chest. There was something unsettlingly womanly about
her, not at all in keeping with the little-girl innocence of
her face. It would be amusing enough, what would happen
between them tonight, for she was new to physical love
and he would be in command. But later, when she was
sure of herself, when she understood her own wants and
needs, she would become aggressive, demanding . . . clinging. If there was one thing he hated, it was a clinging
woman!

Why the devil had he messed things up so badly with Eliza?

He turned away from the river, scowling. Eliza would never have clung to him. Hell, Eliza wouldn't even have wanted him! He would have visited her bed the few times convention demanded, impregnated her with the proper number of children, and gone his own way without a word of protest.

Provided, of course, he remembered to be discreet.

Skye laughed hoarsely. It was just that lack of discretion that had gotten him into trouble in the first place. If only he'd had the sense to keep his hands off that sly serving minx on the Crofte-Johnston estate. But how was he supposed to know Eliza would come along just at the moment he managed to insinuate his hand up that prettily draped English-cotton *longyi*?

Well, lucky for Eliza she hadn't caught him with one of the native boys, whom he actually preferred. She would have fainted dead away, right on the spot. And he would have left her there!

Skye started back toward the ball, then hesitated, his eyes drawn to the gaming room, where the action had grown livelier. It was a good, rousing game—he could tell that by the hoarse shouts and occasional guttural undertones of laughter—and he longed to be a part of it. There was enough of his wastrel father in him to love the sound the cards made slapping against the table. And enough of the daredevil for him to want to pit his skill against all those planters who thought they were better than he was.

Well, why shouldn't he?

The thought appealed as he turned it over in his mind. He had money in his pocket, after all, and a few hours to kill before it was time to meet Celia. Who knows, maybe tonight was his lucky night. Maybe he'd win back everything his father had lost in that other game four years ago.

Maybe he'd win enough so he never had to worry about pretty heiresses again.

He jammed his hands into his pockets, whistling softly as he headed toward the veranda.

3

Down below, the *White Lotus* lay at anchor, sheltered in a deep cove etched out of rocky hills that rose steeply from the ocean's edge. Tall-masted sails shimmered in the moonlight, and a long white hull glowed eerily, like a ghost ship against the darkened waters.

For Teresa Valdes, standing at the edge of a nearby cliff, staring moodily at the sea, the tall clipper was more than a symbol—it was a way of life. The *Lotus* belonged to her, but she belonged to it too, in some deep-felt way she could not have explained, and she sometimes had the mystical sense that she would die when the ship died, not a day sooner . . . or later.

It had been no more than a macabre whim, painting the vessel from stem to stern in gleaming white, the Oriental color of mourning. But the first time they sailed up to a smuggler's junk on a moonlit night and Teresa saw the superstitious terror of the crew as they leapt overboard, plunging into the sea on all sides, she knew that she had stumbled on a weapon far deadlier than any out-of-date cannon on her prow. A pirate, to last more than a few months in those danger-infested waters, had to create an aura of almost supernatural invincibility. And in the three years since she had taken over Lin's broken organization, Teresa Valdes had done just that.

She had not had an easy time of it, especially in the beginning, when money had been scarce and the men threatened to desert at any moment. But Soong had stood by her, and with his help she managed to get the two small ships, the *Black Jasmine* and the *Red Crescent*—later rechristened the *Red Peony*—to a safe harbor on Lantao, the largest of the islands between Hong Kong and Macao. She had to sell everything she possessed, even the magnificent jade collection Lin had given her, and her favorite gold bangle bracelets, but she was able to purchase a swift three-masted clipper, put up for auction by one of the local shipping firms. Fortunately it was in good condition, having been retired only because sails could no longer compete with steam, and once refurbished, with topgallants and royals flapping in the wind, the *White Lotus* was a match for any privateer on the seas.

Her lack of experience was balanced initially by an element of surprise, for no one who knew the fate of Lin and his men expected the phoenix to rise from the ashes again, and certainly no one was looking for two small, relatively insignificant ships that once belonged to him. Her sex, too, proved an unexpected advantage, that and her extreme youthfulness and beauty. Until her reputation spread, she found to her amazement—and utter contempt— that she could pull alongside any vessel on the seas, standing openly in the prow, and not a man on board would have the sense to run for his guns.

Her first successful raid was accomplished in much that manner. The target was a packet steamer bound for Canton, with no passengers and a full cargo of mail and opium. Teresa approached it alone, dressed in Oriental garb in a sampan that looked as if it might sink at any moment. When the crew pulled her aboard, the captain was right there beside them, properly sympathetic at the grisly tale she told of being waylaid and set adrift by pirates—and more than a little aware that this pretty young woman was alone and defenseless on his ship. On the open seas, the captain's word was law, and no one would dare to intervene if he made her a little "more at home" than she wanted to be. If she told stories of rude treatment later, well . . .

The man grinned broadly, enjoying the situation. Who would listen? She was, after all, Chinese. She did not count for much in that part of the world.

Teresa, seeing the lascivious look on those swarthy features, seemed to play into his hands, pleading exhaustion and asking if she could lie down in his cabin. The captain, with a bawdy wink at his mates, was all too ready to agree, staying on deck for a short time afterward, as much to enjoy the banter and lewd jokes that passed among the men as to make sure she was undressed and in bed when he got there.

He would have been considerably less pleased with himself had he known that even at that moment she was making her way from his cabin to the officers' quarters, disabling every gun she could get her hands on and making sure the spare ammunition was dumped overboard. By the time the *White Lotus* appeared and the captain realized what had happened, it was too late. The slaughter that followed was quick and complete.

Deceit became Teresa's hallmark in the months that followed. She soon gave up the idea of making the approach herself, for word of the "pirate princess," as the newspapers labeled her, had begun to cause panic, and even innocent young ladies with a Eurasian cast to their features were denied passage on the better steamers. But there were other ruses at her disposal, and she tried them all, relying heavily on the services of a young Englishman who had been useful to Lin just before his death. She had already noticed that the British had a peculiar way of trusting anyone with white skin and an accent that sounded like theirs—they were not sensibly suspicious like the Chinese; they did not ask questions, even when the unpleasant truth was there in their faces—and that fair-haired, wide-eyed gentleman proved a valuable decoy more than once. He tired of the game eventually, as foreigners were wont to do, but by that time Teresa had learned her craft and did not need him anymore.

Now her operations were more conventional, with well-planned, meticulously timed attacks taking the place of subterfuge. But there were still a few tricks up her sleeve, one in particular, which she was careful to keep a secret, especially from her most dangerous adversary, the American they called the Tiger. Everyone knew about the *White Lotus*, of course—she had deliberately let it be spotted, more than once—but she was reasonably certain neither Brandon Christopher nor anyone else knew of the existence of the two smaller ships. She had used them only a few times, as necessary backup, and she made certain no one was alive to tell the tale when she sailed off again.

Brandon Christopher . . .

Teresa frowned as she looked down the hill to where Soong, her second in command, was climbing slowly up a narrow switchback path. His face was lowered, so she could not make out his expression, but even without seeing, she knew it was pinched with disapproval. Like the other men on that ghostly ship in the cove, he had to be thinking his young mistress was skirting perilously close to disaster tonight.

As he approached, however, he kept his thoughts to himself, calling out only a terse:

"Five minutes."

Teresa nodded. Like Soong, she understood that timing was essential. Dealing with a man like Brandon Christopher, she could not afford to be a few minutes wrong, one way or the other.

"Is everything ready? The dinghy is waiting?"

"It's on the other side of the cove. By the stream. There's no sail, but the oars are strong. I think the wind is not going to rise until later. You will need nothing else."

"And the sentries?" Teresa cast a quick glance at the water. Mindful of the carelessness that had cost Lin and Sebastião their lives, she always insisted on doubling and tripling the watchers.

"Every part of the island is covered, and I have half a dozen of my best men at sea. Not a sampan can get through without their seeing. If anything goes wrong, they will signal with the lanterns."

"Well, then . . ." Teresa shifted the bag she had been carrying to one shoulder. It did not contain much, only an old woolen shawl and a small handgun. "I think it's time to go. Wish me luck, old friend—even if you don't approve of what I'm doing."

Soong's expression did not change. "It is not for me to approve or disapprove. I only follow your orders. The rest is up to you."

Teresa tossed her long black hair back in the moonlight. "You know what's wrong with you, Soong? You never approve or disapprove of *anything*. You are too Chinese."

"Perhaps." Soong had always been completely loyal to his youthful commander—he would lay down his life for her if he had to. But that did not mean he blindly assumed she was right. "What you say is true. One *can* be too Chinese. But the opposite is also possible. And you, I think, are not Chinese enough."

You *think*, Teresa wondered wryly, or you *know*? She did not acknowledge the words; nevertheless they echoed in her ears as she made her way down the rocky path and around a shallow beach to the stream where the dinghy was waiting. Soong was right, of course. There *wasn't* enough of her half-Chinese mother in her. Emotions showed too readily on her face, the way they did with the Europeans; feelings mattered too much in her heart. She ought to be able to let go of the man who had become an obsession with her, ought to let go of the passion and the hatred both, and see him for what he was—a dangerous adversary who would get the better of her if she did not learn to deal with him logically and coolheadedly.

But coolheadedness was the one thing she could not manage when it came to Brandon Christopher.

Even now, three years later, she could still remember, with that same searing anger, exactly how she felt the first time she saw him after the death of Lin and her father. He had been strolling through the lobby of his hotel as nonchalantly as if the entire colony were not talking about the heinous slaughter he had arranged. And she had been so furious, she forgot everything else and followed him up to his room.

"You . . . you monster!" She seized the door out of his hands, forcing her way, eyes flashing, into the room. "You vile, despicable monster! How could you do this to me?"

"To you?" Brandon turned, looking no more than mildly startled. "What, pray tell, did I do to *you*?"

His voice was maddeningly cool, and Teresa, trembling with rage, could only gape at him for a moment.

"Do you deny that you set up that cowardly massacre when everyone was asleep? Do you deny you killed my father? Yes, and my lover too!"

"I deny nothing. Not even that 'cowardly' act, as you choose to label it. But to say I did it to *you*? That's a bit farfetched, my hot-tempered pretty, even for an angry young woman. Surely it must have occurred to you the raid was timed to take place when you weren't there. Obviously I had no desire to hurt you."

"You had no desire to . . . *hurt* me?" Teresa seethed. How could he stand there so calmly, as if nothing had happened? "Do you think it didn't *hurt* to know I was the instrument of my father's death? You tricked me into telling you what you wanted to know. I would never have betrayed my lover's secrets like that. You used me!"

"I gave you what you wanted, Teresa. If that was *using*, then yes, I used you. As you used me. We both had reasons for seeing each other, not all of them honorable. Remember, I never forced you to come to me. I *invited*. You came because you wanted to. And you knew damn well you were betraying your lover when you did."

"Oh . . . *oh* . . ." Anger twisted like a knife inside her, cutting all the deeper because she knew it was true. "I hate you! I wish I had known you were going to be here. I wish I had brought a gun—to put a bullet through your head!''

She lunged forward, provoked into a blind fury by the thought of what he had done—was doing—to her. Her fists beat ineffectually against his chest, her fingers flew upward, clawing at his face, longing to hurt him, as he had hurt her. But he was too quick, and she managed to leave only a single red gash on his cheek before he caught her wrists, wrenching them downward.

Pain shot through her arms, mingling suddenly, unexpectedly, with a warmth that seemed to rise from deep within her. Sick with horror, she realized that no matter what he had done, no matter how she might loathe him, the very touch of his hands, the nearness of that overpowering male virility, was enough to drive all traces of reason from her brain. Destiny, she thought bitterly—cruel, capricious destiny—had played a trick on her, making the only man who could truly satisfy her the one she would never be able to accept.

Then even that thought was gone, and she was in his arms, clutching at his shirt until the fabric ripped in her hands, kissing, crying out for the passion she did not want but could not deny.

Her surrender that afternoon was complete, as was his, though she was too absorbed in her own feelings to realize it, and it was a long time before they lay back, drenched in each other's sweat, on the rumpled, twisted bedcovers. Later, when Teresa finally found herself alone on the dusk-darkened street outside his hotel, waves of humiliation swept over her, reminding her sickeningly how little control she had had of her senses. Helplessness fused with anger, channeling into a hatred so deep it would be the driving force for the rest of her life.

She could not keep herself from wanting him—she realized that now. She could not keep from desiring, or giving in to her desires. But she could see to it that he did not live to enjoy the benefits of his treachery!

This time, caught in the deepening chill of twilight,

Teresa Valdes did not wish for a gun. A gun was too quick for what she had in mind. And too easy. She wanted him to suffer before he died.

The dinghy was on the shore where Soong had left it, pulled up on a narrow ledge of sand. Teresa forced her mind back to the present as she worked it loose. For what she was planning tonight, she needed all her wits about her. She eased the boat away from shore, noting with satisfaction that the ocean was as smooth as glass. The sky above was a deep, cloudless, moon-brightened blue.

She had seen Brandon several times since that tempestuous afternoon at his hotel, always with the same results. At first she had difficulty adjusting to the affair, which they now continued quite openly, since there was no longer any reason to hide. But soon she came to terms with her feelings, deciding, sensibly, to accept what could not be changed and concentrate on what she planned to get out of the relationship.

Before, she had been a naive child whom Brandon Christopher had enjoyed and manipulated. Now she was a woman—a woman who knew what she wanted.

And what she wanted was to ruin the man who had ruined her.

A dark landmass loomed up ahead, and Teresa slowed the boat, dragging her oars through the water. She and Brandon had used the island several times before, and although it was neutral territory, under constant surveillance by her men, she nonetheless approached it with caution. When her eyes detected nothing unusual, she settled back to wait for a signal from the sea, telling her to proceed.

The canvas bag containing the gun was still lying beside her. On impulse, she picked it up and shoved it under the seat. Despite Soong's misgivings, she could not believe she was truly in danger. She did run risks tonight, but they were not the risks he feared. Brandon would not make any overt moves against her, knowing that her men virtually surrounded the area. Just as she wouldn't dare harm him before he had a chance to send whatever signal he had prearranged with his crew. She would be his hostage on the island tonight, as he would be hers.

Games, she thought, suddenly feeling tired. They were playing games with each other. Ostensibly they were lovers, coming together because they could not resist the fires that sparked whenever their bodies touched. But beneath that romantic facade were two deadly sparring partners, each trying to glean the little bit of information about the other's organization that would give an ultimate edge.

Only, that too was an excuse, for on another, even deeper level, Teresa sensed they were in reality the lovers they pretended to be. And the sole result of their meetings thus far had been the physical satisfaction neither of them wanted to admit.

The signal Teresa had been waiting for finally came. Two quick flashes of light from the direction of a promontory to the west, then two flashes again. So Brandon had arrived . . . and he was alone. He would be on the island in a minute or two.

She picked up the oars again and glided silently into a small inlet. Securing the boat on shore, she began walking the short distance to the peasant hut where Brandon would be waiting for her.

Tonight's meeting had been his idea, perfectly timed, as usual. A large shipment of opium would be arriving in a few days from Bengal, and he knew she was frantic to find out what he was planning to do about it. If he was going to wait, attacking the vessel on the China coast, then she would wait too, for these were home waters and she had the advantage here. But if he decided, daringly, to intercept it along the way, then she had to take the risk and follow course.

The lure was an irresistible one, and even recognizing the bait, Teresa had to swallow it. It was dangerous, but only slightly so, for she knew what he wanted in return—to discover where she had relocated their hideout after he smashed Lin's operations on that other, smaller island. He could hope to learn nothing from her arrival, of course, for she always took care to be in position before he came. But perhaps this time, when they parted, she would be too tired, too sated from their passionate lovemaking, to be cautious . . . and he could guess where she was going.

Brandon was already there, leaning casually against the doorframe when she stepped into the clearing that held the small stone hut. As always, on seeing him after an absence, Teresa was stunned by the physical force of his presence. Lamplight spilled out into the darkness, accenting the lines of a powerful physique and setting coppery-brown curls on fire.

"You are prompt, I see." He came forward, greeting her as if they were only lovers, with no thoughts beyond the pleasure they would enjoy in each other's arms. "Dare I presume you could not contain your excitement at the thought of being with me again?"

His voice, deep, faintly drawling, sent a familiar rush of warmth through Teresa's body.

"Of course. I am always excited at the thought of you. You know that."

"And I, you—especially when you look so fetching." He ran a practiced eye down her figure, appreciating the tailor's art that had crafted black silk pants and a high-necked jacket to cling in just the right places. The collar had been embroidered with threads of gold, but that accent was almost lost in the faint light, and the only shimmering brightness came from jet-black tresses floating to her waist. "Did you have that outfit made especially for me?"

Teresa, who had carefully supervised every detail, including the selection of sheer black silk, chosen not only for the way it looked but the way it would feel when he touched her, smiled enigmatically. "You have an inflated opinion of your importance to a woman, Brandon Christopher—and your influence on every detail of her life, including her selection of a wardrobe."

"Hers? Or *yours*? At any rate, the outfit is becoming—

and very appealing to a man of my type. I had hoped, when you put it on tonight, you were thinking of me.''

"Well, perhaps I was.'' She stepped past him into the sparsely furnished hut. Besides the table on which the lamp flickered, and a straight-backed chair, there was only a wide double bed, which Brandon had covered with a sensuous red satin quilt. "I will confess to a certain attraction for you. But then, you already know that . . . don't you?''

"I know that you came tonight''—he slipped up behind her, touching impertinent lips to the nape of her neck—"because you wanted me.''

His voice vibrated through her, dissolving her resistance.

"Yes, I wanted you—God help me. I could think of nothing else all day.''

"You mean you hungered for my strong male body—and couldn't stay away.''

"What else?'' She laughed softly, enjoying the game now that she knew the rules. "Is there any reason why I'd be here, other than that I hunger for the strength of your body? Or am I not supposed admit that—because I am a woman?''

"Admit anything you want . . . only later. Right now, I have other things in mind.''

He drew her toward him, gently but firmly, as expert fingers toyed with the neck of her jacket. Teresa savored the sensation for a moment, then twisted out of his grasp. Even as those brooding dark green eyes caressed her body, she began to undress, slipping out of first the smooth silk jacket, then the loose-fitting pants, under which she wore nothing. Tawny golden skin glowed pink against the scarlet coverlet as she stretched out to watch him remove his own clothes. It was one of the things she enjoyed most about lovemaking, that moment of looking up at the strong naked body of a man standing over her—and seeing that he wanted her.

She was ready when he came to her, her thighs moist with the longing they both shared. It never failed to excite

Brandon, the way she responded, taking her pleasures like
a man, with no need for flattery or coaxing words to talk
her into doing what she had wanted all the time. Without
preliminaries, he buried himself inside her, knowing, but
no longer caring, that he satisfied her deep cravings as
well as his own.

It was only afterward that the loneliness came. Teresa
sat up on the bed and pulled the coverlet around her,
wondering, as she had so many times before, what she was
doing there. Sometimes when they were together, she was
almost happy, managing to forget for an hour or two the
bitterness of the past. But later the anger and self-disgust
always returned, welling inside her until she thought she
would choke on them.

"I should have scratched your eyes out," she said
feelingly.

Brandon raised himself on one elbow. "Don't tell me
my performance wasn't satisfactory. And here I thought
I'd been especially ardent tonight."

"I didn't mean tonight, and you know it. I meant
before. That time after . . . after you betrayed me and I
followed you to your hotel room. I hated you then."

"You hated *yourself*," he reminded her gently, "because you let me make love to you after the way I had
'used' you."

"You did use me! You can twist words around all you
want—you're very good at that—but it doesn't change
anything. You never cared about me. I doubt if you care
now. You're only here because you think you can trick me
into saying something stupid again, the way you did before. That's why you started following me in the first
place, wasn't it? You wanted to get me in bed so—"

Brandon cut her off with a sharp laugh. "I'm hardly
foolish enough to think you could be tricked so easily
now. As to the idea that I followed you with thoughts of
bed on my mind, that's absurd. Quite the contrary. I was
as surprised as you the first time we made love."

"But . . ." Teresa eyed him suspiciously. "You were

always . . . *there*. Everywhere I went, every time I turned around, I saw you.''

"I knew you were Lin's mistress," he reminded her patiently. "You had been pointed out as such several times. It occurred to me you might be useful—though how, I must confess, I had no idea. That first time when I followed you, it was strictly on impulse. Then, seeing your reaction, I decided to keep it up."

"And the night in the grotto . . . ?"

"That night just happened. When you disappeared from the path, I guessed you were heading for the grotto, which I had just discovered myself the day before. I decided to go after you, thinking it might be interesting to shake you up a bit. It wasn't until I saw your eyes in a flash of fireworks that I knew what you expected me to do. And I knew you wanted it."

"You . . . *knew*?" A slow tremor ran through Teresa's body. Was that what this was—a whim of fate? A thing that would never have happened if she hadn't been foolish enough to cross the deserted peninsula at night?

She did not have time to ponder the thought, for he drew her down beside him, and their lovemaking began anew, slowly at first, almost tenderly, rising inexorably to a sweeping, mindless passion that engulfed them both. It seemed to Teresa that Brandon was especially virile that night, as if he, like her, was driven by the need to forget everything else, and by the time they finally finished with each other, his face looked strangely drawn. Tired in ways she had never seen before.

It suddenly occurred to her that she had nearly forgotten what she came for. Now it was almost too late.

"I don't like saying good-bye," she ventured, pouting a little.

"I thought you hated me. Didn't you tell me you wanted to scratch my eyes out?"

"I do hate you, and I'd love to scratch out your eyes. But I need you too, Brandon. No man makes me feel the way you do."

"I know." He laid his hand lightly on hers, looking more tired than ever. "There are times I hate you too, but that doesn't keep me from wanting to make love to you. We are two of a kind, Teresa Valdes. Both damned—or is it doomed? Interesting, how the words sound alike. Well, never mind . . . I'm talking nonsense. I'll be in Hong Kong for a few days, and I have nothing important scheduled. Shall we make plans to meet again?"

Teresa turned abruptly, not wanting him to see her face. If he was telling the truth, if he *was* going to be here for a few days, then he must be planning on attacking the Bengal shipment somewhere in the vicinity of Canton.

"Do you really mean that?" She composed her features as she looked back. "Could we see each other tomorrow if we wanted?"

He must have heard the edge in her voice, for he grew wary. "I can't make any promises. I *do* have something planned, come to think of it . . . though perhaps I can put it off. I don't know, but I will try. Is that good enough for you?"

No. it's *not* good enough, she thought angrily. Damn him! There was a distinct sparkle in his eye now, and he didn't look the least bit tired anymore. He *might* have made a slip, of course. Even cool, self-possessed Brandon Christopher was not perfect. But he might have done it on purpose, too, to throw her off the track.

"I think," she said quietly, "I'll wait and see. There's no telling—is there?—what you're going to do."

She rose and dressed quickly, hating herself for being tricked again, hating herself for coming, even though she knew she couldn't stay away. She should have realized she would never get anything out of him. And even if she did, she wouldn't dare believe it.

By the time Brandon was able to dress and follow her, she had already reached the dinghy and, with her pants legs rolled up to her knees, was pushing it out into the water. He stood in silence on the shore as she turned her

prow toward the open seas, deliberately steering a dangerous course so he could not follow without being seen.

So it was going to be a standoff again.

Brandon smiled grimly, recognizing his defeat and hers
at the same time. He *had* thrown that comment out inten-
tionally, knowing full well how she was going to react.
But she was thwarting him just as effectively now. And
glancing over her shoulder all the while to make sure he
was watching!

In spite of himself, he could not help feeling a grudging
admiration as his eyes followed that slender, erect figure.
Everything about her was evil, in the deepest sense of the
word. She had had absolutely no qualms about cheating on
her lover—her fierce pride was wounded only because she
had been betrayed while she was betraying. Nor had she
had the slightest compunction about the innocent young
lives that were snuffed out every day as a result of the
despicable opium trade she carried on. Yet there was
something touching about her too, a kind of childlike
bravado in the face of adversity, and the maleness in him
could not help responding to her courage and spirit.

It was that response, more than anything else that had
brought him here tonight. He had known when he set out
that he had slim hopes, at best, of learning anything from
her. Had anyone else been involved, he would not have
kept that dangerous rendezvous.

But it was not anyone else, of course. It was Teresa
Valdes . . . and the web she spun with her dark, exotic
beauty was as compelling as it was insidious.

The wind gusted suddenly, blowing cold across the
waters, and Brandon turned up the collar of his jacket as
he headed toward the natural jetty where he had left his
boat. Time to light the lantern that would tell his men he
was safe. Otherwise they would not let the woman through.
And if they didn't, his own life would be on the line, for
her followers were almost certainly within striking distance.

The web she spun . . .

An ironic half-smile twisted Brandon's lips. Yes, "web"

was exactly the word. Beautiful or not, courageous or not, Teresa Valdes was as deadly as a black widow spider. And he had the feeling that, like a spider, the only way he was going to stop her was to kill her.

Before she could kill him.

4

The music and laughter had long since faded away, vanishing with the last of the revelers in a flurry of jangling harnesses and creaking carriage wheels. The only sounds that reached Celia's ears as she huddled in one of the overstuffed chairs on the veranda, her feet tucked under her, came from the direction of the gaming room. But even those were subdued and tense, and she sensed that action at the poker table was reaching a climax.

If only I had stayed with him! she thought, remembering that strange, reckless look on Skye's face when she left. Everything was so perfect until then. He had been so attentive and charming, so wonderfully romantic. Now, all of a sudden, the whole world seemed to be falling apart.

Celia did not need the low, intermittent murmur of male voices to tell her that the game was growing more and more heated and the stakes had gotten out of hand. Nor did she need Ko Taik's hasty whispered accounts whenever he slipped out of the room to get a fresh bottle of liquor or more ice. Her heart had already warned her that her lover had joined the game—and things were not going well for him.

"He is like a man possessed," Ko Taik reported as he paused beside her chair. "There is a demon in him. He loses and loses, yet he will not stop."

"Hasn't he won *at all*?" Celia's heart caught in her throat. She could understand Skye's love of gambling—it

looked exciting to her too. But she didn't understand
throwing good money after bad on a night when luck was
against him.

"He won very much," Ko Taik said. "In the beginning. He had nearly three times what there was when he
started, and the other gentlemen were very angry. They
thought he was going to quit. But he said no, and he
laughed—as if they were saying something very funny.
Then he started to lose, and he did not laugh anymore. But
he did not stop."

Celia watched helplessly as Ko Taik scurried back to his
duties. From his account, it did indeed sound as if her
lover were a man possessed. As if something inside drove
him toward his own destruction.

*They say there are reasons why the Lady Elizabeth
refused him.*

Sin-Sin's words came back, dark and troubling. Could
Skye have inherited his father's obsession? Was that what
the girl was hinting at? He had shown no signs of it
before, but what else could she have meant?

And why else would Ash Claridge warn her she was
making a mistake?

No! Celia forced the thought to the back of her mind.
She had loved Skye Maarten much too long to listen to
idle gossip. She wasn't going to turn her back on him
now.

"Perhaps he'll win after all," she said, stopping Ko
Taik as he passed by with a bucket of ice. "He was
winning before. Perhaps the tide will turn, and he'll win
again."

"Perhaps," the servant agreed dutifully. The lights in
the ballroom had been extinguished, and the peach-toned
gaung baung on his head glowed purplish in the moonlight.

"Perhaps that's why he insists on staying in the game.
You think he's foolish, but he knows his luck is bound to
change. If he's bold enough, he might win in the end."

"Perhaps."

But even as she leaned back, letting her eyes close

wearily, Celia knew she was grasping at straws. By the
time she finally heard the shuffling sounds and low, muttered conversation that told her the game was breaking up,
she was so drained she could no longer pretend. The men
would not be leaving, she knew, if Skye Maarten still had
a ha'penny in his pocket.

And if Skye had lost everything, so had she.

She was ready, a few minutes later, for the stern look on
Ian St. Clair's face as he plodded up the steps to the
veranda after saying good-bye to the last of his guests.

"I am sorry, daughter," he said huskily. "It seems your
young swain has a reckless streak in him."

"You are *not* sorry!" The hurt inside made her lash out,
not even caring if she was fair. "You've always hated
Skye. You know you have. You're glad this happened! It
gives you an excuse to break us up."

Ian recoiled, stung by the force of her anger. "I never
cared for the lad," he admitted. "I made no bones about it
before, and I'll not deny it now. But I cannot be glad of
anything that hurts you so much."

There was truth in his voice, and Celia turned away,
unable to bear the reproach.

"He has lost *everything* then?" she said softly.

"Everything. The cash in his pockets first. Then, when
the others would not accept his note, he sent the coachman
to fetch the rest. It all went on the table, down to his watch
and chain. It was almost as if . . ."

Ian hesitated, recalling that dark, haunted look in the
boy's eyes. At the beginning, he had wanted desperately to
win. But later, when things started to go against him . . .

"It was almost as if he *wanted* to lose."

Celia looked up slowly, not hearing what her father
said, as a new, unspeakable thought came to her.

"You did this on purpose, didn't you?"

"On purpose?" Ian looked shocked. "Of course not!
What are you saying?"

"You never allowed gambling in the house before. And

you never poured liquor so freely either. You knew exactly what was going to happen. And you *wanted* it!"

Ian shifted his weight uncomfortably. There were half-truths in the accusations his distraught daughter was hurling at him. He *had* meant tonight as a test for young Maarten, but it was a test he expected the boy to pass. If Skye had managed to stay away from the tables, it wouldn't have been so difficult considering him as a son-in-law. Or if he sat down and played for a while and then got up again.

"I couldn't have gotten your young man into the gaming room if he didn't want to go. And I didn't mark the cards. You can't blame me for the way luck turned against him. I couldn't have arranged that even if—"

"It doesn't matter." Celia cut him off with a sudden show of spirit. "I wouldn't care if you'd bribed every man there to cheat him out of his money. It won't make any difference. Don't you see? I love Skye enough to marry him anyway. There's nothing you can do to stop me!"

"I won't have to," Ian said quietly. "The boy isn't going to ask you now. He has some pride . . . I'll give him that. And even if that harridan of a mother managed to bully him into it, he knows I'd never give my consent. Let me tell him I'll cut you off—and see if he wants you then!"

"Of course he will. Skye loves me—"

"Love or no, he isn't going to marry you without a dowry. Why do you think he stopped courting Delilah so suddenly?"

"Why? Well . . . because her father told her not to see him. Why else? Skye didn't have anything to say about that. Delilah would never go against—"

"Wouldn't she now?" Ian's voice was sharper than he had intended. He loved his daughter deeply, but it strained his patience sometimes, reasoning with a nineteen-year-old feminine mind. "She had her bags packed to run off with him—I have that on very good authority, mind you! It was young Schuyler who'd have none of it."

"Delilah had her bags packed?" Celia faltered, uncertain. Plain, down-to-earth Delilah with an impetuous heart. "I . . . I can't believe she'd do anything like that."

"She loved the lad. God knows why, but she did. Do you think you're the only girl who's ever been set awhirl by a pretty face and a charming tongue?"

"Well, I don't care! You can say what you want. Skye *does* love me, and I love him. Yes, and I'm going to marry him, too—if he'll still have me."

If.

The word loomed up even larger after Ian was gone and Celia let her guard down again. *If* he would have her.

But of course he wouldn't.

Celia dropped her head to the back of the chair. She loved Skye with all her heart, but even she was not totally blind to his weaknesses. He might have been courting Delilah only because his mother insisted on it, but Papa was still right about one thing. He wasn't going to marry any woman if they didn't have a cent between them.

Not that Papa would keep his threat. If they ran off and got married, if they presented him with a *fait accompli*, he would cave in soon enough and give his grudging blessing. But Skye didn't know that, and he wouldn't take the chance.

Aching and miserable, Celia forced her legs out of the cramped position in which they had been confined for hours and went upstairs to her room. All the joy had gone out of the pretty party dress as she tugged it over her head and dropped it in a heap on the floor, not wanting to ring for Sin-Sin, who would be bursting with curiosity and eager to talk.

It was so unfair! Celia kicked at the dress disconsolately, shoving it aside with her foot. The evening had been so exciting before everything went wrong. It should have been even more exciting now. She should have been breathless with anticipation as she stood there in her chemise, barely able to contain herself until it was time to meet her lover. Now the riverbank would be empty, and Skye would not be there.

Or would he?

The thought struck her just as she finished unlacing her corset, and she let out a little gasp of relief and excitement. She had simply assumed Skye would not keep their rendezvous—but was she right? They had made a deep and intensely emotional commitment to each other tonight. Nothing that happened could change that.

Wasn't it possible, just *possible*, that he would be in the gazebo at the appointed hour? And expect her to be there too?

Her fingers trembled as she removed the corset. She dared not call Sin-Sin to help her lace it up again. And anyway, she did not need it! Corsets were too rigid, too confining. Tonight she wanted to feel as free as the wind.

She wasted a precious twenty minutes pulling nearly every garment she owned out of the tall teak wardrobe and tossing it impatiently on the bed. The dark blue crepe de chine with its tight-fitting basque was her special favorite, and she eyed it longingly for a moment before discarding it with the rest. Even had it not been too dressy for a dawn tryst, she could hardly squeeze into it with her waist unbound. Like most of her prettiest gowns—the pale yellow muslin with its ragged-robin pattern, the piquant dotted swiss trimmed in cherry-colored ribbons, the Persian-print India silk that made her look years older than she was—it was designed to be worn with a tightly laced corset.

On closer examination, only one of her old standbys seemed to fit, an unfashionable sacque made up in a madcap print which Mama called distinctly "bizarre."

In the end, she settled on a brand-new shirtwaist outfit, a recent addition to her wardrobe which had been sent for all the way from London. It was, she thought as she adjusted the snowy cascade of lace spilling from her throat, quite *outré*, and she was not sure she liked it. Still, for all its rather odd blousiness, it was made of exquisitely light lawn, in a flattering shade of powder blue. And it did have a way of clinging, just slightly, when one least expected it.

Well, it will have to do, she thought, eyeing herself in

the mirror. *The color is good for me, and I don't have time to change. If Skye is there and I'm not, he'll think I'm not coming and go away again.*

The night was surprisingly warm as she stepped outside. Although it was still early in the year, it had already turned unseasonably hot, and a scent of frangipani lay in the air, mingling with the honey-sweetness of wild marigolds. The first rains had not yet come, and feathers of yellowish dust stirred faintly as she walked down the path.

How different the world seemed at night. In spite of herself, Celia could not help marveling at the look of her mother's garden in the moonlight. Great croton bushes fanned out on every side, forming dramatic backdrops of black and white, and blood-red hibiscus deepened to splashes of lush, sensuous purple. Zinnias and pansies, all lined up in prim little rows along the rock-edged paths, took on a capricious, wanton air—as if even nature understood what she was about tonight . . . and approved.

She paused beneath a gold mohur tree, looking up at the spreading parasol of branches high above her head. In the daytime, shimmering blossoms would seem bright and beckoning. Now, deep in shadow, they gave a sense of secrecy, veiling her from the watching stars.

Oh, please let him be there, she thought. *Please . . . please let him be there. And let him believe how much I love him.*

But the gazebo, as she approached, appeared to be empty. White-latticed walls were thickly screened with creeping jasmine, and no hint of movement was visible behind green leaves and clusters of pink flowers.

She was about to give up when she heard a faint sound from somewhere inside, and a tall figure appeared in the doorway.

If she had any lingering doubts about her feelings, they vanished at that moment. No one could have been more alluring than handsome Skye Maarten with moonbeams in his hair and deep violet eyes that caught the starlight. He had taken off his jacket, and his shirtsleeves were rolled up, exposing long, graceful arms.

Celia thought her heart would break at the sight of him.

"Oh, Skye," she cried out. "How *could* you? We were so happy tonight. We could have had anything . . ." She broke off, biting back the words of reproach. He had to feel badly enough as it was. He didn't need a shrewish fiancée telling him what he already knew. "Oh, darling, I am sorry. It isn't right to scold you. Not now. But—"

"But how could I be so stupid?" Skye filled in the missing words with good humor. "Go ahead, pretty Celia. Berate me. Call me a fool and a cad—I deserve it. I know I shouldn't have sat down at that table. I knew it at the time."

"And yet you did it anyway."

He gave a careless shrug. "It's in my blood, I suppose. Isn't that what they were saying? All those old biddies as they settled back in their carriages, thanking their lucky stars it wasn't *their* little darlings I was courting. Still . . ." He brightened, throwing her a half-wink. "I might have won, you know. I might have brought out bushels of bills and coins and laid them at your feet. Think how proud you would have been then."

"I would have." Her eyes were shining. "I would have been *very* proud." She couldn't help admiring the way he handled himself, so gallant and uncomplaining. "And I'm proud of you now! I don't care what you've done, or what those old biddies say. I love you. And I still want to be your wife!"

Skye was aware of a vague feeling of surprise as he looked down at her. Any other woman would have been screaming at him, telling him what a good-for-nothing loser he was. Girlish passion might be stifling at times, but there was something to be said for that fierce loyalty of hers.

"I cannot marry you now, Celia," he said rather gruffly. "Surely you know that."

"But you can—if you want to! Think about it, darling.

We could run away. Right now. No one can stop us. As for Papa, he'll come around in time. He's really a soft-hearted old darling—"

"Don't!" Skye cut her off sharply. 'Darling Papa' *might* come around—but then again, he might not. "What you are asking is impossible. For God's sake, leave me my pride at least."

His pride? Celia longed to hurl the words back in his teeth, but she didn't dare. *Pride*? The very word Papa had used—and he had been right. Heaven help any woman who came between a man and his precious pride!

"What are you going to do?" she asked.

To her surprise, he started to laugh, not bitterly, but with genuine amusement.

"I should think that was apparent. It doesn't seem to me I have much choice. I'm going to do exactly what I did before. Go off and get a stake to begin again. It took me better than three years, but that was because I was new at the game. This time, I'll manage in a year."

"A *year*?" Celia's eyes widened with shock. "Another whole year . . . after the time you've already been gone. Oh, Skye . . ." She sought the comfort of his arms, forgetting it was he who was supposed to make the advances. Those last years had seemed an eternity. And that was before she knew what it was like to feel his lips on hers! "I don't think I *can* wait a year. I'd miss you too much."

Skye put his arms around her, feeling a responsive tremor shiver through her body, and he realized she was telling the truth. She had already felt the first sweet stirrings of sexual longing. With her wildness and spirit, it was quite possible she wouldn't be waiting when—and *if* —he returned.

But that was a chance he was going to have to take.

He tensed his muscles, trying without success to extricate himself. "It isn't going to be that bad. Time will pass quickly, and when I come back, we'll have a proper wedding. Not some cheap elopement you'd be ashamed of later. Imagine how funny this is going to seem then. We'll sit back and laugh at how dark and terrible everything looked tonight.''

"No!" The word burst out of Celia's lips. What did it matter, all this talk of pride and propriety, when they loved each other? "I don't want to wait. Take me with you! Time will pass even more quickly if we're together. And I don't care what kind of wedding I have. I just want to be with you.''

She threw her body even more boldly against his, not caring how wanton she seemed. Skye was surprised by the feel of her breasts, high and firm, not flabby, as he had imagined, even without the aid of whalebone and steel. The desire he had felt before returned, and for a moment he was tempted. It could be lonely, night after night in a foreign hotel room. And then, Celia might be useful—if she could be persuaded to give up her scruples and do what he asked.

Still, there was no point pushing fate. Reluctantly he eased her back. His best chances now lay in ingratiating himself with the same people who had helped him before. And if he did, there was a certain attractive young lady who would take a dim view of the blond baggage he was toting along.

"You make it sound so easy, but it isn't. I'm going to have to go to Hong Kong, perhaps even deeper into the Orient. Things can get rough. There's no way I can take a woman with me, especially one who looks like you. If I have to spend all my time protecting you, how am I going to make the money we need?''

His voice was light, but there was a hard edge to it, and Celia felt her heart sink.

"I wouldn't be any trouble. Honestly I wouldn't! I could learn to take care of myself. And if you wanted to go off for a while on your own . . . well, you could always leave me behind. Someplace you considered safe. At least that way we'd be together part of the time.''

Skye shook his head. "What a persuasive child you

are." He smiled. "But that's just it—you *are* a child. All those foolish protests prove it. Don't you understand? If I love you, I can't let you make a sacrifice like this. But never mind. I'll take comfort in the fact that you'll be a woman when I return."

There was no escaping the finality in his tone now, and Celia knew she was defeated. Everything in her body cried out against the loss. He had called her a child, yet that was so unfair! Hadn't he felt the new, intense yearnings he himself had aroused for the first time that night? She didn't *want* to be a child anymore! She wanted to be a woman.

And she wanted to become one with him.

"If you won't take me with you, then . . . then I want . . ." She faltered, her cheeks burning crimson. "I want to be your wife . . . tonight."

The words did not come out the way she had intended, but he understood, and his body, responding to the promise of easy pleasure, prodded him to say yes. If he did not return—he had almost decided to stay away for good this time, and the devil take his nagging mother!—then it wouldn't matter what kind of problems he left behind. And if he *did* come back . . .

Well, it might be handy, having a pretty little heiress all sewed up and waiting.

He bent his head, half ready to give in. But the lips that tilted up to meet him were moist and parted, unexpectedly demanding, and he remembered the qualms he had felt before.

Dammit, he might want an heiress waiting if he came back. But he might want his independence, too! And an irate father waiting at the train with a shotgun was hardly a guarantee of that.

"You keep asking for the things I cannot give," he murmured huskily, "not if I love you."

"Oh . . ." Celia gasped softly. Tears stung her eyes, but she struggled to fight them back, sensing that strength was the one thing that would impress him now. He was going to be gone such a long time. What if he forgot all about her? "I . . . I can't bear to let you go."

The tears that glittered unshed on her lashes, had she but known it, were the one argument that came close to persuading him. Weakness had always appealed to Skye Maarten; helplessness attracted—and he wanted the child he had disdained before, not the woman she was so near to being.

It was with a certain genuine regret that he bid her farewell.

"Be waiting"—he touched her lips at last, but lightly—"when I come back."

Celia stood alone, watching as he sauntered off, so jauntily it tore her heart in two. She loved him so much, so *achingly* much, and there was not a thing she could do about it.

"I will wait," she whispered to the empty shadows. "I will wait forever if I have to."

5

The wind had begun to howl across the water as Teresa Valdes maneuvered her boat back into the sheltered cove where the *White Lotus* lay at anchor. The sea was more temperamental than she had expected, and her arms and shoulders ached by the time she finally tugged the small boat onto the shore.

Soong was not there to greet her, although she sensed he was watching, as usual, from one of the nearby hilltops. She did not call out for him to come and join her. After her meeting with Brandon Christopher, she needed time to be alone with her thoughts.

She frowned as she glanced back at the *White Lotus*, illuminated in the eerie half-light of a waning moon. She disliked the idea of leaving the ship that close to their hideout, fearing it would attract the wrong kind of attention, but she knew Soong was right when he warned her not to move it before dawn. The Tiger's men were sure to be out in force tonight. On dark, still waters, without a whitecap in sight, the *Lotus* would be easy to spot. Better to take it out by day when the stark white hull would blend in with flashes of sunlight glinting off the water.

The tall masts and spotless, gleaming paint gave the vessel a bold, rakish air, and Teresa felt a surge of pride almost as intense as the day she had first claimed it as her own.

She was glad now that she had insisted on calling it the

White Lotus. She had intended the name, at first, only as a kind of secret challenge—an assertion of her abilities as a woman and her right to lead the same life as a man. But to her surprise, it had brought with it another, unexpected advantage, for no one, captain or seaman, heard it without assuming she was connected, however loosely, with one of the secret societies. And no one tangled with the secret societies.

Teresa had always been fascinated by tales of the societies, which she had become aware of as a small child. One on the first things Sebastião Valdes had done when she came to him was insist on hiring an *amah*, an elderly woman who was told in no uncertain terms to make sure the child was instructed in "everything Chinese." Shrewdly Sebastião had sensed that the key to his daughter's acceptance in a European colony lay not in denying, but in emphasizing her exotic Oriental beauty. Teresa, who had no desire to do anything but leave the garlic-and-anise-scented slums of her past behind, had been inclined to rebel. But because Sebastião had been good to her—and because he bought her many pretty things—she agreed.

As it turned out, native tutoring was nowhere near as unpleasant as she had expected. Besides Portuguese, English, and French, she learned fluent Mandarin and Cantonese, together with a smattering of other, more obscure dialects and the written Chinese characters which were common to them all. She also learned other aspects of her heritage. She memorized the teachings of K'ung Tzu—or Confucius, as the Europeans called him—and discovered why the first Emperor of Ch'in slept in a different house every night, and who the characters in *The Water Margin* were. But most of all, she loved stories of the secret societies.

The societies, which were essentially political, at least in rationale, had their roots deep in the past. Originally they had been intended as a protest against tyranny and rigid social conventions. Teresa's particular favorite, the White Lotus—for which she had always had a special secret affinity—was said to have been founded in a Buddhist monastery in the twelfth century, where it was dedicated to the overthrow of the Mongol warlord, Kublai Khan, and the establishment of a Chinese dynasty, the Ming.

Between revolutions, however, the illegal bands found various ways to enrich their coffers and fill their bellies, and young Teresa thrilled to stories of armed robbery and kidnapping . . . and piracy on the high seas.

She was a bright child, and it did not take her long to mark the difference between the Confucian rules of order, which reduced women to a state of perpetual subservience, and the mystical societies. where women were not only accepted as members but also encouraged to seek office. Thus it was hardly surprising that a little girl who wore Chinese robes, but walked with unbound feet and was educated as a boy, grew up dreaming not of marrying some wealthy mandarin or becoming the emperor's favorite concubine, but of riding highways as a bandit, with a sword strapped to her hip and a bold, spirited horse to carry her off when the soldiers chased her into the marsh.

It was a dream that persisted to that day, for in a way, the gun Teresa kept beneath her pillow was her sword, and the *White Lotus* that same swift steed that had captured her heart long ago.

And Brandon Christopher and his men were the soldiers pursuing her into the wilderness.

Teresa left the dinghy where it was and made her way along narrow, twisting paths to the house. She had learned from Lin's mistake, and her dwelling, like the separate quarters she maintained for her men, was set in a secluded valley, not high on a hilltop where it could be spotted by telescope from the sea. The view was not as spectacular from her bedroom window perhaps, the sun did not stream into her halls in the morning, but she was comfortable enough, and more important, she was safe.

The houseboy was waiting when she arrived, but she motioned him back, and he slipped soundlessly down the hall, moving catlike on felt-soled shoes. There were no female servants, not even to tend to her personal needs, for Teresa, a woman herself, was aware of the dissension women could cause among her crew. If the men felt a need of diversion, they had ample opportunity to frequent the brothels of Hong Kong or Macao—but God help the one who tried to bring his liaisons home. No woman, besides her, was allowed on the island.

The main room of the house was open and spacious, for Teresa, whose earliest memories were of cramped slum dwellings where a dozen bodies were frequently crowded into one small room, could not bear the thought of walls that closed in around her. The furnishings, which were sparse but elegant almost to a fault, provided a unique mingling of East and West. Highly polished floors and lacquered red wall posts were distinctly Chinese, as were the scrolled paintings, with gnarled banyans and sheer rock cliffs rising out of clouds of fog. But the couches and comfortable stuffed chairs had been imported from Europe, and the Tientsin carpet, made especially to Teresa's order, was a copy of one that had lain for years in Sebastião's front parlor.

She went over to a low chest of drawers and removed a number of maps and charts, spreading them out on the floor. She was glad, as she squatted down to examine them, that Sebastião had not balked at the idea of engaging tutors for her. It was good to be able to read a map, good to understand the winds and tides and know where a ship was likely to go.

Her eyes narrowed as she traced out a course on the yellowed paper with a long red-polished nail. The ship that carried the Bengal opium was steam-powered, thus not affected by the calms, but the captain still had to avoid monsoons if he wanted to make good time. Bearing that in mind, there was only one course he could take.

And along that course—where?—the Tiger would strike.

She bent forward to study the charts more closely, trying to put herself into Brandon Christopher's head, to think what he would do. It would be a risky matter, pursuing the other vessel into the South China Sea, for he, like her, sailed a clipper and would be at the mercy of the winds, while the steamer was not. A more sensible plan would be to lurk in one of the rocky coves on the coast near Canton and attack from ambush.

But that was what he had implied he would do—when he made that slip that was not a slip at all.

Teresa frowned. Had he been lying, to throw her off the track? Or had he been telling the truth, knowing she would think it was a lie and act accordingly?

She rocked back on her heels, mulling the thing over in her mind. She had assumed it was a hopeless riddle, but was it? Brandon was clever, but he was human, and human behavior always worked itself into a pattern. He had been trying to confuse her when he threw out those words—but how? By picking a choice at random?

Nothing Brandon Christopher ever did was at random.

She turned her attention to one of the smaller charts, reading the lines on it the way someone else might read the letters on a printed page. She was getting to know Brandon better. She had a glimmer now of the way his mind worked. It would amuse him, throwing her off by using the truth.

Yes, he would strike—there!

Teresa tapped the chart with her nail. The perfect choice, an inlet just narrow enough to conceal his presence, but with a strong current to aid him when it came time to sail out again. Yes, that was where he and his men would be waiting.

Only they would wait in vain.

Her eyes glowed. Brandon had one ship, but she had three, though he did not know it. And all three of her captains knew every rock and shoal on that shore. She could risk attacking . . . *there*! A full day ahead of the place he had planned.

A surge of excitement shot through her. Not so much at the thought of plunder, though that was important too, as at the thought of outwitting Brandon Christopher. So far, in their few direct encounters, she had come out distinctly behind. At first Brandon had bested her because he was older and more experienced, later because he had more money behind him, more resources.

But this time the advantage was hers. And she was going to win.

Teresa rose, turning with a soft half-smile to the window, where blackness had begun to ease into the cold gray light of dawn. It would be a challenge, a gauntlet thrown in his face. And if she knew Brandon Christopher, it was a challenge he could not ignore.

He did not like losing any more than she did. He would come after her with everything he had.

And when he did, she would be ready for him.

6

The first streaks of sunrise splashed across the horizon,
bold and capriciously placed, like strokes from a mad
artist's brush. Within minutes they had spread until the sky
seemed to be on fire, and even the muddy Irrawaddy
glowed a rich, warm red.

Celia stared idly at the graceful white pagoda on the
hillside, barely noticing the deep pink glow that seemed to
have been absorbed into its plaster surface. Behind her,
everything was strangely silent, in a way it rarely was
along the riverbank.

Any other day, workers would already be out, bustling
noisily in the rubber groves, and a small army of *malis*
would have descended on the gardens with their scythes
and watering pails. But because last night's party had gone
on until all hours, no one was up, not even the house
servants. Only the *chokra* would be about, seated with his
back to the house, tugging on the rope that worked the
punkah in the ceiling. Later, when the heat rose and the
other servants had gone to rest in their cottages, he would
tie the end of the rope to his foot and lie back on the earth,
wriggling his toes halfheartedly to keep the air stirring
inside.

The morning fire faded slowly, replaced by a clear
white light that muted even the vivid colors of the tropics.
Celia began to wander along the water's edge. The quiet
seemed even more intense now, the solitude deeper than

anything she had experienced before. A faint breeze picked up, cooling the air somewhat, and she was aware, for the first time in her life, of the loneliness and aching beauty of this land she had always taken for granted. She could not imagine what it would be like to leave and never see it again.

Was that what Skye was feeling now?

The thought hurt, almost as much as the raw wound of their recent parting. Was he walking along that same riverbank, thinking how much he loved his home and how long it would be before he came back?

How long *before* he came back?

Celia stopped, realizing suddenly what she was thinking. Before he came back, or *if* he came back? What if he never returned? What if he found someone else, someplace else, and stayed away forever?

The thought clutched like cold fingers at her heart. and she rebelled childishly at the unfairness of a situation not of her own making. Skye Maarten was her whole world, her *life*, and he was leaving her, perhaps never to return. And she who loved him so desperately could neither hold him back nor go with him.

Or could she?

Celia caught her breath, turning the thought over in her mind, wondering why it hadn't occurred to her before. Skye couldn't *ask* her to come with him, of course. He was a man, and a man was expected to sacrifice his happiness, even if it tore his heart apart, to protect the woman he loved.

But that didn't mean she had to accept his sacrifice.

She would go after him! The solution was so bold, so simple, Celia laughed out loud with delight. Her youthful heart glossed over the deeper implications, dwelling instead on practicalities, which were easier to dismiss. Skye had already told her he was going to Hong Kong. Surely it would be a simple matter to find him there. As for how they would manage when she did . . . ? Well, she had a little money of her own, not much, but enough to book passage. And to make sure she wouldn't be a burden on him.

She began to hurry toward the house, half-skipping until she caught herself and forced her feet to move sedately. If someone came out and saw her, which was unlikely, she would say she hadn't been able to sleep and decided to take a walk. After what happened last night, no one would doubt her.

Her main problem, of course, was going to be Papa. But Papa was due in Rangoon on business in a few days. With him out of the way, there was only Mama to worry about, and Celia had always been able to reason with her mother on certain matters, particularly when it came to Schuyler Maarten. There was a definite romantic streak in Mama, something sad and somehow wistful. In her more fanciful moments, Celia imagined she had tragic secrets hidden in her past that made her understand love and young lovers better than anyone else.

No, Mama would not stand in her way. Oh, she might put her foot down for a while, she might plead or even cry, but in the end she was certain to relent. And Celia would be on her way.

And when she got to Hong Kong? Celia hesitated. When she saw Skye again?

The first momentary doubt flickered across her mind, but she brushed it back. Skye would be irritated at first, of course. Men were like that. They hated having their orders disobeyed, even if it was what they had wanted all along. But when he had had time to think it over, when he saw how much she loved him, how much she was ready to give up for his sake, then surely he would be glad.

She closed her eyes for an instant, imagining the scene as he threw his arms around her, whispering between kisses that he adored her and insisted on marrying her at once.

Her head was filled with plans for a hasty but wonderfully exciting elopement as she hurried up the steps of the veranda and into the silent house.

The Tiger Strikes

7

Hong Kong was a world apart from anything Celia had ever known. All the Chinese shops in all the market areas of Burma could not begin to prepare her for those teeming alleyways and steep ladder streets, crowded at any hour of the day or night. The unexpected sights that met her eyes every time she turned a new corner, the sounds that blended one into the other until she could barely hear herself think, even the exotic smells, were so strange and confusing she could never quite get her bearings.

She paused halfway up the narrow, twisting lane to push a strand of windblown hair back from her forehead. The air was surprisingly crisp, and she had had to purchase a woolen mantle from one of the tourist shops on Queen Street. Early spring in Hong Kong, though it lay at much the same latitude, was a far cry from the warmer climate along the Irrawaddy. It was barely past midafternoon, but the day was gray and overcast, and lengthening shadows gave the streets a twilight look. Shopkeepers had begun to set up lanterns for the evening, and flickering gold showed through open doorways as she passed.

For a moment Celia was tempted to give up and go back to her hotel, where even now a tempting tiffin would be laid out on white tablecloths in the ladies' parlor. It had never occurred to her it would be so difficult finding someone in a small colony like Hong Kong. She had had such hopes when she started out that morning after her arrival, inquiring first at the Hong Kong Hotel, which was conveniently located across the Praya from Pedder's Wharf, then at the Victoria in the center of the city, then the Mount Austin on the peak, and finally even the Windsor in Connaught House. But everywhere she asked, no one had heard of Schuyler Maarten and no one recognized his description.

After three days she had been nearly frantic. It was as if the earth had opened up and swallowed every trace of him. She finally picked up his trail at a small private boardinghouse in Victoria View, on the Kowloon side of the harbor, but even that proved a dead end.

"Yes," the woman who ran the place informed her, "a man by that name *did* stay here. But he checked out after a few days. And left no forwarding address."

She had been near tears as she walked back across the small parlor that served as a lobby. The doorman, a tall turbaned Bengali, took pity on her and drew her aside. He had been there when Skye left, he told her. He remembered the occasion particularly because the blond foreigner had been with a Chinese.

No, he did not know the other man's name. Nor would it help if he did, for there were a limited number of Chinese surnames, and all were quite common. But he had seen the man several times before, and he sensed that he was known in native quarters. If Celia wanted to find her friend, he suggested she inquire in local markets and shops, not the fancy European hotels.

At first the information had given her a surge of hope, and Celia was sure she would find Skye in a matter of hours. But two and a half days later, after questioning merchants in their shops and old ladies hawking fish from baskets on the street, she was more discouraged than ever.

What was there about these people that made them so suspicious of outsiders? She had been positive, just an hour before, that she saw a flicker of recognition in an old street vendor's eyes when she mentioned Skye's name. But it had vanished almost instantly, replaced by that same

Oriental passivity she was getting to know all too well—and a sudden inability to recognize a word of English.

She had tried the question again in French, then awkward Spanish, but it was no use. The man was like a rock. She could not even chip that flinty surface.

Celia drew in a deep breath to steady herself. The thought of a butter-dripping scone, or perhaps a light curry dish with condiments of mango and coconut, was even more tempting now, but she steeled herself against it. She had to keep searching as long as there was any daylight left. The hotel where she was staying was more expensive than she had anticipated, and then there was that cloak she had had to buy. If she did not find Skye soon, she would be at the end of her resources.

It was galling to find herself with so little money when she had expected to be at least comfortably fixed on her arrival. But Mama, to her astonishment, had not only "put her foot down," she had kept it there quite firmly, refusing even to discuss the idea of Celia's following her suitor to Hong Kong.

"I know you love Skye, and I do understand. But you're going to have to be patient. He may return, as he did before, and everything will be all right. If he doesn't . . . well, perhaps, in light of what happened . . ."

She let her voice trail off.

Celia, seeing only too clearly what she was getting at, felt betrayed and suddenly helpless. Not only had she lost the support of the one person she thought she could count on, but without Mama's help, she could not get at the money Papa had settled on her when she was eighteen.

She was at her wits' end when help finally came—from a totally unexpected source. Lady Elizabeth Crofte-Johnston.

The small sum Elizabeth brought her—a "peace offering," she said, "to make up for those silly quarrels we had in the past"—was barely enough to cover her passage. But at least it would get her to Hong Kong, and Celia had been about to accept, albeit with trepidation, when she had a second visitor.

"Delilah?"

She was startled, then embarrassed as the other girl explained why she had come. It seemed that she, like her cousin, had heard what Celia was planning to do.

"But how . . . ?" Celia stared at her, dumbfounded. Did everyone know what was going on? "How did you find out?"

"Servants talk, you know. One of the *malis* overheard you quarreling with your mother through an open window. He told Elizabeth's personal maid, who is my maid's sister. But all that isn't important now. What matters is that we have a chance to talk—"

Celia cut her off with an impatient wave of the hand. "I know you mean well, Delilah, but I love Skye, and I'm going to go after him, one way or the other. There's nothing you can do to dissuade me."

But Delilah, surprisingly, seemed to understand. "I'd do the same thing myself," she said, "if I had the courage. And if I thought he wanted me. But it would be a mistake to take my cousin's money. Everything Elizabeth does has strings attached. She'd like to make it easy for you to leave—and hard to come back. With Skye gone, Ash Claridge might begin courting you, and she wants him for herself. Here, take *this* instead."

She opened a pin-seal chatelaine bag with exquisite silver mountings. Celia saw that it was stuffed with coins and bills.

"This was all the cash I could get at short notice, but I'm sure it's more than my cousin offered. If it isn't enough, go to my uncle—my mother's brother. He's a merchant in Hong Kong. His address is in the bag. I'll write and tell him to see that you have everything you need. And, Celia, I hope things work out for you, truly I do. But if they don't, don't be too proud to ask for a ticket home."

Celia had taken the bag, feeling a little strange, but grateful to be able to leave Elizabeth's money behind on the dresser with a note to see that it was returned. Three

days later, when she set sail from Rangoon, she had been
confident, if a little nervous, for she was sure she had
more than she could possibly need. Now she was beginning to worry, and she was glad the uncle was on the
maternal side of Delilah's family. Perhaps he would be
like her mother, gentle and soft-spoken, not sternly intimidating like her father.

Well, no point fussing over things that can't be fixed!
she reminded herself firmly. If she had to, she would
appeal to Delilah's uncle and take him as he was. Right
now she had other matters to worry about.

The lane she had been following ended abruptly at a
corner, and she stopped, looking first one way, then the
other, with a feeling of helplessness. Every street was so
exactly like the one that had gone before, she had no idea
where she had already been . . . or where she wanted to
go.

Fortunately, Victoria, the capital of Hong Kong, had
been built on steep hills that sloped up from the ocean. At
least if she got lost, she could keep going down, and she
would reach the waterfront sooner or later!

Celia picked a direction at random and began walking.
The street she had chosen seemed even more crowded than
the others, if that was possible. Above the shops, wooden
shutters with faded, peeling paint opened onto the street,
and laundry flapped from long bamboo poles, adding a
touch of brightness to the setting. A square-cut wicker
cage dangled from one of the many curtainless windows.
Inside, a prettily colored songbird chirped away, oblivious
of the brash noises below.

Many of the shops were open-fronted, and Celia paused
occasionally to look into them with frank curiosity. In one,
a professional letter-writer, a thin man with wire-framed
spectacles, was scowling intently as he leaned over a low
table. An elderly woman squatted opposite him, her eyes
fixed on the bold Chinese characters that flowed from his
brush. A bill of small denomination was clenched in her
fist.

Next to the letter-writer, sharing the same shop, a fortune-teller piled his craft. Celia studied the face of his customer, a middle-aged, well-dressed Chinese, but she could not guess from those expressionless features whether the man had just heard dire predictions or an augury of good fortune. In the next stall an assortment of paper goods had been set out: houses and cooking utensils, elaborate carriages, horses, complete wardrobes—even piles of artificial paper money. All these and more would be burned at the funeral of someone who had never dreamed of such wealth in life, but would enjoy it now in the afterworld.

As she continued down the street, the brightly colored bottles in an herbalist's shop caught her eye, and she wondered, amused, what was in them. Korean ginseng? Snake glands for the eyes? Dried seahorses for virility? Rows of glass-fronted drawers faced the street, filled with various types of powdered bone, together with herbs and grasses, and on the back wall a large, rather fantastically drawn chart gave witness to the fact that the art of acupuncture was practiced there.

Celia reached the corner and paused briefly. Then, as before, she picked an arbitrary direction and began to follow another narrow, steeply sloping alleyway. Here, too, the shops seemed to have been jammed together with no regard for order. Piles of cabbages alternated with woks and other cooking ware, and gaudy arrays of gemstones were spread out on threadbare blankets. On one side of the street a woman sat on the ground patiently sorting out baskets of bean sprouts; across from her a barber had just wrapped a hot towel around a wealthy patron's face, while a shoemaker pounded on a piece of leather beneath a painted wooden sign in the shape of a giant boot.

If she hadn't been so worried about finding Skye, Celia thought, she would have been intrigued. The sounds were a typically Oriental cacophony: the singsong lilt of voices; the shrill call of hawkers eager to sell their wares; an underlying rumble of wagon wheels coming from a nearby thoroughfare; the constant *clackety-clack, clackety-clack, clackety-clark* of Mah-Jongg tiles. Even the smells were intensified. The scent of jasmine teased her nostrils, of dried chrysanthemums and fresh-baked buns filled with sweet-bean paste, of sweat and urine, garlic and ginger, anise and ginseng, and heavy smoke from braziers and open fires.

Celia stopped halfway up the street, her heart sinking as she caught sight of an old man squatting in front of one of the shops. It was the same man she had seen before—the one she was sure recognized Skye's name.

She had been going around in circles without even realizing it!

Her dismay must have shown on her face, for a young Chinese who had been standing across the lane came over to her. "You are lost, I think," he said quietly.

His voice was well-modulated, almost without an accent, and Celia studied him curiously. He was dressed simply enough, in dark blue pants with a dark blue long-sleeved jacket. But his hair, instead of being worn in a queue down his back, was cropped short like a European's.

"I'm not lost—exactly. I . . . I just . . ." She faltered, suddenly reluctant, though she was not sure why, to confide in this ordinary-looking stranger.

"You are searching for your friend, are you not?" the man said. "The tall blond Englishman."

"Why, yes!" Faint signals of alarm went off in her brain. How could he have learned that, unless he had been following her! "You seem to know a great deal about me. More than I do about you."

"Yes, that's the way it is here." The man smiled apologetically. "You're fair-haired and pretty, so everyone is aware of you. But you didn't see me, even though I was standing nearby." He gestured toward the old man, still squatting in the doorway. "I couldn't help noticing when you told him you were looking for someone. Don't you think that was . . . *foolish*? Surely you can't expect an old man like that to understand English. And even if he did, how would he know where your friend is?"

The words were reasonable enough, but something in his voice set Celia's teeth on edge. More than ever she was sure she had been right. The man *did* understand English. And he knew something about Skye!

"It sounds as if you're telling me not to look for my friend here."

"I was just thinking . . . it might be wisest not to look for him *anywhere*. Perhaps it would not be good to find him."

Dark, intent eyes seemed to bore into her face, and Celia felt herself begin to shiver. What was he saying? Did he know something about Skye that she didn't?

"Was that an observation? Or a warning?"

"Ah, now I have alarmed you." The man smiled again. "I meant only that it is strange for a young man to leave a pretty woman alone to follow after him. Don't you think so? But then, perhaps he has his reasons. It is, of course, none of my concern."

He bowed politely, making a conciliatory gesture with his hands as he backed away, blending into the crowd. Celia stared after him, conscious of a growing sense of frustration. These people had to know where Skye was, yet not one of them would tell her! Why? Because they disapproved of a woman chasing after a man?

She had the sudden uneasy feeling that everyone in that narrow lane was watching her, as if they knew exactly what the strange young man had been saying. More from discomfort than anything else, she picked a doorway at random and ducked into it. If people in this area did know where Skye was, then she was going to question them one after the other until she pried the truth out of them!

The door she had chosen led to a small seasonings shop. Only faint hints of light filtered in from outside, and the interior was dim and musty. A single lantern dangled from a hook in the ceiling, casting elongated shadows on piles of seeds and huge open bags of rice.

Celia worked her way cautiously between the grain-filled sacks and rough wooden barrels that half-blocked the

center aisle. Bins on both sides had been divided into
rectangular sections, and she eyed them curiously, picking
out gnarled, clawlike chunks of ginger root and heaps of
dried lotus seeds, fermented black beans and bright red
jujubes, strips of jellyfish, dried shrimp and squid, and
exotic cloud ears, which would be cooked with tiger-lily
bulbs, or "golden needles." Shelves ran all the way up to
the ceiling, filled with boxes and open glass jars of various
spices—star anise, Chinese cinnamon, fennel, five-spice
powder, hot Szechuan pepper—and rings of dried oysters,
strung on bamboo hoops, were hanging in the doorway.

Along one wall, near a wooden counter with an abacus
on it, Celia noted a large section of eggs. The black ones
with whitish striping, she knew, were "thousand-year-
old" eggs, which were not a thousand at all, but merely
duck eggs that had been soaked in limey clay for eight or
ten weeks until the chemicals had penetrated the shells,
turning the insides to a startlingly iridescent blue-green.
The stripes were made by running forks along the sides to
remove some of the caked-on dirt. There were also a
number of red-dyed eggs, favorite Chinese gifts, especially
at the birth of a child, for red was the color of good
fortune, and tea eggs, with their delicate brown veining,
and smoked eggs, and large jars of bright yellow salt-yolks
to add a touch of contrast to sweet mooncakes or the
blandness of steamed rice.

Celia was so absorbed she did not notice when a man
with pinched features and a thinning grayish queue came
out of the back.

Seeing her stare at the eggs, he said, "You likee?"

She turned, startled. The man's eyes were shrewder than
his face, and she had the feeling he could say more than
"You likee?" if he chose.

"I didn't come here to buy eggs," she replied, taking
care to speak distinctly in case her assessment was wrong.
"I am looking for a friend. His name is Maarten—Schuyler
Maarten. Do you know him?"

A brief light showed in the man's eyes. Recognition?

Celia wondered. Then it vanished, and she had the helpless feeling she was going to be shut out again.

Looking down, she caught sight of the small chatelaine bag in her hand. Perhaps she had been approaching the problem from the wrong direction, she thought suddenly. Perhaps there was a way to reach these people after all.

"I told you before, I don't want to buy any eggs. But I might be interested in buying something else. Information."

Opening the bag, she turned it over, letting a number of small bills and coins spill onto the counter.

The man followed the gesture with eyes that alternated between hesitation and greed. He wanted the money, Celia could tell. He wanted it desperately, but something held him back. Fear?

"Not know this man," he said at last with obvious reluctance. "Not know this . . . Schuyler Maarten."

"But you do know *of* him."

The man nodded slowly, his eyes still on the money. "Schuyler Maarten *was* here," he admitted. "In Hong Kong. But not here now."

He looked up half-hopefully, but her face did not change. Then, sensing that there was only one way he could have the money, he added a last whispered "Lantao."

Lantao? Celia's heart jumped. She barely noticed as the man scooped up the money and hid it behind the counter. Lantao. Surely she had heard that name since she arrived. Wasn't it one of the many islands around Hong Kong?

A few well-chosen inquiries elicited the information she wanted. Lantao was indeed one of the neighboring islands, a fairly large one, located somewhere between Hong Kong and the Portuguese colony of Macao. There was a regularly scheduled ferry-steamer leaving every morning that would drop her at the harbor. From there, the man told her—still with reluctance?—she could hire a local sampan to comb the coves and inlets until she found what she was looking for.

Surely even a large island could not have *that* many coves and inlets! How long would it take to search them?

A few hours at most? By this time tomorrow she could be reunited with Skye.

Her eyes were shining as she ventured out into the street again. Dusk had fallen, and cooking fires glowed in front of several of the shops. Women approached, and occasionally men, carrying large woven-bamboo baskets and earthenware dishes. These were the poor of Hong Kong, who could not afford even the few small coins required to invest in cooking utensils, and they frequented the food stalls each evening, purchasing steaming bowls of soup and noodles, or rice heaped with Chinese vegetables.

The smells were tantalizing, reminding Celia that she had not stopped for lunch. A young girl passed, balancing large baskets on either end of a pole across her shoulder, and Celia tried not to think that the dinner she was delivering to some affluent family might contain duck's-foot soup or grilled snake. Or perhaps fruit bat or fish lips—or monitor lizard!

She had just started to cross the street when she became aware of a slender figure standing a short distance away. Glancing around, she saw the same young man who had accosted her before. There was no way to get away from him, for he had already spotted her and was coming her way.

"You found your friend, I see."

His voice was pleasant, as before, but again she felt vaguely uneasy. No doubt there was a perfectly good reason why he was still there, and that reason had nothing to do with her. Nevertheless . . .

"No, I didn't find him," she said impulsively. Then, realizing the excitement on her face must have given her away, she added hastily: "But I'm sure now that I'm going to. People here know something, even if they won't tell me what it is. Sooner or later I'm going to find out."

He gave her a sharp look but did not pursue the subject. "You shouldn't be out by yourself. Not after dark."

"You mean it's not safe." Celia tried to sound cool, but she couldn't keep from casting a nervous glance over her shoulder. The street seemed to have darkened even in the past few minutes, and the night had an ominous feel to it.

"Oh, you're safe enough here," the man assured her. "This is a crowded street. No one, I think, would harm you. But you're a stranger in Hong Kong, are you not? You might turn a wrong turn and get lost. Then you could find yourself someplace not quite so . . . *pleasant*. Permit me to be your guide."

He did not wait for a reply, but turned and began to walk rapidly down the street. After a moment's hesitation Celia followed, not because she trusted him any more than she had before, but because she sensed he was right. She *couldn't* wander alone through darkened streets in a city she didn't know. Once, he turned into what seemed a threatening, half-empty alleyway, and she was tempted to retreat. But almost at once he led her back onto crowded, comfortable streets, and before she knew it, she found herself on the wide promenade that ran along the sea wall at the bottom of the hill.

He was smiling and affable—just like we were old friends! Celia thought—as he waved down a passing ginricksha and helped her into the seat. All the same, she had the unpleasant feeling those black eyes were laughing at her.

She was sure of it when he grinned suddenly. "Do you have money to pay the fare?"

"Of course," Celia started to snap, then caught herself abruptly. She had given every cent to the shopkeeper! The way this man was looking at her, he seemed to know it. Or had he simply guessed that was the only way she could get information?

"I . . . I didn't bring any money with me. I thought it would be better not to carry cash on the streets."

"Much wiser," he agreed. Reaching into his pocket, he pulled out a ten-cent piece, the usual fare for a half-hour ride. He handed it to the driver with a rapid spate of Chinese, then turned back to Celia. "I told him to take you to your hotel. And please, do not worry about repaying this small coin. It is my pleasure to help a stranger in the city.''

Celia leaned back in the seat, not even stopping to wonder, as she half-closed her eyes, how he had known where to tell the driver to take her. All she knew was that she had never been quite so tired in her life, and it was good to prop her feet up and wriggle her toes out of slippers that suddenly seemed much too tight.

The waterfront was almost completely dark by this time, and Celia stared bewilderedly at lantern-lit storefronts and great hulking warehouses. It was amazing how different everything looked at night. She was glad now that the man, whoever he was, had insisted on accompanying her to a ginricksha. She was not sure she could have found the way by herself.

Beside her, the harbor was a brooding presence, more sensed than seen. Tall-masted ships seemed to loom out of nowhere, only half-visible against an inky sky. Squat sampans were lost in shadow.

Fascinated, Celia turned to look at it.

Tomorrow, she thought dreamily. *Tomorrow I'll climb aboard one of those ships in the harbor—a ferry-steamer—and it will take me to my love.*

Tomorrow Skye and I will be together and I'll never worry about anything again.

8

Hong Kong harbor was bustling with activity the next morning as the ferry pulled away from the dock. Steamers sporting the flags and bright blue funnels of the ocean liners threaded their way between fishermen's sampans and red-sailed junks; and launches of every imaginable type scurried this way and that across the broad expanse of water. To the east, along the shore, gunboats and cruisers of the China squadron lay at anchor, and the flags of a dozen nations could be seen, with the United States and Britain, Russia, France, China, and Japan predominating.

Celia leaned against the railing, watching as the skyline of Hong Kong receded into the distance. The last wisps of morning fog hovered over the island, and the city of Victoria nestled softly into the base of muted hills. Tall buildings seemed to merge, one into the other, and the only landmark she could pick out was the spire of St. Peter's, a mission church on the west side of the harbor. High on the Peak, above the fog, the Mount Austin Hotel caught the sunlight, glittering like a jewel against a backdrop of lush green velvet.

A sudden gust of wind swept across the deck, and Celia shivered as she pulled the woolen cloak tighter around her shoulders. She was glad now she had had the sense to buy it. Who would have thought a semitropical city could be so cold on a foggy spring morning?

She glanced around curiously, sizing up the other passengers. Most were European, perhaps fifteen or twenty on deck, with more inside, sheltered from the wind. As near as she could see, they were all men. Even among the Orientals, who were primarily Chinese and Malay, she spotted only two women. One was middle-aged, a stocky peasant with coarse, impassive features. The other, an elderly woman dressed in a black *sam foo*, was clutching a basket to her breast as if it contained everything she possessed in the world.

Strange, Celia thought, then laughed, realizing it was not that strange at all. The ferry was bound, after all, for Macao, with only one stop at Lantao. Men were more likely than women to be attracted to what was fast becoming a gambling mecca of the Orient.

She had just started to turn back to the rail when she saw a young Chinese standing slightly apart from the others. He was dressed inconspicuously, but short-cropped hair blew in the wind, catching her eye as it whipped across his face.

The man who spoke to her yesterday?

Celia frowned distractedly. It *could* be, though it was hard to tell. She always hated it when colonials said in that condescending way, "They all look alike. You can't tell them apart." But she had to admit, sometimes, it was true. The same slim build, the same coloring, the same general bone structure—how could anyone be sure? And many Chinese nowadays, particularly the young ones, chose not to wear their hair in queues.

"Bloody fools, the lot of them," a voice muttered in her ear. "They ought to know better than to let Chinee on board. Can't think why they do it."

Celia turned to find a tall, lanky Britisher at her side. His hair was graying slightly at the temples, and a monocle stuck in one eye gave him a rather affected look.

"I beg your pardon," she said, startled.

"Risky business," the man went on. "Letting Chinee on a ship. That's an old pirates' trick. They get as many men on board as they can. Put the vessel out of commission before they attack. Can't think what the captain's about, permitting it. It's his skin as well as ours.''

The man's words sent an unexpected shiver down Celia's spine. Even in the few days she had been in Hong Kong, she had already heard stories like that. Just recently, the clerk at the hotel had told her, pirates boarded a mail steamer disguised as passengers and looted the vessel before setting it adrift. Mercifully, everyone except the captain and one steward was unharmed. Other incidents, however, had not ended so fortunately.

''Well,'' she said, trying to brighten the conversation, ''let's hope the pirates don't have their eye on the Macao steam ferry.''

''Don't suppose they do,'' the man admitted. ''We aren't carrying mail or specie that I know of. Still, I'll feel better if we go straight through. Don't stop, you know, unless someone wants to get off at Lantao.''

''Lantao?'' Celia eyed him warily, knowing, as he could not, that at least one passenger was planning to get off there today. ''What's wrong with Lantao? I've heard it's a very pretty place.''

''That may be, but it's a favorite haunt for pirates. Some of the bloodiest have their headquarters there. There or on Cheng Chou.''

''But surely that doesn't mean they're going to attack every steamer that stops for a few minutes in the harbor.'' Celia felt a sudden rush of relief. Plainly the man was an alarmist. ''I understand boats go there all the time. Sometimes twice a day. They wouldn't do that if they expected trouble.''

''Maybe not, but I can't help thinking we'd be safer on another vessel. Wouldn't be here myself if I didn't have urgent business to attend to. I'd any day rather wait for one of the Hong Kong–Canton–Macao steamers. Now, there's a tightly run line. They'd never take on all these Chinee.''

Celia threw a surreptitious glance at the old woman, still clutching her basket as she squatted against the protection of the wall, and wondered what threat that particular

"Chinee" could pose to anyone. Still, there didn't seem much point voicing the thought aloud. Once someone got hold of a prejudice, she had noticed, it was nearly impossible to make him let go.

A few minutes later, the man left, still grumbling about the carelessness of the shipping line, and Celia turned back to the railing. The fog was lifting, and as they entered Sulphur Channel, she could see the banks on both sides, thickly covered with vegetation. The Green Island lighthouse, one of three that guarded the harbor, made a striking sight against the cloudless sky.

During her conversation with the Englishman, Celia had forgotten momentarily the young Chinese she noticed before, and she turned now, curious to see if he was still there. For just an instant, as she caught sight of the empty space at the railing where he had been standing, an eerie sense of foreboding swept over her, and she began to shiver, even though the day had turned so warm she barely needed her cloak.

Laughing a little, she forced herself to shake off the feeling. Even if it was the same man—and that would be the wildest coincidence—there was still no reason to be afraid. If he wanted to hurt her, he had had ample opportunity the night before on the darkened streets of Hong Kong. Today the sun was shining brightly and there were people all around. What harm could come to her here?

The rest of the short voyage passed pleasantly enough, though rather more slowly than she had expected. The ship glided out of the channel and into the sea, following a series of small islands that lay like stepping stones along the water.

At her first glimpse of Lantao, the largest island in the area, twice the size of Hong Kong, Celia felt her heart race with anticipation. Soon, she thought excitedly—in a few hours at most—she would be with Skye again.

But as they drew nearer, and every detail on the island stood out with dazzling clarity, her breath caught in her throat and she realized she was frightened.

What was Skye going to say when he saw her?

The thought had not troubled her before, but she knew it should have. She had been so absorbed with what she was doing, what *she* wanted, she hadn't stopped to wonder how he was going to feel. He *had* told her to stay behind while he got on with his business. What if he was furious with her now? What if he told her to get back on the boat and go home?

Well, if he did, he just did—that was all.

Celia tossed her head back as she slipped off the cloak and laid it over the railing. Skye could say whatever he wanted. He could rant and rave and shout for all he was worth, and in a way she did not blame him. But she was going to use her feminine wiles to cool him down again.

And if he held firm, if he really thought she'd be in the way on Lantao, then she'd agree to return to Hong Kong and wait there. But she would *not* go back to Burma. She had come too far for that.

The steamer began to slow down, and Celia, sensing they were about to enter the harbor, picked up her cloak, draping it lightly over her arm. A number of sampans had gathered to greet the ferry, six or seven at least, perhaps more, and she knew she would have no trouble finding a boat to hire.

Just as they pulled into the shallow bay, a number of Chinese junks sailed out of a secluded inlet at one side, and Celia leaned forward, watching in fascination. There were four at first, then a fifth, and she thrilled to the exotic spectacle they made as they drifted closer. Dark hulls were massive, but gracefully curved, giving the illusion of Chinese dragons floating on the water; blood-red sails swelled in a rising wind.

The Englishman, who had returned to the deck, was standing beside her again, and Celia turned to him with a cry. "Oh, look! Aren't they lovely? Have you ever seen anything so beautiful in your life?"

"Beautiful?" The man's face was a mask of horror.

Celia stared at him in amazement, unable for an instant to figure out what was going on.

Then suddenly she realized.

Pirates! She turned back with a muffled gasp toward the junks, much nearer now than they had been before. She had scoffed when he said there were pirates on Lantao, especially after he admitted the steamer was carrying nothing of value. But pirates had been known to attack ferries just for the jewelry and cash the passengers were carrying!

Celia gripped the rail with both hands, waiting, *praying* for the crew to fire up the engines again. Surely, even with a brisk wind, they would be more than a match for that small fleet of junks.

Instead, the engines seemed to stall, sputtering briefly, then died altogether. The stillness that followed was eerie, with neither sound nor vibration to break the gentle roll of the ocean against the side of the ship.

Stunned, Celia looked up, seeing her own feelings mirrored on the faces of the other European passengers.

The ferry had been stopped. Deliberately stopped! God help them all, the Englishman was right. Some of the Chinese who boarded at Hong Kong *were* pirates. They had probably murdered the captain already, and anyone else with the courage to fight back.

Within minutes the junks had pulled alongside, and Celia felt a terrible jarring crash as they grated into the steamer. Ropes appeared suddenly, as if from nowhere, and men were climbing up them, leaping onto the deck, three and four at a time. A surprising number of the passengers tried to resist, but they were badly outnumbered, and it was quickly apparent they were going to lose. The Englishman, unexpectedly strong despite his prissy appearance, caught one of them by the shirt and might have pitched him overboard had another not come up from behind and given him a sharp clout on the side of the head. Celia cried out in horror as she saw him go down. Seconds later, the action seemed to be everywhere, and the deck was red with blood.

For a moment she could only stand there, too stunned to move or even think. Then, snapping out of her shock, she turned and fled down a short flight of steps. There was no way she could defend herself against the invaders. She had no weapon, and even if she did, they were too well-organized, too well-armed. Her only hope lay in hiding below.

Racing down the narrow passageway, she tried first one door, then the next, shaking them urgently when they would not yield, but it was no use. Sick with fear, she realized they were all locked! Whoever planned this attack had done his job well. There was to be no escape for anyone.

She was ready to weep with despair when she heard a noise behind her. Whirling defensively, she saw a young Chinese—the man she had noticed before—coming out of a doorway at the far end of the passage. Celia pressed deeper into the shadows, terrified he would see her. But he was too caught up in whatever he was doing to throw more than a cursory glance over his shoulder as he hurried up the stairs.

Celia crept stealthily toward the door he had just left. Her hand was trembling as she pressed it against the smooth wood—and felt it slide slowly inward.

The place seemed to be a workroom, or perhaps an officer's cabin, for charts and nautical gear were strewn all around, as if a storm had blown through. A man lay in the center of the rubble, his arms and legs tied with cord. He was wearing a captain's uniform, but aside from a gash on the side of his head where he had apparently been struck, he seemed unhurt.

It crossed her mind fleetingly that it was odd, leaving him like that—not finishing him off. Pirates were supposed to be a bloodthirsty lot. A large metal object, a pin of some sort, was lying on the floor beside him, and she guessed he had been trying to fight off his assailants when he was overcome.

It was a cumbersome weapon, but Celia lunged at it

anyway. If she stood behind the door, hidden from anyone who came into the room, she might be able to bring it down on his head!

She never had a chance to reach it. Just at that moment, a harsh cry sounded in her ear, and she turned to see a swarthy Malay blocking the doorway. A bright red scarf had been knotted at his brow, half-restraining black hair that flew around his face, and his eyes were glazed with feverish brightness.

Horrified, Celia realized she was not going to get the pin. She had no weapon, nothing to save herself, and he was coming toward her!

Her fingers tightened around the cape she was carrying. Instinctively she wrapped one end around her hand, waiting grimly as he drew nearer.

Then suddenly she flicked it out like a whip, catching him around the legs.

The man gave a grunt of surprise and stumbled back, but he did not fall. Frantically Celia lashed out again, but this time he was ready for her. Within seconds he had caught hold of the cape and wrested it out of her grasp. Defenseless now, she felt strong arms close around her, half-lifting her off the ground, dragging her, kicking and screaming, up the steps to the deck.

The battle, which had been brief but savage, was over by the time they got there. Celia swayed faintly as she saw the congealed blood and crumpled bodies that seemed to be everywhere. Several of the waiting sampans had joined in the fight, coming to the aid of the defenders, but theirs had been a useless gallantry, and not one of the crewmen seemed to have survived.

The passengers, at least the Europeans, had fared better. Except for the Englishman and one stout gentleman who was holding a bloodstained handkerchief to his head, they were all huddled together against the wall. A handful of Chinese were with them, including the old woman, still clutching her basket dazedly to her breast.

The Malay dropped Celia roughly to the deck and gave

her a shove toward the others. Two men who seemed to have been standing guard looked up curiously, and he let out a barrage of words in some guttural language she could not understand. His gestures, broad and coarse, told her he was describing her resistance. And laughing as he did!

Anger burst inside her, flooding away even the fear and anguish. It was bad enough, the barbaric deeds these men committed in the name of plunder. But to laugh besides . . .

She took a step toward him and spat in his face.

The defiant gesture accomplished nothing. The man only laughed as he wrenched her wrists again, thrusting her crudely against the wall with the others. Terrified and humiliated, she was forced to stand and watch while they finished what they had come to do.

It was, for a girl who had always led a sheltered life, brutal beyond imagining. The men worked quickly and methodically, but the very calmness of their behavior only made them seem more cold-blooded. They sifted through bodies on the deck, the wounded as well as the dead, then turned their attention to the Chinese passengers, selecting some—seemingly by whim—shooting them and tossing their bodies overboard. From time to time, they paused, throwing questioning glances at a slightly built man who appeared to be their leader.

Startled, Celia recognized the man she had seen before. The wind was blowing his hair back from his face, and now that she could see him better, she was sure her first instinct had been right. He *was* the man she had spoken to yesterday.

A sharp cry drew her eyes back to the deck, where the Malay, together with several of the others, was tending to the wounded. He straightened up, gesturing downward as he gave one of the bodies a nudge with his boot.

The man with the short hair turned, staring for a moment at the badly wounded Chinese with a strange expression on his face. Then he said something that sounded like "Sung," or perhaps "Soong," and before Celia realized what was happening, the Malay had drawn his sword, bringing it down in one swift motion to sever the man's head from his body. Nausea welled up inside her as he threw first the decapitated body, then the head, into the sea, where it floated like a grotesque mask for a minute before sinking.

By the time she looked back again, the Malay had moved over to the place where the Englishman lay. Celia cringed, certain the man was about to meet a like fate. But to her surprise, two of the men picked him up, moving with surprising gentleness as they lowered him into one of several sampans, now tied with the junks at the side of the ferry. The stout man with the wound on his forehead was next, then the rest of the passengers, one by one, as their attackers herded them onto the waiting boats by means of rope ladders secured to the rail. As each sampan was filled, the cord was cut and it was allowed to drift slowly toward the beach.

For the first time since the men had boarded the ship, Celia dared to let herself hope. Could it be that, whatever dark urges had driven them, they were quelled now, and the terrible bloodletting was over? Robbery did not seem to be a motive, for the passengers were not searched as they moved onto the sampans. And clearly the pirates intended to put them ashore, leaving them unharmed to wait for rescue.

Her hope was short-lived, however, for as the last of the passengers, the old woman with the basket, was guided down the ladder, the sampan began to move, and Celia was left on deck. She glanced over at the pirate leader, trying desperately to question him with frightened eyes, but the man did not look her way.

It suddenly occurred to her that all the decisions today had been his. The choices between life and death. And he made them arbitrarily. What if she had been wrong when she assumed he was trying to warn her yesterday? What if he had taken a dislike to her instead? What if he had no use for bold females who went after the men they loved?

She began to tremble, but if the man noticed, he gave
no indication. Stepping over to the rail, he paused briefly
to speak to the Malay, then started down one of the
ladders. A second later, the other man turned, and Celia
realized, horrified, what had happened.

He had been told to fetch her.

He was grinning from ear to ear as he approached, but
he took care not to get too close, and Celia sensed he had
no desire to be covered with spittle again. She managed to
hold her head high as he shoved her toward the railing and
down a rope ladder. But the minute she felt her feet touch
the deck and knew she was on one of the pirate junks, the
largest of the five, courage deserted her, and she started to
shake again, almost uncontrollably.

They were taking her with them!

The idea was horrifying but inescapable. There was no
other reason why they would have brought her here. She
was the only white woman on board the ferry—*and they
were taking her with them*!

She felt herself sway weakly, and caught hold of the
rough wooden railing to keep from falling. Why, *why*,
hadn't she listened to the man when he talked to her
yesterday? He *had* been trying to warn her, whatever his
motives, and she was a fool to have dismissed him so
lightly. Now she was paying for her folly.

The door to the interior opened suddenly, putting an end
to her thoughts, and Celia turned to see a powerful sun-
bronzed man stride onto the deck. He was not as tall as the
Malay or as dramatically dressed as some of the other
pirates, with their gaudy scarves and bright beads, but
there was something so compelling about him, so utterly
magnetic, that she forgot everything else, even the fears
that had held her in thrall a moment before.

Clearly this was the true leader of the pirate band.
Everything about him, his bearing, the way he walked,
even that quick, assessing look he cast up at the ferry,
bespoke the confidence of a man accustomed to being in
charge. She wondered briefly why he had stayed behind

while the others risked their lives; then she saw him glance at the man with the short hair, giving him a slight, barely perceptible nod, and she thought she knew. He had held back not because he was afraid of danger, but because he had given command to the other man and did not want to undermine his authority.

Fascinated in spite of herself, Celia found her eyes drawn toward that boldly arresting face. His skin was deeply tanned, not leathery, as she might have expected, but surprisingly smooth; his features were strong and sharply chiseled, giving him a rugged, craggy look. He was not what she would have called truly handsome, certainly not handsome in a *classical* way, yet there was something distinctly exciting about him, something that stirred her blood in ways she did not recognize. Long burnished-auburn hair blew back from his brow, and his eyes, a piercing emerald green, seemed to take in the entire deck, pausing when they came to her, narrowing with interest.

A slow tremor ran through her as she felt the impact of that searing gaze. Never before had she been so aware of the sheer maleness of any man: the broadness of his shoulders straining an immaculate white linen shirt, the lean hard lines of his thighs beneath tightly cut burgundy breeches, the way his collar had been left open at his throat, revealing tangled hints of red-brown hair.

Any other time, she thought helplessly, any other place, she would have been intrigued by him. Now she could think only how very like a highwayman he looked.

Or a pirate.

The wind ruffled his hair, catching the sunlight until red streaks buried in the auburn seemed to shimmer like gold. Strong masculine lips turned up just slightly, a rakish look, and Celia had the feeling he knew what she was thinking . . .

Red hair!

The realization came like a bolt out of nowhere. This man had red hair—and he was a pirate!

Memories came rushing back, stories she had heard and

half-dismissed about a redheaded American adventurer, a sea captain turned opium pirate who in a few short years had made his name a symbol for daring and lawlessness throughout the Orient. How, she asked herself dazedly, could he ever have seemed so glamorous to her? So romantic?

This time when a tremor ran through her body, it was a tremor of fear.

She had been captured by the Tiger.

9

The last thing on Schuyler Maarten's mind that brisk spring afternoon was the fiancée he had not seen for several weeks. He was sprawled comfortably on a satin-brocaded couch, oblivious of the subtle Chinese decor around him as he stared admiringly at a slim young woman across the room, her profile dramatically highlighted against the sun-shimmering windowpanes.

"Well, Teresa," he said softly, "time has treated you well, I see. You were always an uncommonly pretty little thing. Now you've taken on an aura of mystique that's absolutely irresistible."

"And you, I see, have the same honeyed tongue." Teresa turned, half-smiling. "You were always able to charm me before—even though I saw right through you. Do you expect to be as successful this time, I wonder?"

"You sound as if you're not glad to see me." Skye stretched out his long legs as he looked up at her.

"Oh, I'm glad enough to have you back—but then, you already knew that. You wouldn't have gotten anywhere near this place if I hadn't permitted it. Though why I should have, I don't know, after the way you went all over Hong Kong blabbing my name to anyone who would listen. That was hardly wise."

"It didn't do any harm, either." Teresa was almost paranoid sometimes, with her insistence on secrecy, even when it didn't make sense. "Everyone in Hong Kong already knows who you are. The 'pirate princess'—they were talking about you long before I came to add fuel to the fire. Besides, you aren't looking at things from my point of view. How was I going to find you if I sat around all day in a cheap hotel room and never opened my mouth? But if you think someone was using me to get at you, forget it. Even if I were stupid enough to let myself be followed—which I'm not—that dragon you sent to fetch me would never have permitted it."

"No. Soong is my best man. That's why I chose him. I hope, Maarten, you did what he said and kept quiet after he contacted you. I wouldn't like to think you'd been spreading—"

"You don't give me enough credit," Skye cut in rather crossly. In reality, he *had* been talking. It had been necessary to float a small loan those last few days in Hong Kong, and it had helped to pretend he was in tight with the dreaded White Lotus gang. Still, even if someone did believe those hints he threw out about Lantao—a wild guess which later, to his surprise, turned out to be correct—it wouldn't matter. The island was large and the hideout too well-secreted to be easily found. "I couldn't have given you away if I'd wanted to. Soong was too cautious to tell me where you were. Good God, the man blindfolded me before he put me on the sardine can that brought me here! If you hadn't told me yourself, I wouldn't even know what island we're on."

Teresa nodded her approval. "I can always count on Soong. I wasn't worried. Not really. It's just that my nerves are on edge today."

"So . . ." Skye rose and went over to where she was standing at the window. He could smell her perfume, sweet and musky, but he was careful not to touch her. "Something is up, is it? Something big?"

She glanced back, dark eyes flashing with an excitement he had not expected.

"Bigger than you can imagine."

"And that's why you kept me cooling my heels all these days since I arrived?"

"That's part of it. I did have other things on my mind. But I also wanted time to decide what I was going to do with you."

"What a polite way to put it." Skye laughed harshly. "Come, Teresa dear. Why don't we be blunt? You never minced words before."

"Before?" Teresa went over to a small end table and lit up an American cigarette. "Before, as I recall, you stayed just long enough to get the money you wanted—and then walked out on me. And I wasn't aware that I was 'mincing' words. What I said was the truth. I did need time to decide what I wanted to do with you."

"Which means—correct me if I'm wrong—you were trying to decide whether you could trust me."

"What an idea!" Teresa looked amused. "Trust you? Of course I don't trust you. Anyone foolish enough to put his faith in you would pay a price for it, I think. You're a prostitute, Maarten—and I don't mean that just in the obvious sense. You'll always sell yourself to the highest bidder. Your services, your friendship, your loyalty. I have to remember that someone might outbid me."

"Aren't you going to offer me a cigarette?" He lit his from hers, then gave it back, holding his hand steady. She was trying to bait him, but it wouldn't work. "I gather all this means you're not going to tell me what you're planning."

"If you're interested—why not?" Teresa flicked her ashes carelessly into a centuries-old Ming bowl. "I don't have to trust you to talk about my plans. You can't leave the island without my permission—and I'm not going to give it today."

"Good." Skye settled back on the couch, propping his feet up on a low drum table. "All right, begin at the beginning now. And don't leave out anything."

Teresa laughed. "You are too melodramatic, but that's good. You make me see the humor in what I'm doing. It's not a very complicated story. I'm afraid you'll be disappointed. Several weeks ago, I finally managed to get the best of the Tiger, stealing a shipment of opium right out from under his nose. He, of course, is looking for vengeance now. And I'm looking to repeat the coup—only on a much grander scale. Recently I learned that a large purchase had been made in Calcutta, one of the biggest ever. The drug will arrive soon in several vessels, but I don't know what shipping firm is carrying it.''

"And . . . ?"

"And there's only one way to find out. A few discreet inquiries must be made in Hong Kong. Who has been working longer hours lately, who has put on new hands at the dock—that sort of thing. Naturally, I can't ask the questions myself. Nor can Soong do it, for not only is he Chinese, his English is awkward and would arouse suspicion.''

"Dammit, Teresa, that's where you could use me!" Forgetting himself, Skye jumped up and began pacing back and forth. "No one would think a thing of it if I started chatting with some guy next to me at a bar or discussed her husband's hours with a bored middle-aged woman at a party." He whirled to face her. "You said before you'd be a fool to trust me, but I think you're a fool not to. Oh, all right. I am for sale. Why the hell not? But think about it! In this case, *you* would be the highest bidder.''

"Would I? I'm not so sure." Teresa took the place he had vacated on the couch and sat with one knee tucked up to her chin. "The shipping companies would pay a nice reward to find out what I'm up to.''

"Maybe—but they don't know me from Adam. How much are they likely to offer for a fanciful little story with nothing to back it up? And even if they did match your price, which I doubt, it'd still be a one-time deal. I'm looking for something more substantial.''

"So you can lose it again?" Her lips twisted mockingly. "Really, Maarten—a poker game?"

Skye shrugged. "Poker is as good as anything else—and the stakes were high."

"And you, of course, needed the money. But not, I think—in your case—to buy the affections of a woman."

"No, to buy my way *out* of the clutches of a pretty woman with matrimony on her mind. An even more powerful incentive, I assure you. When I sat down at that poker table, I had it in my head to win so much money I'd never think about her confounded dowry again. Later, it occurred to me, if I lost enough, her father would get his back up and I wouldn't have to marry her anyway."

Teresa could not keep from smiling. "You are so predictable. That's part of your charm. You asked me before if I wasn't glad to have you here. I am—*very* glad."

"Then you'll let me in on this operation?" Skye took a drag from his cigarette, holding in the smoke. It wasn't just the money he wanted. It was the excitement. God, it had been boring, stuck in Burma like that! "Trust me with this assignment, and I'll show you what I'm made of. Hell, Teresa, I want to get in on the action again!"

"I think, if I *could*, I would. Unfortunately, it's too late. I've already sent Soong into town with a crew of men, none of them too promising, I'm afraid. Only one, a new man, speaks good enough English to pull it off, and he's still going to have trouble because he's Chinese, even though he acts more like a European. Whatever they learn—or don't learn—they have to be back on today's ferry, tomorrow at the latest."

Skye leaned back against the window frame, taking another drag and letting the smoke out through his nostrils. "Then we take to the seas a day or two after that—if they're successful."

"Not *we*," Teresa corrected. "Me and my men. I have other plans for you. That's what kept me awake half the night."

"Thinking how you were going to fit me into the organization?" He put out his cigarette and went to the couch, bending teasingly over the back. "Or thinking how you would enjoy sending the houseboy to fetch me while everyone else was asleep?'' Her shoulders were temptingly close, soft beneath thin silk, but he made no attempt to move. The first advance, as always, would come from her.

''No,'' she said truthfully. She felt the nearness of his hands, and she knew he wanted to touch her, just as she knew why he was holding back. ''That did not occur to me *then*. I was thinking only what a fool Lin was, four years ago, when you first came to us. He should have used you to better advantage.''

''Perhaps he would have if he'd lived longer. Though you're right—I doubt it. I wasn't Chinese, and Lin never trusted anyone not of his own race. Even your father.''

Teresa let the comment pass. She had always known that whatever influence Sebastião had with Lin came not from himself but from his beautiful part-Chinese daughter.

''Lin used you as a decoy to lure men into his net. So did I, though on a larger scale. I wouldn't do that again. It was a waste of your talents, putting you in the prow of a boat so captains would not be suspicious when we approached—or sending you as a passenger on a ferry. I should have had you get a job in a shipping office instead. Then I would have known the comings and goings of every steamer on the line.''

''That would have been an even greater waste.'' Skye laughed. ''What you should have done was stake me to a good hot poker game, with plenty of liquor flowing.''

''Yes, yes, and you'd have won so much money we'd never have to—''

''Won, hell! I love poker, but I'm not hooked on it the way my father was. It's a means to an end for me. In this case, I'd have made sure I lost.''

He paused, grinning at her reaction.

''Men like a cheerful loser—especially when he loses to them. They'll sit around for hours afterward and talk their heads off. A few weeks of that, and I'd know the movements of every ship on every line in this part of the world.''

Teresa rested her head against the back of the sofa, chuckling softly. "I think you're right, Schuyler. You do have a way of talking. It's what you do best. More and more now, I'm happy you came back."

"Because I can get you the information you need?" He leaned closer, his breath warm against her neck, provocative, but not too bold.

"Because of the information—yes."

Her voice lay deep in her throat, and they both knew what she was saying, without words. He would give her more than information . . . more than promises for tomorrow or the day after. She arched her body backward, pressing deeper into the cushions, a subtle invitation for him to touch her, as he had wanted to before.

It was an invitation she did not have to repeat. Light hands brushed against her shoulder, the barest hint of a caress, still time for her to back out if she wanted. Then, when she did not, he grew more daring, sliding downward, playing with slender, almost boyish breasts that barely filled his fingers. A few gentle tugs inched up the silken fabric of her shirt until he could feel warm naked flesh against his hands.

Sighing softly, Teresa twisted away, knowing as she rose that she was going to give in to the baser instincts of her body, even though she had not planned on dallying with him that evening. She turned to face him, not bothering to draw the curtains as she unfastened her mannish shirt, for she knew none of the men would approach the house without her permission. It took her only a moment to undress, a moment longer to stretch out on the chaise longue she kept for just that purpose, her legs spreading slightly in anticipation of what she was about to ask.

Skye saw the way she had begun to look at him, her eyes lingering on his mouth, her tongue flicking moistly across her own lips, and he knew what she had in mind. It always intrigued him, the directness with which she approached her passions, with no pretense, no apologies for what she wanted.

He began to laugh, a low guttural sound. Kneeling between her legs, he eased them apart. Teresa reached out with one hand, laying her fingers on cheeks that were only lightly whiskered, yet distinctly masculine to her touch.

"I think I *will* be the highest bidder," she murmured huskily. "At least tonight. Please me now, and perhaps I'll give you the present I sent for this afternoon."

"What?" He looked up, half-teasing. "Here I thought you were wrapped up in shipping lanes and sea charts— and all the while you were thinking of ways to win my loyalty. Let me guess. Is it a nice dirty shade of green? Will it crinkle in my fingers?"

Teresa giggled in spite of herself. "No, it is not green at all. What are you thinking of? American dollars? It is what you would probably call 'yellow.' And I hope it will not crinkle in your fingers. Did you by any chance notice the boy who opened the door when you came?"

"No," he lied. "I was too anxious to see you." In fact he *had* noticed, with a distinct warming in his groin. The boy was slim, the way he liked them, more brown-skinned than yellow—and he had not turned away when Skye looked at him. "Don't tell me you bought that pretty little plaything for me?"

"Why not? Do you think I'm so enamored I cannot bear the thought of sharing you?"

"Hardly," he replied dryly. Even in those first months after Lin's death, when she had been barely more than a child, Teresa had already begun to enjoy the company of a wide variety of men. As far as he knew, she had never been with one often enough to feel jealous. Still . . . "It does seem a bit more generous than one ought to expect."

"I'm not being generous. Only sensible. If I'm not ready to give fidelity, then why should I expect it? It builds resentment and . . ." And? She hesitated, remembering all too vividly the consequences to Lin when she had been forced to keep her own love affair a secret. "And deceit. Men are so stupid. They make the rules—then they don't want to play by them. It is better this way."

Her hand lingered on his cheek a moment longer, then fell back, telling him she was tired of talk. Yes, it *is* better, he thought as he leaned forward. He would have sought the boy out anyway, with unpleasant consequences perhaps, for her as well as him. How much better—and wiser—to give her blessing.

He rested his fingers on dark curls that nestled between her thighs, brushing them aside to expose the soft, moist lips of flesh beneath. As he did, he felt his body begin to swell, hardening with the beginnings of an erection, and he knew he was responding not to her, but to the memory of that slim brown figure in the hall. Would she let him have the boy tonight? he wondered. Or would she make him finish the act with her?

Bending forward, he touched her, first with his lips, then his tongue, even his teeth—carefully, but not too carefully—the way he knew she liked it. The female smell of her was heavy in his nostrils, the wetness and warmth provoked his lips, and he knew suddenly that it did not matter. Teresa or the boy. One way or another, he was going to be satisfied tonight.

Teresa began to writhe, slowly at first, then more urgently, following the rhythms he set with skillful thrusts of his tongue. She was aware every second of the calculation and timing that were so much a part of his lovemaking, yet she was swept away, too, as if every act, every motion, were spontaneous and unthinking. Perhaps it was the very lack of excitement, of abandon on his part that made him so attuned to her wants, her needs.

She held on one last second, relishing the sense of mastery over her passions, then let go as floods of sheer physical energy surged, one after another, through her body. Trembling almost convulsively, she twisted her fingers in his hair, pressing him closer, making him do it again, and then again, before she finally let him go.

His face, as he drew back, was a mirror of his feelings, and Teresa, satiated now, found it hard to keep from laughing. How smug he looked, as if he had just been very clever. Did he really think she didn't know what was going through his mind?

"Run along, then." She spoke indulgently, like a mother to a small child. "I know you're thinking about the boy I got for you. You'll find him in a house of his own—not very big, but enough for what you have in mind—just at the end of the path."

Skye demurred, feigning reluctance at the last moment—as if it were expected of him! Teresa thought—and she had to send him away. Now that he had served his purpose, she was just as glad to be rid of him as she got up and pulled on her clothes. What was there about a woman that made a man think she wanted to clasp him to her bosom after they finished making love?

Did he think her fragile ego would be shattered when he left?

Ego, indeed! Teresa turned toward the mirror, checking to make sure her shirt was straight. What did ego have to do with lovemaking? If deeper feelings were involved, then it was a thing of the heart. If not, it was an affair of the body. Either way, ego did not enter into it.

She glided soundlessly across the room, staring through the window at shadows that were beginning to deepen in the trees outside. Obviously, for whatever reason, Soong had not made the ferry that day, and she found herself vaguely disappointed. She had been half-joking before, when she said she was glad Skye was back. She had been neither glad nor sorry. Now, however, she was beginning to think he might have his uses—and not just in her bed.

The poker games were too obvious, of course. They would appeal to a man like Skye, but that was because he never thought things through. There were, however, many ways to befriend a man and make him talk. Skye had a certain gift of charm . . . and other gifts too, if that should prove necessary.

Trust him or not, Teresa thought, she was going to have to use him, relying on him more heavily than she had in the past.

But then, that might not be a problem.

She turned away from the window and looked back into the room, golden now with the late-afternoon light. She would just have to be sure she was always the highest bidder. There were two things Skye Maarten cared about— money and pleasure. She would dangle both in front of him.

Only not too much.

She frowned as she leaned for a moment against the wall. Yes . . . that had been her mistake last time. She had paid Skye Maarten too much—and always in cash. She had made it easy for him to leave her.

This time, she would handle things better. She would offer just enough so he would not be tempted to go to anyone else, but not enough to satisfy.

This time, when their relationship dissolved, it would not be because he had walked out on her, but because she was through with him.

Celia huddled miserably in the only chair in the small stone hut the pirates had taken her to. Faint light filtered through cracks in a boarded-up window, and she sensed that dusk was approaching, but she was too disoriented to be sure. She had thought, when they forced her out of the junk and onto the shore, that she wanted nothing more than to be out of sight of them, but now that she was alone and her imagination had free rein, she found herself more frightened than ever.

True, they had not harmed her . . . not yet.

She looked around the room, trying half-heartedly to get her bearings. All those dire things she had imagined when she saw the pirate captain and sensed that aura of leashed-in masculine virility had not come to pass. But it was still early, and she couldn't help noticing that the only piece of furniture, other than the chair on which she was seated and a flimsy wooden table, was a surprisingly comfortable-looking double bed, incongruously spread with a flaming scarlet coverlet.

What if they do this all the time? she thought. What if they bring young women here and have their way with them? And bury them afterward on the rocky hillside so no one will know what happened!

The sound of footsteps came from outside, and Celia's heart skipped a beat as she heard them stop in front of the door. When it opened a second later, she saw a young boy, a Caucasian of about twelve or thirteen, with a large tray balanced in his hands.

The boy hesitated, looking around awkwardly, then headed toward the table and set down the tray, which contained a large bowl of steaming stew and several pieces of crusty white bread. A chipped earthenware mug was filled to the brim with something that looked like mud, and the bitter odor of coffee filled the air.

Celia's stomach balked at the smell, and she felt like retching as she watched the boy back out of the room, staring at her with large, curious eyes. He had been gone only a few minutes, barely time to recompose herself, when the door opened again, so abruptly this time it slammed against the wall.

Starting nervously, Celia looked up to see a man standing on the threshold. It was the same man she had seen on the junk—the pirate captain. The one they called the Tiger.

Celia gulped, trying to conceal her fear as she and the man eyed each other in silence. He seemed even more dramatically compelling now than he had been before. His lean, muscular body loomed up in that compact doorway, built to Oriental specifications, and the vibrant redness of his hair, the green of those bold, penetrating eyes, shimmered in the twilight. Despite her fears, Celia could not help feeling a strange fascination. It was almost as if something inside her, some deep, primitive instinct she did not recognize, was drawn toward the sheer physical vitality he exuded with every breath. As if destiny had deliberately brought her to that spot and intended them to meet.

The thought frightened her, and she spoke quickly to dispel it. "What . . . what are you going to do?" She rose, trying to look braver than she felt. "Why did you bring me here? What do you want?"

The man ignored her questions as he glanced at the tray, still untouched on the table.

"Our food isn't fancy, but I think you'll find it savory enough. Freddie—the boy who brought it—serves as cook sometimes when we're on land. He manages quite well, I think, for a lad of fourteen."

Celia stared at him, too confused for a moment to speak. The way he was behaving, so casually, so matter-of-fact, he might have been an innkeeper stopping by her table to inquire how she enjoyed the fare.

"I asked what you're planning to do to me," she said, finding her voice again. "Are you deaf, or don't you think I deserve the courtesy of a reply?"

The man leaned casually against the door frame, the beginnings of a raffish half-smile showing on his features. Either he had not noticed her sharpness or it amused him.

"What do you *think* I'm going to do?"

His eyes ran slowly, insolently down her figure, and Celia felt a chill of horror run through her. Sweet heaven, she had been right about him all along! He might offer shelter and a tray of food, but he was civilized in no other way!

"You can't treat me like this!" she burst out. "I'm a British subject. The government has laws to punish people like you! It will go hard enough on you when they find out you've kidnapped an Englishwoman. But if you . . . if you dare . . . ."

"If I dare *what*, madam?" He had begun to laugh softly. His eyes, still toying with her body, paused for an instant on the ripe curves of her breast. "You seem to have some . . . uh, colorful notions about pirates. Have you been reading too many romantic novels? Or is this an exaggerated estimate of your own charms? Do you think every man who looks at you automatically has 'designs'?"

Celia caught her breath, realizing he was playing games with her, and hating him for it.

"I *was* the only woman on the ferry," she reminded him heatedly.

"Hardly. There were two others, as I recall. Or don't you consider Chinese to be women?"

"Well . . . well, yes, of . . . of course they are!" She hated him even more now, the way he was twisting her words around, making her look like a fool! "But they were . . . well, they were older. I meant I was the only *young* woman on board."

"No, you didn't," he said coolly. "You meant you were the only white woman . . . but we'll let that pass. As for my 'lecherous intentions,' put your mind at rest. I want only one thing from you. To know what you were doing in Hong Kong."

Celia tilted her chin up, looking him square in the eye. "None of your damned business."

"Ah?" He raised a mocking brow. "They told me you had spirit. I see they were right. Any other time, I'd be suitably impressed. Right now, I don't have time for girlish humors. Let me rephrase my question. I hear you spent the last several days inquiring after a man named Schuyler Maarten. I want to know why."

"Do you?" Celia continued to meet his gaze. "Well, then, let me rephrase my answer. It'll be a long, cold day in hell before I tell you!"

Her defiance seemed to anger him. He reached out, catching hold of her arms, as if to shake the truth out of her. But as he drew her toward him, something happened between them, a sudden electrifying sensation that seemed to run from his body into hers, then back to his again. Celia gasped, recalling belatedly how she had felt when she first saw him, how acutely aware she had been of him as a man.

His eyes changed, darkening suddenly, burning as they probed her with piercing intensity. Then slowly he released her arms, still throbbing from the bruising force of his fingers.

"So . . ." he said softly. "You're not as innocent as

you look. I had wondered. Well . . . we'll leave it for now. I have more important matters to tend to, but I'll be back in the morning. If you're not ready to talk then, perhaps we can find . . . uh . . . *other* ways to negotiate.''

"*Ooooh*!'' Celia seethed with fury as she watched him head arrogantly toward the door. He was baiting her again, just like he had before. He knew perfectly well she *was* innocent, and he was using that to get what he wanted.

She picked up the closest thing at hand, the dish of stew, and hurled it furiously in his direction. He reacted just in time, ducking outside. The last thing she saw was a flash of teeth, white against bronzed skin, then the door closed and the bowl shattered against it, sending bits of meat and vegetables all over the room.

Oh, she *did* hate him! She dropped her head into her hands, shaking so badly she could barely contain herself. The man was a scoundrel! A vile, egotistical scoundrel who didn't care how many people he hurt. She hated him more than she had ever hated anyone in her life. Or ever would. And yet . . .

And yet . . .

Celia drew her hands down, still trembling, but able to think more clearly now that he was gone. And yet there *was* something about him, some indefinably magnetic quality that brought out all her passions, rage and fascination both.

Helplessly she realized she had been a child until that moment, blissfully imagining physical yearning as some gently sweet emotion that enticed rather than commanded. With Skye, her fantasies had been romantic, centering more on what it would feel like to float in his arms on the dance floor than be carried off to his bed. Even the first sense of sexual awakening, when he kissed her in the garden, had been just that—an awakening. With this man, she felt something deeper, more intense. It was as if for the first time she dared to let herself truly think and *feel* as a woman.

And this man was a pirate. A kidnapper and a killer. A blackguard with the morals of a snake.

"Damn him!"

Teresa Valdes stared through the window, barely seeing the first hints of sunset red above the hills.

"Damn, damn, *damn* him!"

They had brought her the news a short time ago, and she was still seething with fury. Some of her best men had been on that ferry! Men she trusted and valued. And the others, waiting on the sampans? Instead of running for their lives when they saw what was happening, they had rushed in to help, the fools! Now they were lost too.

"How could he have known?" She whirled to face Skye Maarten, who had been called back from other interests and was lounging with sullen carelessness on a couch across the room. "*How*? The other passengers were all released. Even the Chinese. *My* men were slaughtered! How could he have singled them out like that, without making one mistake?"

"I can think of several ways," Skye replied calmly. He was as aware as Teresa of the devastation the Tiger had caused in her organization, just as he was aware of the impact on his own ambitious plans. But there seemed little point brooding over it now. "One possibility leaps to mind. Maybe there was a traitor among your men. Didn't you tell me one of them was new?"

"Kwan," she agreed thoughtfully. "I took him on because he speaks perfect English, with hardly a trace of accent. But he knows nothing about our operations. He's never even seen the headquarters on Lantao. And he was recommended by his cousin, one of the men killed on the ferry!"

"Be reasonable, Teresa." Skye picked up a half-empty glass from the table beside him and took a sip of excellent French brandy. "The bodies were tossed overboard. You don't know who's dead and who isn't. You only know your man wasn't among the group stranded on the beach.

He might have sailed off with the pirates. Perhaps he only brought his cousin in in the first place because—''

"No!" Teresa cut him off angrily, hating the thought he might be right. "That man was with me for two years! He was always trustworthy. If he was going to betray me, he would have done it long ago. Besides, I paid him well. Better than he had ever been paid before—''

"How you do persist in assuming everyone can be bought." Skye grinned. "You were right about me, but then, I've never tried to deny it. Perhaps this man wasn't up for bids, at least not for money. There are subtler kinds of pressure, remember—especially in the Orient. You know how these people are. Loyalty to family is more important than anything else, and family networks go from city to city all over the world. If a man had to choose between you—a Eurasian woman—and a member of his family, what do you think he would do?''

Teresa turned away, not bothering to argue. She was part Chinese herself, but she had always been an outsider, and the Chinese way of thinking was almost as alien to her as it was to Skye Maarten. Soong had understood better, of course—but even Soong miscalculated this time.

And Soong was no longer there to advise her.

She was surprised to feel tears burn her eyelids, she who never wept. In her own way, she had loved the man who had just died, loved him almost as much as she loved her father. And Brandon Christopher had taken them both from her!

"But why did he attack *there*?" She turned back, controlling the tremor in her voice. "Why Lantao . . . why that particular ferry? And why today? Soong was too closemouthed to tell anyone his plans in advance. None of those men—*none of them*—could have known until the last minute how and when he was going to travel."

"A lucky guess perhaps," Skye hazarded. "If the Tiger figured out what you were up to, then he had to know timing was essential. You could hardly bring the men back later than today—or perhaps tomorrow. And you almost *had* to rely on public transport rather than risk discovery by sending in a boat. As for why he chose that particular ferry, no doubt he received a signal from the deck.''

"Yes, yes, of course there was a signal!" Teresa said impatiently. "But why was he waiting *there*? On *that* bay? If he had exact information, why not hit us here? If not, why assume our headquarters were on Lantao? Why not Cheng Chou? Or one of the other islands?''

"Another lucky guess?" Skye squirmed, knowing full well why the Tiger had settled on Lantao. Who would have thought that anyone would pay attention to those ridiculous hints he threw out about the island? He'd only settled on it in the first place because it sounded believable. "Everyone knows that Lantao, with its coves and hills, is a natural pirates' hangout. Cheng Chou is much smaller. It might be that the Tiger had already been able to eliminate it by means of a careful search. At any rate, there's no sense worrying about what's over and done with. The point is, what are we going to do now?''

Teresa glared at him, stung by the cool reason in his tone. Picking up a pillow from a nearby chair, she flung it irritably across the room.

"If only those fools in the sampans hadn't thought they could help! They walked right into the Tiger's trap, just as he knew they would. Now, instead of ten men, I've lost nearly thirty—the crew for an entire ship! And we were shorthanded as it was.''

"Well, then, it seems to me there's only one thing to do. You've got enough men to crew the *White Lotus*. Use that ship, and keep the other two in port until you've had time to rebuild your forces.''

"And walk into the Tiger's trap a second time?" Teresa tossed her head contemptuously. "You don't know the first thing about me if you think I'm going to do that. The *Black Jasmine* and the *Red Peony* are my secret strength. Without them, I'd be no match for Brandon Christopher with his superior manpower and financial backing. Fortunately, the captain of the *Jasmine* was on board his ship

supervising necessary repairs in the rigging, and the first
mate of the *Peony* is capable of taking over. As for the
Lotus . . ." Her voice trailed off as she threw him a cool,
appraising look. "What do *you* know about ships, Maarten?"

"Not a damn thing." Skye put his glass back on the
table and leaned forward, looking amused. "But then, I
don't have to . . . do I? You can read the charts and plot
our course well enough; no one else has to be involved in
that. And the men can handle the actual sailing, provided
they have someone to crack the whip over them. And,
yes—if that's what you're really asking—I'm very good at
cracking whips."

Teresa eyed him thoughtfully, sizing him up and deciding he was correct in his assessment of himself. "There's
still one problem. We can't set out forty men short. I'm
going to have to do what everyone else does. Buy some of
my crew."

"Shanghaied men don't make the best sailors," he
warned.

"Maybe not, but I'll pay them generously. *Every* man
may not be for sale, but most are—particularly the ones
who hang out in bars along the waterfront. When they
wake up and find themselves with more money than they
expected and plenty of food for their bellies, maybe they'll
know they're well off. At any rate, I'll purchase more than
we need. If some of them prove difficult, we can always
pitch them over the side."

Skye chuckled softly, enjoying the way her mind worked.
"That'll solve the problem of troublemakers in two ways.
The worst will be dead, and the others will be considerably
less likely to rebel."

Teresa stepped over to the window, barely hearing what
he said as she looked out at the hills again. The sunset was
well advanced now, and the earth was shrouded in a deep,
rich light as crimson as the blood of the men who had died
on the ferry.

"I remember once when I was a little girl . . . I must
have been eight or nine, because I had been with my father

for about a year. I saw a length of fabric in one of the shops along the Praya Grande, an exquisite silk, woven with threads of gold, and I wanted it more than I had ever wanted anything in my life. It was much too old for me, and my father refused to buy it, but that didn't keep me from wanting. I used to go there several times a day and just look and look. One afternoon the shopkeeper was busy in the back, and there was no one to see, so I took it.''

She turned, smiling almost sweetly in the soft light.

''I hid it under my bed. You have no idea how terrified I was that someone would find it and I would be punished. It did me even less good there than in the shop—I didn't dare take it out and look at it—but I kept it anyway because I couldn't bear the thought of destroying it. Then one day the maid found it and took it to my father. I was trembling all over when he called me in to see him. Do you know what he did?''

Skye shook his head. ''No. What?''

''He laughed. I'll never forget—he just stood there and laughed. Then he had the seamstress make the fabric into a dress for me. I wore it everywhere, even in front of the shopkeeper, for he couldn't prove it was his—and besides, he didn't dare protest. Even then, my father was associated with dangerous men, though none so powerful as Lin.

'' 'Little daughter,' he told me—and those words have stuck in my mind—'Little daughter, if you want something badly enough, don't be afraid to go after it.' ''

Skye leaned forward, beginning to understand what she was getting at. ''And what do you want now?''

''I want Brandon Christopher's head in a bamboo basket.''

10

The light was gone by the time Celia finally gave in to her weariness and stretched out on the bed. Her stomach still churned, and she did not regret the stew that clung in congealing pieces to the floor and walls of her small, clumsily constructed prison. Or that vile-smelling coffee, cold in its cup!

It was a long time before she fell asleep, and then only fitfully. The coverlet was temptingly thick, but she could not bring herself to crawl under it, as if somehow that would be surrendering to her fate, and several times she woke to find she was shivering.

Once she thought she heard voices outside the window.

"What are we going to do with her?" one of them seemed to say, though his English was so bad she couldn't be sure.

"Wait and see," the other replied. She sensed it was the man with the short-cropped hair, for he had almost no accent. "The Moonwind comes tomorrow night."

The Moonwind? Celia sat up, trying to focus her eyes, but she could not make out even the vaguest outlines in that pitch blackness. Who or *what* was the Moonwind? Chinese secret societies, she knew, often had exotic names like that, though she couldn't remember any of them, except the White Lotus, which was reputed to include a pirate band headed by a woman! Could the Moonwind be something like that?

She lay awake for an hour or so longer, but although she strained her ears, she heard nothing else. She had just begun to wonder if she wasn't dreaming it all when she fell at last into another restless sleep.

When she woke again, it was morning. The room was filled with a faint grayish light, but it seemed even colder than before, and every muscle in her body ached as she got out of bed.

If I didn't know I'd dozed off at least a dozen times, she thought wearily, I'd swear I hadn't gotten any sleep at all.

A slight rapping startled her at the door, and she glanced up, puzzled. The Tiger had shown precious little consideration last night. Surely he wasn't developing manners now!

But as the door swung open, she saw not the redheaded pirate she had half-expected, but the young Chinese who had accosted her two days before on the street. He was dressed like a European, in denim pants and a loose cotton shirt which somehow suited his style. In his hands he carried a tray laden with platters, cups, and three small china pots.

"I didn't know what you liked for breakfast," he said amiably, "so I brought everything I could find. Perhaps it's just as well . . ." He looked around, taking in the broken bowl and hardened splotches of stew. "You can't have had much to eat last night."

"I didn't have *anything*," she admitted. To her surprise, her stomach began to rumble as she surveyed the contents of the tray. He had indeed brought a little of everything. The platters held a number of eggs, cooked to perfection, a thick slice of grilled ham, fresh vegetables, and crusty bread, together with a choice of jellies and marmalades. One of the pots seemed to contain tea, another coffee, and the third something that smelled deliciously like sweet chocolate.

"Well, then, I hope you enjoy this." The man set the tray on the table, smiling tentatively as he noticed her hesitance. "You don't need to be afraid of us, you know.

If we were planning to hurt you, we'd have done so
already. Besides, why would I take such care with your
breakfast?''

Celia sensed he was trying to be kind, but she was too
tired and too tense to respond.

"What are you going to do with me?" she asked,
repeating the question that had gone unanswered the night
before. "Please, *please*, what are you going to do?"

The young man shook his head regretfully. "I can't tell
you that. I'm sorry. But I do promise, no harm is going to
come to you. Eat your breakfast now, before it gets cold."
He picked up last night's tray and headed for the door.
"I'll send someone to clean up this mess."

He stopped at the last moment, turning, as if on impulse.

"Your name is Celia St. Clair. I already know that, but
you don't know who I am. They call me 'China' Kwan.
The boy who brought your dinner last night is Freddie
Brown. And the man you spoke with later, the one who
seems to have gotten you so angry—"

"I know who he is," Celia interrupted, not wanting to
be reminded. "He's the Tiger."

"That's the name he's known by, yes. But he is really
Brandon Christopher." China Kwan smiled again, warmly
this time. "There, now—we all know each other, so everything is all right. You can't be afraid of someone you
know."

He closed the door behind him, leaving Celia more
confused than ever, though not, she had to admit, quite so
ill-at-ease. She knew better, of course, than to trust the
word of a pirate. Still, why *would* he worry about her
breakfast if they had some evil fate in mind for her?

She turned to the tray, tackling the meal with relish. The
ham was a bit too salty for her taste, but quite edible; the
eggs were even better than they looked; and she polished
off every bit of the bread and jam. Finishing the tea with
regret, she poured out a cup of chocolate, but left the third
pot strictly alone. Obviously the coffee had been brewed
for Brandon Christopher. Americans were positively bar-

baric sometimes, making it so strong you could feel the grit against your teeth.

The meal soothed her anxieties, giving credence to Mama's theory that nothing ever looked quite so bad on a full stomach, and she was almost in a good mood a half-hour later when the door opened again and Brandon Christopher strode into the room. Without, she noted wryly, taking the time to knock. Like his lieutenant, he had changed to dark blue denims and was sporting a casual red-checked shirt, open at the neck.

He paused a few feet away, casting an amused glance at the tray in front of her. "I see breakfast meets with your approval. I must say I'm glad. I'd hate to think I'd sent in more ammunition for you to use against me."

Celia was surprised to find herself smiling. There was something infectious in his humor, especially with those little lines that formed in the tanned skin around his eyes, as if he were used to laughing.

"I might have saved something," she confessed, "if I had known you were coming. But I doubt it. I was too hungry to think of anything else."

"Good. Then maybe you'll be ready to listen to what I have to say."

Celia eyed him warily. "More questions?"

"No, actually an apology of sorts. I stalked in here last night like a raging bull. There were reasons for my impatience, but that's beside the point. I could have been a damn sight gentler. Oh, hell, I *should* have been gentler. I hope you'll let me make it up to you now."

"You're not going to question me again?" Celia looked doubtful. "About what I was doing in Hong Kong? And why I was searching for Skye?"

"I have every intention of questioning you," he replied with disarming frankness. "But not now. I *am* in a hurry, but I think I can wait an hour or two before pressing you again. In the meantime, China Kwan is sending the boy in to clean up the mess you made last night. I thought you might like to take a walk around the island with me.

Unless of course you'd rather stay and watch him scrape
that confounded stuff off the walls."

"No." Celia was already up and at the door before he
finished making the offer. She had been in that room only
a few hours, but already it seemed like a prison. "I'd do
almost anything to get out of here. Including going for a
walk with you!"

He looked startled, then laughed. "Well, under the
circumstances, I guess that's the best I can hope for."

The morning sunlight felt wonderfully warm as Celia
stepped outside. The air was scented with flowers and
greenery, a welcome change from the damp chill of the
hut. As he had promised, Brandon did not question her
again; in fact, he almost seemed to have forgotten she was
there as he strode on ahead, leaving her to follow as best
she could. They cut across a shallow plain, then started up
a steeply winding path to the top of what appeared to be
the highest hill on the island.

Brandon paused only once, near the crest, to throw an
impatient glance over his shoulder. "You're going to have
to step on it if you want to catch up," he called down to
her. "Or can't you manage a rugged place like this? If it's
too much for you, there are some flat rocks over there
where you can wait. I should only be a few minutes. I
want to check some things from here."

"Of course I can manage," Celia shouted back, trying
not to let him see the way she slid and stumbled with each
step she took. "And it's *not* too much for me! What do
you think? That women are fragile little flowers who can
never keep up with a man?"

"Only some of them." He grinned, not quite nicely, it
seemed to her. "Especially the ones who are dressed like
that."

Celia glared at him. "What's wrong with the way I'm
dressed?" She had on the same pale blue shirtwaist she
had worn the last time she saw Skye, which she had
decided by this time was definitely fetching. And emi-

nently practical, too. "The skirt is an inch and a half from
the ground. A perfect length for walking!"

"Oh, the skirt's all right, if a bit frilly—and at least
you're not laced in so tight you can't breathe. Nothing is
as tiresome as females who faint all the time because they
can't get enough oxygen into their lungs. But those shoes
are ridiculous. How the devil do you expect to walk in
them, much less climb hills?"

"My shoes are just fine, thank you!" she snapped,
knowing full well that at least three-quarters of the reason
she was lagging behind was those pointed toes and dainty
little heels that seemed to catch in every crevice. "Anyway, they don't make sturdy footwear for women like they
do for men. The only boots I own are for riding, not
walking."

"They make sensible shoes for golf and tennis," he
reminded her reasonably.

"Well, I wear them—when I play tennis!" She was
beginning to dislike him thoroughly again, and she wondered how she could have forgotten, even for a few minutes, how furious he made her before. He might have been
pleasant enough when he showed up that morning, but
obviously his good moods didn't last for long. "I didn't
leave my hotel yesterday expecting to go for a walk, you
know."

"No, I daresay you didn't." He relented enough to
smile as he stretched out his hand, helping her over one of
the steeper spots. "I *am* sorry. I promised myself I was
going to be a perfect gentleman this morning, but you do
have a way of bringing out the worst in me. Little girls
who don't like to be teased should learn not to show their
tempers."

Little girls? Celia bit her lip, choking back a hot retort.
She would have loved to tell him just what she thought of
his "teasing," but that would be playing into his hands.
Besides, she reminded herself, trying to be sensible, it
would be foolish to forget she was in his power. She

couldn't risk the possibility that one of *her* barbs might hit home.

Brandon did not speak again, but he slowed his pace, and they reached the top together. Gusts of wind caught Celia's hair, threatening to pull it out of its pins, but she barely noticed as she looked around. Every cove on that small island was visible from the hilltop, every narrow sandy beach, surrounded by miles and miles of ocean. The view was so breathtaking it was hard to think of anything else.

"What is that?" she asked, pointing toward a patch of green on the horizon. "It's so big it looks more like the mainland than another island."

"*That*," he said softly, "is Lantao." A strangely thoughtful look came over his face. "I've been on this island several times, but never in daylight, and I've never had a chance to explore it thoroughly. If I had, I'd have noticed a few things that might have saved me a great deal of trouble. You see that inlet over there?" He pointed toward a barely perceptible break in the Lantao shoreline. "And that narrow gully that seems to run to a valley deep in the hills? Somewhere in there, I suspect—though it's too late to matter now—there's another exceptionally pretty little girl named Teresa Valdes . . . with some very evil thoughts on her mind."

He broke off, smiling as he changed the subject. "Over that way, about half a day by steam ferry, is Macao, a colony that was founded by the Portuguese more than three hundred years ago. People have a way of calling it an island, but actually it's a narrow peninsula attached to China . . . And back that way, to the east, is Hong Kong."

Celia turned to gaze in the direction he indicated, but all she could see was ocean. "I don't know much about Hong Kong," she admitted. "Was it always British?"

"No, it's been in English hands for only a short time. Half a century or so. China ceded it to Britain as part of the Nanking peace treaty after the First Opium War, which ended in 1841. Before that, it was of little interest to anyone. Just a few rocky hills occupied by a handful of fishermen and smugglers. You might say its entire economy was based on opium. In many ways it still is.''

"Oh, but surely you can't mean opium is traded there now! Not legally!'' She knew, of course, that it was peddled in back alleys of Chinatowns all over the world. But to call it the base for an entire economy? "That sounds so . . . so tainted.''

"Doesn't it though?'' Brandon remarked dryly. "The English have a way of being wonderfully fastidious—on the surface. Hong Kong is the jewel in the eastern imperial crown; I daresay they didn't much care for the idea of having it contaminated by the 'filthy trade.' But then, they could hardly refuse to allow British opium from British India to be brought into British Hong Kong, now could they? Even before the Second Opium War, when the stuff was formally shoved down China's throat, drug transactions were carried on quite openly. After that, of course, with the Chinese being forced to declare importation legal, it's been impossible to put a lid on the traffic.''

"But you make it sound as if the British created the problem,'' she protested indignantly. "Colonials are much more . . . more *noble* than that. We try to leave the empire a better place than we found it, not worse.''

"You personally, perhaps.'' Brandon made no effort to conceal his skepticism. "But don't try to make every British trader into a Sunday-school teacher. Like it or not, opium was promoted in China in the first place to even out an unfavorable balance of payments. The fact that the drug had long been illegal in England—for damn good reason! —didn't mean a thing to those 'noble' gentlemen. You see, British shipping lines were being forced to shell out large sums of gold and silver for all the tea, silk, and spices that were so popular at home. And the Chinese, ungrateful wretches, wouldn't buy anything in exchange. It was getting to be a drain, leaving all that cash in a foreign country. They had to come up with something the heathens wanted. Eventually they found it.''

"Opium?" Celia shuddered. "But even if that's true, surely it wasn't just the British who were involved. Others must have taken part too.''

Brandon grimaced wryly. "I see you could do with a short history lesson. The First Opium War came about when the Chinese decided, sensibly enough, to put a stop to the trade. That most unusual oddity in Chinese public life, an uncorruptible official, actually went so far as to seize all the supplies in foreign warehouses and destroy them. He made such a thorough job of it, it took twenty-three days to accomplish. Every ball of opium was broken into pieces, thrown into a trench filled with water, quick-lime, and salt, and sluiced out to sea. Would you be interested in knowing who lost the most in that little transaction? The good old British firm of Jardine, Mathieson. Second? Why, Dent and Company—also British. Care to guess who was third?''

He broke off, grinning.

"Russell and Company—American as apple pie. Christopher Shipping Lines, I am chagrined to admit, didn't have an ounce to lose.''

"*Christopher* Lines?" She looked at him inquiringly.

"Not a coincidence, no. The firm was founded by my grandfather, Levi Christopher, an old reprobate who ought to have done better for himself in the Orient—and would have if he hadn't been so busy defending the slave trade, which was already in the process of being outlawed. I'm doing my best to make up for his shortcomings. Officially, of course, we've kept our hands clean. But unofficially . . .'' He laughed as he caught sight of the puzzled look on her face. "Pirates are in business too—only the stakes are higher for us. You didn't think we spent all our time raiding passenger boats with no hope of profit?''

"Well, n-no . . .'' Celia felt the warmth drain out of her cheeks as she recalled that hideous scene on the ferry. "No, of course I didn't. I'm not stupid. But—''

"But how can I speak of it so calmly?" His face took on an unexpected softness, and she had the feeling, just for an instant, that he understood. "For the second time today, I have to say I'm sorry. I keep forgetting how terrifying the experience must have been for you. Women rarely travel on that particular line. I had hoped there wouldn't be any yesterday when we attacked."

"But there were," she reminded him. "Three of us—as you took such pains to point out."

"Yes, but I wasn't worried about the others. They were—as *you* pointed out—considerably older. You were the only young woman there. And unlike you, I really do mean young . . . Dammit, Celia St. Clair, do you have to stand there and stare at me as if I were a monster? I'm trying my best to apologize."

"*Apologize?*" Celia turned away, too shocked to look at him. Apologies were for treading on someone's toes when you danced! And Brandon Christopher *was* a monster. She'd be a fool if she let herself lose sight of that, no matter how amiable he might sometimes seem. Or how attractive. "I don't think you can ever apologize for what you did yesterday."

He stared at her rigid back for a moment, then stepped up behind her, close but not touching. "Would it help if I told you those men deserved exactly what they got? I wasn't being altogether honest with you before. I *did* reap a profit from the raid, though it wasn't the kind that can be reckoned in dollars or pounds. And every one of those 'poor little lambs to the slaughter' had slaughtered at least one other human being with his own hand."

He paused, waiting for a response. When it did not come, he took hold of her shoulders, turning her around. "I'm afraid we've put this off as long as we can. I am sorry—there, that's three times today, a record for Brandon Christopher—but I have to ask you again. What were you doing in Hong Kong?"

"And I have to tell you again—it's none of your busi-

ness! You're not going to get the information you want.
Why don't you stop trying?''

"Ah, but I will get it, whether you help me or not. If
you thought it over, you'd realize that. I've already learned
a great deal about you. I know your name and where
you're from. Your father is Ian St. Clair, and he owns a
plantation on the Irrawaddy, not far from Rangoon. Your
mother's name is Serena, and she had silver-blond hair
like yours until it started to go gray.''

"But . . . but how . . . ?'' Celia looked up, stunned.
"How can you know all that?''

"It's simple really. Your name was on the register at
your hotel, and you had talked to one of the clerks,
mentioning you were from Burma. Then there's that mar-
velous little invention—the telegraph. It took only a few
hours to get most of what I was looking for. The rest, I
admit, was a matter of luck. I found an employee at one of
the shipping lines who had been in Rangoon and knew
your father. He even remembered you. Said you were a
'spunky little thing.' ''

Celia turned her head to the side, trying to hide the stab
of fear that raced through her. If they had gone to all this
trouble, then they must be holding her for ransom! Her
father would be beside himself when they got in touch
with him. He'd do anything to raise the money, even if it
meant losing the plantation.

"My father isn't a rich man,'' she said miserably. "He
can't afford to give you much. Even if he sells everything
he possesses. And if you're thinking of Skye . . .'' She
closed her eyes, feeling suddenly sick. Skye had been
most emphatic when he told her not to come—because he
was afraid she'd be a burden! "Please . . . he isn't rich
either . . .''

"I didn't take you for money, Celia,'' Brandon said
gently. "There isn't a price on your head, if that's what
you're worried about. And I didn't mean to frighten you
like this. All I want are a few facts—which I can get
anyway, without your help.''

Celia was embarrassed to feel tears running down her cheeks. When he was kind like that, she almost had the feeling she could trust him and that he really didn't mean to harm her. Besides, as he said, there was hardly any point trying to hide what he could find out for himself.

"Schuyler Maarten is my fiancée," she said simply. "I came here to be with him." Then, mustering as much dignity as she could, she went on to tell him everything, from the moment Skye had first returned to the night he left again, after losing his entire stake in a poker game. It was a long story, but Brandon did not interrupt, listening with unexpected patience until she had finished.

"He lost everything . . . gambling?" A faint hint of sarcasm drew her gaze upward.

"Yes," she admitted warily.

"And you still want him?" The mockery was open now, sparkling in his eyes. "Ah . . . and I was beginning to think you had a little sense."

"Of course I still want him!" Celia felt her spirit return. He had lulled her into almost liking him for a moment, but that wasn't going to happen again! "Do you think I'm so shallow I wouldn't stand by the man I love just because he did something I don't approve of? Skye is young and reckless—I know that—but he'll grow out of it. And I don't want him any less because of it, either!"

"So I see," he replied dryly, "but I wonder—do you know what you're getting into?"

Probably, he thought, looking down at those hotly indignant features. She could hardly be as naive as she appeared. Maarten must have told her all about the money he brought back with him. That kind of braggart always talked. And then, she *was* a passionate little creature. He had sensed that before, when he caught hold of her arms and felt the startling heat of her reaction. Passionate little creatures didn't go halfway across the Orient pursuing men who were not already their lovers.

"It's time we were getting back," he said gruffly as he

started down the path. "It's late, and I have to figure out what to do with you before the *Moonwind* comes."

"The . . . *Moonwind*?"

Brandon heard the catch in her voice and turned. "What do you know about the *Moonwind*?" he asked sharply.

"Nothing. I . . . I just heard . . . I *overheard* some of the men talking. In the middle of the night. But they didn't say anything. Just that it was coming."

"My men should learn to be more discreet. Well . . . no harm done, I suppose. You'd have found out for yourself tonight anyway. The *Moonwind* is my ship. She used to be the Christopher Lines' proudest vessel, one of the swiftest on the seas. When clippers went out of fashion and steamers came in, I commandeered her for . . . uh, other uses."

"Oh, a ship."

Celia breathed a sigh of relief. She had been so afraid the *Moonwind* was some sort of sinister secret society. A ship sounded relatively innocuous. Still . . .

"You said you had to figure out what to do with me. Why? You told me you weren't holding me for ransom."

"I told you I wasn't holding you for *money*. I didn't say I wasn't hoping you'd have your uses. When the *Moonwind* sails in tonight, she'll have a full load of opium in her hold, bound for . . . new markets. I had been toying with the idea of taking you with us. Now that I've heard your story, I'm not so sure. I might just ship you back to your father."

"Ship me *back*?" Celia stared at him in horror. "To Burma?" But she couldn't go back there! Once her father got her home again, he'd watch her like a hawk. She'd never be reunited with Skye. "No! I won't go. If you put me on a ship, I . . . I'll jump overboard and swim to shore! You can't make me go back!"

"I can if I decide to," he reminded her grimly. "Even if I have to keep you under lock and key. But relax, I haven't made up my mind yet."

"But . . . I don't want to go! I'd rather do *anything*

than go back there. I'd . . . I'd even rather sail with you on the *Moonwind*!''

"Well, you might get your wish."

He turned and headed briskly down the path. Celia scrambled after him, trying desperately to keep up. Her shoes *were* ridiculous for walking, but she'd have died before she admitted it, especially to him!

They had almost reached the bottom when her ankle twisted, and she gave a little cry as she felt herself lurch forward. Brandon whirled instinctively, reaching out to steady her.

The touch of his hand was startlingly strong, provocative somehow, and Celia caught her breath as she looked up into dark, haunting eyes that seemed to hold her in a spell. Long, slow shivers ran through her body, frightening, uncontrollable, yet not altogether unpleasant. She had the sudden irrational feeling that he was going to draw her into his arms and kiss her, and instead of resisting, she wondered only what it would be like to feel those mocking masculine lips hard against her mouth.

The sensation lasted barely the space of a heartbeat. Then Brandon released her hand and took a step back, not a retreat but a challenge as his taunting lips curved faintly upward. Horrified, Celia caught her skirt in both hands and began to race back toward the small stone hut. She did not care what he thought. She did not even care that he was laughing out loud, the insultingly sarcastic sound following her as she fled. All she wanted was to get away.

God in heaven, what was she doing?

She slammed the door and leaned against it, trying to still the frantic beating of her heart as it thumped against her chest. She had almost let that man kiss her. *Let* him? She had *encouraged* him! And he would have done it, too, if she hadn't come to her senses just in time.

It was not as if she *loved* him. Celia pushed away from the door and went over to sit on the edge of the bed. She loved Skye. She always had, and she always would. This man was no more than a stranger—and a dubious one at that! Why, then, did her body respond every time he touched her or she even thought he was going to?

She sank down on the bed, burying her head in soft pillows. She was not ignorant of what went on between a man and a woman in the privacy of their bedroom. Serena, being a dutiful mother, had explained it all long ago, managing the business with a minimum of Victorian embarrassment. But Serena had emphasized the gentler aspects of love, hinting that 'the other' was more in the nature of duty than pleasure—though the faint flush on her cheeks when she spoke about it gave Celia the idea, even then, that there might be more to it than she was telling.

What Serena had not taught her daughter, however, and what was troubling her now, was that love and desire were not always the same thing. A woman's heart and mind could ache with yearning for one man, while her body hungered for another.

It was all so confusing! Celia wrapped her arms around the pillow, hugging it against her breast as she tried to concentrate on Skye, calling up an image of what he had looked like, his face, his eyes, his smiling lips, that last night they were together.

But all she could see was Brandon Christopher.

China Kwan was waiting a few hours later when Brandon made his way down to the small cove where the *Moonwind* was due to arrive shortly after dusk. He had been standing with his back to the path, staring out across the water, but he turned, troubled, at the sound of footsteps.

"It was a mistake, I think," he said, lowering his voice as Brandon drew near. "Coming here. It is too dangerous."

"Because this is the island Teresa chose for our trysts?" Brandon shrugged nonchalantly. "No, my friend, I think you're wrong. Our pretty pirate lady is too involved in her own concerns right now to worry about where I am. Nor would she come here if she did. This particular kind of boldness is not part of her nature."

No, but it is a part of yours, China thought—and the

lady is getting to know you quite well of late. He kept the thought to himself, however, sensing that Brandon had been right. Teresa Valdes *would* need more than a day or two to regroup her shattered forces. By that time they would be gone.

"What about *her*?" He inclined his head in the direction of the stone cottage.

"Not quite what we had in mind, I'm afraid. Apparently the little minx came to Hong Kong on her own. She just assumed that her fiancé—which word is, I suspect, a euphemism—was going to be delighted to see her. She says, and I'm inclined to believe her, that he has no idea she's here." He grinned suddenly. "Can you imagine the scene if that ferry had gotten through yesterday and those two young ladies had come face to face? Would Maarten have had more trouble explaining Teresa to Celia, do you think, or Celia to Teresa?"

The other man did not laugh. "Why don't you send her back, Bran? What do you say? She's been through enough as it is, what with that bloody raid on the ferry. Women are softer—they can't take things like a man. She might already bear scars for life from this."

"Women are *softer*?" Brandon laughed shortly. "Ah, you mean like Teresa Valdes."

"Teresa is different. She's lived a man's life so long she has begun to think like a man. It's not fair to judge every woman by her."

"I suppose it isn't. But . . ." Brandon picked up a flat stone, skipping it across the water. "Dammit, China, that girl might come in handy. If we hang around the Orient, we're going to keep coming up a stalemate. We've been through this over and over, and we always come to the same conclusion. Sure, we win a few rounds—like yesterday—but Teresa comes back stronger than ever. We've got to lure her to U.S. territory, where she can be arrested. And hanged, as she deserves."

"That's what this raid was about," China reminded him. "It wasn't just those few men we were after. We wanted to hit Teresa where it hurts. She's like a wounded animal now—and wounded animals lose their caution when they come after a hunter. All we have to do is set sail and—''

"And she'll follow. Yes, yes, I know—and you're right! She probably will. But I wouldn't mind a little added insurance."

China's dark eyes narrowed. "You mean the girl, of course. Do you really think Skye Maarten cares enough about her to—"

"Hardly," Brandon cut in. "From what I've heard about Maarten, he wouldn't lift a finger to come after her. But Teresa might."

Seeing the puzzled look his words evoked, he went on, "The lady is very liberal when it comes to her lovers. She's notorious for that. But she does like to control the situation. If she thought Skye had sent for Celia behind her back . . . well, it could be like waving a red flag in front of an angry bull. And that might be just what we need at some point in the future."

"It might," the other man agreed. "But are you sure that's why you want to bring her along?"

"You doubt my motives?" Brandon threw him a wry look. "You've been with me a long time, China. Do you think I'm the sort to be taken in by fluttering lashes and big wistful blue-gray eyes?"

"I've seen the way you look at the girl. And I know what that means. She is very beautiful . . . and very young. A deadly combination when a man needs to keep his head."

"Well, you could be right about that." Brandon flicked another stone at the water, watching as it skimmed across a near-glassy surface. They were going to need more wind tomorrow if they expected to take off on time. "I *am* drawn to Miss Celia St. Clair. I won't deny that." More drawn, he thought, than he had been for a long time—to any woman. "But that doesn't alter the facts. Whatever my motives, we still might be able to use her. I can't afford to let go of anything that could help us. Not at this stage of the game."

His voice was firm enough to stop further argument, but later, after China Kwan had gone off to prepare for the arrival of the *Moonwind*, he found himself brooding uncharacteristically over things he had thought were already settled. A slight breeze had come up, fragrant with flowers, faintly disturbing . . . like the scent of Celia's perfume in his nostrils.

Dammit, why hadn't he taken her when he had the chance? That was what this was all about. A physical need that could have been easily satisfied. He should have gone after her into the hut and taken her by force if she turned coy and tried to resist. She was experienced. He was sure of that. And she *had* wanted him. They had both felt it.

But wanting a man, he reminded himself, and surrendering to him were not necessarily the same thing. His lips twisted into a grimace as he squinted out at sun-shimmering water, searching for traces of the *Moonwind*, which would not appear for hours. Didn't every woman, even an experienced one, have the right to say no if she really meant it?

And she would have, too. He knew that, just as he knew she desired him. She would have cried and pleaded and said "*Please* don't"—and meant every blasted word of it!

For an instant he was almost tempted to listen to China Kwan and send Celia back to her father. What were the odds, after all, that she would make any difference, one way or the other? But those same sooty lashes he had disdained before, those misty blue-gray eyes, came back to haunt him, and he could not let go.

Oh, hell, he had already committed himself. Right or wrong, he was going to stick by his decision.

The woman was coming with them.

11

The *Moonwind* glided into the cove shortly after nightfall and departed again the next morning with the first gray haze of dawn. Celia, who had been hurried across the deck and down a narrow staircase, barely had time to form a jumbled impression of scurrying men and tangled ropes before the first lurching motion warned her they were under way.

Helplessly she watched as the men who had brought her below turned and went back on deck. Alone again, she tried desperately not to think that, of everyone aboard that ship, she was the only one who had no idea where they were going.

Or what the Tiger had planned for their arrival.

At least, she thought, clinging to the only comfort she could find, she seemed to be safe enough for the time being. They had not harmed her on the island, nor did they appear to have any evil intentions toward her while she was on the ship. After that, she was not so sure.

Her first few hours on board were spent in a small cubbyhole fitted out as a carpenter's shop next to the galley, for Brandon had been adamant about allowing no one but working hands on deck when they set sail. Not that she minded. After what had happened between them the day before, she thought, she would be just as happy if she never had to see him again! She settled down on a rough wooden packing crate, ready to spend the rest of the voyage there if that was what he had in mind.

But by the time morning had dragged by and the cook, a small wizened Chinese, had brought her a share of hard tack and salt beef, the place had begun to seem unbearably confining, and she was almost glad when Brandon appeared, asking her with surprising geniality if she would like to see the ship that would be her "home" for the next several weeks.

That a cramped, smelly ocean vessel could hardly be "home" was an observation Celia kept to herself as she followed Brandon up on deck. Back talk, she noticed, always seemed to set him off, and it occurred to her that the best way to handle the situation was to be coolly aloof whenever she was with him.

One look at the deck, however, swarming with activity, and she nearly forgot her resolves. Everything seemed even busier now that they were at sea, and she took an instinctive step closer to Brandon as men bustled past, hurrying back and forth with no apparent order to their actions. Sails seemed to explode as they slapped in the wind, and taut rope lines creaked and groaned.

"It certainly is . . . imposing," she admitted. It made her dizzy just to look up at the rigging, soaring above the deck.

Brandon laughed. "A good choice of words. I remember the first time my grandfather brought me aboard one of his ships. I stared up at the rigging, like you're doing now—and all the way down the deck—and thought I'd never seen anything so *massive* in my life."

"How big is it?" Celia asked, curious in spite of herself.

"About 1,500 tons. Actually that's small for an American vessel. Most of the later clippers that came out of New England were two thousand tons, though British ships tended to half that size. But my grandfather had the *Moonwind* designed as much for grace and maneuverability as carrying power."

Celia, whose idea of "big" was an elephant that weighed

in at three and a half tons, found the numbers he was throwing at her impossible to grasp.

"It's hard to believe anything that large can even float."

"Not only can she float, she's the fastest thing on the water. The art of shipbuilding was at a peak in the mid-sixties when she was constructed, although even then, the appeal of the clipper was waning. Windjammers are sturdier and carry five or six times the cargo, and of course steamers were already beginning to prove they could cut days off a long voyage. I'm glad in a way the old scoundrel didn't live to see the end of the sailing era. He would have been bitterly disappointed."

"But . . . I don't understand." Celia looked puzzled. "How can steamers make better time? You said the *Moonwind* was the fastest thing afloat."

"She is," he agreed, "when the wind is right. But overall, steamers are more dependable. They aren't affected by calms, nor do you have to reef in the sails during a storm, so their day-to-day average tends to be better. Now that there's a reliable network of coaling stations, a steamer can go almost anywhere. There's no reason to use sailing ships on regular routes."

As Brandon showed her around, Celia began to catch a glimmer of the way his grandfather must have felt about sailing. In spite of herself, she could not resist a secret liking for the "old scoundrel" who built his ship with such pride and care. Every detail was meticulously executed, right down to the boards on deck, which fitted neatly into each other with no sign of warping.

"Various types of hardwood are used in ship construction," Brandon explained. "On the *Moonwind*, you'll see primarily white oak from Massachusetts, though there's rock maple too, and live oak, even a bit of Malabar teak. The timber comes from trees that were felled in the winter, when most of the sap—which causes rot—is in the roots. First the bark is stripped off, then it's steeped in hot water to remove the rest of the sap, then dried out in the sun.

Later, it has to be soaked in metallic salts to inhibit dry rot.''

A laborious process, Celia thought, yet well worth the effort. Not only was the *Moonwind* practical, it had a certain raw beauty, even an elegance of sorts. The deck had been holystoned until it gleamed, and dark mahogany woodwork and polished brass fittings shimmered in the sunlight.

Everything about the vessel was tightly constructed, and Celia was fascinated by the manner in which every inch had been put to use. Below the water level, in the keel, was the hold, a vast damp-smelling cavern containing the cargo, about which she was careful not to inquire—knowing full well she didn't want to hear the reply!—and the supplies. Next came the lower deck, or tween deck, with a small but efficient galley and shops for the carpenter and sailmaker. The crew's quarters were located deep in the bow, in an area that seemed to be dark and windowless, though Celia couldn't be sure, for Brandon did not escort her inside. Directly above, on the main deck, was a small wooden structure which he pointed out as the ''necessary house.''

''That is what they call it, isn't it? In proper Victorian novels?''

Celia, who had no idea how novelists referred to the thing, eyed it with suspicion. It might be ''necessary,'' but it certainly didn't look inviting. Nor did it seem adequate for a crew that always numbered at least forty! She sincerely hoped there were more agreeable facilities for guests somewhere else. Perhaps near the captain's cabin at the back of the ship or—as Brandon persisted in correcting her—aft.

''If you're going to live on board, you have to call things by their proper names. Back is not back. It's aft or abaft. And front is fore.''

''I'm not 'living' here by choice,'' Celia reminded him tartly. ''So if you don't mind, I think I'll just call things what I want!''

But because she hated that way he had of looking down his nose at her, and because she didn't want to make a fool of herself in front of the entire crew, Celia stored the terms in her mind anyway. Aft was the back of the ship, and fore was the front, and the place where the crew had their quarters was the forecastle—or fo'c'sle, as it was pronounced. Starboard was right, with a green light attached. And port or larboard was left, with a red light.

"Is that to keep boats from running into each other in the dark?" she quipped sarcastically. "Or is it so the men will know which side is which when they get drunk at night?"

"This isn't a *boat*, dammit." His grumbling, she noted, was relatively good-natured. "It's a *ship*. And no one gets drunk on board the *Moonwind*, or any oceangoing clipper, for that matter. Liquor is strictly rationed, consisting primarily of watered-down rum for cold nights on deck. The crew lives in close quarters: tempers are short enough as it is. We don't need anything to set off the sparks."

They had been strolling back toward the rear of the ship—no, *aft*, Celia reminded herself—when they reached a narrow door opening onto yet another downward staircase.

"Officers' quarters," Brandon informed her, then went on to explain that he had had his things moved out of the captain's cabin, which she would be using for the duration of the voyage.

"I'll be bunking in with China Kwan, the chief mate."

The second mate, it seemed, a wiry Filipino who had followed Celia with lewd eyes a moment before when they passed him on the deck, would be hanging his hammock with the rest of the crew in the forecastle. She was vaguely sorry to think she had inconvenienced the man, but she couldn't help being glad he was sleeping at the other end of the ship.

The stairway opened directly into the saloon, a small chamber that divided the captain's cabin from the mates' quarters. Shallow benches were built into the walls, and in the center, a wooden dining table was littered with instru-

ments and charts. Light flooded in through a row of square
glass panes on one side of the low ceiling.

By contrast, the captain's cabin, which had no outside
apertures, seemed strangely dark, for it was illuminated
only by a single lantern set on a red mahogany desk in the
corner. Although it was undeniably snug, Celia had to
admit it looked comfortable. A neat bunk had been tucked
into one wall, with storage drawers beneath, and a wash-
stand, made of the same dark wood, stood next to the
captain's desk.

It was a minute before she noticed that her luggage,
which had been left at the hotel, was lying on the bed,
together with several paper-wrapped parcels which looked
as if they had come from Hong Kong shops.

"What . . .?"

She did not have time to finish the question, for Brandon had already crossed the room and was—without so
much as a "May I?"—tugging open the largest of her two
valises.

"I had one of the men bring these from Hong Kong,"
he said as he riffled through her things like so many old
rags in a rag bag. "Not that I hoped for much, and by
God, I was right! Look at this." He pulled out a pale
yellow muslin gown trimmed with yards and yards of
French ribbon, one of the prettiest of the outfits she had
brought with her. "And this . . . and *this*!"

There followed a lime-green organdy, sprigged in white
and royal blue, with a daringly low neck, made only
slightly more modest by the insertion of several tiers of
lace. Then the dark blue crepe de chine—her favorite!
—packed in anticipation of that first evening with Skye in
Hong Kong. And then a pair of petticoats, knife pleated in
rustling taffeta, which Celia considered the height of fashionable elegance—but which Brandon, judging from his
expression, regarded with the utmost repugnance.

"No wonder they call the damned things 'street sweep-
ers,' " he snorted contemptuously. "Walk down the road
in one of these and you'll pick up more than your share of

mud and manure, I'll warrant! They're not only unaesthetic, they're unsanitary! Why the devil do women have so little sense? No man would be caught dead in anything so foolish."

Celia refrained from mentioning the absurd starched collars that men affected, and their tightly knotted ties, as she watched him sling the pretty dresses and petticoats over his arm.

"What . . . what are you going to do with those?"

"Toss them overboard, if I have any sense!"

"Toss them *where*?"

"You heard me. Over the rail. We're cramped enough without having to make room for useless gewgaws. Yes, and *this* too!" He picked up a fabulously expensive whalebone corset, which Papa had sent for all the way from Paris, and shook it in her face. "I'll not have you lacing yourself so tight you can't breathe. There's no place for swooning females on a clipper."

Celia was so horrified at the sight of that intimate garment in coarse masculine hands, that she very nearly *did* swoon. Only the thought of the exquisite blue crepe de chine held her back.

"Oh no you don't!" She caught hold of the fabric and tugged it out of his grasp. "I adore that dress. My father paid a fortune for it. I won't let you cast it into the sea!"

Brandon glowered. For a moment she was afraid he was going to take it back again, but to her relief, he pitched it on the bed. "Very well. Keep it if you insist, though I'll be damned if I know what use you're going to make of it on board. But the rest of these have to go!"

Without giving her a chance to protest again, he turned and strode forcefully to the deck. Celia, still clutching the blue crepe de chine, trotted helplessly after him, watching as he arranged everything in a wooden crate and tied it with a sailor's knot.

"You're really going to throw them overboard?"

The sound of her voice caught his attention, and he

whirled around, looking faintly annoyed, as if he had not expected to find her there.

"You don't have to take everything I say so literally," he replied gruffly. "No, of course I'm not going to toss them over the side, though God knows I should. They're going into the hold, where they'll be out of the way." He had started toward the cabin even before he finished speaking, and Celia, her jaw clenched, had no choice but to follow.

Plainly, she thought as she headed miserably down the stairs, this voyage was going to be even worse than she had imagined. She could just picture herself, week after endless week, wearing the dress she had on now. Why, she couldn't even take it off to wash it! It wouldn't dry overnight, and she could never squeeze into the crepe de chine without her corset, which was in the hold with everything else.

When she reached the cabin, however, she saw that Brandon had torn open the packages, and a number of new garments were strewn on the bed.

While they were hardly what she would have chosen for herself, she could not deny, as she sorted through them, that they did look reasonably decent. A light pearl-gray shirtwaist blouse, much like the one she had on, but softer and prettier, was complemented by a deeper gray sport skirt with pleats stitched partway down. Black kid ankle boots seemed to go with the costume, although there were also two pairs of low-heeled golfing shoes, sensible, with nonskid soles and a set of gaiters for warmth.

The rest of the clothes appeared to be men's styles, or perhaps boys', for they were a small size, and Celia was almost certain they would fit. She noted two pairs of long denim trousers, another of white duck fabric, three checkered shirts in various shades of blue and blue-green, a pullover sweater, and a heavy dark blue woolen jacket.

She was about to admit grudgingly that they had been well selected when her eye fell on something she had not noticed before.

Picking it up, she found herself gazing at the oddest garment she had ever seen. It seemed to be a shirt, or perhaps a sweater of some sort, a loose, shapeless tube of blue-gray knit with sleeves sewn into it.

"Why, it looks like a potato sack!"

Brandon laughed, an unsettlingly mocking sound. "It's called an 'athletic jersey,' or so the shopkeeper in Hong Kong claims. Apparently it's the latest thing. Practical, too—which goes to show that fashion isn't all bad." He ran a practiced eye down her figure. "I have a feeling it's going to look better on you than around a few pounds of potatoes. Go ahead, try them on. If the sizes aren't right, we'll borrow a needle so you can make alterations."

Celia, who could manage passably well when it came to embroidery but had never done any real sewing in her life, eyed the garments warily. Fortunately, however, when Brandon had gone and she was alone again, she found that everything fit, except for the shoes, which were a half-size too large but would do well enough with bits of paper wadded in the toes. The pants seemed a little strange, for she was not used to anything tight around her legs, but they were not nearly as confining as she had imagined. And the "athletic jersey," for all its ugliness, felt remarkably loose and free.

She had just begun to think the outfit wasn't so bad after all when the door opened and Brandon barged into the room. Without knocking, too! she thought indignantly. She had just opened her mouth to remind him sarcastically that small courtesies were sometimes appreciated—especially in a lady's dressing chamber—when she caught sight of the expression on his face.

Why, he's looking at me as if I were naked! she thought, too shocked to move.

Suddenly the shirt that had felt so comfortable before seemed almost embarrassingly obscene, and she sensed, without seeing, the way it clung perversely to every contour of her body.

Against her will, her eyes drifted downward, mesmerized by the slow bulge that had begun to form in the front of his trousers. Then, horrified, they snapped up again as she realized what she was doing.

Brandon did not miss the flood of crimson that rose to her cheeks. "A basic masculine reaction." He followed her gaze with a roguish leer. "Quite uncontrollable—and since it's also unconcealable, I refuse to apologize. But rest assured, madam, I am capable of keeping my lusty impulses under control. You are in no 'danger' from me—assuming, of course, that's the way you look at it."

His eyes gleamed wickedly as he lingered in the doorway.

"Some of my men, however, may not show quite the same restraint. Don't forget, we're going to be at sea a long time. Perhaps you have some . . . uh . . . underpinnings that might . . . minimize the effect."

Celia felt her flush deepen. If she had had anything at hand, she would happily have thrown it at him, and not even cared if he laughed. She was never so glad of anything in her life as to see the door close behind him and know he was finally gone.

It was positively boorish, she thought furiously, the way that man acted! Clenching her hand into a fist, she beat it ineffectually against the door frame. And what made it worse was that unspeakable way he had of looking at her as if he thought she enjoyed his lewd insinuations!

It wasn't until considerably later, when the embarrassment had abated somewhat and Celia's usual sense of humor returned, that it occurred to her what Brandon had said. Rather to her surprise, she found herself laughing.

Underpinnings, indeed! What a quaint way to put it. Could it be that Brandon Christopher, a man who rummaged freely through women's luggage—and gaped at corsets without blinking an eye—actually drew the line at saying "chemise" or "small clothes"?

The thought restored her confidence somewhat, and she turned her attention back to her wardrobe. Fortunately he *had* left her enough "underpinnings" to make do. She took off the jersey and put on a chemise, then a second to

be on the safe side before she pulled the jersey on again.
Feeling a little more modest, she ventured up on deck.

The air was crisp, even though the sun was still bright,
and Celia did not mind the extra layers of clothing at all.
She wandered over to the railing and was staring out at the
water when China Kwan joined her. He did not say much,
chatting idly of this and that, but as before, she sensed he
was trying to be kind, and by the time he left, she was
feeling at least a little more at ease.

When Brandon appeared a few minutes later, she was
relaxed enough almost to forget how angry he had made
her before. He too seemed in good humor, and she noticed
that he treated her with exaggerated courtesy, as if to make
up for his earlier rudeness. After he had talked a little
about the ship, pointing out things he thought she might
have missed, he told her, with none of his usual conde-
scension, the rules she would be expected to follow while
she was on board.

There were, it seemed, only three things she had to keep
in mind. She was to stay out of the way whenever things
got hectic, which sounded fair enough, and she was under
no circumstance to enter the forecastle—scarcely a hardship, since she had no desire to go into that dingy hole
anyway. Nor was she to explore the ship unless Brandon
or China Kwan was with her.

"But that's absurd! At that rate, I'd spend the whole trip
in the saloon with no one but the cabin boy to keep me
company."

"It's for your own protection," he told her, looking
suddenly serious. "And incidentally, I don't want you
encouraging Freddie to hang around either. He delivers the
food and picks up the dishes. That's it!"

"Freddie?" She stared at him, incredulous. "Surely
you can't say *that's* for my protection. Didn't you tell me
the boy was thirteen?"

"Fourteen. An age at which adolescents are increasingly
preoccupied with things that didn't concern them before.

And Freddie shows signs of being an especially nasty-minded little boy.''

"Well, yes, but even so, he's not going to *try* anything. And if he did, I'm capable of taking care of myself.''

"I'm sure you are,'' he remarked dryly. "But Freddie is a hard worker, and he shows promise of being able to take over when Cook gets too old to go to sea. I'd hate to have something happen that would force me to leave him behind next time we hit port.''

Celia leaned back over the railing, staring gloomily at the horizon. "It sounds like I *am* going to spend the whole trip in the saloon all by myself.''

"Hardly.'' His humor seemed to have returned. "You can go anywhere you want on deck. In the daytime. All I ask is that you don't let anyone show you the cargo in the hold. And don't wander much past midship after dark. It's harder to keep an eye on things then.''

Not an unreasonable request, Celia had to admit, but not exactly practical either. That unappealing little house he had pointed out before seemed to be the only one on board, and it was well past the middle of the ship.

Brandon seemed to guess what she was thinking, for he waved down one of the crew and sent him to fetch something from the hold. When the man returned, he was carrying a parcel wrapped in old newspapers.

Brandon opened it, revealing a large brass pot, which he presented to Celia with a mock-comic bow. "For you, m'lady. The Indians call it a *lota*. In small villages all over the country, you see women heading for the fields just after dawn with these tucked under their arms—unless their men keep them in *purdah*, in which case lower-caste servants take care of the business for them. I bought three last time I was in Calcutta. For my three maiden aunts in Boston. I thought I'd tell them they're planters.''

"Planters?'' She looked at him curiously.

"Can't you picture the look on some poor sea captain's face when he pays a duty call on one of the old dears and finds himself eyeball to eyeball with this!''

Celia struggled to keep her mouth from quivering. "It doesn't seem right, making fun of your maiden aunts like that. Do you really have three?"

"Technically, only one," he confessed. "The other two were married, but their husbands had the decency to die early on. They've lived down the stigma."

"And you think they'd be so easily shocked? I find that hard to believe."

He grinned. "You don't know Boston."

"But surely, even in Boston, ladies sometimes feel the call of nature on a cold winter's night. They must have chamber pots there too."

"Yes, but not in the middle of the front parlor—with geraniums sticking out of them!"

Celia gave in to her laughter then, unable to help herself. Of anyone she had ever known, Brandon Christopher was certainly the most enigmatic. He was, without a doubt, the most *aggravating* man on earth, yet there was something so natural about him when he wanted to be—so much fun!—it was hard to remember she was determined to dislike him. And even harder to remember that unsavory cargo in the hold.

Within a few days she had grown accustomed to life on board ship, which turned out to be surprisingly pleasant, if a bit tedious, once the first qualms of seasickness were over. Time was measured differently at sea, and she found herself listening for the bells that chimed on the hour and half-hour, dividing everything into four-hour periods corresponding to the four-hour watches.

The day began for Celia at eight bells, the hour at which a light breakfast of rice porridge and tea sweetened with molasses was brought into the saloon. When eight bells sounded again, it was noon, time for cold salt beef and sea biscuits with the men on deck or, if the day was bitter and Cook could be persuaded, a hash of those same ingredients, stirred up in a skillet with potatoes and plenty of black pepper to make it palatable. Dinner was served at four bells, or six o'clock, midway in the dogwatches, and either Brandon or China Kwan would join her for a meal that was tasty and surprisingly nourishing. Poultry coops had been constructed on the forward deck, and pig pens were located under the stairway, so there was an ample supply of fresh eggs and pork, and even an occasional roast chicken, together with tinned vegetables and the inevitable preserved limes that Brandon insisted were the British way of staving off scurvy. She didn't care for them herself, but she ate them anyway, "just in case," and she had to admit she remained in excellent health.

Everyone on board, with the exception of the "idlers," the cook and cabin boy, carpenter and sailmaker, were divided into two watches, the so-called "port" and "starboard" watches. This had nothing to do with where the men were positioned, but came from the method of assigning duties. On most merchant vessels, crews were changed with predictable regularity, and watches were set at a traditional ritual the first day out of port. The men lined up on deck, and the first and second mates took turns choosing among them, the first mate sending his hands to the port side of the ship, the second thumbing his to starboard, until the division was complete.

On the *Moonwind*, where the crew remained essentially the same, no such ceremony had taken place, and the terms were merely a convenience, the "port" watch being the first mate's, or China Kwan's, watch, the "starboard" watch belonging to the second mate, Jorge, the Filipino.

The watches, like the bells, were set up in four-hour blocks, with one group standing from midnight until four in the morning and the next from four to eight, when the first came on again. The dogwatches—four to eight in the evening—were broken into two two-hour segments so the same men would not always be on duty for the unpopular early-morning shift.

It came as a surprise to Celia to discover that sailing was considerably more challenging than it had looked those few times she went with Papa to Rangoon and watched tall clippers glide gracefully into port. There was little free

time, even off duty, for there always seemed to be sails or
rigging that required mending, clothes in need of a stitch
or a patch, decks to be holystoned, brass fittings that had
lost their sheen. Brandon was too busy to spend much time
with her, but China Kwan proved remarkably patient with
her endless questions, and she found herself looking on
him more and more as a friend.

It was China who taught her about the rigging of a ship.
The *Moonwind*, he told her, was a full-rigged vessel, with
three masts—foremast, mainmast, and mizzenmast—each
carrying five sails. The lowest sail was known as the
mainsail, with the topsail above it, then the topgallant, the
royal, and finally the skysail. In the bow, flying jibs
angled out over the water, and staysails flapped noisily on
several of the taut lines, or stays, between the masts.
Additional canvas could be put out—though why it would
be needed, Celia could not for the life of her imagine—in
the form of studding sails, which ran on extended yards to
the sides, as high up as the royals.

It fascinated her to stand on deck and look up, which
she could now do without feeling giddy, as men scrambled
out to the ends of the long yards, checking lines and
shaking out heavy canvas sails or reefing them in, accord-
ing to the whims of the wind.

She had assumed that it took years to learn to work
effectively at such dizzying heights. But when she asked
China Kwan about it, he told her the men were expected to
perfect their technique on the spot. ''On most ships, new
hands are sent up immediately after they sail. There's no
time to get used to the idea or work up to it gradually.''

That bit of information increased Celia's admiration,
and she watched those catlike climbing figures with awe.
It was hard to believe that most of the men, perhaps all of
them, had gone to the top of one mast or another the first
day they were at sea. Surprisingly, the best hands in the
rigging were not the brawniest men, but the light, wiry
ones, who seemed to swing from rope to rope like mon-
keys in a tree.

"Why, I could do that!" she said one day when China Kwan paused to speak with her for a moment. "It doesn't look nearly as hard as it did at first."

"It isn't," he agreed. "But it isn't easy, either."

"No, I'm sure it isn't. Still . . ." Celia broke off, staring at sails flapping in the wind as a sudden new thought came to her. "China, do you suppose I could try? I'm sure I could do it, and I wouldn't get in the way. Besides, I heard Brandon say he was shorthanded. Maybe I could take over some of the lighter chores."

"You? Certainly not." China looked shocked. "It's much too dangerous. I couldn't allow it. Working the rigging is a man's job."

"Some of those 'men' are barely boys," Celia protested, gesturing toward a particularly slight figure on the main topsail yard. "Look at that one. Why, he's not much bigger than I am. I know I'm not strong enough to reef in a sail, and I suppose I couldn't handle the canvas when it's wet. But I could manage if it was . . . well, a tangled line or something like that."

"I don't know . . ." China's eyes narrowed speculatively. They *could* use the help, especially when it came to putting more lookouts in the rigging. But a woman? "I still think it's too dangerous. I don't—"

"Oh, please, China," Celia pleaded. "*Please* say yes! You don't know how tiresome it is standing on deck all the time doing *nothing*! It's not my fault I'm here in the first place. If you have to keep me prisoner, at least give me something to do!"

The outburst surprised him, and China felt his resolve weaken. Something in those high spirits appealed to him, reminding him a little of himself at that age. Not that he had been particularly eager to go up in the rigging—but then, he hadn't had a choice.

"Very well," he conceded. "I don't suppose it could hurt to let you go up to the mainsail, maybe even as high as the topsail. But not today. The wind is strong and it seems to be rising. Wait until it calms down. Then I'll take you up myself and show you what to do.''

Celia lowered her lashes demurely as she thanked him, but the instant he was gone, her eyes turned up again, sparkling with mischief as they took in the rigging. Wait until the winds ease off, he had told her—only they had been at sea for over a week, and the winds seemed to get stronger every day. If she waited, she might never have a chance.

And really, why should she? She *could* do it, she was sure of that. China's reluctant concession had only strengthened her faith in herself. She could do it, and the time was *now*, before the wind got even worse.

She bided her time, waiting until the watches changed and the second mate, the Filipino, was on duty. Jorge was a good sailor, even the men who disliked him did not deny that, but he was plodding and slow-witted, and Celia was certain she could get around him. She was just mulling over various methods of approach when she heard him call out to one of the men, ordering him in English, which was the language of the ship, to free a tangled shroud on the mizzenmast.

"I'll do it," she burst in impulsively. Then, seeing the startled look on the mate's face, she added, "China Kwan has been teaching me the rigging. He says I have to learn to pull my weight."

Jorge's swarthy features struggled with the words, and Celia sensed that, like most of the men, he had only a limited sailor's vocabulary and caught barely the gist of what she was saying.

"Woman in rigging," he muttered darkly. "No good. No. You say China Kwan—"

"Yes, China Kwan!" Celia smiled her prettiest, deliberately confusing him with her femininity. She had not forgotten the way his eyes had a tendency to run up and down her body. "I'm sure you wouldn't want to defy China Kwan. He's a very important man. After all, he *is* the chief mate, and Captain Christopher listens to him."

She emphasized those two words, *Captain Christopher*, and they seemed to produce the desired effect.

Jorge still looked suspicious, but he nodded gloomily. "China say you go, you go. You fix line—there. Mizzen royal."

The mizzen *royal*? Celia looked up, feeling suddenly light-headed as she saw the spot where he was pointing. The royal was almost to the top of the rearmost mast, well above the topsail, which was the highest point China had told her she could go. For an instant she was tempted to back down, but she could feel Jorge's dark eyes on her again, slimy and bold, and she sensed it was too late. She had already thrown out the challenge. If she did not win his respect now, she was going to have trouble with him for the rest of the voyage.

She tried to look casual as she strolled over to the ratline. No, not "strolled," she thought self-consciously— "swaggered" was more the word. She was only vaguely aware of rough hemp scratching her hands as she began to climb upward. All she could think of was the one piece of advice she remembered from everything China had told her about working the rigging.

"Don't look down," he had said. "That's what they always tell the new men. *Don't look down.*"

As if she would even consider it! Celia's stomach churned just at the thought, and she kept her eyes fixed on the rope as she moved upward, passing first the mainsail, then the topsail and the topgallant, stopping at last at the royal. Forty feet up at least, she thought, perhaps even fifty, though she'd never had a head for distance or measurements.

She was glad now she had watched the men so closely, for she was able to mimic them reasonably well. Grabbing hold of the yard with both arms, she hung on for dear life as she searched for a hold on the footropes. It seemed to take forever, but finally she worked her way, inch by inch to the the end of the spar. The shroud, which had snapped loose and become tangled in the rigging, was, mercifully, easy to work free, and she breathed a sigh of relief as she dropped it to the deck, where one of the hands would catch it and tie it up again.

It was then that instinct failed her, and forgetting everything, she let her eyes follow that swift downward motion. Every inch of her flesh turned to ice as she saw how small the men looked, like little insects scurrying over the deck—and how sickeningly long the drop was. The sight was too much for an already queasy stomach, and to her disgrace, she lost the lunch she had just consumed.

Thank heaven the wind is blowing! she thought weakly. She could just imagine the effect on all those laughing upturned faces.

Somehow—later she would not even remember how she did it—she managed to get back to the mast. She had one brief moment of panic when the wind gusted suddenly, but she held on as hard as she could, and in a few seconds it had passed. By the time she reached the ratline, she was surprised to find her confidence returning, and she scrambled down almost as nimbly as the men, not even minding when she caught occasional glimpses of the deck.

She was greenish as she leapt down at last, but she had done what she set her mind to, and she was beginning to feel quite smug—until she looked up and found herself face to face with a livid Brandon Christopher.

"What in hell do you think you're doing?"

Celia gazed into those dark, angry eyes, and something inside her snapped. She was sick to death of the way this man treated her, as if she were a mindless little nitwit who was only there to obey his orders. She might be his prisoner, but that didn't mean he was going to reduce her to sputtering incoherence again. Or bully her into submission.

"I went up to untangle a shroud in the mizzen royal. And I made a damn good job of it, too! Or don't you think *my* work counts for anything—because I'm a woman?"

Brandon took a deep breath, controlling his temper. The last thing he wanted her to know was the way he had felt when he looked up and saw her caught in that gust of wind.

"Who the devil told you you could go up there?" he said through clenched teeth.

"Jorge—but don't blame him. I tricked him into it by telling him China said it was all right. I was just so bored sitting around all the time with nothing to do!"

"Ah, you were *bored.*" An edge of sarcasm crept into his voice. "That explains it then. Bored young ladies must be amused at any cost. Did it occur to you that you might fall into the sea—and I'd have to risk a boat and men to try to rescue you? Not that it would do much good. You probably can't swim, and once that sweater got water-logged, it would be so heavy you'd sink like a rock."

"I wasn't the least bit concerned," Celia lied. "I knew I wouldn't fall. Anyway, I swim very well. And I do have enough sense to get out of heavy clothes in the water." There—at least that was the truth! "And China really did say I could do it. Well . . . he said I could when it was calmer and he had time to teach me. It isn't fair, treating me as if I were totally useless just because I'm a female!"

"I'm not so sure of that." Brandon's mouth twitched just slightly. "But I do admit China was right. If you want to learn the rigging, you ought to be allowed to. Or anything else that interests you. I would prefer, however, that you do it the way he suggested—on a calm day and under proper supervision. In the meantime, since you're so eager to become a sailor, we might get started on a course of navigation."

"You mean . . ." Celia hesitated, not sure she had heard him right. "*You'd* be willing to teach me?"

"None other. We can begin tonight, as soon as the dinner dishes are cleared from the table. That is, *if* you're a good little girl and stay out of the way now. With this wind, I may have to reef the sails, and I don't want to spend all my time worrying about what you're up to when I'm supposed to be running the ship."

It was, for a man like Brandon Christopher, a conces-sion, and Celia recognized it as such. For the first time since he had taken her captive, he had actually admitted she was a person in her own right, with needs and feelings that had to be considered. And abilities that might even be respected.

She was humming a gay little tune under her breath as she hurried across the deck and down the steps, taking them two at a time. She did not even care how gruff he had been or that he had told her to be a "good little girl" and stay out of the way. He was giving her what she wanted, and that was all that counted.

She was already at the bottom of the steps before it occurred to her, quite irrelevantly, that she hadn't thought about Skye Maarten for days.

12

The wind died down by nightfall, and dinner was a pleasant affair, especially after those last few days when Celia had felt as if she were constantly snatching at plates and mugs as they slid past her down the long polished table. Cook had prepared a casserole of leftover roast chicken, mixed with vegetables and white rice, and any other evening she would have welcomed the chance to linger over it. But tonight, mindful of the treat Brandon had promised after the dishes were cleared away, she was too excited to more than pick at her food.

Brandon, seeing the eager glow in her eyes, generously hurried his own meal and did not even insist on finishing the vile cup of strong black coffee he always consumed after dinner. Celia, as usual, had been offered a pot of tea, but she waved it aside when she saw him bring out a large scrolled map and several of the strangest-looking charts she had ever seen in her life.

He opened the map first. Celia found it easy to read, even with the sea lanes marked on it, for Ian St. Clair had insisted that his daughter study geography and she was already familiar with the continents and islands. But the charts, with hundreds of little arrows going off in all directions, were something else again.

"Those indicate the prevailing winds," Brandon told her, laughing at the puzzled expression on her face. "A captain can chart his course on the map, then use one of

215

these, this for example"—he picked up a chart at random—"to check the direction of the wind."

"But that's silly!" Celia took the chart and squinted at the squiggly lines. "I haven't been at sea very long, but even I've seen the way the wind changes, sometimes quite suddenly. How can anyone pick a certain spot, like *that*"—she jabbed her finger arbitrarily at the chart—"and say what direction the wind is going to blow?"

Brandon laughed. "I asked the same thing myself when I was twelve and went to sea for the first time. I still remember the way my grandfather glowered. 'I didn't say the wind, boy,' he bellowed at me. 'I said the *prevailing* wind.' Of course winds shift from time to time—and you're right, they're influenced by a number of different conditions. But at any given spot there's a general trend that can be observed and recorded. By looking at these charts, I can steer a course with the weather instead of tacking into stubborn headwinds. I can also pick the narrowest point to cross the calms, which on a sailing ship saves several days."

Celia turned back to the chart in her hands, intrigued now that she was beginning to understand it. "But who made these charts?" she asked. "And where did he get his information? How can anyone know the prevailing winds all over the world?"

"A good question." Brandon gave her a look out of the corner of his eye. He had suggested navigation lessons only as a diversion, assuming she would quickly tire of them, but she was proving a more apt pupil than he had expected. "The man who did this was a naval lieutenant, Matthew Fontaine Maury. After he was disabled—broke his leg on leave, I understand, and it never healed properly—he was shunted off to a desk job in Washington. That might have been a dead end for someone else. But Maury had access to ships' logs from every vessel that ever sailed for the U.S. Navy. Literally thousands."

"That's how he found the trends, then. By examining all those logs and consolidating the information."

"Precisely. In the mid-fifties he published his first volume, *The Physical Geography of the Sea*. That, along with wind and current charts, is the sea captain's bible. Those of us who are young enough to have grown up on it can't even imagine what life was like before."

He sorted through the charts, picking several that corresponded with the sea lanes the *Moonwind* had been following, and spread them out on the table next to the map. As he traced their course, pointing out the arrows that applied and showing her in the ship's log how accurate they had been, Celia found herself distracted by his nearness on the bench beside her. That coarsely knitted sleeve brushed against her bare forearm, the male smell of hemp and leather tingled in her nostrils, and it was all she could do to concentrate on what he was saying.

Sometimes, the things he told her were easy to follow, and he would give her a nod of approval as she came up with the answer he had been looking for. Other times, however, the concepts seemed hopelessly complicated, and he had to explain things over and over in that same cool voice before she finally grasped what he was getting at.

"You're being remarkably patient," she said after they had been at it for an hour. "I expected you to be glowering and bellowing like your grandfather by now. You make a good teacher."

"Only when it's a subject I'm interested in, and then only for short intervals. Patience has never been one of my strong points. And I have no experience at teaching."

"You didn't have little brothers or sisters at home? To teach the ABC's or how to buckle their shoes?"

"Actually, I have four sisters. All younger." In spite of himself, he began to laugh. "And, yes, that does teach a certain degree of patience. I was never responsible for shoes or ABC's, but just taking them for a drive was an exercise in self-control. Have you ever heard four females talking at the same time in a closed carriage? Like a bunch of damned birds twittering in an aviary! To say nothing of the skirts and petticoats that seem to be all over the place, and those absurd little bonnets with feathers that keep getting in a man's nose!''

Celia laughed with him, sensing the affection beneath his grumbling. ''No brothers?'' she asked.

''One.'' His expression softened. ''He was six or seven the last time I lived at home, and I remember him chiefly as a little red-haired monkey with big yellow-green eyes and an impossible way of following me everywhere I went. I used to threaten him with dire consequences if he didn't stop—which, of course, he never did. And which, I am embarrassed to admit, secretly fed my ego. There's nothing like being a big brother and having someone look up to you absolutely without qualification.''

His face changed again, turning serious as he looked back at the charts.

''But enough of this, young lady! I may not be much of a teacher, but I know when someone's procrastinating. No more idle conversation. I have to go on deck, but I want you to look through this section I've marked in Maury's *Geography* and be prepared to discuss it when I get back.''

He pulled on a dark blue woolen jacket and was gone, leaving the cabin with a strangely empty feeling. Celia was disturbingly aware, as she opened the book and tried to focus, of the effect this man had on her, as powerful now when he was gone as it had been before in his presence.

Yet it wasn't merely a physical sensation, she thought, helpless to control her feelings—it was emotional too, as if somehow a bond were being formed between them every time they talked.

Fleetingly an image of Skye Maarten came into her mind, not quite as dazzling as it had been before, and it occurred to her suddenly that they had never really talked. Oh, they had flirted and teased and gossiped, but they hadn't *talked*. Not the way she had with Brandon Christopher.

Sighing, she bent over the book, forcing her mind back to the task at hand.

The next morning, Brandon continued the lesson, teaching Celia the instruments of navigation. She laughed out loud when she saw the "binnacle boy," a whimsical figure that held the captain's compass in a polished brass receptacle, but she soon learned to respect its importance, together with the less colorful chronometer, used to calculate longitude within a fraction of a degree, and the sextant, which measured angles of celestial bodies above the horizon.

Noon-to-noon "sightings" were taken each day and the results entered in the log, which recorded both position and distance traveled. Speed was measured by a primitive but surprisingly accurate method. A long cord, with knots at even intervals and a weight attached to one end, was wound around a large wooden spool. While two men held the spool, a third threw the weighted end into the water and, turning over an hourglass, noted the amount of rope that went out in the allotted time, using that to calculate speed in "knots," or nautical miles per hour.

After a few days, Brandon turned the navigational instruments over to Celia, telling her that she would now be in charge of the daily sightings. The responsibility was unnerving, especially at first, although she noticed that Brandon was always there to check her calculations. Still, she was pleased to see that he rarely made corrections.

By this time Celia was standing her share of the watches. Brandon had been making do with almost no sleep, but now that she was available to be the "extra eyes" for China Kwan, he slackened off slightly, taking his turn on deck primarily during the starboard watch. The wind had picked up again, so she was rarely allowed in the rigging, and then only as high as the mainsail yard with a lookout's glass in her hand, but she was accustomed to the height now and no longer felt the same queasiness she had before. Her duties consisted primarily of running errands or helping to fetch grog for the crew on a cold night watch, though Brandon still insisted she remain in the mid and aft sections after dark.

She found herself looking forward to her time on deck,

enjoying especially the first hour of dawn, when great surging waves rose mystically out of the darkness. Staring at that vast, timeless expanse of water, always changing, always different and new, she understood how so many men had been seduced by the sea.

Sometimes the loneliness seemed so intense she almost felt as if she had been absorbed into the landscape, until she was at one with ocean and sky as they merged on the horizon. Other times, the sheer emptiness terrified her, reminding her that her own life was adrift, with no familiar landmarks, no way to find her bearings. She knew where she was only by virtue of a little spot marked on the map, which changed every day. And she had no idea at all where she was going.

She was standing at the rail early one morning when a heavy fog blew in out of nowhere, cutting her off from everything around her. She had just turned to grope her way back to the saloon when the sound of voices stopped her.

"Do you suppose she's out there somewhere? Or is all this for nothing?"

The voice was Brandon's, but there was something different about it, a brooding quality that made Celia reluctant to announce her presence.

"Perhaps," China Kwan replied quietly. "I wonder sometimes myself, though there's nothing we can do about it. My cousin is in a better position to guess. Shall we ask?" Without waiting for a reply, he called out something in what sounded like one of the Chinese dialects. Celia could barely hear the answer, but she sensed it came from that other Kwan, a stocky middle-aged man she had noticed on deck.

Brandon did not seem to understand the dialect either, for when the men had finished speaking, China translated.

"He says yes." His voice was still soft, but there was a note of excitement in it. "He was with her long enough to know her moods and patterns, and he says yes. She *is* there. He is sure of it."

"Well, my friend"—Brandon sounded grim—"let's hope he's right."

The men wandered away, and the rest of their conversation was lost, but Celia could not keep from thinking about it even later as she lay in the narrow captain's bunk drifting off to sleep.

She?

What had they meant by that? She knew, of course, that sailors often referred to ships as "she." They might have been doing something like that. Speculating on another vessel . . . wondering if *she* was there, about to appear on the horizon.

But there was another possibility, too—and it was that new and totally unexpected thought that disturbed her now.

Could it be Brandon had a woman somewhere? One he did not truly like, judging by the tone of his voice, but one who had become an obsession?

One he hoped had followed him?

Ugly, jealous pangs twisted inside her stomach, and Celia hated herself for not being able to fight them back. It didn't help in the least to realize she was being irrational. Brandon Christopher was a strong, intensely virile man. Of course he had a woman somewhere! Or *women*!

And anyway, that had nothing to do with her. She was attracted to him, of course—she couldn't deny that—just as she supposed he was attracted to her, though on a more superficial level. But there was nothing *real* between them. Nothing deep and permanent. A few weeks more, a few months perhaps, depending on what he had planned, and then they would never see each other again.

At breakfast the next morning, Brandon was more attentive than usual, and Celia found to her distress that last night's twinges of jealousy were still with her. She didn't see much of him throughout the day that followed, and she was busy enough to get him out of her mind, but when he sent word that evening that he would not be able to join her for dinner, she was so disappointed she barely touched her food.

Why am I letting him do this to me? she thought as she leaned against the rail an hour later, waiting for her turn to go on watch. It was foolish to fret like this, doubly foolish to let her thoughts dwell on Brandon Christopher! This was exactly the way she had behaved with Skye, mooning over him every night in the garden, unable to think of anything else—and now, a few weeks later, she had forgotten all about him! What was wrong with her? Was she so shallow her affections automatically belonged to the handsomest man at hand?

She was in that same introspective mood a short while later when Brandon stopped to lean against the railing beside her.

"What are you doing?" he teased. "Daydreaming? I hear that's a favorite pastime for females."

"Do you indeed? What a way to put it. Tell me, did you get a rise out of your sisters when you threw out comments like that?"

"Always." He laughed. "Are you suggesting it isn't going to work this time?"

"Not on me. And in case you hadn't noticed, it isn't day anymore, but well past nightfall. So it would have to be 'nightdreams,' which has a rather silly sound to it. Actually I was just . . . curious." She hesitated, not wanting him to guess she *had* been daydreaming, and about him at that. "What made your grandfather call his ship the *Moonwind*? It seems such a fanciful name, not at all what one would expect from an 'old tyrant.' "

"Ships often have fanciful names. The *Flying Cloud* comes to mind, or the *Sea Witch*. But, yes, I suppose this one is rather more poetic than most. However, my grandfather didn't choose it. I did. And in my defense, I was fourteen at the time."

"You named the ship?" Celia looked puzzled. "But I thought . . . Didn't you tell me it was built in the sixties? Why, if you were fourteen then, that would make you—"

"A very old man. Past forty, which no doubt sounds ancient to you. But never fear"—he broke into a grin—"I'm not well-preserved for my age. In reality, the ship had another name when it was put into use. The *Charlotte Lee*—after an elusive beauty who captured my grandfather's heart. Much to my grandmother's disapproval, I might add. There was a quarrel of some sort between them—I'm not sure, perhaps the lady disappointed him. Perhaps he disappointed her—who knows? At any rate, he took a chisel in one hand and a sanding stone in the other and personally scraped every trace of her name off the hull.

"I had been to sea with him only once, but we hit it off well—there's more than a little of the old scoundrel in me—and he told me I could choose the new name."

"But why *Moonwind*? I mean, it seems a peculiar choice for a boy of fourteen."

"Not at all. The ship was moored in an old whaling harbor off the Cape at the time. Grandfather took me up by coach to see it. It was after midnight when we arrived, and thin wisps of something—half cloud, half fog—were floating in the air. For a moment they parted, letting a shaft of moonlight strike the ship. I thought then, and I still do, that I'd never seen anything so beautiful in my life. Or so eerie."

He looked out over the ocean, lost for a moment in the past.

"I remembered what the wind had felt like, those long moonlit nights at sea. Different from the winds of day somehow, capricious, almost supernatural—as if it had a will of its own. I used to pretend that fairy ships floated on night currents, drifting off to worlds beyond the imagination. And the *Moonwind* seemed such a vessel."

He broke off, laughing at boyish reveries that were easily called back, and just as easily shrugged off. But after he was gone, the mood he had set persisted, and Celia found herself thinking about what he had said.

A moonwind? Was there such a thing? In nature as in

life? A dark force . . . willful . . . capricious . . . drawing vessels on unseen currents toward unknown destinations.

She felt a sudden kinship for the old clipper, built to be queen of the seas, reduced now to pirating for her keep. It was only a fancy, she knew—like Brandon's fancies when he was a boy—but she couldn't help feeling they were two of a kind. She too, like the ship, had had her life disrupted, until nothing of the old remained. She too had been caught on a moonwind, carried off on tides beyond her control.

But where was she going, she wondered, on those dark night currents? And what would happen when she got there?

"Where *are* we going?"

Celia caught Brandon the next morning as he was heading up the stairs to check on the starboard watch, which had just gone on duty. Ordinarily she would never have been so bold, but it had been a long night and she was too tired even to think of being cautious.

"It really is exasperating," she went on as he turned halfway up to look back at her, "not having the vaguest idea when we're going to see land—or where! Or isn't a prisoner allowed to ask such questions?"

If Brandon noticed the tartness in her tone, he did not seem annoyed. "Quite the contrary," he said, sounding quite amiable. "It's a natural question. In fact, I'd have brought it up myself, but I assumed you had it figured out, judging by the course we're steering. We've been heading for Hawaii, or as you English put it, the Sandwich Islands— named, incidentally, after the Earl of Sandwich, who was the first man with the sensible idea of slapping his dinner between two slices of bread. If I could find a way to keep flour from going moldy on board, I'd have Cook do the same for us." He was already at the top of the steps by the time he finished speaking, and Celia had to raise her voice to pursue the subject.

"But why the Sand . . . ?" she called out. "Why Hawaii?'' The place looked uninteresting on the map, nothing but little dots strung out in the middle of the ocean. "What's there?''

"Sugar plantations, for one thing. The planters have been having trouble with the local royalty. Since their markets are in America, it's possible the islands will be taken over by the United States. There's no guarantee, of course, but if that happens, I want to be there. I have some . . . uh . . . business to transact.''

His voice lingered on the last words, sending a shiver down Celia's spine. Business! She could well imagine what that meant. There was a dark look in his eyes, a kind of sardonic amusement. Almost as if he had expected her consternation, she thought as she watched him turn and disappear through the doorway onto the deck. Sometimes, for hours, days on end, she almost managed to forget what they were doing in the middle of the Pacific Ocean and what cargo the *Moonwind* was carrying in her hold. But somehow he always found a way to remind her just what it was she distrusted most about him.

It's possible the islands will be taken over by the United States.

The words remained, even after Brandon had gone, and Celia found herself dwelling on them, wondering what it was that had given his tone that faint edge of excitement when he uttered them. She would have thought, American laws being what they were, that U.S. jurisdiction would make things even more dangerous for an opium pirate. But perhaps it would drive the price up too, by frightening away the competition.

The thought was still on her mind as she peeled off her spray-dampened clothes and tumbled bone-tired into bed. It was hard sometimes to reconcile these two Brandon Christophers, they seemed so diametrically opposed. Which was the real man? The cool competent sea captain who took pride in his ship and had the patience to teach a young woman how to sail? Or the hot-blooded pirate seeking a fortune from one of the foulest evils the world had ever known?

"Why do you do it?" she asked, abandoning caution for a second time later that afternoon when she ran into him on deck. She was careful to keep her voice flippant so he wouldn't guess how deeply he had disturbed her—or how much she had been thinking of him of late. "Trade in opium, I mean. Is it that much more profitable than carrying legitimate goods? Say tea, for instance."

Brandon gave her a sharp look, then seemed to relax. He had been making a careful inspection of the brasswork, which had to be polished every day, even when, to Celia's eyes, it didn't need it.

"Considerably more profitable, and less of a nuisance. Tea has to be carefully loaded to make sure the seawater that seeps into the hold doesn't get at the chests. Even then, some of the more delicate varieties are ruined by moisture if the voyage takes too long. Opium is easier to handle, though it's so light it requires considerable ballast."

"Ballast?" Celia had never heard the term before.

"Sandbags, rocks, anything with enough weight to hold the vessel steady," he explained. "As a matter of fact, the rage for *chinoiserie* that swept the States back in the 1700's began when the old *Empress of China* pulled into New York harbor with her hold half-filled with porcelain, which had been used as ballast."

"But there's not as much profit in that?"

"As in opium, you mean?" His eyes took on a brittle look, and Celia felt her blood turn cold. "Hardly . . . nor as much of a challenge." For just an instant she was tempted to tell him what she thought of the vile trade he was carrying on, but she could just see the way those mocking lips would turn up at the corners, cutting her down to size if she tried.

"Which is it that attracts you most?" she asked, thinking again how much more dangerous it was going to be for him in American-controlled territory. "The money or the challenge?"

"Ah, well . . ." He paused, looking at her in the oddest way, almost as if he expected something. "They both have their appeal."

Appeal? It all sounded so callous. "I can understand the challenge, in a way. But money? Surely you could make everything you need, and then some, from the shipping line."

"Everything I *need*?" Brandon laughed shortly as he turned back to the brasswork, apparently not burnished to his demanding specifications. "There's little you can do with money beyond a certain point, and I'm well past that. Though I must admit, there's a certain . . . fascination with great wealth. Don't tell me you've never felt it?"

For all her attempts at sophistication, Celia could not help being shocked. To be fascinated with wealth was one thing, to sell one's soul to get it quite another matter. Once again she longed to lash out with her tongue, but as before, something in his manner, that careless aloofness he wrapped around himself like a mantle, held her back.

"I would think," she said, trying to sound cool, "that your passion for riches might stop this side of utter recklessness. If I were a man, I'd find a less hazardous way to make my fortune."

"Ah, but you aren't a man." He was looking at her in that probing manner again, searching, as it were, for something he did not seem to see. "Women are most sensible when it comes to achieving wealth. They find a man who already has a fortune—and marry him."

Celia had the distinctly unpleasant feeling he was talking about Skye Maarten, though that, of course, was ridiculous. Skye was the one who had had something to gain from their prospective union—and she had wanted him anyway. Still, there was no point explaining delicate feelings to a man like Brandon Christopher.

"What a good idea," she said icily. "I'll have to do that."

She tried to keep her composure as she glided across the deck, but she had the feeling she was flouncing instead, like a little girl about to throw a tantrum. Why was it, she asked herself when she was alone again, that she hadn't told him what she thought? Why hadn't she looked him right in the eye and said, "I think it's rotten and despicable, the way you're making money from the suffering of others"? What was there about him that made it so hard for her to speak freely, even after she had thought they were finally coming to terms with each other?

Had she been a little older, a little more experienced with men, it might have occurred to her to wonder if Brandon, like herself, had noticed their growing closeness and was deliberately setting up barriers between them. But because she was not, he continued to confuse her, and despite the obvious physical attraction, which she no longer attempted to deny—or perhaps because of it, she thought wryly—she found herself half-dreading the times they were alone together.

That same discomfort was still there in the evening when they met briefly in the saloon. Brandon had not joined her at dinner, but he sat down for a few minutes now, throwing his jacket on the bench beside him as he gulped down a mug of his usual bitter-smelling coffee.

He seemed to be in an uncommunicative mood, or so Celia thought, until she looked up to catch him watching her with a curious expression on his face.

"I notice you haven't mentioned your parents since you came on board," he said unexpectedly. "They must have been frantic with worry when they didn't hear from you, yet you seem totally unconcerned. Were you telling the truth before, when you said you came to Hong Kong to find Schuyler Maarten? Or were you running away from them as well?"

Celia stiffened, sensing the disapproval in his tone. She *had* been concerned about Ian and Serena, and feeling guilty too for what she had put them through. But that was not something she was going to discuss with him.

"I'm not running away from anyone or anything," she said sharply. "Though I don't see that that's any of your business. As for my parents, there isn't much I can do about them, is there? I can hardly send a telegram or a letter from the *Moonwind*.''

''Well, then, perhaps I can put your mind at ease.'' He set his mug down, sliding it across the table. ''I took it on myself to communicate with them. Before we left Hong Kong.''

''You . . . took it on yourself?'' Celia could only gape at him. How dare he so something like that, without even asking how she felt! ''What did you say to them, pray tell? That I'd been taken hostage by pirates and was being held on a ship with a cargo of opium? That must have made them feel much better!''

''Hardly. I wrote as owner of the Christopher Lines, telling them you were being cared for. Ah, but I seem to have offended you again.'' His expression did not look as if he were the least bit sorry. ''And here I thought you'd be pleased to know your parents had been reassured.''

Celia bit her tongue as she saw him draw on his jacket and return to the deck. Any other time, she *would* have been pleased, but the way he was treating her, so arrogantly, so offhand, made her furious all over again, and it seemed to her she hated him almost as much as she had that day she first laid eyes on him.

Still, she had to admit, when she cooled down a bit and objectivity returned, that was not quite true. She didn't *hate* Brandon Christopher—she just didn't understand him. And she didn't know how to control her feelings when she was with him.

If she hadn't had an outlet, someone to talk to during those long, bewildering weeks, her situation aboard the *Moonwind* might have been intolerable. Fortunately, however, in China Kwan she found the friend she desperately needed, and she spent long hours with him on deck, trying to sort out her thoughts and feelings. At least with China she dared to say what was on her mind, without being afraid he would laugh or be insulted by her bluntness.

''I don't see how either of you justify what you're

doing," she said that night as she came up from the galley
with a cup of steaming coffee, which he, like his captain,
seemed to prefer. "Brandon is a complete enigma to me,
and you're even worse! He at least has depths I can't
fathom, but you . . . well, you seem so open, so sensitive
and kind . . ." She broke off, handing the coffee to China,
who leaned back against the rail as he reached out to
accept it.

"And you can't see me as an opium smuggler? Is that
it?"

"It doesn't make sense," Celia admitted. "Why take all
these risks? You don't have a fortune to gain, the way
Brandon does. This isn't going to make *you* rich."

China wrapped his hands around the mug, studying her
over the brim as he took a sip of the warming liquid. "I'm
well paid for what I do," he parried. "I couldn't make this
much money at anything else."

"But to be involved in . . . piracy?" Celia knew she
must sound naive, but she couldn't keep the horror out of
her voice. "And *opium*?"

"Why not opium? Because it's illegal? Is that what
bothers you? Or do you believe, like so many others, that I
have tainted my hands because it's a dirty business?"

"Isn't it?"

"I only transport the opium." He turned away, staring
out over the water as he recomposed his features. It was
easy enough saying the words—he had heard them many
times before. But it wasn't easy lying to a woman he liked
and respected. Dammit, it was Brandon's place to deal
with this, not his! "I make it available to men—for a
price. It's their choice whether they buy or not. I don't put
the stuff in their pipes and ram it down their throats."

"And that absolves you of responsibility?" Celia stared
at him, aghast. "Because you only *supply* the drug? Hasn't
it occurred to you that if the supply weren't there, the
addicts wouldn't be either? My God, China, think of the
lives that have been ruined by opium."

"Lives have been ruined by liquor too," he reminded

her. "Does that mean no alcoholic beverages should be
made available to anyone? Tell me, don't you enjoy an
occasional glass of wine or champagne with your dinner?
How would you like it if some self-righteous prig told you
you couldn't have any more because a few people can't
handle it?"

"But that's just it, China! A *few* people can't handle it.
Most of us only drink a little every now and then—and
hardly get tipsy at all. That doesn't do any harm."

"I've known a number of men who smoke a pipe every
now and then, too. That doesn't harm them either. And
what about getting 'tipsy,' as you put it—have you ever
seen anything as disgusting as a drunk? They reel in the
streets; they shout out abuse and fall down in the gutter—or
go home and beat their wives. Even the worst addict
doesn't do that." He paused as he looked at her again.
"Don't you think every man has a right to his own vice, as
long as it's by his choice . . . and not yours?"

"Well, I suppose . . ." Celia hesitated, confused. It
seemed to her he was twisting things around, making
opium smuggling all right because she couldn't defend
alcoholism. "I can't help thinking you wouldn't be saying
these things if you had begun smoking yourself and hadn't
been able to stop."

"Wouldn't I?" China's voice was steady, betraying
nothing of what he felt. "I think you're wrong. I think I
would." And I did, he wanted to add. I did say those
things, and I did begin smoking. And, yes, God help me, I
couldn't stop.

But because he had given his word, he remained silent,
though he knew the same troubling thoughts were still on
her mind a few minutes later when she took up the lookout's glass and climbed with the ease of a seasoned sailor
to her post on the mizzenmast. Damn Brandon, he thought
again as he took a last swig from the cup. He should have
told the girl the truth, right from the beginning. It wasn't
fair, keeping her in the dark like this. Nor was there any

reason for it. She could hardly betray them while she was on the ship, even if she wanted to.

He set the cup down where the cabin boy would find it and turned up the woolen collar on his jacket. The air grew warmer as they approached the Hawaiian Islands, but the wind was still crisp and the nights had a tendency to be bitter. He hated the position he found himself in, hated not being able to admit what he was, what he had been—what he was doing now. But there were still debts that had to be paid, loyalties that could not be questioned.

He leaned over the rail, resting gloveless hands on cold metal as he stared out at dark undulating waves, barely visible in the rays of a slim crescent moon. For the first time in many months his mind drifted back to the past, reviving old memories, pondering once again the chain of events that had brought him to that place at that particular moment.

13

The journey began, for China Kwan, twenty-nine years earlier in the homeland of his ancestors, though he had but secondhand knowledge of his origins, for his young mother was barely six months pregnant when she stood on the docks in Canton and looked misty-eyed over her shoulder at the distant mountains she would never see again.

It was not an impromptu move. The matriarch of that particular branch of the Kwan family had long since looked around the walled compound where she had spent most of her adult life and, foreseeing little future for herself as the widow of Number Eighteen's Seventh Son, had persuaded her firstborn to leave his wife and children and sign on as a laborer in the sugar fields of a faraway island with the unpronounceable name of Hawaii. After twelve years of toil and careful savings, the family was gathered amid a pile of bundled possessions on the dock waiting to join him, their number including the pregnant widow of the youngest Kwan son, a slip of a girl who wept and pleaded to be left behind.

The long sea voyage was a difficult one, the landing in Honolulu less than encouraging, for the waterfront was crowded and dusty, and the Chinese section of town looked little better than the slum streets they had passed through on their way to the docks in Canton. But Old Grandmother, as she was already known, although she was a still comparatively young woman, refused to be daunted. The old year had just ended as they moved into a small shanty which, with the addition of rooms from time to time, would eventually become a comfortable home, and the Year of the Rat was beginning. An auspicious omen, as she never tired of reminding them, for it marked the beginning of the twelve-year cycle, a time for renewal and hope, a time to dare and reach out and to try new things.

Shortly after that, young Kwan Suan-fong, Fortunate Winds Kwan, made his appearance in the world, his first breath coinciding almost exactly with his mother's last, for that debilitating journey had taken its toll on the fragile child who had never wanted to come. Her passing was not deeply mourned, for she had not been well liked by the others; attention centered instead on the child, the first of his family to be born in the new year, and the first to claim allegiance to a new land.

The Kwan-family fortunes prospered in the years to come, due largely to the shrewdness of Old Grandmother. Each of her sons had begun life in Hawaii on a sugar plantation, with most of the earnings going to buy plots of land and stores and restaurants on the waterfront; but one by one, they were called back to run the family businesses and cultivate the family farms, and the grandchildren, as they grew, were given their share of responsibility.

Had he been born into a different family, the boy's fate might have been the same, but Old Grandmother, whose keen eyesight was legendary, and whose mind was twice as sharp, had long ago decided that soup stands and vegetable wagons wheeled around on the streets would not be enough. In China the Kwan family had boasted more than its share of scholars; things would be the same here.

Because there was little ready cash in the family coffers, and because extra hands could not be spared, the old woman decided craftily that only one of the boys would be educated. There had been no doubt in her mind which it would be. Young Suan-fong was the brightest of her grandchildren, and true to his name, the most fortunate. Had he not been the first to be born on the new soil? Did he not see the light of day almost at the beginning of the propitious Year of the Rat?

The teachers at the mission school welcomed the boy, recognizing in him an exceptional student, and they were encouraged to groom him for the role they sensed would be his in the new society of the islands. "Stop looking like a Chinese peasant," they urged with more practicality than tact. "Cut off your hair. Dress in white man's clothes. Let everyone *see* what you are!"

The idea was appealing, but it was intimidating too, and in the end the boy listened to his grandmother, who had been viewing the changes in his character with increasing alarm. Thus he was dressed as his ancestors had been dressed, long hair braided neatly down his back, when it came time to go to America and complete his schooling at one of the universities that accepted foreign students of other races.

There, for the first time, he found out what it was to be different. In Hawaii everyone had been accepted, to some extent or other, and if there were barriers of color, they were barriers that frequently broke down. But in the United States, although he gained respect for his intelligence and willingness to work, young Kwan found himself increasingly isolated from the mainstream of life, held strictly to his own kind except for the most superficial contacts. When he came home again, he looked almost white on the outside, dressed in the denim pants and stylish dark red shirt that would have pleased his teachers, his hair cropped short around his face. But on the inside he was more Chinese than ever.

It was the way he felt on the inside that prompted him to press his grandmother for permission to visit China, the homeland he had never seen; it was the way he looked on the outside that prompted her to agree. It was, for her, a difficult concession. Much as she loved the boy, he was an investment, and she was anxious to begin drawing dividends. But she was even more anxious to keep him from losing a sense of himself as Chinese, and for that reason she loosened the purse strings enough to give him the passage money.

He could not have said himself what he had expected, but whatever it was, he didn't find it in the land that now proved a bitter disappointment. The valley his family had lived in for generations was not green and spacious, as Old Grandmother had described it; it was shallow and parched, yielding little in the way of viable crops. And the "great buildings" of the compound were not great at all, but cramped and badly in need of a coat of paint. Even the ancestral hall was a shabby, spiritless place, with nothing to inspire the awe and sense of continuity he had longed for.

He made only one friend while he was there, a girl cousin who had been married, tragically, though unwittingly, for her parents were people of great compassion, to an opium addict. He had been deeply shocked to find her living with her one surviving child in a small hovel, desperately close to starvation, and it was that outsider's viewpoint—and his expression of it—that resulted in her being taken back into the family compound. When it came time to leave, he could see tears in her eyes as she walked him to the main road, moving slowly because her feet had been bound as a child, and he knew he would miss her—but he would miss nothing else. He was ready to go home.

He spent his last night before sailing in a dark smoke-stained bar along the waterfront, his passage money pinned in the pocket of his shirt, for he dared not leave it in a dingy hotel room shared with others. He had been a bit nervous as he entered, but after the first few minutes, when no one paid any attention, he began to relax and enjoy the drink the bartender had poured. The glass looked filthy, but the whiskey was surprisingly good, though it had a bitter taste as it went down, and he drained it in a single gulp. There was a picture hanging on the wall behind the bar, a lewd representation of a naked dark-haired girl sprawled out on a couch, and he found himself staring at it, wondering suddenly why his eyes seemed out of focus.

It was the last conscious thought he had.

When he came to, his head was throbbing as if someone were pounding from the inside with a hammer, and his mouth was so dry he could barely swallow. At first he was disoriented, and he had difficulty making things out. He seemed to be in a dark enclosed space, but if it was a room, it was one without foundation, for he was aware of a faintly swaying motion.

Slowly his head began to clear, and he realized he had been placed in the hold of a ship. He was not alone, for as he turned, he could see bodies lying all around. A few inches away was a grotesquely distorted figure, a man surely, yet he looked like an oversized doll with broken limbs. One arm had been twisted, and the sleeve was strangely flattened, almost as if there were nothing inside. Then suddenly the cuff began to move, rustling slightly, and as he watched, a rat crawled out.

He was still retching a second later when the hatch cover burst open and shafts of light flooded the darkness. As men leapt into the hold, he realized at last what had happened. He had been shanghaied. That drink in the bar had been drugged, and he had been carried off to the docks. His hands reached up automatically, feeling for his pockets, but he knew what he would find. There was nothing there.

The burly team of sailors worked quickly, sorting through the bodies on the floor, pushing aside those who were still unconscious and forcing the others to their feet. When they reached the man with the twisted arm, one of them let out a curse, giving the body a kick with his boot.

The man seemed to disintegrate, dissolving into a pile of old rags and wisps of straw that floated on the air.

It was, as young Kwan later learned, a favorite dockside trick. Shanghaiers were paid by the head for their wares, and they made their deliveries at night, when small discrepancies were likely to go unnoticed, especially since no one was anxious to dig through a pile of vermin-infested bodies. Fresh corpses were often mixed in with living men, and if these were unavailable, old suits of clothes might be stuffed with straw and rags, sometimes with a rat or two tied into the bundle to give the look of a drunk's limbs twitching in sleep.

Life on board the vessel, which had been christened inappropriately the *Star of the East*, was harsh and unrelenting right from the beginning. Every man who could stand, however wobbly his legs, was herded onto deck. There the mates singled them out, sending them one by one into the rigging, without even a few minutes to get their bearings.

"Hey, you there! China!" one of them called, giving the young man the name that would follow him for the rest of his life. "Lay aloft! There on the mainmast. Up to the top, you hear?" There was enough stridency in his voice to be intimidating, and China scrambled to do as he was told, clinging to the yards and footropes as he reached the top. The rolling motion of the ship, easy enough on deck, was exaggerated at that height, and he retched painfully, but there was nothing in his stomach to come up.

Hard work was a way of life on the *Star of the East*, and free time virtually nonexistent, even on Sundays, when most captains allowed their men a measure of rest. The decks had to be scrubbed every morning with chunks of sandstone, then swabbed until they were clean; the broad canvas sails required considerable attention, reefing in foul weather, unfurling in fair; the taut lines that held them seemed in constant need of repair, even on the coldest days when numb hands could barely hold the ropes; and more than once China Kwan found himself "laying aloft" with a bucket of foul-smelling grease to slush the mast.

Rations were in short supply, and drinking water was doled out with an exceptionally light hand, but even though he was often weak from thirst and hunger, China learned, like the others, not to complain. Discipline at sea, never gentle, was particularly strict on the *Star*, and the captain and his mates strolled the decks with lengths of tarred rope or belaying pins in their hands. A man might be dunked in the lee scruppers for nothing more than grumbling under his breath, then tied to the rail and left to shiver for hours in the wind.

As long as he lived, China would never forget the way he felt that first time he heard the dreaded call: "All hands on deck to witness punishment!" Still half-asleep, he tumbled out of bed, pulling on his trousers with more haste than usual when he saw how everyone else was moving. Even so, he was the last man to take his place beside the others in that long line on deck. One of the port watch, a stocky young Portuguese, had been forced, face in, against the shrouds. His hands were tied to the ropes above him, his jacket torn off so the tanned skin on his back was exposed.

China watched, sickened but not daring to look away, as the captain raised his hand, flicking back a knotted piece of rope, jerking it forward again. The sound it made as it came down on naked flesh seared through the body of every man on deck.

A wave of anger rippled through the watchers, so intense it was almost audible, though no one had made a sound. Every instinct in China's body urged him to go forward and help the fellow. He wasn't an animal, to be beaten like that! He was a man—and men had a right to their dignity.

But before he could move, he felt a hand on his arm. Glancing around, he saw that he was standing next to a tall, lanky blond who went by the name of Swede. There was no expression on that weather-beaten face, but the hold on his arm tightened, and China realized with a surge of frustration what the man was telling him.

Leave well enough alone, he was saying. There's nothing you can do. You'll only make it hard on yourself if you try. And on the rest of us.

The beating lasted longer than usual, for the Portuguese was stubborn, and the captain had made up his mind not to leave off until he cried out. When at last the mates moved forward to cut him down, he could not stand upright, but staggered, doubled over like a hunchback, into the forecastle. One of the veteran sailors, a feisty old salt who wasn't afraid of anyone, asked the captain for some salve, but the request was denied, and there was nothing they could do to ease the man's pain. He lay all day in his bunk, not making a sound, but when night came and he drifted occasionally into sleep, his moans filled the air.

China Kwan lay in his own bunk, a short distance away, feeling drained and strangely emasculated as he listened to those low, barely human sounds. What kind of man was he, letting something like this happen? Standing there watching, not raising a hand, not speaking a word of protest. Yet what was there he could have said—what could he have done?—that wouldn't have brought the captain's wrath down on the rest of the crew? Bitterness lay like bile in his mouth, and he was conscious of nothing so much as a desire to get out of there, to jump ship at the first port and head for home, where he would never ask himself questions like that again.

When they finally reached land, however, a few days later, it was not the port China had imagined, but a small fishing settlement on the coast above Canton. His watch, the starboard, had drawn first liberty, and he was put ashore with the rest of the men in boats. Only one other ship was visible, a squat, untidy-looking steamer, anchored, like the *Star of the East*, well out from shore, and he knew he could never get to it without being seen.

Not that it would help if he could, he thought, realizing for the first time how few and far between were the ways out for a shanghaied sailor. How likely was it that the captain would take him on without asking questions? Even the roughest renegades were reluctant to encourage desertion. And without the money that had been stolen from him, he couldn't hope to pay for his passage.

He lingered on the beach after the rest of the men had gone, wading for a while barefoot in water that lapped up around his ankles. Then, putting on his shoes, he wandered halfheartedly toward the settlement, an unappealing motley assortment of bars and fisherman's huts. He had just paused to cast a last glance back at the steamer, wondering if he shouldn't swim out after all and take his chances with the captain, when he became aware that someone else was there. Turning, he saw the tall Scandinavian who had kept him from getting in trouble before.

The man seemed to read his thoughts, for he said grimly, "Not here, boy. Wait for a bigger town, if that's what you have on your mind. Canton, Hong Kong, Manila maybe. Not here."

China sensed the truth in his words, but it was hard to let go. "I suppose you're right. But dammit, Manila seems a long way away."

The Swede's expression eased somewhat as he recognized in the young man things he himself had not felt for many years. He didn't take to most people, but he liked this boy's spunk—though it would do him no good. On impulse, he stretched out an arm.

"Hey, China boy, you come with me." Ordinarily he kept to his own company on shore, putting distance between himself and his mates, but this time he would make an exception. "I know that old tub out there. She's nothing but trouble. One ship, another ship—what's the difference, eh? You do what you have to, and take your fun where you can. You want fun? Come on. I'll show you fun."

China, assuming he meant one of the local brothels, was about to decline, when he thought better of it. This was the first overture of friendship anyone had made since he had been forced to sea, and he couldn't afford to reject it. Besides, the town seemed a dreary place, the land around it even drearier. What could he do there all by himself?

The house Swede led him to on the outskirts of town was constructed, like the others, of bamboo tied together with what appeared to be long strips of dried grass. Inside, the large single room was even filthier than he had expected, and he was tempted once again to say "no, thank you," and leave. But as his eyes adjusted to the dimness, he saw figures lounging on rough wooden bunks, not women at all, but men, and he realized with a shock that he was not in a bawdy house. This was an opium den.

The color drained from his face, and he was aware, out of the corner of his eye, of Swede, grinning broadly. Sensing that his naiveté would be the butt of many a joke at sea if he didn't redeem himself, he forced his eyes to run coolly around the room, taking in the details he had barely noticed before. As he did, he felt not so much the disgust he had expected, though that was there too, but a certain warped fascination, and he found to his surprise that he was curious—not merely curious to see what was going on, but to try the stuff himself, to taste it, to feel it, to know what it was that drove men to crave it so desperately they lost all control of their lives.

The thought frightened him a little, and he realized that without even thinking about it, he had already made up his mind. He tried to tell himself he was doing it only because his shipmate was watching, but even then he knew that wasn't true. Life at sea was unbearably oppressive—the long, monotonous days seemed to drag on without end. A few hours of drug-induced dreams would be a welcome change from the cheap whiskey that burned a hole in his gut.

Even with two ships at anchor, the den was relatively uncrowded, and he found a couch near the door where the air was slightly less fetid. Taking a small portion of opium on the point of a long needle, the way Swede showed him, he tried to twist it into a ball, but he was so awkward the other man laughed.

"Hey, you don't do good like Swede right away," he said, enjoying his role as mentor. "It takes many times. Much skill. Here, you watch—I show you what to do." He swirled the pasty substance on the needletip, holding it over an open flame until it was bubbly and caramel-colored, then pressed it into the bowl of a bamboo pipe, which China eyed with distaste. He was not normally prissy, but the long stem was charred with age and use, and he could almost see the hundreds of lips that had slobbered over it in the past.

Swede, catching his expression, laughed again. "You want a new pipe, eh, boy? Take it from Swede—old pipes are better. The opium, it soaks in here." He tapped the stem with a callused finger. "You stay away from new bamboo—and fancy-priced ivories too. They don't sweeten with age."

China drew the pipe reluctantly to his lips. He was more than a little apprehensive now, and sorry he had started the whole thing, but he knew he would lose face if he backed down. Acrid smoke burned his nose and throat, but only slightly, no more so than the tobacco the men passed around the forecastle, and he finished the pipe in several short puffs and leaned back, waiting for something to happen. When it didn't, he took another pipe, then another, filling them himself by this time, for Swede had gone across the room to tend to his own indulgences.

He consumed four pipes before he began to feel the effects. At first he was aware only of a vague dizziness, accompanied by nausea, slight but decidedly unpleasant. Then, even though that had not passed, he felt a kind of exhilaration, not elation exactly, but a quiet contentment that prompted him to continue.

A few pipes more, and the physical sensations began to be distressing, but there was nothing he could do, for he had already absorbed a considerable amount of opium into his system. His pulse was racing at an alarming rate, perspiration poured profusely from his body, and he seemed to itch everywhere, his eyelids, his nose, his scrotum, the damp area under his arms. When he tried to get up, he had trouble moving his limbs, and a wave of giddiness swept over him. Turning his head to the side, he vomited copiously, though with less discomfort than he might have imagined.

The effects of the drug were still with him when he

returned to the ship. He could walk more easily, but that earlier sense of contentment was gone, replaced by an almost paranoiac edginess. Every noise made him jump, and he developed an irrational fear of the deck, sensing illogically that he was going to jump over the rail, even though he had no urge to do anything of the kind. Fortunately, they were still at anchor, and he was able to spend the entire night in his bunk, though even there he was uneasy, afraid to doze off for fear he might walk in his sleep.

It was fully twenty-four hours before he felt like himself again, and in that time he vowed he would never touch the stuff again. But the next time they went ashore and Swede invited him to come along, he found, to his surprise, that he was inclined to accept. Later, when he tried to figure it out, he was hard pressed to come up with a reason. Perhaps he was still curious, perhaps he had to prove something—perhaps he was just so bored, so filled with despair, he hungered for anything that would create a diversion. At any rate, he did try it again, and again he had the same reaction. This time when he vowed to stay away he was sure he meant it, but it was only a week before he pressed a pipe to his lips again.

After a few attempts, the distressing side effects eased, and for the first time China experienced the dreamlike euphoria that lured addicts to the couch again and again. He had left the *Star of the East* by now and found a berth on another ship, but the change, as Swede had intimated, brought little improvement. The new vessel, a hermaphrodite brig, was in slightly better condition, but life on board was still harsh and monotonous, and the perfumed breezes of Hawaii seemed farther away than ever. His only solace was opium, and he turned to it with greater and greater frequency.

He had been on the drug somewhat less than a year, requiring ever-increasing doses, when the pleasant sensations began to fade, disappearing altogether after a month or two. Now when he smoked, it was not for pleasure but to stave off the discomfort he felt if his usual pipe was even a few minutes late. His mind was still alert when he was not smoking, and he saw all too clearly what was happening. He was addicted, and he knew it.

Thoughts of home were even more distant now, for he knew that the shame of his addiction would never allow him to show his face in Hawaii. Sometimes he would look at his pipe and hate it, even though he couldn't keep from picking it up again, and then he would tell himself he was going to break the habit. Perhaps he would try that old Chinese remedy he had heard about. A bottle of rice wine spiked with opium, a glass poured out at the hour he usually took his pipe, pure wine to top the bottle off again. Each day's dose thus became weaker and weaker, dependency was eased, and after a time the smoker was cured. He would try that too, China promised himself. He *would* try it one day—when the time was right.

Only the time never seemed to be right. It was a vicious circle. He couldn't go home until he was cured; yet there was no point seeking a cure until he found a way home. Few ships seemed to be bound for Hawaii, fewer still were willing to take on new hands—and on a sailor's meager pay, how could he save the passage money?

The pattern might have continued, the excuses and the procrastination, had fate not brought him to a particularly sleazy waterfront town on the day a tall clipper with no name painted on its prow anchored to take on supplies. More out of curiosity than anything else, China wandered down to the docks and asked one of the older hands what it was.

When he heard, in slightly awed tones, "That's the *Moonwind*, mate," China found himself staring at the ship with new interest. In the short time Brandon Christopher had been in the Orient, he had made a reputation for himself, especially among sailors. He was a hard master, it was said, but a fair one: life on board his ship was decent, and wages were good. Impetuously China decided to ask the man to take him on. Any other time he might have been out of luck, but Brandon was shorthanded and signed him up without the usual questions.

China Kwan had been away from Hawaii for more than three years the day he stepped on board the *Moonwind*, and in that time he had come to accept the fact that he was never going to see his home again. But as he looked around at the immaculately clean deck, the mahogany woodwork gleaming in the sun, the brass fittings that had been polished until they shone, he found himself daring for the first time to hope. He had even tucked a bottle of rice wine into his bag, thinking this time, perhaps, he would really use it. But he had not minded as much as he should when Brandon's men discovered it and took it away. And he had been relieved when they didn't find his stash of opium.

For a pirate, Brandon Christopher ran a surprisingly tight ship. Not only was liquor forbidden, no drugs were allowed outside the cargo hold, and none of the men smoked even an occasional pipe. At first China tried to find a quiet corner to indulge his habit, but privacy on board was nonexistent, and he was forced, a little nervously, to light up in a section of the work area behind the carpenter's shop. Men passed occasionally, looking at him strangely, and he, not recognizing the pity in their eyes, was sure they were on the verge of reporting him. When he looked up, his third night on board, and saw a raging Brandon Christopher towering over him, he was certain they had. He did not realize that the hatch was open, and a sickeningly sweet odor had drifted up on deck, reminding Brandon of a dim, smoky den in Shanghai.

Brandon, as always, acted quickly and decisively. Without a word, he rummaged through China's things, finding and removing the rest of the opium. Then, as the younger man followed, dazed and horrified, he took it up on deck and made ready to throw it overboard.

"No!" China reached out, trying desperately to snatch the parcel from his hands. "You can't do that! I . . . I need it. Don't you understand, I can't live without it. If you take it away from me, I'll . . . I'll die!" His voice sounded whining even to himself, and he cringed as Brandon turned slowly, dark green eyes filling with disgust.

"Very well," he said after a moment's pause. "I can't force you to act like a man. Keep your supply if you must. But you'll take it into steerage—and you'll stay there under lock and key until I put you off at the next port. I won't have you contamininating my men."

Those angry, hypnotic eyes seemed to bore into him, and in their depths China Kwan saw an image of himself he did not like. Suddenly, more than anything, he wanted to be the man Brandon had taunted him with, wanted to free himself of the devil riding on his back. He glanced down at the parcel, then out to sea, then back at the parcel again, and suddenly he knew the choice was clear. Be rid of it now—or lose hope forever.

"Go ahead," he said, his voice hoarse with bravado. "Pitch it overboard. I don't care. I was planning on breaking the habit anyway. Now is as good a time as any."

Brandon started to move, then hesitated, sensing that the other man did not understand what he was letting himself in for. But he sensed, too, as China himself had a moment before, that this was his last chance.

"You're sure?"

"Pitch it overboard," he said again, and Brandon dropped it into the water.

As he stood there watching dark ripples close slowly over the only source of drugs on board, China felt an immense sense of relief, almost as exhilarating as the most enticing of his opium dreams. He had done it—with Brandon's help, of course—but still, he had done it. Now he was going to have to kick the habit.

The feeling lasted throughout the evening. Although he was acutely uncomfortable, the pains were nowhere near as bad as he had imagined, and as he tumbled into bed, so tired he knew he would go right to sleep, he was congratulating himself on finally having found the courage to do what he should have done long ago.

An hour before dawn he woke to violent convulsions

racking his entire body. A sudden chill turned his flesh to
ice, followed almost immediately by waves of heat so
intense he felt as if he were on fire. Whimpering sounds
were coming out of his throat, but he was so ill by that
time, he was not even aware of them. Nor was he aware of
the men who had gathered around him, for he had begun
to hallucinate, and to him, those were not human faces at
all, but animals with blood-red eyes and fangs bared to
devour. It was a measure of his weakness that he couldn't
even try to get up and flee.

By morning he was in a pitiable state, his bed completely drenched, his clothing fouled with sweat and excre-
ment. Looking up in a relatively lucid moment, he was
surprised to see Brandon Christopher leaning over him.
Only later did he learn that Brandon, hearing of his plight,
had come into the forecastle himself and carried him off to
his cabin. He tried to say something, tried to make a joke
about the rice wine that had been taken from him, the
easier cure he had planned for himself, but everything
came out garbled, and he was certain the other man couldn't
understand a word he said.

Brandon had understood, however, and he was kicking
himself, not for the wine, which could be replaced from a
store kept in the captain's saloon to be doled out on special
occasions, but for the opium he had tossed into the sea. He
had been in such a fury it had not occurred to him he
might want some of it later to ease the symptoms of
withdrawal. Any other time, there would have been an
ample supply in the hold, but he had just sold a small
amount to maintain his image and dumped the rest into the
harbor under cover of darkness. There was nothing he
could do now but stand by and pray that the boy was
stronger than he looked.

For the next two days China continued in the same
condition. He was exhausted, but he could not seem to
sleep, and although he was hallucinating less, he com-
plained of pain and weakness in his limbs. All he was able
to keep down was a little chilled champagne, which Bran-

don held to his lips himself, giving him a few sips before coaxing him to swallow the water he needed to survive. By the third day he was feeling a little better, and he managed a cup of tea, though he was still not up to trying the tinned biscuits Cook had found for him in the galley. It was a good two weeks before he took his first turn around the deck, another month after that before he felt well enough to go ashore.

The town, ironically, was one he had been to before, and he knew its seamier aspects all too well. When they landed, he half-expected Brandon to accompany him, or perhaps send one of the men along to make sure he didn't get into trouble, but to his surprise, he was allowed to go off on his own. His feet wandered toward the section of town he knew best—out of curiosity, he told himself, though something deep inside warned there was more to it than that.

He had not realized until he stood outside that rough bamboo hut, so like the shack where he had been initiated into the forbidden world of opium dreams, how hard it was going to be to turn around and walk away. Beads of sweat stood out on his forehead, but still he remained, staring for a long time at the door, longing to go inside . . . praying that he wouldn't.

When he returned to the *Moonwind* two hours later, clear-eyed and clean, Brandon was waiting for him. The older man did not say anything, but clapped a hand on his shoulder as they walked together toward the bow, and he knew everything was going to be all right.

From that moment on, China dedicated his life to the man who had saved it. It was not a conscious choice; it was simply a fact, something he could not have changed, even had he wanted to. Within a few months he was initiated into that small select circle aboard the *Moonwind*, the few men who knew what the ship's mission really was, and no one could have been more loyal. Whatever Brandon Christopher wanted, whatever he demanded, no matter how illogical, how unreasonable it might sound, it was his for the asking. Whatever Brandon needed, China Kwan was his man.

14

The wind had died down. The air had an almost tropical stillness, with only a faint breeze blowing as China Kwan turned away from the sea, leaning for a moment with his back against the railing. The sound of bells broke into his thoughts, echoing across the darkened deck. Eight bells, time to change the watch. He pushed away from the rail and was just heading toward the stairway when he saw Brandon come up from below.

Stopping, he grinned suddenly. "A ghost from yesterday," he said.

"What?" Brandon gave him a puzzled look.

"You caught me stargazing. I had just been thinking about . . . times long ago. Things in the past."

He started toward the steps again, but Brandon caught his arm, holding him back. "Some things," he said with a gently raised brow, "are best left in the past."

China laughed again, shrugging off the comment, and Brandon watched enviously as the other man turned and hurried down the stairs. How simple it was to come to terms with yesterday, when yesterday had been resolved to your satisfaction. What would his friend have said, he wondered, if he'd told him he hadn't been thinking of "yesterday" at all when he'd uttered those words, but of other, more painful ghosts, buried even deeper in the past?

He was in that same introspective mood a few minutes later when he wandered forward, barely nodding to one of the men as he passed on his way to the afterdeck. The mainmast topsail was flapping faintly in the breeze, and he looked up to see Celia still perched at her post on the lowest yard. She had evidently heard the bells, for she had lowered her glass and was staring out to sea.

Faint rays of moonlight played on her features, leaving deep blue shadows to accent the strong, yet softly feminine lines of her face. She had tucked her hair under a cap Freddie the cabin boy had given her, an odd little tam that managed to look charming in spite of itself. Stray curls peeked out around the edges, little wisps of silver that gave her a fetching elfin look.

"Hello up there," he called out. "The watch is over. Why don't you go back to the cabin and get some rest?"

She looked startled for a moment, then tucked the glass into her belt, another gift from Freddie—the boy seemed positively enamored of her—and scrambled down the ratline.

"How friendly you're being tonight," she said as she leapt onto the deck. "And very considerate too."

"Aren't I always?"

"Not lately. As a matter of fact, I'd begun to think you were deliberately trying to annoy me—or keep me at arm's length."

Touché, Brandon thought, surprised but pleased at how quickly she was learning to banter with him. He had forgotten how sharp she was. He was going to have to watch his step in the future.

"I'm afraid all this must seem strange to you," he said, deliberately changing the subject. "I wonder if we weren't crueler than we realized, cutting you off from everything—and everyone—you know."

"It's not so strange now." Celia took off the cap, letting her hair tumble down her back. "I'm getting used to it. In fact, I'm even beginning to enjoy life on board—but yes, at first I *was* confused. It was very hard for me."

There was enough of that initial struggle left in her voice to make Brandon feel guilty. "I forget sometimes why you ran away . . . uh, pardon me, why you *left home* in the first place. Do you mind very much, having been waylaid before you could find Schuyler Maarten?''

"Nooo . . ." Celia hesitated over the word, not quite sure how she felt. She had wanted to be with Skye so desperately when she came after him. But now she hardly thought about him. "No, I . . . I don't think I really do."

"You don't love him, then?"

"I did once. At least, I cared very much. Only now . . . well, now I almost feel like a different person. I hardly remember that little girl who came to Hong Kong a few weeks ago." Then, feeling disloyal, she added hastily, "But I really *did* care. And I'm sure I would again, if I could just see him, spend some time with him . . ."

Her face turned thoughtful, almost misty in the pale moonlight, and Brandon found himself beguiled by that same soft sensuality he had noticed more and more these past few days. What was there about a woman, he wondered wryly, that made her so appealing when she spoke of another man? The hint of passion in her voice? The sense that she was unattainable?

He raised his hand, not even aware that he had moved until he felt it linger on her cheek. Just a friendly gesture, or so he told himself. But as he did so, his blood stirred, and he sensed, without dwelling on it, that there was something deeper in his feelings than mere desire.

God, she was beautiful when she looked at him like that, sweet . . . somehow trusting.

Suddenly he was caressing her face, cupping it in both his hands, easing it up until her lips were inches from his own.

Celia felt as if her heart had stopped beating, so light was that touch, so unexpectedly tantalizing. Then it started again, fluttering outrageously, a wild, frightening feeling, yet she could no more control it than she could the winds that swept across the deck. She knew he was going to kiss her, knew she should pull away—she should cry out in protest at the liberties he was taking—but she could not bring herself to move or even breathe.

The feel of his lips was achingly tender, lulling away every other sensation. Her eyes closed; her neck arched upward to flow with the rhythm he had initiated. From somewhere deep inside she felt a slow fire begin to burn, spreading to her breast, her thighs, her limbs. How could a man be so sweetly sensitive and yet so forceful? Touching her only lightly with his mouth, but calling out to yearnings so intense they threatened to devour?

Without thinking, without even realizing what she was doing, she reached up, her arms coiling around his neck. Her body seemed to move of its own accord, pressing closer, savoring the warmth of him, the male hardness against her own yielding femininity. His hands were in her hair now, twisting in the thick tresses that cascaded over her shoulders. A little moan started somewhere in her throat, slipping through her lips as she felt them part.

His mouth responded, turning hard, demanding, and she had the sudden terrifying feeling that she was drowning as he ravished her completely and thoroughly with his tongue.

Brandon was intensely conscious of that moment of surrender, of the feel of her mouth, her body, her will succumbing to his assault, and a feverish heat coursed through his veins, robbing him of the power to reason. The strong masculine instincts of his body took over, and enveloping her in a ravenous embrace, he let his hands run down her back, following the contours of her hips, resting a moment on rounded buttocks, firm beneath tight denim pants. He had never wanted anyone as much as he wanted this woman, never *needed* anyone as much. He longed to sweep her up in his arms and carry her off to the narrow cot where he had spent too many nights alone.

But he could not, he reminded himself, reality intruding again. He dared not.

With a wrenching effort he forced himself to pull back. Catching hold of Celia's arms, he tugged them away from his neck more roughly than he had intended. "Didn't your mother ever teach you not to kiss a man like that? Unless of course you want me to pull off your clothes and have my way with you right here!''

Her eyes clouded, shimmering with a sudden spate of tears, and Brandon, seeing the flood of color in her cheeks, wished he could call the words back, make them gentler somehow, less unkind.

All he could do now was try to soften them.

"Don't be a fool, Celia. I'm not the man for you, and you're not the woman for me. If you have any sense in that pretty head of yours, you'll run away as fast as your legs will carry you. If you don't, I warn you, I'm going to take you in my arms again. And this time I won't let go."

Celia hesitated a fraction of a second, soft blue-gray eyes still troubled as she looked up at him, and Brandon had the idiotic feeling—the idiotic *hope*—that she was going to stay. Then, blushing again, she turned and ran toward the stairway that led to the saloon.

"Damn!" Brandon cursed softly under his breath as he watched her disappear into the darkness. Why the devil had he let himself touch her like that? He had sworn he wasn't going to. And why did he feel so empty, now that she was gone?

He started forward, seeing as he did that one of the men had left a length of rope tangled on the deck. Ordinarily he would have been infuriated by such sloppy seamanship. Now he was grateful for something to do.

He seemed to have a knack for picking the wrong woman, he thought as he leaned down, working the line into a tidy coil. First Teresa Valdes, as evil a little baggage as he'd ever run across. And now pretty pink-and-silver Celia St. Clair.

Only with Teresa, he reminded himself ruefully, it had been purely a physical affair. He had always known that, right from their first encounter, though he suspected she did not. For all that she took her pleasures like a man, there was something distinctly feminine about her, and feminine little creatures had a way of cloaking their lust in the guise of prettier passions.

With Celia, his feelings ran deeper, touching him in ways he had not expected, ways that unsettled.

His hands smelled faintly resinous as he finished coiling the rope, and he rubbed them briskly on the side of his trousers. Not that he could compare the two women. Celia was not evil, not like Teresa, but there was something disturbingly amoral in her choice of lovers. She had been wildly infatuated with Schuyler Maarten—hadn't she admitted it herself just a few minutes ago?—and the relationship had obviously progressed beyond a few sweet kisses. She would hardly have come so far to find him if it hadn't. Now that she was tired of him, she was perfectly ready to throw herself into the arms of a man she thought was a pirate and a dealer in drugs.

Or was he being too hard on her?

Brandon began to move again, his eyes running automatically across the deck to make sure everything was in order. A woman was different from a man. She didn't have the same control over her life. First she belonged to her father; then she took orders from a husband or a lover, as the case might be, with little choice as to where she went or how she lived. Could he blame her if she said: I'm going to follow my heart, and the devil take the consequences!

The prow was deserted when he reached it, a welcome sight, for he was in no mood for idle chitchat. The waves were almost still now, the ocean ebony dark, hiding whatever lay beneath.

Dammit, no matter how he rationalized, there was still something wrong with her, some lack of moral fiber that led her to be attracted first to a snake like Maarten, then to the man she believed Brandon Christopher to be. He didn't want that kind of involvement in his life, didn't want his thoughts to keep drifting back to her, even against his will. He didn't want to *want* her.

He didn't want to—but God help him, he did.

*   *   *

Celia, huddled alone on the afterdeck, was wrestling with much the same thoughts as Brandon, and finding them every bit as difficult to resolve.

When she had left him, she intended to go back to her cabin, but a faint shaft of light flickering up the stairway had reminded her that China would still be in the saloon, and sensing the expression on her face would give her away, she turned instead to the privacy of the shadows next to the chicken coop. There she wouldn't be noticed even if anyone ventured that far aft.

She did not waste time trying to deny her feelings for Brandon—things had gone too far for that, especially tonight—but she did not truly understand them, and because she didn't, they frightened her. How could she care so much for a man she didn't trust? she asked herself again and again. Why did her body insist on responding when her mind said: No, hold back, take care.

Almost against her will, her fingers moved to her lips, tracing the warmth that still lingered from that single searing kiss. Her entire body seemed to ache, as if he had bruised her with his roughness, and she felt the hungers he had roused begin to swell again, a bittersweet reminder of what had passed between them.

With a flood of shame she realized that she would have gone with him if he had urged her—she would have done whatever he asked. She would go with him now if he sought her out in the darkness and tempted her with strong, enveloping arms.

But he was a pirate!

A wave of weakness swept over her, and she was lost for a moment in the terrible sense of guilt and self-recrimination that would have eased Brandon's doubts had he only been able to see it. He was a pirate. He had had men murdered in front of her very eyes, a despicable deed no matter how he claimed they deserved it. He was a pirate. The hold of his ship was filled with opium.

And yet . . .

Celia stirred slightly, her back rubbing against the slats

of the coop. The chickens squawked a faint protest, then sensing no danger in that intruding presence, settled down again.

And yet there was something else in him too, something deep and strong and honest. It was hard to believe he was really what he seemed. It was almost as if . . . as if . . .

She broke off the thought, realizing suddenly what she was doing. She was making up stories in her head, trying to explain away things that couldn't be explained . . . trying to turn Brandon Christopher into something he wasn't. And all because she needed to justify her feelings!

Sighing softly, she tucked her knees up, resting her cheek against them. Why was it, she wondered, that she felt such a need to be scrupulous now? With Skye Maarten she had found it easy enough to pretend away the little flaws she didn't like, to ignore the weaknesses others found so glaring. With this man, for the first time in her life, she was compelled to see everything clearly. With this man she wanted honesty, no matter how it hurt—and she knew only too well what that meant.

The unthinkable had happened. She was falling in love with Brandon Christopher.

15

"Sail ho!"

The cry should have come from Celia, for she was stationed at the lookout's post on the mizzenmast, but she had been so wrapped up in thoughts of Brandon and what had happened between them the night before, she hadn't been paying attention. Now she raised her glass guiltily, squinting through it at a cloud of white sails so far away they looked like a child's toy on the horizon.

Odd, she thought as she drew the glass back. It isn't showing any colors . . .

"Sail ho!" the cry came again, "Sail ho!" with a sharp new urgency, and suddenly the deck was swarming. Even the hands who had been off duty were tumbling out of their bunks and hastening up from below. Alarmed, Celia scurried down the ratline and went off in search of Brandon. There were too many men on deck for mere curiosity, and they were moving much too quickly. Could it be that that other vessel was a renegade? Was that why it wasn't flying a flag?

She found Brandon on the afterdeck with China beside him. Several of the other men were standing a short distance away, but he paid no heed as he turned his eye to a shiny brass telescope. The approaching ship carried three masts, square-rigged like the *Moonwind*, but it was moving faster, closing the gap between them with each passing minute.

"So she *is* there after all."

The words were muttered under his breath, barely audible, but they sent a shudder down Celia's spine. *She* again. The same thing he had said before, when she overheard him in the fog. Only now it sounded more than ever as if he were talking about a woman.

Before she could say anything, China Kwan reached out and touched him on the arm. "You're sure it is she? You couldn't be mistaken?"

Brandon shook his head grimly as he handed the glass to China. "There's no mistaking that ship. See for yourself."

"But how can you identify anything at that distance?" Celia interrupted, unable to contain herself any longer. "It's too far away to make out details. And it's not flying any colors."

Brandon and China turned at the same time, both looking startled to see her there.

It was China who recovered first. "She doesn't need to fly her colors," he started to explain; then Brandon cut in, adding:

"She has her colors painted on her hull—or lack of color, I should say. That's the *White Lotus*."

"The *White Lotus*?" Curious in spite of herself, Celia looked back at the ship. "But isn't that the name of a Chinese secret society?" And wasn't it one that was supposed to contain an outlaw band headed by a woman? "Are they pirates, then?"

Brandon laughed harshly. "How you spit that word out. You make it sound very sinister and mysterious. Have you forgotten? You're riding on a pirate vessel yourself."

"N-no, of course not . . ." Celia faltered. In her turmoil over her feelings about Brandon, she *had* forgotten— and she had forgotten what it might mean to her. "Is there . . . is there going to be trouble?"

"Not if I can help it." Brandon's jaw tensed, and it seemed to her he looked worried, no matter what he said. "But as a precaution, I want you out of the way—do you understand? You might be perfectly adequate as a lookout, but you'd be no use at all in a fight. Go back to your cabin, or the galley if you prefer, and stay there until I tell you to come up.''

Celia squirmed. She *wasn't* an adequate lookout, at least she hadn't been this morning, and she would certainly be in the way if anything happened. But she couldn't bear the thought of huddling below in semi-darkness, listening to the sounds on deck and not knowing what was going on.

"I don't want to go down there," she protested. "I'd feel so . . . so cooped up. It would be more frightening than being out in the open. Please . . ."

Brandon's eyes narrowed as he recognized an instinct truer than his own. If it did come to a showdown, if the *White Lotus* aimed her cannons in their direction, anyone belowdeck might be trapped with no hope of escape.

"Very well," he relented. "Stay up here—I daresay it's for the best. But for God's sake, keep out of the way. I'm not going to have time to worry about you."

He sensed as he turned back to the rail, half-lifting the telescope again, that he had hurt her with his brusqueness, and he knew she was trying to be quiet as she slipped away, assuming he had forgotten all about her. Yet even without turning, he was conscious of every move she made, every feeling she was too unsure to put into words. He leaned forward, gazing out at the water but not seeing it, seeing only the tears in her eyes last night when he had been too sharp with her, the faint quivering she had tried to hide on her lips. Damn, he thought angrily. Why hadn't he anticipated this?

China, watching, caught the tension in his manner. "I did warn you," he said quietly, "not to bring her."

"And I wouldn't listen. I know, my friend, I know. Now, because of my stubbornness, I have put her in mortal danger."

China's eyes drifted back to the *Lotus*, close enough now so he could see the gleaming white on her hull without a glass. "What's going to happen, do you think? What is she going to do?"

"I wish I knew," Brandon said softly. "I wish to God I knew."

Teresa Valdes stood motionless on the prow of the *White Lotus*, long ebony hair streaming out behind her as she stared through her glass at the tall clipper on the waves ahead.

This meeting of the two ships was not her idea. She had spotted the *Moonwind* several times in the past few days—at least she had thought it was the *Moonwind*, though it was too far away to be sure—and she had taken great care to pull back before the other vessel could get a sighting on her. Now a trick of the winds had caught her unaware, blowing her so close it was impossible to slip away unseen.

"Fools!"

She drew the glass back from her eye, scowling as she thought of the men on watch. Maarten had been right, it seemed. Shanghaied men didn't make the best sailors. They should have called her the instant they saw sails in the distance; instead, they had let her sleep.

"My, my, how angry we sound," a brittle voice came from behind. "I should have thought this was just what you were looking for." A few feet away, Skye Maarten was lounging indolently against the railing, as nonchalant as if the entire matter were of little concern. "The advantage is yours, you know. You have only to pull close enough to engage the Tiger in combat—and then bring up the *Black Jasmine* and the *Red Peony*. He'll never know what hit him."

"And you think that's what I want?" Teresa whirled, dark eyes bright with scorn. Didn't he know she had already flashed a message by mirror to the other two ships, telling them to hold back? "You think I want to end it here? In one swift battle?"

"That's what you *said* you wanted. Your words exactly, as I recall. 'I want Brandon Christopher's head in a bamboo basket.' "

"Yes, and how do you suggest I do that? Brandon is

captain of the *Moonwind*. He'll fight to the death with his
men if he has to. Not a one of them will be taken alive.
I'm not looking for anything that quick—or that easy. I
want him on his knees when he goes to his maker. And I
want him in pain.''

Skye stared at her in fascination, seeing the intensity of
her hatred, seeing something else too that she wasn't
admitting, perhaps even to herself.

''So we're going to back off, then? We're going to give
the *Moonwind* a wide berth and just sail away?''

''No!'' Contempt flared in her eyes again. ''Do you
think I would let Brandon Christopher believe I was afraid
of him? No! We're going to sail right up to the *Moonwind*,
so close we could reach out and touch the railing if we
wanted to. Then—and only then—will we sail away again!''

Skye whistled through his teeth. ''Isn't that taking quite
a chance?''

''A chance?'' Teresa flicked her hair back from her
face. ''I'm not afraid of chances! Besides, who knows?
Maybe it won't be an empty gesture after all. I haven't
forgotten that the Tiger killed my best man—Soong—on
that raid on the ferry. Perhaps, when we get close enough,
I'll find a way to make him pay.''

She turned her head quickly, not wanting him to see that
the bravado was a mask, the words mere empty defiance.
It would, of course, be the wildest coincidence if she
found a way to exact satisfaction today, and she was too
intelligent not to realize it. The truth was, she was going
closer not because she thought she would accomplish anything, not because there was any logical reason for it at all,
but because she was compelled to.

Because Brandon Christopher was there, and no matter
what he had done, no matter how she hated him, she could
not stay away.

The foremast mainsail was far from the most protected
position on the *Moonwind*, yet to Celia somehow it seemed
safer than anyplace else, and she sought it out almost

instinctively. When she had left Brandon and China, she had tried to find a quiet out-of-the-way corner on the deck, but no matter where she went, she always seemed to be stumbling into the middle of some frantic activity or other.

At least here, she thought, looking down at scurrying figures below, I'll be out of the way. And I can see what's going on.

Even ten minutes ago she would not have been able to claim that lofty perch, for Brandon, in a last attempt to outrun the *White Lotus*, had ordered every inch of canvas unfurled, and men had sprung into the rigging with cries of "Sheet home the mizzen topgallant!" "Weather sheets home!" "All clear there?" and "Aye, aye, sir, all clear!" ringing on all sides. Soon staysails were flapping briskly in the wind, and studding sails showed at the end of every yard, all the way up to the royals.

The added canvas had given a heartening burst of speed, and for just an instant Celia dared to hope they were going to make it. Hadn't Brandon told her the *Moonwind* was the fastest thing afloat? But the pursuing vessel had continued to draw closer, and reluctantly she was forced to dismiss his boasting as a captain's vanity. She could not know that the *Moonwind* was badly overburdened, for Brandon Christopher had had no chance to jettison his unsavory cargo before they sailed, and the ship was bound so taut she was not fit for a race. Otherwise no one could have outrun her.

The men who had been occupied only a few minutes before in the rigging now turned their attention to the cannons, and as Celia watched from her vantage point, they pulled off heavy covers, cleaning and loading the weapons with grim efficiency. She had left her glass behind, but did not need it, for the *White Lotus* was so near she could make out details on the deck with her naked eye.

Like the *Moonwind*, the other vessel's cannons were at the ready, and men stood beside them, prepared, or so it seemed to Celia, to fire at will.

Her fingers tensed, clutching at a sturdy cord that had been wrapped around the yard on which she was sitting.

One end was securely fastened, but the other was loose, and this she unwound, looping it deftly in one hand. She could not have said herself what she was planning to do; she knew only that she felt safer this way. Perhaps if the fighting came too close, if the cannon volleys she feared were aimed at the foremast, she could use the rope to slide to the deck.

In spite of herself, her eyes were riveted on the approaching vessel, which had already overtaken the *Moonwind* and was beginning to pull up on the leeward side. The silm, pale hull had an otherworldly look about it, especially so close. Everything on board, with the exception of the decking itself and a few pieces of polished brass, had been painted the same ghostly white.

The two ships held even for several minutes, the silence between them almost eerie. Not a human sound could be heard, neither captain's cry nor sailor's shout above the wind as it whistled through the rigging and slapped sturdy canvas back and forth. The men on the *Lotus* were clearly visible now—Celia could make out even the expressions on their faces. They seemed to be exclusively Oriental, Chinese for the most part, though she spotted a few who could have been Indian or Malay.

Then a flash of something bright showed at the far side of the deck, and she was startled to see a man with yellow-gold hair disappear into a tangle of ropes and sails. In that one split second she had a strange sense of recognition, as if something about him were familiar, though that, of course, was impossible. How could she know anyone on a pirate ship? She had just been taken aback seeing a fair head among all those dark Oriental ones.

She did not have time to pursue the thought, for a sudden commotion broke out at the rear of the vessel, a loud barrage of sounds, repeated again and again, like sporadic bursts of gunfire. Every man on deck rushed aft, concentrating on the port side until the ship began to list, and she had to throw her arms around the yard to keep from falling.

As she did, her eyes flicked back to the *Lotus*, and she caught sight of a slim figure standing in the prow. The lad, or so he seemed—he was hardly big enough to be a man—was wearing a sailor's cap, so Celia couldn't make out his hair, but his features were delicate, almost pretty, and his skin had a faintly yellowish cast. There was something stealthy about his motions as he climbed over the rail and began to descend a rope ladder to the water. No sooner had he reached it than a small wooden boat glided around from the other side of the ship, and he leapt into it.

A trap?

Celia's mind began to whirl. All that hubbub at the stern had been a ruse then, a ploy to draw everyone's eyes away from the bow, where the real action was taking place. But to what point? Aside from the boy, she could see only one other occupant of the boat, a burly, dark-skinned oarsman.

What threat could those two possibly pose to the *Moonwind*?

She glanced around nervously, hoping that one of the men had wandered forward, but as before, the deck below was empty. Then, just as she was about to scramble down the ratline and run for help, she saw China Kwan hurrying along the leeward rail. One look at his face was enough to tell her he had seen what was happening, and she breathed a sigh of relief, certain everything would be all right.

But as she looked back, she saw to her surprise that the small vessel was moving much faster than she had expected. Already it had rounded the *Moonwind*'s prow and was hugging the boards on the side of the hull. The rower had pulled in his oars; now something else was in his hands, a length of rope with a metal hook attached to one end. He swung it over his head, catching it in one deft motion on the rail, and began to climb.

Terrified, Celia tried to cry out a warning, but the wind carried her voice away, and no one could hear. China had almost reached the spot by that time, but it was too late, for the intruder already had both feet planted on the deck as he emerged from behind one of the staysails. Lunging forward, the man caught him in a choke-hold, squeezing a muscular forearm over his throat.

Gasping with horror, Celia watched as he dragged China over the rail and down into the waiting boat.

At last she realized what they were up to. It *was* a trap, but it was even more treacherous than she had imagined. They knew all along they were going to be spotted. They *wanted* to be spotted. Only a senior officer would be sharp-witted enough to see what was going on and come forward—and they would have him at their mercy!

But for what purpose? To kidnap one of Brandon Christopher's ablest lieutenants? Or to kill him so the *Moonwind* would be shorthanded?

Uncoiling the rope in her hands, Celia let it drop to the deck. She had to get help for China, and she had to get it now! Thank heaven she had had the sense to bring gloves, she thought as she tugged them out of her pocket and put them on. There was no time to go down the rope carefully, hand over hand. She would have to slide to the deck.

Below, in the boat, China Kwan was even more aware than Celia of the deadly danger he faced. The choke-hold had taken his breath away, but he was still conscious, and as his attacker thrust him forward, pushing him onto his knees, he looked up to see a figure he recognized standing over him.

"Teresa Valdes?"

A gleam of triumph showed in black eyes as she watched him struggle to his feet. "Did you think, friend Kwan, we would not meet again?" There was a soft, almost purring quality to her voice, a gloating realization that her sudden impulsive gambit had paid off. "Did you think you could betray me and just turn around and walk away? No one does that to Teresa Valdes."

"If you didn't want to be betrayed, you shouldn't have made it so easy." China kept his voice steady, sensing that coolness was his only hope as he stalled for time. "You took me on not knowing the first thing about me."

"I knew your cousin—or I thought I did. But it seems he betrayed me too."

"No, he did not." China spoke quietly, trying not to let his eyes move visibly as he looked around the boat. The man was a few steps away now. If he moved a little farther back . . . "I tied him up before the raid on the ferry and left him in one of the cabins. Afterward he was given a choice. He could have his freedom if he promised not to join you again. Or he could come with us."

Teresa did not ask what choice the cousin had made. In her world, money bought loyalty, and the Tiger had always had the means to outbid her.

"Well, it doesn't matter. I don't have time to worry about that now." Her hand slid slowly into her pocket. As China watched her draw it out again, he realized he had waited a second too long. Even if the man moved farther away now, he wouldn't dare leap over the side. Not while she was holding a gun.

"I assume you intend to use that."

She acknowledged his words with a wry half-smile. "A reasonable assumption."

"Why? To get revenge on me?"

"Not revenge, retribution. Brandon Christopher killed my most trusted friend that day on the ferry. I intend to even things up." She raised the gun, aiming it with cool precision. "A fitting gesture, don't you think? One able lieutenant for another."

Celia, still watching from the mainsail yard, gasped in shock at the menace inherent in that slow, deliberate motion. Automatically her fingers tightened around the rope she was holding, while her mind clutched frantically at half-formed plans. She could not go for help now—it would never arrive in time. But she had to do something to save her friend.

Without giving herself time to think, she jumped off the yard and began to slide down the rope. If she could just swing out to the side, she thought desperately—if she could catch the railing with her foot and shove away from it—she might be able to land in the center of the boat.

She was so frightened she didn't even notice the sickening sense of falling as the rope slipped much too swiftly through her fingers. Her gloves held until she had nearly reached the end; then friction burned through the leather, and with a cry of pain she let go, dropping the last few feet.

Her aim was not true, but the impact as she crashed onto the boat was enough to throw Teresa off balance, knocking the gun out of her hand. At the same time, her cap fell off, spilling an abundance of jet-black hair down her back.

A woman!

Celia was so stunned she could only stand there and stare. Not a boy at all, but a woman! She should have guessed before, when she first caught a glimpse of those delicate features. A woman—and an exceptionally beautiful one at that. Something sick and ugly twisted inside her, and for just an instant, irrationally, she forgot everything else, even her fear. So this was the *she* Brandon had spoken of with such intensity in his voice. She was looking back at Celia now with the same shock, the same sudden recognition in those dark, exotic eyes.

Waves of faintness washed over Celia, holding her immobile as she stared into what felt like a mirror of her own jealousy. She tried not to remember the way Brandon's arms had caught her up, the way his lips had felt, hot and passionate against hers, only a few hours before. Every instinct in her body warned her he had shared those same sweet kisses with this woman.

Kisses . . . and much, much more.

She was so engrossed in her thoughts she had lost all sense of danger, but China, fully recovered now, was alert to everything. Teresa seemed as stunned as Celia—nor was she a threat any longer without her gun—but the oarsman had drawn a wicked-looking knife and could be counted on to use it. Catching Celia by the arms, China half-lifted, half-pushed her into the water, leaping after her.

"I hope you were telling the truth," he said as he appeared for a second beside her, "when you claimed you could swim." Then, gripping her shoulders in both hands, he ducked her under the surface.

Celia barely had time to take in a gulp of air before she felt the water close over her head. Fortunately it *was* the truth. She had always been as supple as a little fish—Papa's words exactly, from the day he first taught her to swim. With a strong kick she twisted her body nimbly around, plunging as far down as she could.

The hull ran deeper than she had expected, even that close to the prow, and for an instant she almost panicked, sensing no end to those rough wooden boards beneath her groping fingertips. Then suddenly they gave way, and slipping under, she rocketed to the surface on the other side, lungs bursting as she gasped for air.

By the time she got her bearings, she saw that the enemy vessel had begun to drift backward, easing around the stern to the other side of the *Moonwind*, where even now the small boat must be heading toward it. Angry and frustrated, she realized their assailants were going to get away. She was much too weak and hoarse to call out anything coherent, and China, thrashing beside her, managed only raucous shouts for help.

Brandon was the first to reach her when at last she climbed up a knotted rope that one of the men had tossed down from the deck. His arms were around her at once, his face ashen as he bent to look at her, and it was several minutes before she could get him to listen to the confused explanations she was trying to make. When at last he understood, he sent several men to check on the situation, but as she had feared, they found no trace of the mysterious woman or her oarsman. The boat was still there, but it was empty, drifting loose on the water.

"They must have swum back to the *Lotus*," China suggested, shivering as he wrapped himself in a blanket that had been brought up from the forecastle. "It makes sense. In the boat, they'd have been too easy a target."

"I wonder . . ." Brandon's eyes had a faraway look as they drifted back to the water. "She was a good swimmer when she was a child, I understand, at least in calm water, but she never tried it again after she got to Macao. Maybe it reminded her of her humble origins. Still, you're probably right. The *White Lotus* is beginning to pull away—and at a brisk clip, too. The crew wouldn't leave if she weren't safely on board."

She. Celia looked up, recalling the terrible jealous feeling that had swept over her when she caught sight of those exotic Oriental features. Now here was Brandon speaking of her again, and quite intimately, too—as if he knew her well indeed.

"Who . . . who is she?" she asked, gasping so badly she could barely make herself heard. "Who is she—and what does she want from you?"

"It doesn't matter who she is," Brandon replied, hearing only half of what she said. "Nothing matters as long as you're all right. When I looked down there and saw you in the water . . ." He broke off, embarrassed by emotions he had never expressed so openly before. "Well, you're safe, thank God—and you'll be safe from now on, I promise. No one is ever going to take chances with your life again."

Without giving her even a moment to respond, he picked her up in his arms and carried her across the deck toward the stairway that led to the cabin. The men, seeing the expression on his face, grinned and winked at each other as they stepped aside to let him pass, but Celia, her head resting on his shoulder, was unaware of the relief and anguish written on those strong masculine features.

He had come so close to losing her that afternoon. His arms tightened as the thought flashed through his mind. So very close! Damn, what kind of bastard was he, playing games with her life as well as his own?

He kicked open the door, and laying her gently on the

bed, began to strip the wet garments from her body. He was so concerned, he barely even noticed her nakedness as he bundled her up in an old flannel shirt, much too large, but warm and wonderfully soft. He had just finished and was tucking the blanket around her when he saw raw red marks where the rope had burned her hands.

Turning them palm-up, he raised them tenderly to his lips. "You little fool." His voice was suddenly turned hoarse. "Whatever possessed you to do a crazy thing like that? Don't you know what might have happened?"

"I had to do it," Celia murmured weakly. "There was no other way. They were going to kill China. He's the only person who has been kind to me all this time. How could I let something happen to him?"

The only person who had been kind to her. . . . Brandon laid her hands back on the clean sheets and rose to find a jar of salve in one of the cabinets. She had not meant the words as a rebuke—she was too gentle for petty vindictiveness—but nonetheless they were. Many things had passed between him and this beautiful young woman—passion, fascination, excitement, curiosity, sometimes even a genuine liking. But kindness had not been among them.

He began to rub the salve into her hands, trying with that one gesture to erase weeks of brusqueness and inconsideration. Fortunately the wounds were less severe than he had thought, and as he examined them, he realized they would heal nicely in a few days. Still, he insisted on finding a pair of freshly-laundered gloves, not so much because he believed they would help as because it was the only thing he could think of to do.

Celia was already groggy, even before Cook brought in a steaming pot of tea, and she managed only a few sips from the cup Brandon held to her lips. But she seemed quite warm by now, and he noticed her color was good, so he did not force her to finish.

He was aware, as he rose to put the salve back in its drawer, that his hands were shaking badly. He, who had always been strong enough to handle any situation, to endure any fate, had been brought to his knees at last—and by a slip of a girl.

"You have captured my heart, sweet Celia," he said softly. "I didn't mean to fall in love with you, God knows—or with any other woman—but it seems to have happened. What are you, a witch, that you have crept up unawares and stolen my heart away?"

He paused, a little surprised at the words, for he had never spoken them before. Love had always seemed an elusive will-o'-the-wisp, a pretty concept that applied to other people. How could it have happened to him?

"Yes, a witch—surely that must be it, for why else would I feel this way? And yet, my darling, I must confess I do not truly mind the enchantment."

He turned, half-expecting to see laughter or perhaps a glint of mockery—and didn't he deserve it?—in those wide gray eyes. Instead, they were closed, her head nestled deeply in a pile of soft pillows on the end of the bed.

He stared at her for a moment, startled, then began to chuckle under his breath. Poor child, she was so exhausted, she must have fallen asleep the instant he left her side. She had been sleeping all this time.

He had poured out his heart, and she had not heard a word he said.

16

The next morning when Celia ventured up on deck, considerably later than usual, for she had been relieved of watch duties until her hands healed, the air had a different smell to it, warmer somehow, if air could actually *smell* warmer . . . balmier . . . and she sensed that land was near.

It appeared the following dawn. At first it showed itself only an elusive haze on the horizon, drifting miragelike in and out of a shimmering pink sunrise. But by noon the shoreline had begun to take shape, and by midafternoon she could make out silhouettes of palm trees along the beach, their gracefully curving trunks and jagged leaves outlined against the clearest blue sky she had ever seen.

"Is that Hawaii?" She grabbed hold of the rail, pulling back as a sharp pain reminded her that her hands, which had responded nicely to the salve, still had soft scabs that broke under pressure.

Brandon laughed at her excitement. "It can't be anything else—unless, of course, you miscalculated in those noon-to-noon sightings."

"I could hardly have done that," Celia countered, enjoying the teasing. "You checked me much too carefully. It has to be Hawaii then, but . . . well, it does seem awfully . . . small."

"It *is* small." He laughed again. "The largest of the islands isn't a fiftieth the size of Burma, and the smallest is considerably smaller than Hong Kong. But don't confuse size with importance. There isn't another piece of land for miles in any direction. The little Kingdom of Hawaii—if indeed it's still a kingdom when we arrive, the state of royalty being rather precarious at the moment—has a unique significance as a stepping stone between America and the Orient.''

Celia squinted into the distance, trying to recall what she had heard about Hawaii. Papa had told her once that the Sandwich Islanders, as he called them, were too open and friendly for their own good, and their culture was being submerged into that of foreign powers, particularly the United States. Neither politics nor ethics, however, had appealed overmuch to a young girl prone to romantic daydreams, and she had listened with only half an ear. Now she was keenly aware of how little she knew about the place they were about to land.

"Well, I don't care whether it's important or not," she said impulsively. "And I don't care how small it is. I'm just going to be glad to get off the ship and walk on the ground again."

"So will we all''—Brandon grinned—"when we get our land legs back.''

Celia, who had no idea what "land legs" were, laughed anyway, relishing the prospect of going ashore so much that it almost didn't matter where—or what Brandon Christopher had in mind for her when they did.

They arrived well before sunset, but to Celia's surprise, they did not land immediately. Brandon insisted on circling the area for some time, studying the shoreline thoughtfully through his glass, and it was almost dark by the time they anchored just outside the mouth of a protected inlet. A small party of handpicked men went ashore first with instructions to scout the area. Only when they were satisfied did the boat return to take the others off the *Moonwind* in shifts.

Brandon and Celia were among the last group to leave the vessel. The shallow bay that had been chosen for the camp was edged by a surprisingly narrow beach, with grayish sand dulled slightly by the windward waves. As they approached, Celia saw that the men had already begun to build small fires, and makeshift shelters were taking form in the flickering light. Freddie, the errand boy even on land, had detached himself from the others and was laughing good-naturedly as he raced along the beach gathering scraps of driftwood by the armful.

Celia had already slipped off her shoes, assuming that she and Brandon were going to join that small band already on shore. But no sooner had the other men climbed out of the boat, wading thigh-high through the water to the accompaniment of laughter and hoarse shouts of encouragement, than Brandon took up the oars himself, guiding them to a smaller, more secluded cove a short distance away.

"The men have been confined for a long time under rigid discipline," he explained as he eased the small boat expertly onto the sand. "The first thing they want to do when they hit shore is let out some of that pent-up steam. I try not to interfere, as long as it doesn't get out of hand. They're good men, but they're going to get very drunk tonight. And very wild. It's no place for a lady."

"No, I . . . I suppose it isn't," Celia admitted reluctantly. "I can see why you wouldn't want me there, but . . ." Her voice trailed off as she watched Brandon jump out and tug the boat over the tide line. She knew he was right, but she hadn't expected to be alone with him tonight, and she wasn't prepared for the violent emotions he churned up in her. Besides, the memory of that strange, exotic girl was still too fresh, reminding her that she wasn't the first woman who had ever hungered for Brandon Christopher. And no doubt she wouldn't be the last.

"But you'd feel better if we were with them now?" Brandon grinned rakishly, as if he knew what she was thinking. "Is that it?"

"Well, it does sound like they're having fun." Celia was careful to keep things light, not intending to give him an excuse to laugh at her. "I know it makes sense, what you said, but I can't help thinking I'm missing out on something. Tell me, are we . . . uh . . . are we going to stay here all night?"

"No." He saw her look around at the deserted beach, barren in the light of a rising moon, and sensing her confusion, he backed off. "I knew you wanted to come ashore, so I thought I'd arrange it for an hour or two. But we'll be staying on board ship until . . ." He hesitated, not wanting to alarm her. He had left a skeleton crew on the *Moonwind*. Everything would be secure there, but he didn't know what to expect on land. "Until I can make other arrangements. A grass hut is remarkably comfortable, but only if you've had time to prepare it properly. Come on, now. Don't you want to try out your land legs?"

Celia let him take her hand, but the instant her feet touched the ground, she drew it back again, trying to tell herself that the sudden flush of warmth she felt was just the last trace of rope burn on her palms.

The sand, still wet from the afternoon tide, oozed invitingly between her toes as she took her first tentative steps. Brandon had not been joking, it seemed, when he warned her she would have to get used to walking all over again. Her legs were almost wobbling, they felt so shaky, as if the earth were swaying beneath her.

Laughing, she threw her head back, wishing she had left her hair loose so she could luxuriate in the sultry feel of the breeze, so different from the brisker winds at sea. She had enjoyed those weeks on the *Moonwind*—they had been fascinating in spite of her initial fears—but it was good to feel her feet on terra firma again. She had decided to wear the pretty pearl-gray shirtwaist Brandon had given her, thinking it added a festive touch to the occasion. Now she was glad, for she felt wonderfully free in the loose lacy blouse and shirred skirt that blew up around her ankles.

"This isn't at all what I expected," she said, searching for something neutral to talk about as she glanced at the shadowy shrubs that cut the beach off from whatever lay inland. She was relieved that Brandon didn't plan on keeping her there all night, but she couldn't help remembering the effect he had on her whenever they were alone.

"I don't know much about the Sandwich . . . about Hawaii—only what I've read in books. And what Papa told me, of course, though I'm afraid I didn't listen very well. Still, I pictured something green and lush. You know, with exotic trees and tropical flowers splashing color all around."

"And your romantic soul is disappointed?" Brandon took off his boots and rolled his trousers up to his knees as they strolled along the edge of the water. "Actually, most of the island *is* green, and every bit as lush and exotic as your heart could crave. The shore tends to be starker, especially on the windward side, where the beach is frequently battered by storms. But here—stop and take a whiff. See if you can't catch a scent of flowers mingled with the salt spray."

Celia paused, tilting her nose up. "You're right. I *do* smell flowers. That's frangipani, I think—"

"Plumeria here—or melia, as the Hawaiians call it."

"And there's something else, too . . . something familiar, though I can't make it out. But, oh, it smells like . . . like Burma." There was a faint catch in her voice, and Brandon picked it up.

"You say that so strangely, as if it weren't what you intended."

"No, actually it wasn't." Celia wandered back away from the water. Finding a dry patch of sand, she sat down, her knees tucked up to her chin. "I started to say it smelled like home. But then all of a sudden it felt funny, calling Burma *home*."

Brandon sat beside her, taking her hand so gently she didn't even think of pulling away. "You must feel very lost right now . . . and lonely. It has occurred to me, more and more of late, that it was unfair—what I did to you."

"I did it to myself, too." Celia smiled a little as she forced herself to be objective. "When I ran off to Hong

Kong, I didn't think about what I was doing. I didn't care. Nothing mattered, because I was going to Skye. I thought all I wanted was to be with him.''

"And you don't think that now?" He said it quietly, but there was a hint of something sharp in his tone.

"Not anymore. I know I'll never see him again—and I don't really want to—but I don't want to go back to my parents either. I wouldn't fit in, not after everything that's happened. Only, you see, I don't know where I *do* want to go. Sometimes I feel like there isn't anyplace I can call home. I know that sounds funny, but—"

"No, it doesn't. If there's a man on earth who understands the way you feel, it's me. I left Boston myself when I was still a boy. I've never settled in one place long enough to say, 'Here I am. This is home.' But then, I've always been a natural nomad—you might say I was born under a wandering star. Being homeless doesn't seem so strange to me."

"You've never thought about staying anywhere?" Celia studied those strong masculine features in the moonlight. "Making a home for yourself?"

"Sometimes." He shifted his weight, moving subtly closer. "But only idly, only as a passing fancy, until . . . recently."

"Recently?" Celia sensed the change in his voice, his manner, and she tried to set herself on guard, but it was hard when he was so close.

"These islands have a way of getting under your skin. They've lured more than one old salt away from the sea. I wouldn't be surprised if they got me too when I . . ."

He caught himself, laughing. When I find the right woman? God, how often had one or another of his sisters said that to him, and he had always scoffed. Now, it seemed, he *had* found the woman he wanted, and if fate hadn't stepped in, he would have told her so that night before she fell asleep—but he wasn't ready to commit himself, not yet. There were still too many things to be settled between them.

"When I give up my restless ways," he said instead. "I'll tell you what. In a few days we'll go inland and I'll show you the Hawaii I've come to know these past few years. The cool green valleys and the beach at Waikiki— the playground of the royal Hawaiians. Perhaps then you'll understand why I love this garden paradise."

And perhaps you'll love it too, he thought, surprised at the turn his mind was taking. Why was it so important that this woman who had been a stranger a few weeks ago share the passions of his heart?

Celia sensed the unspoken questions in his eyes, and while she did not understand them, she realized instinctively that he was reaching out to her. She was tempted to give in, to let herself drift into his arms as she knew he desired, but she was afraid too, and fear won out.

"It really is very . . . pretty here. I can see why anyone would love it." She felt no resistance as she pulled her hand away, but she was aware that he was watching her.

"You're uncomfortable with me," he said gently. "Why? Because I kissed you before?"

"Well . . . yes," Celia admitted, blushing as she recalled how completely she had responded. "Partly because of that. But partly because . . . because of . . ." She took a deep breath, then blurted it out. "Because of *her*!"

"Her?" Brandon frowned for a moment. "Ah, you mean our beautiful pirate lady."

Celia nodded. "Who is she, Brandon? I tried to question you about her before, do you remember? Right after I saw her. But you wouldn't tell me anything."

"Is it so important?" he asked gruffly. Then, when she did not reply, he realized it was. Standing up, he brushed the loose sand from his trousers and paced restlessly away from the water. "She's just what I said—a pirate lady. Her name is Teresa Valdes, if that means anything. She is as evil as she is beautiful—and as dangerous. We are mortal enemies."

"I wonder if that's quite the word." Celia fixed him with troubled eyes, but he did not look back. "I saw the expression on her face when she caught sight of me—it wasn't the face of a woman who had come to confront her 'enemy.' There's something else between you, isn't there?''

Brandon stared at the shrubbery, waxy green with rich red flowers deepened almost to black in the moonlight. It would be so easy to lie to her, so easy to say the words she wanted to hear, but he could not bring himself to do it.

"There *was* something between us." He reached out and snapped off one of the blossoms as he turned to face her. "I'm not particularly proud of it, but I'm not ashamed either. There have been many women in my life—I refuse to pretend they don't exist. Teresa and I . . ." He broke off, smiling ironically. Had a fling? A trite way to put it, not exactly accurate for all that intensity of passion. "You might say we 'used' each other, though I did more of the using, perhaps, than she. Teresa is self-absorbed, cruel in many ways, but she was young when I first encountered her, and I think she didn't understand what was going on. I did. She hates me for that."

"And loves you too?"

"Perhaps," he admitted, "in a warped way."

"And you? Do you love her?"

"Love?" Brandon stared out at the ocean, forcing himself to confront feelings he had never examined before. "No, love never entered into the matter, at least not on my side. It was more like . . . fascination. The way the moth comes back again and again to the flame." He laughed hoarsely. "A dreadful cliché, but apt in this case. It was not mere beauty or sensuality that drew me to Teresa Valdes. It was a sense of danger, of something beyond myself I couldn't control, of . . . Ah, well . . ." He came and squatted beside Celia, looking into her eyes. "Whatever it was, it doesn't matter anymore. It's all over. I feel nothing for her now. Nothing."

"You are . . . sure?"

"I am sure." He held out the flower, a sweet temptation. "I am very sure. And I think you know why."

Celia took the flower and tucked it in her hair. The deep

purple-red caught the pink of her cheeks until they seemed to glow. "Why?" she asked softly.

"Because I have a new fascination to replace the old. Because a new—and much prettier—witch has cast her spell on me. Because from the moment I laid eyes on you, devilishly beautiful Celia St. Clair, I could think of no one else . . . want no one else. . . ."

He drew her toward him, arms tender, yet so strong she could not have pulled away if she wanted to. There was, in those hardened muscles, a leashed-in virility, frightening but exciting, tantalizing in ways her body seemed to understand.

She laughed softly as his lips brushed hers lightly—as if he, like her, was not quite ready to let go.

"I thought you said you weren't the man for me," she reminded him. "And I wasn't the woman for you."

"And you're not going to let me forget it?" He laughed, a deep sound, rough somehow. "Very well . . . I was wrong. Is that what you're waiting to hear? You *are* the woman for me. And I, I hope, am the man for you." He eased back just slightly, and Celia sensed that he was waiting for a reply, that he would not touch her again until she spoke.

"Yes . . ." She barely whispered the word. "Yes . . . you are the man for me."

His arms tightened around her, not gentle now, but harsh, demanding, staking the claim they both knew she would not deny. Impatient fingers tangled in her hair, pins scattering as he ripped it out of its tidy coil and buried his head in thick, luxuriant tresses. A low, muffled moan, as much surrender as longing, escaped from lips that sank hungrily to the base of her throat.

One last quiver of alarm ran through her body. She could not let this happen, she *must* not—not so quickly, so roughly. Not with a man who had never offered a single promise, a single sweet word of love.

Then his mouth was hard on hers, and whatever protests she might have made were stilled. His tongue became a

weapon of assault, as it had that one time before, driving
away even the will to reason. She felt his hands run down
her back, bold and insolent, undoing the little buttons on
her blouse; felt the searing warmth of probing fingers
burning through the sheer fabric of her chemise; felt the
sinewy strength of his body, taut and relentless as he drew
her to her knees beside him on the sand.

Odd little whimpers seemed to float in the air, sounds
she did not even recognize as coming from her. But Brandon recognized them, and he grew bolder, daring the
liberties he had only hinted at before.

Somehow—Celia did not know how—her blouse was
off and in his hands; then suddenly it was on the ground.
Now he was slipping the chemise partway down one shoulder, lowering his head to the cleavage of her breasts,
teasing with his lips, his tongue.

Her body arched toward him, erect pink nipples rising
beneath the gauzy silk to meet his fingertips. She was no
longer more than dimly aware of what she was doing, nor
did she even care. She knew only that he was pressing her
back onto the sand, knew that she wanted him to.

Brandon, leaning over her, was keenly aware of every
muscle in his body throbbing with pain and yearning. He
had wanted this woman the first time he saw her. He had
looked at that silver-blond sensuality and he had grown
hard just at the sight. He wanted her even more now.

Celia felt the roughness of his hands as he tugged at her
skirt, too aroused now to think of niceties, and for just an
instant she stiffened, her doubts returning. But the subtle
warmth that had begun low in her belly grew more intense,
radiating outward until she seemed to be on fire. A strange
moisture spread between her thighs, drenching her under-
garments, and she flushed with embarrassment, not knowing whether that was normal.

But if Brandon noticed anything wrong, it did not show
as he slipped his hand between her legs, coming to rest
there, where she longed to feel him, though still through a
veil of silk. Even inexperienced as she was, Celia realized

that the long, slow shudder racking his body was one of passion, not surprise or revulsion. His lips felt feverish as he touched the corner of her mouth, half-kissing, half-whispering his desire.

"You are ready for me, my darling," he murmured huskily, "and I am ready for you."

He took her hand and drew it toward him, planning on proving his words by pressing it between his own legs. Then, thinking better of the gesture, recalling that this was their first time together, he raised her fingers instead to his mouth, kissing each one tenderly, letting it go.

Time enough later for the wantonness and wild abandon he relished so much as a natural part of lovemaking. Time enough to lie on the beach, open and unashamed, as they explored every inch of each other's bodies. Tonight he would allow her a degree of maidenly modesty, though maiden she was clearly not, not if he was any judge of female behavior. Tonight he would offer the sweet illusion of secret intimacy.

Celia's body went limp as he swept her up in his arms, and she sensed, even without opening quivering eyelids, that he was carrying her toward the shadowed shrubs, away from the windswept sand. Somehow her arms found themselves around his neck, grasping, clinging. His shirt felt coarse against the softness of her cheek; the male smell of him was heavy in her nostrils.

She was so caught up in bewildering new sensations that she did not even notice the moment he stopped. Later she would ask herself how it could have happened and she not have been aware. She knew only that suddenly everything had changed, and there was a coolness in his manner as he set her down, found her blouse and slipped it on again, fastening it with expert fingers.

Not until he had finished did she turn to see a man standing a short distance away, near the water.

He made an incongruous sight, there on the beach, in a dark suit, the jacket open at the front. His boots had a polished military look, toes dulled slightly by the edges of the waves that lapped up against them. Though he was rather taller than average height, rounded shoulders and a belly sagging over his belt made him look smaller than he actually was.

Brandon stared at the man in silence for a moment, neither acknowledging his presence nor seeming to expect a response from him. Then, turning back to Celia, he tucked a finger under her chin, still ignoring the stranger as he tilted her face upward. "Go to the *Moonwind* and wait for me there. You can manage the oars by yourself, I think. The sea is calm tonight. If you have trouble, call for one of the men to come and help you. I want you to stay in your cabin until I arrive. But leave the door unlocked—that is, if you still want me."

His features twisted wryly, acknowledging the distinct possibility that she might not, but other than that one cryptic look, he made no effort to persuade her. Celia's pulse was racing as she turned and fled down the beach, feeling something cold and heavy settle over her heart.

God help her, what had she almost done? Self-disgust welled up inside her as she recalled the intensity of her emotions, the ravenous yearning that had made her forget everything else. If that man hadn't come along when he did . . .

She was shuddering by the time she reached the boat and shoved it with difficulty along the sand. Brandon had not told her who the intruder was, but he didn't have to. Plainly the man was some sort of "business associate" involved in an unsavory drug operation. Who else would feel the need to meet on a deserted beach at night?

How could she have forgotten what Brandon Christopher was?

Celia got the boat into the water and picked up the oars, finding them heavier than she had expected, but she was too proud to call for help. How could she have been such a willing accomplice in the seduction that had almost taken place tonight? Not only had she come within minutes of giving herself to a man who had never breathed a word of love or marriage, she had not even remembered he was a scoundrel who made his fortune from the suffering of others.

She paused for a moment, resting her arms as she glanced over her shoulder. The rowing seemed easier, now that she was getting used to it. Ahead of her the dark outline of the *Moonwind* blended into the sky, a subtle invitation, hard to resist.

Now was the time to get away. Every instinct in her body warned her she would never have a chance like this again. She was free now—she ought to pick up the oars and go with the current, around the next curve to a beach where no one could keep her from landing.

And yet she knew so little about this island they had taken her to. Her mind caught hold of the thought, toying with it, not sure what to do. She did not know what kind of terrain she might encounter in the darkness, or how far she would have to go to the nearest settlement; she did not know whether the natives were friendly or hostile.

And most of all—she drew back the oars, holding them a second longer—yes, most of all, she did not know if she wanted to.

17

"Your timing, as usual, is excellent."

Brandon's voice was laced with sarcasm as he turned to face the man at the edge of the water. Colonel Robert Quarrie remained where he was for a moment, then stepped forward, coming just near enough so he could be heard without raising his voice.

"I wish I could say the same about yours. I've been waiting at the appointed place, assuming you'd come as soon as the ship anchored and you'd seen your crew ashore. I didn't realize you'd been . . . uh . . . detained."

"It's none of your business what I was doing!" Brandon exploded. "Dammit, Quarrie, you don't own me. I'm not one of those blasted little privates you're used to, hopping to attention at your command. You didn't need to see me tonight. Any business we have could have waited until morning."

"Could it indeed?" Quarrie's dark eyes snapped uncharacteristically. "Didn't it occur to you, just in passing, that the *White Lotus* might be only a few hours behind . . . maybe less. Timing is an essential part of this operation. I have to know exactly what's going on at all times."

"Yes, and I sent my man to you." Brandon turned impatiently to the water, staring out at the small boat that was carrying Celia slowly toward the *Moonwind*. "China Kwan. He's perfectly capable of briefing you. As I said before, you didn't need me."

Quarrie started to remind him that a briefing from the lieutenant was hardly the same thing as a briefing from the captain. Then, sensing the tension in the other man's mood, he changed his mind. "Kwan is a good man," he said in tones intended to be conciliatory.

"Yes." Brandon nodded absently. Celia had hesitated, holding back, and for a moment he had been alarmed. But she had the oars in her hand again and was continuing toward the ship. "Yes, he is."

"He said the raid on the ferry went very well, although I must say I'm not surprised. I know you well enough by now to be sure everything was carefully planned. He did mention, though, that you'd had a bit of luck. Something about a relative of his working for Teresa Valdes."

The words were vague, but a certain edge to his voice caught Brandon's ear, and he glanced over his shoulder. "A cousin," he confirmed. "He'd been with Teresa and her gang for two years."

"How convenient that he managed to change loyalties so quickly. First Teresa, then you. One does wonder if his conscience rests quite easy of a night. That was a particularly bloody raid he participated in."

"He didn't *participate*." Brandon snapped the words out irritably. "In fact, he didn't know about it until it was over. The two cousins had never met, incidentally, though China was acquainted with the younger sister. She had been married with predictably unpleasant results to an opium addict, and he was instrumental in having her taken back into the family living quarters. The elder Kwan was grateful—it seems she had always been his favorite. So when China looked him up in Hong Kong, down on his luck and needing a job, it was natural for him to help."

He turned back to the *Moonwind* just in time to see Celia climb up a ladder one of the men had thrown down. He and China had debated long and carefully before deciding how to deal with the cousin. In the end, they opted to keep him in the dark until after the raid, then offer him a choice—his freedom if he agreed not to return to his former mistress, or the opportunity to switch sides and come over to Brandon Christopher.

"And of course you paid him well," Quarrie quipped after Brandon had explained the situation.

"I paid him exactly what he was getting before. Not a penny more—or less." He and China had debated that too, and it proved a good move. The man had lost nothing monetarily, but neither was his sense of honor tarnished. He had no reason to reproach himself: he had not sold his soul for cash.

"Ah, a good gambit." Quarrie's face twisted ironically. "But I wonder . . . If Cousin Kwan hadn't wanted to come to you—and hadn't promised to forsake his beautiful young commander—would you have had him put to death?"

"Hardly." Brandon eyed him coldly. "That's not my style."

"I was afraid of that." He shook his head. "An admirable stand, but not very sensible. You're too softhearted for your own good."

"Call it softhearted if you like. I call it practical. How could I command undying loyalty from my ablest lieutenant if I tricked him into using his own cousin, then had the man murdered? Or from the rest of my crew, for that matter—who'd be waiting for me to sell them out too!"

Quarrie chuckled. He was used to giving orders and he liked having them obeyed, but he enjoyed the younger man's spirit, though this hardly seemed the time for it.

"I understand you had a bit of a skirmish a few days back," he said, changing the subject. "Came close to a battle at sea, I hear. Too bad you couldn't turn it more to your advantage, though it may work out in the end. Kwan tells me your lovely blond captive was the heroine of the day." He made a soft sound, like laughter under his breath. "By Jove, that must have been a sight. I wonder what our pirate thought when she got her first glimpse of the lady."

And what the lady thought when she saw the pirate, he added mentally, but he kept the observation to himself. No doubt the subject had already come up. He couldn't imagine it had gone over well.

"What Teresa thought," Brandon said, hating the mention of Celia on Quarrie's lips, "is no concern of mine. Or yours."

"Ah, but it is. I think you underestimate Senhorita Valdes' passion for you. One sight of that pretty face, and quite sumptuous body, I might add—you have excellent taste—and her blood must have been boiling. If there was any doubt in my mind that she'd follow the *Moonwind*, it's gone now. I'd be willing to bet she'd do anything, risk anything, to come after you and avenge herself on the girl who shares your bed."

"Dammit, Quarrie . . ." Brandon's jaw tightened as he gaped at the man, disgusted. "Do you think I'm going to use Celia as bait to trap Teresa Valdes? I have no intention of endangering her life—"

"What I think is that you don't have a choice." Quarrie's tone was crisp now, militaristic. "Teresa has already seen the lady. You can't go back and alter that little fact. She *is* going to come after her, whether you will it or no. All you can do is be alert and turn the situation to advantage. For your sake as well as hers."

The color drained out of Brandon's face as he recognized in those calculated words a bitter truth he did not want to accept. "You're a bastard, Quarrie. All that matters to you is winning this damned game of yours. Haven't you ever cared about anyone? Haven't you ever been in love?"

"In love? Oh, yes . . ." Quarrie's lips turned up, not quite pleasantly. "I haven't always been middle-aged, though it must seem that way to you. I know what it is to love . . . and desire . . . and I understand what you're feeling right now. But that doesn't make things any different."

He turned away, plunging his hands into his pockets as he moved a few paces down the beach. His jacket felt heavy, much too warm for a sultry evening, but he had never been comfortable in casual garb.

"The situation has changed since we last spoke," he said, turning back. "Hawaii, I'm afraid, hasn't turned out the way we expected. Oh, you can stay for a few weeks if you like. As a matter of fact, it's better that way. A . . . rest will do you good." And give the hot-blooded *senhorita* a chance to see you gamboling with your new mistress on the beach, he thought, though he took care not to utter the words aloud. "But after that you're going to have to run up your sails and head for the West Coast. With or without the lady, that's up to you—though I would recommend without, if you care about her safety."

"What the devil are you talking about?" Brandon glowered at him, surprised. "The arrangement was for me to get Teresa to Hawaii, where—"

"The arrangement was for you to get her to U.S. territory, which Hawaii would have been had annexation come about on schedule. But with Cleveland winning the election this past November, we haven't a Chinaman's chance. As long as Benjamin Harrison was President, the sugar planters had a sympathetic ear in Washington, and the islands were almost certain to come under the 'protection' of the United States. But the damned Democrats, without knowing the first thing about what's going on, are determined to respect the natives' 'sovereignty.' A noble idea, but one that, I'm sure you'll understand, I don't relish under the circumstances. There's even talk of restoring the monarchy—"

"Damn," Brandon muttered softly.

"My sentiments exactly." Quarrie lifted a grizzled brow as he caught sight of the dark red blossom that had dropped from Celia's hair onto the sand. "This couldn't have come at a worse time. No matter what happens, the law isn't going to be on our side. If Liliuokalani gets her throne back, unlikely, I admit, considering her outlandish behavior—she has not only refused to grant amnesty to the *haole* revolutionaries, she insists that they be put to death—the first thing she'll do is sell opium monopolies to beef up the royal coffers. And if the sugar planters continue their provisionary government . . . Well, despite their missionary background, they do have a habit of looking the other way when it's convenient. So you see, if we want to get Teresa Valdes, we have to lure her to the West Coast.''

Brandon looked thoughtful for a moment, then shook his head. "No, that's asking too much. Get someone else to do your dirty work this time, Quarrie. I'm out of it.''

"You'll never be out of it." Quarrie raised dark eyes to stare almost pityingly at the other man. "Not until the last member of that gang has been rounded up and hanged. After that . . . perhaps.''

He bent down and picked up the flower, touching it briefly to his nose. The scent of sand and salt was on it, but he could still detect a trace of sweetness.

"You asked before if I had ever loved anyone. I did once, very deeply, as only a plain man can love, who never expected that sort of bounty in his life. She was my wife, and she was very beautiful, as beautiful as your lady—no, more so. She was just nineteen when she started smoking opium.''

He paused, looking up, making sure, unnecessarily, that Brandon was listening.

"She wanted me to go to the dens with her, and because I doted on her—and because I was afraid of what she'd do if I said no—I agreed. I won't tell you the things we did there, not so much because they degrade me as because they degrade my memory of her. Within a few months we were both addicted. When I realized that, I insisted on going for a cure at one of those fancy private hospitals, very exclusive. Expensive, too. She didn't want to come, but I forced her.''

He looked down at the flower, wilting slightly in his hand. "It didn't take, of course—her cure. It never does unless you want it to. A few weeks later, she ran away. I went after her—three times. The third time, I found her with another man, right there in the open, sharing a wretched wooden bunk in one of the sleaziest cellars I'd ever seen. Their clothes were in disarray, half on, half off, as if the whole thing didn't matter. Do you know what it does to a man, standing there, watching his wife have sexual relations with someone else?

"That's the devilish thing about the stuff, you know, at least at first. It increases certain . . . appetites. We had done that sort of thing before—together. But somehow it was different without the haze of opium over my eyes.

"I never tried to find her again. Call it cowardice on my part, and perhaps you're right, but I couldn't bring myself to do it. I don't even know if she's still alive. I rather doubt it—she was always a frail woman. But either way, she's dead to me."

His shoulders seemed to cave in, even rounder than before, making him look older, tired.

"So you see, I *do* understand. I do know what it is to love, and to fear the loss of love. I also know what it is to be commited to a cause. And you, my friend, are committed."

"Perhaps . . ." A picture flashed in front of Brandon's eyes. An opium den on a late afternoon, straw-colored hair clinging to a skull-like brow, yellow-green eyes glazed as if in death. He had made a promise to that boy.

"Perhaps," he conceded again. "But it's not the same thing. My commitment is not yours."

"But it *is* a commitment. You're in this to the end."

Brandon let his breath out slowly. "Yes." He *had* made that promise. And he would keep it. "Yes, I'm in to the end. But I warn you, Quarrie, it ends with Teresa Valdes. I'll lure her to California for you. I'll see her hanged—or worse. But then it's over."

"That's all I ask. See this through. After that the choice is yours." His manner changed subtly, the mood lightening as he held out the flower in his hand. "Your lady seems to have dropped this. You might want to take it—if you're going back to her."

18

Brandon waited until Quarrie had gone, then clenched his hand into a fist, crushing the flower and scattering the red petals on the sand. He would not have considered bringing it to Celia now, not after it had been contaminated by Quarrie's touch—even if he thought she wanted it.

Which, it occurred to him, she very likely did not.

His jaw clenched slightly as he glanced out at the *Moonwind*, barely a shadow in the pale rays of a crescent moon. He had not missed that look she gave him just before she turned and ran down the beach, and he had the feeling she was already regretting the intimacies that had passed between them.

Pulling out a flint, he struck it, flashing the signal for a boatman to come and pick him up. The boy who appeared a few minutes later was a young but trusted member of the crew, and he came eagerly, anticipating the banter he and Brandon usually shared on the rare occasions they were alone together. Noting the brooding expression on the older man's countenance, however—and seeing the rigid way he sat in the boat, looking neither right nor left—he wisely remained silent, not wanting to provoke an undeserved tongue-lashing.

Plainly the captain was in a dark mood tonight. As they pulled away from shore, the boy couldn't help wondering what had happened between him and the pretty lady with

the blond hair. Like everyone else on board, he had come
to admire Celia for her spunkiness and ready laughter, and
he had shared in the knowing grins that passed among the
crew when she went ashore with Brandon. Then, barely an
hour later, she had come back—alone.

Well, he wouldn't want to be her if she had done
something to put the captain in a rage like this. The boy
eased the boat alongside the *Moonwind* and held it steady
as Brandon climbed the rope ladder. Any other time, no
matter what was on his mind, he would have paused at the
top, calling out at least a cursory thank-you to the crew-
man who had served him, but tonight he was too preoccupied even for that.

No, the boy thought again, he wouldn't like to be the
person who had crossed Brandon Christopher.

That same anger was visible on Brandon's face as he
strode across the deck, heading for the stairway to the
saloon, though it was not, as the boy assumed, directed at
anyone on board. He was still thinking of the man he had
left on shore, hating him for having the audacity to take up
a flower and press it to his nose.

Not that it was fair to blame him. Brandon paused at the
head of the stairs, his rage cooling as he made an effort to
be objective. Quarrie was not at fault in this. He was only
doing what he had to—just as he, Brandon, would do what
he felt was right.

Only, dammit, why did the thing have to concern Celia?
Or more to the point tonight, why did it concern his
relationship with her? Why couldn't he just go for a walk
on the beach with a beautiful woman and let nature take its
course, as it had so pleasantly seemed about to? Now that
delightful prospect looked highly unlikely.

Unlikely, indeed! He started down the stairs, his face
twisting into a wry half-smile. He knew enough about
women to know that once the moment of passion had
cooled, "reason" had a way of setting in. And there was
nothing more hopeless than trying to reason with a woman
who was sure she had reason on *her* side.

He stepped into the saloon, expecting to find the cabin
door closed, the bolt holding tight when he tried it with his
hand. But to his surprise, it was ajar. A faint flicker of
gold shimmered through the narrow crack.

She must have heard his approaching footsteps, for she
was already looking up as he eased the door inward. She
had changed out of the fetching shirtwaist she had been
wearing before and was now garbed in a nightdress of
some sort, a filmy white concoction with pearl buttons
down the front and a flare of lace at her throat. A matching
robe of more modest fabric lay across the foot of the bed,
but she made no attempt to reach out and pull it on. Her
hair was loose and golden in the lamplight, framing her
face and half-hiding the round curves of her shoulders.

Like a bride, Brandon thought unexpectedly. Like a
virgin bride on her wedding night.

He stepped inside and shut the door behind him, groping
with one hand for the bolt to ensure their privacy.

"I thought I might find the door locked against me."
He was surprised at the faint hint of a quaver in his voice,
he who had always been so sure with women.

Celia, too, seemed confused, for she lowered her eyes.
"I . . . I thought so too—in fact, I hoped you would."

"You . . . *hoped*?" Something tugged at his heart, but
he tried to ignore it.

"I am a little afraid of you," she said, looking up
shyly. "Afraid of . . . what's happening between us."

Brandon squatted beside the narrow bunk, searching her
face with his eyes. He was consumed with longing for her
now—every muscle, every nerve ending in his body ached
with the need he could barely control—but he cared for
her, too . . . cared more than he ever had for any woman
. . . cared too much to take advantage.

"Did you *want* me to stay away, Celia?" he asked
softly. "Did you want me not to come?"

"No." She smiled, her lips warm and full, enticingly
womanly. "No, I tried to want to, but I couldn't."

"You're sure?"

She raised her hand, tracing the sensuous outline of his mouth with steady fingers. A bold gesture, unexpected. "I'm sure."

He leaned toward her, drawn by her words, the sudden sensuality in her tone, and Celia thought for a moment he was going to kiss her. Instead, his lips found her forehead, running along the edge of her hair, nibbling at soft pink earlobes, sinking with a sigh to the place where her hair barely covered her shoulders. Little shivers of anticipation ran through her, not frightening now, the way they had been on the beach, but eager, as if her body already understood what her mind had only guessed at.

"You're so beautiful . . ." Brandon drew back, his eyes caressing her hungrily, frankly. "God help me, the first time I saw you, I wanted to rip the pins out of that absurdly fashionable upsweep and tousle your hair in my hands. I wanted you here—in my bed—just like you are now." He chuckled, a warm sound, low and husky. "Well, not *just* like you are now. I wanted you naked, with not a stitch of clothing on your body."

He laid his hand on the top button of her gown, twisting it in his fingers, only half-teasing. "May I?"

Celia looked down, blushing. Every propriety she had ever learned told her she ought to be outraged by the way he was talking to her, ought to protest at the liberties he was taking—certainly she shouldn't enjoy them so much!

"I . . . I don't know. It seems so . . . well, somehow so . . . wanton!"

Brandon laughed, a little harshly. "You mean a gentleman isn't supposed to look at a lady's body, is that it? Especially when the lights are turned up."

He wondered if Schuyler Maarten had been content to possess her in long sleeves and a high lacy neck. He doubted it, though he had to admit her modesty seemed genuine enough. Dammit, why did he keep dredging up the past, trying to make her into the virgin she so clearly wasn't? Sweet little innocents had never held any appeal for him.

"I've seen your body before," he reminded her, somewhat more gently. "Have you forgotten? I was the one who undressed you when you burned your hands on the rope. And a very pleasant task it was, too."

Celia's flush deepened. "I had forgotten," she admitted. "But you were so matter-of-fact about it then. You hardly seemed to . . . well, to *notice*."

"I didn't—at the time. I was too worried about you to think of anything else. But it did occur to me later that you have an exceptionally beautiful body . . . and I wanted very much to see it again. When I could give it my full attention." All the while he was speaking, his fingers were slipping down that filmy negligee, pausing briefly to undo each of the dainty buttons, easing the sheer fabric away until her flesh was exposed to his eyes.

Celia held her breath, not quite so sure now, but unable to protest as he rose and looked down at her with an expression that could not be misinterpreted.

Something deep inside seemed to respond, a primitive warmth she could not control, burning especially in the places where his gaze touched her. Passionate eyes, deep green in shadow, played with the swollen curves of her breasts, slid to her belly, her hips, her thighs . . . lingered on that soft golden-brown shadow between her legs.

He had already begun to remove his own clothes, not taking his eyes from her for an instant as he did. The boots came off first, then the crisp white shirt, which tore as he tugged at it with impatient fingers. His chest, startlingly naked now, was even more powerful than Celia had imagined. Rippling muscles were plainly visible beneath tangled curls of auburn hair.

Fascinated, she watched as he unbuckled his belt and tossed it aside. Then his hands were on the front of his trousers and a soft gasp slipped out of her lips.

Brandon reacted to the sound, hesitating as he saw an expression he had not expected on her face. Innocence again. An illusion, he knew—but, ah, how sweet. Keeping his trousers on, he sat beside her, so close she could feel his body trembling.

"One last chance," he said huskily. "Tell me to go . . . and I will. If you let me stay, I'm going to lay you back on this bed and make love to you . . . and nothing will get me to stop."

Celia's eyes were clouded as she looked at him, but there was no doubt in them, no fear. "I wouldn't want you to."

Her arms found his neck, twining instinctively around it; her fingers clutched at the naked flesh of his back, drawing him down beside her, finding, surprisingly, that their limbs seemed to mesh. How easy it is, she thought, marveling at the way her body seemed to know what to do. She had agonized over this man so many times; she had asked herself: Should I? Shouldn't I? Can I—or can't I?

Now they were together, and it seemed so right.

His hands felt hot on her breast, greedy, devouring hands, pinching her nipples so they were hard when he sought them with his mouth. She had not dreamed it would be like this, had not anticipated the smell and texture of a man's body, the way his hands would feel as they left her breast, caressing the taut skin of her belly, moving down to her thighs, coaxing them apart. Then his hands left her, just for a second, and Celia knew he was groping with his pants again, and suddenly her hands were there too, helping him, ripping away the unwanted fabric even as her voice begged, whimpering, wordless, for him to come to her.

He did not hesitate. With a single swift stab he drove into her wrenchingly, painfully, and Celia felt herself draw back, confused and hurt, not knowing why he had suddenly turned so rough. He seemed to sense her change in mood, for he relented, but only briefly, lying still within her for an instant before beginning his assault again. This time, the pain was less, ebbing into a sweeter, more urgent agony as her hips began to move, slowly at first, awkwardly, then faster and faster, keeping time with those deep, rhythmic thrusts.

She was no longer aware of what was happening to her, of what she had dared and surrendered. All she could do now was feel and react as he carried her with him, soaring to heights she had never expected, never even imagined. All she knew was that she had to cling to him, had to follow wherever he led, trusting, knowing he would bring the release she craved but could not yet understand.

Then suddenly the passion burst in one great explosion, and at last she did understand. *This* was what she had wanted all along. This was what she had sensed whenever he came near her; this was what it was to be a woman . . . and to love a man. Her own sharp cry at that final moment of sweetness was muffled by a low masculine moan as Brandon too surrendered, sinking, spent and satisfied, onto her body.

He did not pull away immediately, but continued to hold her, as if he craved the closeness as much as she. His lips were achingly tender when at last he kissed her, softly this time, lovingly, masking the moment of loneliness as he retreated gently from her body.

Celia, lost in wonderful new sensations, nestled in his arms, too contented to speak or move. Brandon, recognizing the satisfaction inherent in that gesture, was inclined to feel pleased with himself and would have said so had he not looked down at that very moment and seen blood spreading out on the sheets between her thighs.

Why didn't you tell me? he started to say, not minding in the least—he had wanted her enough not to care what time of month it was for her—but surprised nonetheless, for women usually set great store by such things. Then, startlingly, the truth came to him.

"My God—you were a virgin."

He sat up abruptly, stunned. Now he uttered the words he had started before, meaning them quite differently. "Why didn't you tell me?"

Celia's lip began to quiver as she saw the incredulous look on those dark, handsome features staring down at her.

For one last moment she did not understand; then suddenly all the happiness she had felt before, all the sweet contentment, was washed away in a flood of shame and humiliation. Dear heaven, what must he have thought? She had come to his arms so quickly, had welcomed him into her bed without a visible hesitation. No wonder it hadn't occurred to him she might be a virgin!

"What did you think?" she cried out unhappily. "That I do this all the time? Because I was so easy with you?" All she had wanted was to share this beautiful experience with him, the most beautiful experience of her life—and he had looked on her as a whore! Tears welled up in her eyes, spilling hotly down her cheeks.

"Good Lord, Celia . . ." Brandon faltered, unable, like many a strong man, to cope with feminine tears, especially the ones he was only too aware of having caused himself. "You did come to Hong Kong, all the way from Burma— you told me so yourself—just to be with Schuyler Maarten. Naturally I assumed . . . well, what the devil was I supposed to think?"

"But I followed Skye because I loved him," she said plaintively. "Not because I . . . because I had done *this* with him." She had managed to stop crying, but drops of moisture still glittered on her lashes, catching at his conscience, making him feel guiltier than ever.

"I seem to have a rather warped view of the world," he said wryly. "And a dismal understanding of the way a young woman's heart works. It should have occurred to me that you might be innocent. It didn't—but it should have." Hadn't he thought, just fleetingly, how shy she looked when he came into the room, how virginal? "Ah, Celia, did you think I was judging you because I believed you had lain with another man? There's nothing wrong with being a woman, my sweet, with being warm and loving and responsive. Though I must confess I'm secretly glad you chose to experience these things for the first time with me."

She looked surprised—though at which of his words, he could not tell.

"Secretly . . . glad?"

"I don't like to admit it"—his lips turned up, faintly mocking—"but every time I thought of you with Maarten, something snapped inside me." Damn, he had never worried about virginity before. If anything, it was a nuisance, to be patiently overcome if he wanted a woman enough. But with Celia . . . "All I had to do was imagine his arms around you, and I was so jealous of the son of a bitch I couldn't see straight. There, does that make you feel any better?"

Celia laughed softly. It did indeed make her feel much better. And really, did it matter what he had thought before? As long as he knew the truth now. "You almost sound as if you cared."

"I do care," he said, turning suddenly serious. "I care very much for you. And I want you very much . . . all to myself."

He stretched out again full length beside her, his hands incredibly gentle as they traced every curve of her body, sweetly familiar now, yet still so new. Celia gave a little sigh, not knowing quite what he was doing, not even knowing what she wanted, feeling only the same compelling sensations he had stirred in her before.

Shyly she began to respond, allowing herself to explore his body, playing with it as he had played with hers, though not so boldly. He encouraged her to touch him, helped her hands find his thighs, dared them to linger for just a second.

Her eyes widened as she caught sight of that part of him, grown hard again and quite unbelievably large.

"I hope you are looking at me in fascination," he teased. "For that is a part of my body I intend you to see often in the future."

"No . . . well, yes . . . perhaps . . ." She could feel her cheeks turning a vivid shade of pink. It *was* fascinating, though she didn't know if she should be staring quite so openly. "It's just that it's . . . it's so . . . big! I'm glad I didn't see it before. It would have frightened me."

Brandon laughed, charmed by the naiveté he had not expected, had not even thought he wanted. "I'm glad I did something right. God knows, I would have been more understanding, gentler, had I known. Did I hurt you very much, my dear?''

"No," she lied, then caught herself, realizing he was too knowing to be so easily deceived. "It did hurt at first, but not for long. And it didn't matter, because . . . oh, Brandon, you made me so very happy."

"I want to make you happy, darling, and I want to please you. This time, I'll be gentler . . . I promise."

"This time?"

Celia squirmed with pleasure as she felt his hands begin to work their magic again, keeping his promise, caressing her slowly, with great tenderness. It surprised her a little, making her somehow uncomfortable, to realize how quickly he could rekindle her passion.

"But . . . can we?" she murmured, confused. "Is it all right ? . . . Again? . . . So soon?"

Brandon tried not to laugh as he nuzzled her neck playfully with his mouth. "Of course it's all right. Again and again—and again." He thrust his hand boldly between her thighs, hurting her a little, for she was still sore from before, but she could not bring herself to object. "And it's not too soon. Not for you. See, my love, how wet you are. . . .You're ready for me."

Celia giggled a little, recalling suddenly how embarrassed she had been earlier. "So that's what that means. I thought when it first happened that something was wrong."

He laughed then, but gently, careful not to make fun of her. "Didn't your mother explain anything to you?"

"Of course she did," Celia retorted, defending Serena. Then, laughing with him, she added, "She told me everything that goes on between a man and a woman. Only it was . . . oh, you know, rather vague, and I didn't really understand."

"Well, you're going to understand now—and I am going to teach you."

He took her in his arms, holding her close for a moment, then began patiently, lovingly, to do just that.

INTERLUDE

19

Time, as Celia was to discover, had little meaning in Hawaii. Clocks might repose on carved wooden mantelpieces in the elegant homes of missionary descendants, but none could be seen, save as nonfunctioning ornaments, in simpler native huts or in the lush rain forests and sun-shimmering beaches where the heartbeat of an older, more traditional culture could still be felt. Here the days moved with deceptive slowness, drifting by like orchid petals on a languid breeze; yet as they turned into weeks, then one month, then two, and Celia looked back, she could not imagine where they had gone.

There had to be something in the air, she decided dreamily, a perfumed opiate that made it hard to remember other lands across the sea—and harder still to think of returning to them.

Those first two nights, she and Brandon had remained on board the *Moonwind*, crowded together in the narrow captain's bunk, not minding in the least, for sleep was the last thing on their minds. Then, on the morning of the third day, they moved ashore, taking possession of a small grass house which had just been completed the afternoon before.

It was a light, airy place, much prettier than she had pictured, and Celia was enchanted the instant she saw it. The style was vaguely reminiscent of native huts in Burma, though cooler and cleaner, and there was a faintly rustling sound as breezes stirred the thatched roof. The supporting poles were slender tree trunks—brought down from the mountains, Brandon told her—with smooth, fragrant pandanus matting stretched between. More matting covered the tamped-earth floor, on which stood a bed, its wooden legs set in saucers of water to discourage insects, a small chest of drawers, and a table with two caned chairs.

Gauze curtains, gaily colored, quivered in the unglazed windows, and Celia went over to one, brushing the fabric aside to look out. A spacious lanai, half again as large as the hut itself, ran all along one side; beyond it she could see a large shade tree, bright with blossoms, spreading a carpet of colorful petals across the lawn.

"Oh, it's so pretty!" She whirled back to the doorway. "I love it, Brandon. Really, I do! It's just like . . . like a playhouse!"

Brandon laughed, enjoying the novelty of the place through her eyes. It *was* like a playhouse, he thought, amused, and they were like children playing at a life that was only theirs through fantasy.

"I want you to like it here," he said, picking her up and tossing her impulsively in the air. "I want you to like being with me."

"As if I didn't." Celia smiled as he set her back on the floor, looking at her in a way that promised a speedy introduction to the comforts of the new bed, an idea to which she was not at all averse. "You know I like being with you—always."

Brandon did not disappoint her, and for the next hours she was too engrossed in feelings of the moment to think of anything else. Only later did reality intrude again, and as they sat at the table slicing into ripe papayas he had just picked from a tree in the yard, Celia found herself wondering what life was going to be like now that they seemed to be settling into a routine on the island. Clearly Brandon planned to stay with her, for a while at least—though how long "a while" might be, she had no idea, nor could she bring herself to ask. She was happy now with things as they were. Questions could only bring back the doubts she was not ready to face.

But there were other, everyday concerns about which she was intensely curious. And on these matters she did not hesitate to pester him with endless questions.

What were the people like who lived here? she wanted to know. Did they all have grass houses like this one? Did they eat lush tropical fruits, and fish from the sea every evening? When was he going to take her to see the rest of the island, as he had promised that first night on the beach? And when—oh, *when*—was he going to give her back the clothes he had stashed in the hold of the *Moonwind*?

"I don't think I can put on these ugly denim pants one more time! Oh, Brandon, I brought such *pretty* dresses with me! One especially. It's yellow muslin with the loveliest French ribbon—all pink and white. I can't wait until you see it!"

Brandon, who secretly liked the way she looked in those "ugly denim pants," just tight enough to accent the lines of a firm but delectably rounded derriere, demurred. "You can wear your finery when we go into town—if you think it's still in style. Though from what I've heard of female fashions, even a month is enough to make the most extravagant ball gown hopelessly out-of-date. But I'll be damned if I'm going to have you sitting around the house all boned-in like some blasted fortress, or carrying half a ton of petticoats every time we go for a walk on the beach!"

Celia, who had noticed that her gowns were at least half a year behind those on the streets of Hong Kong, and whose skin prickled at the very thought of all that extra fabric in such a sultry climate, might have been inclined to agree had it not been for one thing.

"I don't care what you say, Brandon. I'm so bored with dressing in trousers. And looking like a man! I want to wear something pretty again, just for a while—even if I suffer every second."

"Hardly like a man, my dear." Brandon raised one brow as his eye ran over curves that were distinctly unmasculine in form. "But I do get your point. As a matter of fact, though I couldn't resist teasing you, I've already taken care of the matter. Give me another twenty-four hours, and if you're not satisfied with the arrangements, I've made, I'll go into the hold personally and fetch your beloved gowns."

True to his word, he disappeared early the next morning, refusing, no matter how she coaxed, to say anything about where he was going or what he had in mind. When he returned an hour and a half later, a rainbow of exquisitely colored silks and cottons was strewn over the seat of the carriage.

Celia ran out to greet him, exclaiming with pleasure as she picked up one dress after another, holding each to the light so she could see it better. The gowns looked funny at first, for they were all loosely fashioned, with flowing lines and no proper waists at all, but the styles were so deliciously feminine, the colors such a tempting contrast to blue denim and wash-faded checks, her heart could not help rejoicing.

The design, Brandon told her, as she went inside to try them on, was patterned roughly after the *holoku*, a garment introduced by the missionaries shortly after their arrival.

"It seems," he said in dry tones, "they didn't like the way the ladies of the island were dressed."

"Why?" Celia was curious. "What were they wearing?"

"Essentially . . . nothing." Brandon grinned raffishly. "Imagine the affront to missionary propriety when those good gentlemen caught sight of their first massive brown-skinned woman with great bare breasts sagging to her waist, around which she might—or might not—have been wearing a belt of shells."

"And that was all?" Celia tried not to let it show, but like the missionaries, she too was shocked.

"Not even sandals," he agreed wickedly. "The ladies of the church soon put a stop to that, however. Before you could say 'John Calvin,' native femininity was swathed from head to toe in quaintly unflattering Mother Hubbards. Not a sinful ankle peeped from beneath those modest hems, nor a shapely wrist from long sleeves. Mercifully, native taste at least dictated that the things be made up in bright fabrics.''

And equally mercifully, Celia thought as she slipped the prettiest of the gowns over her head, Brandon had had the good sense not to follow the pattern too closely. The rounded neck dipped quite low, scandalously but flatteringly immodest, and little puffs of silk barely covered her shoulders, leaving both wrists and elbows bare. The front was slightly fitted, showing off curves that a man like Brandon Christopher would never willingly have disguised, even for comfort, but the back flared out in the subtle suggestion of a train.

The colors were perfect, suiting not only his taste but also hers. In place of the gaudy prints that so captivated the native eye, Brandon had selected pastels, delicate shades of pink and lavender and pale blue, the perfect foil for soft gray eyes and platinum hair.

"Oh, Brandon, I adore them. You were right. They're absolutely wonderful! I'd never ask for my old clothes back if I could always have things as pretty as this. Why . . ." She spun around, catching a glimpse of herself in a small mirror propped up on the chest. "I could wear this dress forever!"

"Not exactly . . . forever."

Brandon's lids drooped suggestively, giving his eyes a hooded look as he slipped the garment off her shoulders. The neck was just wide enough to allow the fabric to slide unimpeded to the floor.

"It's a fetching dress, my love, and you look beautiful in it . . . but you look even more beautiful like this."

"Ohhhh . . ." Celia shivered, sensing the provocative warmth of his hands a second before she felt them touch her breast. "You're impossible, do you know that? Don't you ever think of anything else?"

"Not often." He laughed as his fingers found her nipples, turning them into hard little peaks. "At least not when I'm with you." He drew her down on the ground then, not even waiting to move the short distance to the bed, making love to her right there, with an intensity that was completely, utterly satisfying.

It sometimes seemed, in those first blissful days together, that Brandon did indeed have little else on his mind; though, if she were going to be honest, Celia had to admit she hardly minded. When she woke in the morning, she would find him watching her, waiting only until her eyes opened to take her in his arms and do those things she had been dreaming about all night long. And often—quite shamefully, it seemed to her, though not at all unpleasantly—they didn't get out of bed until noon.

"You're a terrible influence," she teased one afternoon when he had lured her back into the hut with that look in his eye again. "I shouldn't let you do this."

But let him she did, and willingly, for once freed of the inhibitions that had been imposed on her by Victorian conventions, Celia found herself turning into quite a wanton—and enjoying every second of it!

Theirs was a shared passion, in the truest sense of the word, and if Celia was too naive to recognize the rarity of the relationship, Brandon was not. She might have forgotten the earlier conflicts that had held them at arm's length, but he remembered all too clearly, and he knew that the fragile loveliness of their soap-bubble world would not endure for long. It was a bittersweet awareness, one that gave their days and nights a certain savor, making him perhaps more attentive than he would otherwise have been.

Those early days were spent close to the hut. Later, Brandon promised, he would take her to explore the island—"when we can bear to be more than five minutes from a bed." For now it was enough to be together, to take the time to discover each other's wants and needs.

Something in his voice when he uttered those words, something in the way he nibbled only half-teasingly at her earlobe, made the proximity of a bed more appealing than ever, and Celia did not argue.

Often they would pass an entire day in the gardens surrounding the hut, or wander off to find a nearby pool where they could splash naked in crystalline waters rippling down from the hills. It was the contrasts Celia found most fascinating. The rise of the *palis*, deep green and brown in the distance. The flatness of the water, stretching blue and gem-bright to the horizon. The gentle roll of meadows dotted with green *ti* leaves and lemon-fragrant white hibiscus, with bougainvillea in rich shades of magenta and salmon pink, and yellow alamaneda and orange trumpet vine and snowflake-petaled star jasmine. The trees intrigued her, though she could not tell them apart, the *kous* and the *haus*, the *halas* with their narrow leaves, and the *milos*, out of which poi bowls and great canoes would one day be sculptured.

Other times, they strolled hand in hand along the deserted beaches, Brandon in a light shirt and trousers, Celia in one of her pretty new *holokus*, or sometimes the bathing costume he had had made for her when he learned she loved to swim.

It was an odd, unfashionable outfit, rather like a short dress with pantalettes beneath, and at first glimpse Celia had been tempted to refuse it altogether. Still, she had to admit when she finally put it on, it was more practical than the bulkier garments ladies usually wore to the beach, though it did have a disconcerting way of clinging, ocean-wet, to every contour of her body when she came out of the surf.

The day after he gave her the bathing dress, Brandon returned from one of his many short trips to check on the crew with a smooth curved board under his arm. This, he claimed, was a great favorite of the natives, who spent a good deal of time playing with it in the water. "They use it to ride the surf," he explained, and proceeded to demonstrate, swimming a fair distance out, waiting for just the right wave, climbing up on the board—and falling with a loud whoop into the water!

He was laughing good-naturedly a few seconds later when Celia plunged waist-deep into the surf to help him retrieve the board. Together they passed a delightful afternoon trying to master the sport, though neither of them proved very good at it. Brandon at least managed to stand for several seconds at a time, but Celia gave up after the first few tries and rode the great waves on her belly, shrieking with excitement when she splashed up on the sand.

"Well, never mind," Brandon said later as they lay exhausted and laughing on the beach. "The Hawaiians are better at it, but they have the advantage. A man's bathing suit is more sensible than a woman's, but it's still much too restrictive. We'd be more graceful too if we could try the thing naked—the way the natives do."

"Don't they wear anything at all?" Celia asked, fascinated in spite of herself. She had seen natives frolicking in the surf, and off in the distance, against the horizon, their bronzed bodies did look as if they might be displayed as nature had created them.

"Not a stitch. They used to come out on their boards to meet the whalers, in the ports at Lahaina and Honolulu, naked as jaybirds."

Celia, who had no idea what a jaybird was, and could not for the life of her imagine why it would be more naked than any other bird, found herself giggling at the image. "Anyway, I'm glad *I* have a bathing outfit. I wouldn't like to stand up for the first time and see a ship on the horizon—and have the captain and his crew waving at me."

"Neither would I, my love." Brandon laughed softly,

as though they had just shared a private joke no one else could understand. "I adore the sight of your body, free and unencumbered. But I don't want to share it with anyone else, even if I'm there to protect you."

The possessiveness of his words escaped her at the moment, for just then Brandon picked her up and carried her into the house, where shadows had begun to lengthen and curtains closed out the rest of the world. But later, lying in his arms, listening to the night sounds all around, Celia remembered what he had said, and suddenly she felt warm and safe.

It was almost, she thought as she drifted off to sleep, as if Brandon Christopher loved her . . . as she loved him.

The next morning, when she finally roused herself out of bed, Celia was surprised to see sunlight streaming across the matted floor of the hut. The divided doorway had been closed on the bottom to deter small animals, but the top was open, letting in a welcome breeze. Brandon was nowhere in sight, and she yawned lazily as she went over to the dressing table, which she had coaxed him to buy a few days before, telling him, only half-teasing, that a woman could never make do with one tiny mirror on a chest of drawers.

She had just finished brushing her hair and was coiling it in a loose knot on top of her head when suddenly she heard a hoarse cry from somewhere outside.

Jumping up, she hurried over to the door. Surely that was Brandon, she thought, alarmed. But all she heard now was a loud peal of masculine laughter. Pulling a pale lavender print dress over her head, she raced outside, curious to see what was happening.

Brandon was standing on a nearby knoll, his head turned away as he looked down in the direction of the beach. Celia reached him just in time to see the last of a long, straggling line of men, women, and children emerge from a grove of coconut palms. Sounds drifted up the hillside, shouts and chatter, mingling with laughter and spontaneous bursts of song.

That strange procession was led by a man and woman, Hawaiians of the most enormous proportions Celia had ever seen, though size was only part of their extraordinary effect. For a moment all she could do was stand there and stare at them in amazement.

They made a vivid picture. The man was clad in a broad *malo,* a scarlet girdle with a short yellow skirt dangling from it, presumably for modesty, though the gesture was muted by a broad expanse of brown chest, only half-hidden beneath a garland of *maile* leaves. The woman, like Celia, was wearing a *holoku,* but more traditionally cut, with long sleeves and a long regal train trailing behind her in the sand. The color was a bright pinkish red, startling enough in itself, but made even more so by an overprint of lustrous purple-red flowers. In her hand she carried an elaborate fan crafted of feathers in still another shade of red.

Brandon had already started forward, and Celia, not wanting to be left behind, hurried after him. As she approached, she saw that most of the merrymakers were natives, though there was a generous sprinkling of Orientals as well, especially among the younger people, and she was startled to catch sight of her old friend China Kwan. He had on a white shirt, with buttons open halfway down and sleeves rolled up to his elbows; below it was a patterned cotton skirt, not unlike the leader's, but simpler and longer, and his feet were bare. On his brow she saw a wreath of dark green leaves, brightened with red flowers, an almost exact mate to the one worn by a lithe and exceptionally beautiful Polynesian girl walking beside him.

Brandon got there first and almost immediately was so enveloped Celia could not even see where he had gone. She barely had time to be bewildered, for a pair of brown arms opened suddenly and she found herself clasped against an enormous red-and-purple-flowered bosom. The overflow of warmth and affection seemed natural to everyone else, for openness was a part of island life, but to a young girl raised with proper British restraint, it was distinctly disconcerting.

"You save Luka's boy," the woman said majestically as she released Celia to catch her breath. Her voice, like her person, was large, but pleasing, with a melodic lilt. "You Luka's daughter now. We all one big happy family, yes?" And with that cliché she pressed Celia to her breast again, half-stifling, as before.

China was there laughing when she finally extricated herself. "This is Luka," he said unnecessarily. "I told her how you swung down on a rope to rescue me, and she was most impressed. And this"—he gestured toward the large man, whose mouth opened in a broad toothless grin—"is her husband, Iopeka." He paused, eyes crinkling with merriment. "Luka is . . . my mother."

Celia laughed, assuming he meant the words as a joke, but as they started down the beach, following behind the boisterous procession, she learned that that was only half-true. The woman was, of course, no blood relation, but she was the closest thing to a mother China had ever known. His real mother, he told her, had died a short time after he was born, and Luka had been pressed into service as a wet nurse, for she had just given birth to a son of her own and had more than enough milk in her ample bosom for two. As he grew, the bond continued, and whenever he could, he had escaped to the cool interior valley where Luka's house was always overflowing with children and laughter.

"Luka and her husband were very good to me. Of course, that's not unusual here. Hawaiians always have room in their hearts—and their homes—for another child. It doesn't matter if he's Hawaiian, or a *pake* like me, or a *haole* like you. A child is a child. There's love enough for all."

The extent of that love became apparent a few minutes later when they arrived at a wide stretch of beach where markings in the sand showed that a pit had been gouged out of the earth, although it was now filled in again. The warmhearted couple had learned only two days before that China was back after an absence of nearly five years, but, typically, they had dropped everything and gathered their friends for a welcoming feast.

"But how could you do it so quickly?" Celia asked, looking wide-eyed as Iopeka came over to point out the *imu,* or barbecue pit, of which he was enormously proud. "Surely you must have work to be done. Were you able to leave it? Just like that?"

The man grinned, raising big brown shoulders in a careless shrug. "Work, it be done byem'bye," he said, introducing her to her first phrase in Hawaiian. "Byem'bye, it all gonna happen. Mo' bettah now we be with friends."

It was not, strictly speaking, a truly Hawaiian phrase, yet it typified the spirit of the islands. *Byem'bye,* something between "later" and "maybe" and "not at all, but does it matter?" A casual way of life, totally impractical, but with a certain charm all the same, and Celia could not help being intrigued.

"I suppose it's only natural," she said when Iopeka had gone off again, "that he would want to greet you as soon as possible. After all, you call Luka your 'mother,' so Iopeka must feel like he's your father."

"Not quite." China gave her a teasing look. "As a matter of fact, I never laid eyes on him before yesterday."

"But you said Luka and her husband were *both* kind to you."

"A slight misrepresentation." He laughed. "I should have said 'Luka and her *husbands.*' Hawaiians have a different way of looking at things, a kind of morality that's more . . . well, more generous than Europeans are used to." Celia saw him glance at the pretty girl who had been walking beside him, wondering perhaps if she shared the same instincts. "Luka's husbands always disappeared after a year or two. The next time I showed up, there'd be someone new at the table. They were all the same, big and jolly and full of laughter, and I thought the whole thing was great fun. I loved having all those Hawaiian 'uncles' to complement my serious, proper Chinese uncles in town.''

Celia did not have time to digest those rather startling words, for Brandon appeared just then, carrying a circlet of fresh frangipani, which he draped around her neck.

"Plumeria," he reminded her as she sniffed the familiar perfume-sweet scent. "Or *melia*, if you prefer. The natives often make garlands out of it, *leis*, as they are known here. Iopeka wanted to give me a strand of *maile* from his own neck—'for Luka's daughter,' he said—which, I assure you, is a great honor. *Maile* is reserved for close friends and honored guests. But I persuaded him that plumeria would suit you better." A wise choice, too, he thought, as he stepped back to look at her, for the waxy blossoms with their delicate pink-red veining brought out the fragile prettiness that had so captivated him the first time he saw her.

He, too, was wearing a *lei*, though his was somewhat more masculine, being fashioned of the same shiny green leaves that graced China's forehead, with only a few blood-red blossoms. Celia could not resist a smile as she saw it on him. Anywhere else, a man would have seemed vaguely effeminate, wearing flowers like that.

"I can't believe Luka and Iopeka arranged everything in only two days," she said, looking around at the surprisingly large crowd that had gathered to welcome China home. Some of the younger people had gone off along the beach, but children were playing nearby in the surf, and a small impromptu orchestra of native instruments had formed not far from the barbecue pit.

"You haven't seen anything yet," Brandon told her, laughing as he described the elaborate preparations that had been taking place for the last two days. As soon as the location for the *luau*, or feast, had been chosen, the *imu* was gouged out of the ground and lined with heated stones. Into it went the *kalua* pig, skinned and eviscerated and seasoned inside and out with soy sauce and salt water; together with *laulaus*, little bundles of pork and butterfish wrapped in *ti* leaves, and yams and tender taro shoots. Everything was then doused with water, covered with banana leaves and earth, and allowed to cook slowly until done to perfection.

"There was once a *luau* for a visiting king," China told her, "that took two hundred people a full day to prepare. Seventy large turtles were served, and there was a wall of kava root higher than a man and thirty-five feet long—and another wall containing thirty-five thousand yams."

"We can't expect anything quite as elaborate today—" Brandon cut in.

"Thank goodness!" Celia said, breathless at the thought.

"—but there'll be an enormous quantity of food. Most of the guests will stay for several days, until everything is gone."

"But that's so extravagant," Celia protested. "Can Luka and Iopeka afford all this?" It seemed a sensible question, but to her surprise, the two men burst out laughing.

"Hawaiians don't think of money the way Europeans do," China said. "There's no such thing as saving for a rainy day. If a *kanaka* comes into some cash, there's a feast for the entire village—and pretty soon it's all gone."

"A *kanaka*?"

"A native," Brandon explained. "That's their term for themselves. And China's right. Hawaiians *don't* look at things the way we do, from a self-centered point of view. Sharing is a way of life on the islands. Whatever one has, they all have—food, clothes, tobacco."

China nodded his agreement. "It's said that if one *kanaka* has money, all have money. If one is rich, all are rich."

Yes, for about twenty minutes, Celia thought, shaking her head at a life-style that was so different from anything she had experienced. She didn't know if she admired these people for their warmth and generosity or was appalled because they didn't have the sense to put aside even a little for a "rainy day."

Knowing that the feast would not be ready for some

time, China went off in his own direction, while Brandon and Celia strolled along the shore. Brandon rolled his pants legs up, as he had that first night when they had just come off the *Moonwind,* and Celia, not at all self-conscious now, hitched her skirt up in one hand, holding it almost to her knees as the water splashed over her feet and ankles.

Farther out, natives were swimming with their surf-boards, choosing the perfect wave to rise out of the water, and Celia paused to follow supple brown bodies as they leaned gracefully to one side or the other, moving with incredible ease. It seemed so simple when the *kanakas* did it, as if even a child could manage on the first try. And so much fun!

She had just turned to ask Brandon if they could try again the next morning, when she caught sight of a particularly lithe figure skimming with stunning skill across the water. Fascinated, she looked back, forgetting everything else as she watched.

It was the girl she had seen in the procession, the one who had been walking beside China Kwan. Wet hair flowed behind her, and a dark, glistening body seemed to fly, as if her feet had wings to carry her above the surface of the wave. It had just begun to crest, frothing white at the edge, when Celia realized suddenly that she was naked.

Even then, she could not tear her eyes away. There was something strangely compelling about the sight, more like a work of art, a statue by some ancient master, than a naked body to cause embarrassment. The girl was exceptionally tall, nearly six feet, but she was well-formed, with large firm breasts and surprisingly slim hips tapering into long, perfectly shaped legs. An aura of sensuality surrounded her, yet in a strange way she seemed innocent too, as if her nakedness were the most natural thing in the world.

A soft chuckle sounded in Celia's ear, warning her that Brandon was watching not the girl, but her—and he was amused at her reaction.

"I *am* shocked," she said, blushing belatedly. "And I

can see why the missionaries were horrified. But . . . oh,
Brandon, she is beautiful, isn't she?''

"She is indeed," he agreed, secretly pleased at the
nonjudgmental way she was coming to accept the islands.
"And we aren't the only ones who think so." He nodded
toward the spot where China Kwan was standing on the
shore, so mesmerized he had not even noticed that his long
gingham skirt was wet all the way up to his calves.

Celia laughed as she recalled the way he had looked at
the girl when they were talking before. "He does seem
taken with her," she said.

"Her name is Kalani," Brandon told her. "Iopeka mentioned it before, though I'm sure I would have picked her
out anyway. She's an orphan, like China, and Luka raised
her—so in a way she's a sister to him. She was still a child
when he went away, but even then she was lively and
vivacious, and he's told me more than once that he was
curious to see how she turned out."

Celia watched skeptically as Kalani leapt from the board,
spinning around to catch it in her hands.

"It doesn't seem to me he's looking at her at all like a
sister."

"Oh, I don't know," Brandon replied wickedly. "Islanders have their own way of doing things. The royal
Hawaiians often married their sisters—and of course, China
and the girl aren't related by blood."

Kalani had tossed her surfboard on the sand and was
running along the beach, shaking the water out of her hair
as she headed for China. Just before she reached him, she
stooped and in one graceful gesture caught up a bright
length of cotton and draped it around her body. The fabric
clung as she moved, creating an even more sensuous effect
than her nudity of a moment before.

She was taller than China, but they made a striking
couple as they turned and walked slowly away from the
beach. China had one hand on her waist; now he dropped
it, letting it rest suggestively on the rounded curve of her
buttocks. Far from being annoyed, she began to laugh,

bending her head to whisper something in his ear. Then quite openly, without a backward glance, they headed toward a cluster of shrubs that separated the sand from the more sheltered inland fields.

Celia stared after them, so shocked for a moment she couldn't speak. It was Brandon who broke the silence, resting both hands on her shoulders as he turned her gently to face him. "There's nothing wrong with physical love, my sweet," he reminded her with a teasing half-smile. "Even in the middle of a *luau*. After all, they aren't doing anything we haven't done ourselves."

In spite of herself, Celia had to smile back. She *was* being a hypocrite, looking down her nose at someone for doing boldly what she was all too ready to do in secret. Still, try as she would, she couldn't imagine herself walking off with a man that way—even the man who was openly her lover.

She and Brandon continued to wander along the beach, speaking every now and then, but for the most part enjoying each other's company without words, until an hour or so later when the tempting aroma of roast pork drew them back to the *imu*. The *kalua* pig had just been exhumed, and as they approached, they could see it lying in full splendor on a bed of banana leaves. The smell was even more heavenly now, and Celia's mouth began to water, reminding her suddenly that she had had no breakfast and was very hungry.

Brandon flattened out a wide leaf to form a makeshift platter they could share. "The natives don't bother with such niceties," he said, "but we *malihinis* cling to our tableware." Laughing, he tore off a few pieces of the roasted flesh, laying them beside a small pile of *laulaus* and other intriguing-looking items. Celia found a patch of shade beneath a coconut palm, and as Brandon sat beside her, set out to explore the new dishes with relish.

The pork was every bit as delicious as it looked, melting on her tongue almost the instant she put it in her mouth, and the fish, though seasoned only with salt water, took on a delicate flavoring from the leaves in which it had been wrapped. Even the yams, odd-looking tubers, rather like yellowish potatoes, had an unexpected sweetness when she bit into them. There was also a calabash of raw fish, "cooked" in a marinade of lime juice and coconut cream, and great salty black mollusks, and tender morsels of chicken and taro tops. Huge chunks of breadfruit were barely warm now, for they had been cooked earlier in the day, but they had a smooth, pleasant texture and delectable raisinish taste.

"How greedy you are," Brandon said, amused, as he watched her lick the last traces of pork fat from her fingers. "It's lucky I had all those *holokus* made. If you keep eating like this, you won't be able to fit into anything else."

Celia grinned, enjoying the attention—and trying not to think how true it was going to be if she had many more meals like this. She was still laughing a few minutes later when Iopeka came over, beaming as he held out a beautifully carved wooden bowl.

One look at the chalky substance it contained—and one whiff of that sharp, spicy aroma—was enough to convince Celia that it might not be such terribly bad manners to shake her head and politely say no.

If Iopeka was offended, he did not show it. In fact, the way he was chuckling, it almost seemed to Celia he had expected the refusal. He extended the bowl next to Brandon, who accepted it, but took only a sip or two before handing it back.

"Just as well you didn't try it," he whispered, winking broadly as Iopeka moved on to offer the bowl to other guests. "That was *awa*, spelled with a W, but pronounced, as many of the island words are, with a V. It's the ceremonial drink of Hawaii, made from the root of the pepper shrub. The men prepare it by chewing—their saliva converts some of the starch to sugar—then spit it into a bowl and mix in water."

"They *spit* it into the bowl." Celia ran her tongue over

her lips, almost tasting the stuff, even though she hadn't touched it. "You're right. I'm glad I *didn't* try it."

Brandon did, however, insist that she sample one of the other native dishes. It came in a large calabash, generously filled to the brim, and was an odd purplish-pink, looking like a runny paste that had been artificially dyed.

"It's called *poi*," he informed her. "And you'll be glad to hear that while it's also made from a root, the taro root, it isn't chewed, but boiled. It looks a little like Rocquefort when it's fully cooked, and incidentally, it's quite tasty like that, but the islanders prefer to pound it with a lava hammer on a *poi* board until it turns into a glutinous goo. Luka will have spent hours preparing this for the *luau*. It'll hurt her feelings if you don't at least taste it."

Sensing he was right, Celia pressed two fingers together and dipped them into the calabash, the way he showed her, swirling them around and bringing them to her lips with an appropriate smacking sound.

"Ugh!" she said, careful to control her face in case Luka was watching. "This stuff not only looks like paste, it tastes like it too."

Brandon laughed. "It's an acquired taste," he admitted as he licked it off his fingers, seemingly without revulsion. "It's not a bad one to develop, though. *Poi* is a remarkably nutritious starch, more digestible than potatoes and more nourishing than rice. They say an infant of two weeks can eat it safely, and it won't harm an elderly stomach ravaged by ulcers."

"I am sure that's true, my dear," Celia said demurely, "but right now, as you pointed out, I've had more than enough to eat—and I'm sure we could coax some of these little urchins to carry off the calabash and destroy the evidence."

Brandon agreed, laughing as he beckoned to a nearby lad, who was so delighted at his good fortune, he didn't stop to question the strange behavior of *haoles* who chose not to finish their portion of *poi*.

"I was hoping you wouldn't want it," Brandon murmured, his voice dropping so low only Celia could hear. "For I had it in mind to lure you off someplace where we could be alone."

Celia looked puzzled; then her cheeks burned hot. "Oh no, Brandon!" She couldn't keep a scandalized note out of her voice as she recalled the way she had felt earlier, when China and the pretty Hawaiian girl wandered off into the shrubbery. It occurred to her suddenly they had not yet reappeared, though that had been fully two hours before. "We shouldn't . . . I mean we *can't* do something like that."

"Ah, but we *can*—and we're going to." He had already coaxed her up, even before she knew what was happening, and she could feel him leading her almost in the direction those other two lovers had taken. "I've longed to be alone with you all afternoon—and you know it, vixen. The sight of you, so close, so untouchable, has been driving me mad."

"But, Brandon . . ." Celia tried to pull away, but he was too strong. Or perhaps, she thought helplessly, she wasn't trying as hard as she meant to. "Everyone is going to see where we're going. They'll guess—"

"They won't guess," he said, laughing. "They'll *know*— and they won't give a damn. If they say anything, which I doubt, it will only be: 'What a lucky devil, finding a beautiful woman like that.' "

Celia held back one last moment, sensing that what he was asking was wrong, though why, she had no idea, if they wanted each other and it didn't bother anyone else. Then they were behind the screen of white hibiscus, and it was too late to protest, nor did she truly want to, for her own blood, like his, had begun to boil, stirring with the unquenchable emotions he always sparked in her.

"There, you see?" He sank to his knees on the sand, drawing her with him. "No one will intrude on us here. And no one will see what we're doing—unless, of course, someone is watching from the hillside with a captain's glass . . . which I very much doubt."

"You are incorrigible." Celia was surprised to find her arms opening, willing accomplices to the assault he had planned. "You have no shame."

"None at all."

She shivered as his hand slipped under her skirt, finding just the right spot, moving with a sure instinct, honed by the weeks they had been together.

Her first soft cry dissolved a second later into little whimpers as he forced her back on the ground. The graceful Hawaiian robe offered no protection, yielding as he urged it up, baring her hips, her breasts. His tongue sought her nipples; his lips traced a course of searing kisses down her belly, coming to rest where his fingers had touched her with such devastating effect before.

No longer were her responses her own. Brandon was manipulating her, playing her body like an instrument, knowing just when and where to touch her . . . when to draw back for an instant. Her legs coiled around his neck, instinct guiding her as she clasped him in a tender vise. Her fingers tangled in his hair, and she was clinging, daring him to try to get away.

Then suddenly it was there, the moment she had been waiting for, and she surrendered, trembling, to the sweet torment he had devised for her. Her entire body seemed to quiver with a thousand tiny convulsions, then relaxed as she felt him slide upward, taking her lovingly in his arms.

"Now who's incorrigible?" he murmured. "And insatiable."

He shifted his weight on top of her, trying to be gentle, but not succeeding, for he was too inflamed by her beauty and passion to hold back as he had intended. Celia responded almost immediately, sensing even before he moved that he was preparing to take her, just as he had sensed that she was ready again, with no need for interludes or preliminaries.

She sighed as she felt him penetrate her, deeply, urgently, driving everything away, until there was no more ocean crashing against the shore, no sun burning down on the sand . . . just she and Brandon Christopher alone in their own private world.

20

Unless, of course, someone is watching from the hillside with a captain's glass, Brandon had said. A playful quip, which Celia had not taken seriously—though perhaps she should have, for even at that moment a polished brass telescope was trained on them from behind a clump of tall grasses halfway up the slope.

Teresa Valdes stared down at the lovers for a long time. Then slowly she lowered the glass, her pretty features contorting with rage and hatred.

The blond bitch!

Anger exploded inside her, flooding in a torrent that only half-masked a sudden searing stab of jealousy. The glass was powerful: she had not failed to see every detail of the sheer pleasure on Celia's face when Brandon laid his head between her legs, ravishing her with the same skillful tongue that she, Teresa, knew only too well—and that even now, though she hated herself for it, she burned to feel again.

Yes, and she had seen the way the slut responded, too, when Brandon—without a moment's respite—had mounted her the way a dog went after a bitch in heat! She wouldn't have minded so much if Celia hadn't relished it, if she had surrendered passively to Brandon Christopher's male urges, loving him perhaps, but not enjoying him so completely. Not wallowing in his masculinity the way she herself had so many times in the past.

Her fingers tightened around the glass, and she raised it again, steadying her hand with an act of will.

The lovers had finished now and were lying there panting, short heavy gasps that made the woman's full breasts rise and fall disgustingly. They had not even undressed completely, so eager had they been to get at each other. Celia's lavender-flowered gown was bunched up around her neck, Brandon's pants pulled halfway down—that was all. Now they seemed to be laughing as they remedied the situation, easing off the offending garments, cuddling naked in each other's arms.

"Well, if it isn't the little voyeur. I wouldn't have thought this was your game, Teresa—peeping at other people's passions. You always preferred your ecstasies firsthand."

The voice jolted into her thoughts, and Teresa folded the telescope with a snap and spun around. "What are you doing here, Maarten? Spying on me?"

"While you're spying on them? An intriguing thought. Actually, I was taking a walk when I noticed you crouching in the grasses. I must admit I was curious—and a bit surprised when I saw what you were looking at. Not that I blame you. It is an . . . amusing scene."

"Hardly *amusing*." Teresa retreated a short distance, taking cover in a grove of saplings. "Only you would choose such a word."

"*Titillating*, then." He followed her into the grove, laying a hand on the front of her blouse, bolder now than he had been early in their relationship. "Don't tell me that little tableau didn't excite you, because it's written all over your face. Whatever he was giving her, and I can make a damn good guess, you want it too. Lucky for you . . ." His hand began to move slowly, deliberately massaging her small breasts through the sheer silken fabric. To his surprise, she twisted away, her head snapping back as black eyes flashed a warning.

"*Lucky* for me? What do you think, Maarten? That all

you have to do is fondle my bosom and I'll swoon in your arms? Get away from me! I'm in no mood for you today."

"So . . ." Skye whistled under his breath as his eyes drifted down the hillside. The lovers were quiet now, as if they had fallen asleep. Ordinarily Teresa showed little discrimination when it came to relieving her physical needs. But today, with *them* down there . . .

"I had wondered," he said softly, "but I couldn't be sure. Not until now. You're in love with him."

"Love?" Teresa spat out the word. "What a fool you are, Maarten, if you think that! I don't *love* Brandon Christopher. Haven't you eyes to see? I hate him!"

"Do you indeed?" Skye took a step backward, eyeing her with amusement. "Perhaps. But then, love and hate are very close, don't you think?"

His lips curled up as she turned and started angrily down the hill, not even bothering to hide behind the foliage now. The smile was not a mirthful one. It had already occurred to him that this little obsession of Teresa's could be dangerous. God knows, it had been foolhardy in the extreme, tearing after the Tiger like that, when the smart thing would have been to stay in Hong Kong and regroup their forces. And now that she had actually seen him with his blond mistress, now that that tender scene was no longer merely in her imagination, there was no telling what she might do.

Still, it was . . . well, interesting the way things had turned out. He began to move slowly down the slope, making no more effort than Teresa to conceal himself from the lovers, who were too self-absorbed to notice anything else. It had come as quite a shock, catching his first glimpse of the woman Teresa had been ranting about since that skirmish with the *Moonwind*—and learning that she was none other than vivacious little Celia St. Clair.

He had not given a thought to his absent fiancée since he left Burma; now, it seemed, she had not been thinking of him either. He would have given a penny or two to find out what had brought her here. Had she come to Hong

Kong looking for him and gotten tangled up with the Tiger instead? Not that his curiosity was likely to be satisfied, for the time being at least. Still, whatever had occurred, one thing was plain. The lady had other things on her mind than fretting over Schuyler Maarten.

He caught up with Teresa on the narrow dirt path that wound inland from the base of the hill, but he did not try to press his company on her, sensing from her demeanor that she was still angry. He was a bit sorry now, thinking it over, that he hadn't taken advantage of the opportunity Celia had given him that last morning on the banks of the Irrawaddy. It would have been diverting, feeling all that smoldering sensuality erupt into passion for the first time at his hands.

Diverting, too, to look down at the couple in the grassy hollow and know that *he* had had her first.

And that Brandon Christopher was aware of it.

The noise of the *luau* barely penetrated the cool interior glen that Teresa had entered. As Skye followed a few paces behind, he was surprised to see a small girl standing in the center of the path, sniveling, quite unpleasantly, it seemed to him. He had assumed all the local children were on the beach listening to the music, begging, no doubt with those same snuffling sounds, for handouts from the revelers.

To anyone else the little waif might have appeared winsome, but Skye disliked children, especially toddlers of three or four, and he found nothing particularly appealing in those round dark eyes and swarthy features, bespeaking a mingling of Polynesian and Oriental blood. Teresa, however, had stopped beside the child, bending to examine the scraped knee that had produced those god-awful howls.

Any other time, Skye would barely have noticed, for Teresa, surprisingly, was fond of youngsters, relating to them in a way she rarely did with adults. But today he would have thought she was too caught up in her own moods to care about anything else.

Teresa remained with the child for several minutes,

speaking in soothing tones until the crying finally subsided. She had just stood up, though her hand was still on
that tousled mop of hair—probably licey too, Skye thought
with a shudder—when a boy appeared in the thick undergrowth that rimmed the side of the road. He could have
been no more than eight or nine years old, but the instant
he saw a stranger touching the little girl, he leapt onto the
path with as menacing a look as he could muster.

Teresa drew her hand back but made no move to retreat.
"Your little sister?" she asked gently.

She waited a few seconds, then dipped her hand into her
pocket and held out a coin. The boy did not move, but
stared at it in silent suspicion.

"Here, take it," she pressed. "Buy the little girl something good to eat. She's hungry. You too."

The boy continued to stare at the coin, conflicting emotions showing in his face. He was not used to kindness—he
feared a trick—yet obviously he wanted to believe. Then,
greed getting the better of caution, he grabbed the money
out of Teresa's hand, and clutching the girl by the arm,
pulled her back into the undergrowth. One last glimpse of
bright eyes showed through the foliage, curious now, not
quite so frightened, before he vanished altogether.

"They are so timid," Teresa said softly, as if to herself,
"these children who live by their wits, with no one to care
for them. They want the food at the *luau*, but they are
afraid to go and ask for it. They want the coin in my hand,
but they are afraid to reach out and take it."

Skye raised a curious brow as she glanced back at him.

"Very generous, Teresa," he said dryly. He had not
failed to see the size of the coin she had given the boy.
"That was more than enough to buy a good meal—or
two."

"I know what it is to be afraid, Maarten. You, who
were born in a big house with all the food you ever
wanted, cannot understand that. I also know what it is to
need friends, and if I stay here, I'm going to need every
friend I can get."

If she stayed. Skye suddenly felt cold. A premonition? "You're seriously considering such recklessness, then? A bold raid is out of the question, you know—the Tiger has his men all around. I thought by now you'd have realized how much wiser it would be to meet him on the open seas."

"Where I have the advantage—as you reminded me before? Yes, of course it's wiser. I know that, Maarten—I'm not stupid. But the choice may not be mine. I wish now . . ."

She broke off, recalling the one chance she had had to defeat Brandon Christopher at sea, and hating herself for not taking it. Something ugly and twisting, like a knife blade, tore at her gut as she saw him again in that blond hussy's embrace. Damn, she had been a fool! She'd see him dead before she subjected herself to such torture again!

"Well, never mind," she said abruptly. "The Tiger seems to be settling in quite comfortably—it doesn't look as if he's planning on leaving Hawaii, at least for a while. I think, like it or not, we may *have* to face him here. And for that"—she smiled darkly as she glanced back at the underbrush, motionless now—"I'm going to have to gather my forces."

Skye looked amused. "Children, Teresa? Are you as hard up as all that?"

"Hard up? Come, Maarten, think about it. You saw that crowd at the *luau* today. That man of Brandon's—that China Kwan—knows people all over the island. If I try to recruit someone, how can I be sure it isn't a friend of his? Or a relative of one of those *kanakas* on the beach? But children? Little strays no one knows? They couldn't betray me if they wanted to."

"True," Skye admitted, seeing the validity of what she was saying. "But even so, what use can you make of them?"

"To run errands perhaps, to spy for me, to ferret out information anyone else would have trouble getting. Children can be very wily, Maarten—make no mistake about that—and they do have a certain advantage. They are always underfoot, you see. Everyone takes them for granted. No one *sees* them.''

A new brightness had come into her eyes, warning Skye not to press her. He still didn't like the idea of confronting the Tiger on land—they were too close to equal there, didn't have the *Black Jasmine* and the *Red Peony* to back them up—but he had a feeling she was right. The choice wasn't going to be theirs. Not if she couldn't let go of Brandon Christopher.

''Then you think it's going to be here?'' he said slowly. ''In Hawaii?''

''I think it's going to be here.''

21

A few days after the *luau*, China Kwan appeared at the small grass house, almost with the first morning light, to extend an invitation to Brandon and Celia.

"The daughter of one of our neighbors is getting married," he said, smiling apologetically as they dressed and hurried out to greet him. "They're a poor family, so of course it won't be a grand occasion, but I think you might find it interesting. We Chinese are a thrifty people, but we have our extravagances too, like the *kanakas*. And ceremonies are important to us."

Brandon, who had never attended a Chinese wedding, though he had often seen the elaborate processions pass him on the street, was quick to accept. He did not always understand the Oriental cultures, but he had a deep respect for them and rarely missed an opportunity to study their most solemn customs. Besides, he had been making plans of late, albeit sketchily—plans that increasingly included Celia—and he was eager to have her learn more about these islands he had come to love.

"All you've seen so far are the beaches and coconut palms," he teased. "And the only ritual you've experienced is a native feast. Very charming, to be sure, but there's more to Hawaii than that. People from many backgrounds have come together here, not always comfortably, but with an intermingling I've never found anyplace else. Even the Polynesians were immigrants originally, paddling up on the beaches in their dugout canoes. Then the whites came, missionaries and whaling captains who stayed on to found the great sugar empires and trading firms. Now Chinese laborers are descending in droves, and it doesn't look as if they're going to be content to work out their contracts and go home again.''

China grinned. ''Upstarts, all of us. And you're right— there *is* a unique intermingling here. But we cling to our own ways too, as you'll see today.''

He had brought a hired carriage, and the three of them crowded together on the narrow seat as the coachman prodded the horses into a slow trot. The ride into town was a long one, but Celia did not mind, for the terrain of the islands changed with each passing mile, and she was fascinated by everything she saw.

''Look at that!'' she would cry as they rode through an irrigated valley dotted with shaggy banana groves and stands of mulberry trees, whose bark was used for making *kapa* cloth. Or, ''Oh, how pretty!'' as she spotted a dazzling shower tree, its showy mantle of yellow blossoms catching and reflecting the sunlight. Trumpet vines, with tongues of orange flame, seemed to grow wild by the sides of the road, mingling with hibiscus hedges and rare white bougainvillea and scarlet-plumed royal poinciana, which Brandon said had been imported all the way from Madagascar, an island she knew only vaguely from the maps in her geography book.

The red dust of the plains gave way after a while to majestic *palis*, rising, sometimes gently, sometimes in sheer rock walls out of the earth. The air was cooler as they rose on twisting trails that threaded through the hills, and Celia was chilly enough to appreciate the embroidered silk shawl China had brought for her.

''I knew you'd dress too lightly,'' he explained. ''You *malihinis*—you newcomers—think the sunshine is always warm on the islands.''

Celia laughed, enjoying the thoughtfulness of the gesture. She was feeling relaxed enough to tease him just a

little about the beautiful Hawaiian girl who had caught his
fancy at the *luau,* though she was tactful enough not to
mention the way they had gone off together.

"She really is quite lovely, China," she said, her eyes
lighting with mischief. "Should Brandon be worried? Are
you thinking of leaving the sea and settling down?"

"I would never leave the sea—as long as my captain
needs me." China's voice had turned unexpectedly serious, but only for a second. "Besides, I'm the ablest man
on the *Moonwind.* Brandon could never manage without
me."

"True," Brandon agreed, laughing.

"You'd give up Kalani, then?" Celia watched for his
reaction. "That pretty girl. Be honest, now—can you look
me in the eye and tell me truly you haven't thought of
marrying her?"

China looked flustered. "Well, yes, I have *thought* of
it. You see . . ." He glanced over at Brandon, whose face
seemed to tighten just for a second. "Kalani . . . works in
town, and I do not approve. I'd give a great deal to get her
out of that life and bring her home—where she belongs."

That one word, "works," so plainly distasteful on China
Kwan's lips, brought a smile to Celia's as she recognized
the masculine prejudices that had prompted it. She was
intrigued, too, for never in her sheltered life had she been
exposed to the world of working women, but try as she
would, she couldn't coax either of the men to talk about it.

"But if you disapprove so much," she persisted, "if
you want to get Kalani out of 'that life' so badly, I would
think you'd be all the more anxious to marry her."

"I might consider it," he admitted, "if it weren't for
two things. I don't think Kalani is interested in marrying
me. And I'm sure my grandmother wouldn't permit it."

"Your grandmother?" Celia said, surprised. China had
always seemed so independent to her. She couldn't imagine his asking permission for anything, especially from a
female relative. "Didn't you tell me you had several uncles? I assumed one of them was your guardian."

"Officially, yes." His eyes crinkled with amusement. "Eldest Uncle. But Chinese women are very strong. It's not at all unusual for one to be the real head of the family, even though she bows to her man in public." The laughter broke in his voice, spilling out. "Wait till you see my grandmother. Then you'll understand."

The road sloped down, angling through one last shallow pass and opening onto a parched grass plain. The scent of the sea had grown strong again, and Celia leaned over the edge of the carriage, craning her neck for her first glimpse of Honolulu. She had been completely happy these past weeks alone with Brandon, but she couldn't help being excited at the idea of seeing crowded streets again, bustling with people, and elegant homes and pretty shop windows.

That first view of the outskirts of town, however, was a disappointment. Neither the houses she had so wistfully imagined nor the land on which they were situated held any great appeal. The weather was hotter here than on the windward shore, the air oppressively humid, and the ground was covered only with the scantest vegetation. It came as no surprise when Brandon told her that the missionary wives had hated the place, complaining bitterly of the heat and dust.

"It's the harbor that makes the city," he explained. "No, not aesthetically—don't look at me like that, I know it's not particularly attractive. But there's a good channel through the coral reefs, and the water is deep right up to the shore. It's large enough, and sheltered enough, so a hundred ships can lie at anchor at one time."

Celia wrinkled her nose distastefully, though she had to admit the town looked slightly more presentable as they began to roll west along Beretania Street. Houses here, for the most part, were simple, rather boxlike wooden structures, but they were large and well-tended, with coral foundations and cool covered *lanais* running all around. The lots were large, the structures set well back, with broad grassy lawns and neatly planted gardens giving evidence that the descendants of those first missionary wives took pride in their homes.

The city changed character again as they turned left on Nuuanu Street, passing Hotel and King, then right on Merchant, heading for the waterfront. Now they were entering the section known as Chinatown, and narrow rutted dirt lanes had a disconcerting way of jogging around open cesspools in the ground. Buildings were crammed together, an indiscriminate assortment of stables and open-fronted restaurants, houses, pig sties and privies, all without ventilation or proper drainage. The gutters were particularly unpleasant, swarming with lice and fleas; and scrawny brown rats lurked in the shadows, waiting only for darkness to come out and scavenge.

The carriage pulled to a stop in front of a house that looked dismally like all the others. Cheap wooden slatting faced the front, some of the boards coming loose, others held precariously by rusty nails that jutted out of the surface. All that seemed to hold it together in places was an odd assortment of long bracing poles.

Was this where China lived?

Celia gaped at the place in dismay. She had not realized, though perhaps she should have, that his family was so poor. It occurred to her what a sacrifice it must have been, scraping together enough money to send one of the boys to be educated in America. No wonder China felt so close to them. And no wonder he was ready to defer to whatever they asked.

Brandon's hand touched her arm, and she thought she caught a glimmer of laughter as he said, "There's an old saying, my love, trite, but very true: Don't judge a book by its cover. Wait till you see what's inside."

Celia was still skeptical, but said nothing as China helped her out of the carriage. At least she could be grateful for one thing, she thought, lifting her skirt to raise it out of the dust. The rains didn't come as frequently here as on windward Oahu. Otherwise, the streets would be rivers of mud and refuse.

Once through the gate, however, she was forced to reevaluate her thinking, for the house, as Brandon had hinted, was clean and surprisingly elegant. True, the doors were not set in a straight line, giving the rooms an oddly asymmetrical look, but that, as she later learned, was to keep the dragon of happiness from escaping. And if the ground sloped noticeably downward—toward, never away from the house—it was so that good fortune could not slip away.

The central room, opening off the entry court, was shared by the entire Kwan family, whose private chambers were located elsewhere in that surprisingly large complex. Here, as in many Chinese homes, simplicity and practicality vied with a love of garish color. Imported teak floors, exquisite as they might be, had been chosen more for their durability than their sheen; the walls were plastered and whitewashed twice yearly to control the mildew in that humid climate, and furnishings were kept to a minimum. But the rounded support poles had been lacquered a high-gloss red, and red wall scrolls with gilded sayings from Confucius hung in various places on the walls. From her shrine in the far corner, Kuan Yin, the Goddess of Mercy, flanked by meticulously arranged tablets bearing the names of honored ancestors, looked down on daily offerings of incense and fresh-cut flowers.

China laughed at Celia's frankly astonished expression. "You expected garbage on the floors? Rats scurrying all around? Well, never mind—you're supposed to. Old Grandmother, as everyone calls her, says we must not tempt the jealousy of the gods by flaunting our wealth on the outside. Of course, she's a shrewd lady, and it may also have occurred to her that it's wise not to let the riffraff on the street guess which houses may contain possessions of value."

He was still laughing as he led them into the kitchen, a large room comfortably cluttered with rice barrels and chopping boards, jars of pickles on the counter, and bunches of dried vegetables and glistening oil-covered ducks hang-

ing on bamboo rods from the ceiling. A pot of water was
kept boiling day and night on the great iron cookstove that
dominated one end of the room. Above was the shrine of
the Kitchen God, a most important deity, for it was he
who reported to the heavens every New Year's on the
family's conduct.

Old Grandmother was stooping over a block on the far
side of the room when they entered, her hands moving
deftly as she chopped up strange-looking seasonings Celia
did not recognize. At first glance there was nothing to
distinguish her from all the other elderly Chinese women
on the street. Her dress was typical, a pair of threadbare
black trousers and a black tunic buttoned up the side, and
her thinning gray hair had been pulled into a bun at the
back of her head. As she set aside her work, however, and
came forward, rubbing her hands briskly on her pants,
Celia was aware of alert dark eyes taking in everything at
once.

Why, she's like her house, Celia thought, amused. Shabby
on the outside to fool thieves and jealous gods, but trim
and tidy inside. And definitely above average in quality.

The old woman moved slowly, but there was a bustling
air about her as she sat them at a rough wooden table,
China on one side, Brandon and Celia on the other. Going
from the counter to the stove, then back to the table again,
she insisted on fussing over them, setting out a row of
blue-and-white cups into which she poured a pale musky-
scented tea. She seemed especially fond of Brandon, for
she hovered over him a good part of the time, alternately
chattering and scolding, speaking sometimes in the Pid-
gin English that served as a common denominator on the
islands, sometimes in Chinese, which, to Celia's surprise,
Brandon answered in kind.

She had just started to ask him about it, when he broke
off the conversation, reaching out with one arm to draw
her toward him. "Well, Old Grandmother, what do you
think?" he said in English. "Here I have brought a beautiful woman home to meet my Chinese family, and you

haven't said a word about her. Tell me, do you approve of my taste?''

Shrewd eyes turned to Celia, studying her carefully, *judging*, it seemed, for the briefest of seconds. Then her wrinkled features relaxed, breaking into a broad smile, and she let out a spate of what sounded like approval. At least Celia hoped it was, for she was getting to like the old woman.

"She says," Brandon translated, "that you are very pretty." He leaned closer with a wink. "And right she is, too—not that I needed anyone to tell me."

Celia flushed, enjoying the compliment, but confused all the same. "How do you know what she's saying, Brandon? Do you speak Chinese?"

"I do and I don't." He laughed. "In the years I've been in the Orient, I've managed to learn Mandarin, which is one of the more important dialects, though not the one Old Grandmother speaks. She knows only a few words, but she makes a point of using them, more I suspect to humor me than for any other reason. It's a little game we play."

"I don't understand." Celia wrinkled her brow. "You sound as if you've met China's grandmother before." But when? she thought, puzzled. He had rarely been out of her sight, and then only for short times—never long enough to make the trip into Honolulu.

Brandon looked sheepish. "I have," he confessed, then went on to explain that he had visited the Kwan household several times on previous trips to Hawaii. China had been obliged to remain with the *Moonwind* in Hong Kong—he was in command whenever the captain was absent—but Brandon, realizing that his family would be worried, made a point of calling to reassure them.

And made a point of not mentioning it, too, Celia thought, smiling to herself as she remembered the way he had gotten in touch with her parents, knowing they too must be beside themselves with worry. It was funny, how sensitive and considerate Brandon Christopher could sometimes be—and how embarrassed he was to be caught out in his kindnesses.

Platters of rice cakes appeared on the table, and little steamed buns filled with sweet bean paste, which smelled delicious and tasted even better, for they had brought nothing with them in the carriage but a few pieces of fresh fruit. Brandon took time between mouthfuls to tease the old woman, telling her she was too shrewd for her own good—which she took as a high compliment—and warning her she would never have a chance to enjoy her riches if she hoarded every penny to invest in land and new businesses.

"You should use some of the money to buy yourself a pretty dress, Old Grandmother." He grinned. "A nice slinky *cheong sam* with a slit up the side to show off your legs."

The old woman was still chuckling as she went over to the stove to steam up another portion of buns, not at all insulted apparently by the comment or the mode of address. But to Celia it seemed strange, and she leaned over to whisper to Brandon:

"I know China said everyone calls her Old Grandmother, but isn't that disrespectful? Anyhow, it sounds so . . . well, so impersonal. Doesn't she have a name?"

Brandon laughed. "Presumably, but I wouldn't dream of using it. A Chinese woman is never known as herself: she's known by her relationship to others. She is 'Ful-ai's Wife' or 'Fats-ai's Mother' or perhaps 'Ninth Aunt' for her position in the family. The old grandmother is simply that—'Old Grandmother'—and the only disrespect would be to ask her what her name is. I doubt if her grandsons themselves know, perhaps not even her own sons."

At that moment China, who had gone out to check on the impending festivities, came back to report that they were about to begin. The women would soon be dressing the bride, he told them, a highly ritualistic ceremony which he and Brandon naturally could not witness. But

Celia, as an honored guest of the powerful Kwan family, was invited to attend.

"We have to hurry," he warned, "if you don't want to miss it."

The street outside was even more crowded now, with passersby pausing to listen to haunting strains of music that drifted out of a nearby gateway. As Celia followed China into the narrow walled courtyard, she was shocked to see how small and shabby it was. The earthen floor had been cleaned of debris, and there was some attempt to brighten the mud-plastered walls with paper decorations for the occasion, but she was keenly aware of the poverty she had expected to sense when she stepped into the Kwan compound.

For all the plainness of the setting, however, an air of gaiety prevailed. At a table along the far wall, a group of musicians in green costumes with red-tasseled hats had just laid down their instruments to enjoy a sip of tea. Theirs was an important role in the festivities, for by the various motifs they played throughout the afternoon, not only the guests in the courtyard but also men and women in the street would know what part of the ceremony was taking place.

A tall, graceful girl detached herself from a group at the side of the yard and came toward them, arms extended. Celia was surprised to recognize Kalani, looking even prettier now, with a cluster of red hibiscus in her upswept dark hair.

She laughed infectiously as she caught Celia's hands and drew her toward a small open doorway. Her presence at such an occasion was a rarity, for while she was friendly with the Chinese families in the area and spoke several of their dialects fluently, she was usually too busy to attend. Today, however, at China's request, she had come to interpret for Celia the bride-dressing ceremony, which had already begun.

The room in which the bride was being prepared was just off the courtyard, but the walls were thick, and even though the music had started up again, the sound was dull and muted. As her eyes adjusted to the dimness, Celia saw a slender wide-eyed girl seated solemnly on the *k'ang,* a raised platform that took up most of one end of the room.

"But she's so young," Celia whispered, shocked. She hadn't expected such a little girl, or one who looked so frail. "Why, she can't be more than ten or eleven."

"She would say fourteen," Kalani whispered back. "Though that's twelve as you and I reckon age. Her birthday is short—just before the new year. Chinese count themselves as a year old the day they are born and add another year at each New Year's celebration."

"Twelve?" Celia pinched her lips, disapproving. Twelve was barely older than ten or eleven. Surely she was not mature enough to deal with the physical aspects of marriage, let alone the psychological ones. "How can a child like that make decisions that will affect the rest of her life?"

"Actually, the decisions aren't hers," Kalani explained. "Marriages are arranged by the matchmaker—in this neighborhood, the man who carries out the night soil. He doesn't care how things turn out, of course—all he wants is his commission—but if the parents are loving, they look into the character and circumstances of the man he has recommended. The girl, of course, has no say in the matter. Often, as in this case, the bride will see her new husband for the first time when she peeks through her fingers as they carry her out to her sedan chair."

Celia shook her head sadly. "Twelve years old. It seems so . . . inhumane. Does she even know what's going on, I wonder?"

"I doubt it," Kalani replied, unperturbed. "I think now she's just excited, having all this attention paid to her and wearing a pretty dress. But really, it's not as cruel as it seems. The marriage won't be consummated tonight or for many nights to come. If the bridegroom is young, they can be playmates for each other. If he's older, he'll be a kindly uncle whom she can get to know and learn slowly to love.''

''And if she doesn't?''

''There are many kinds of love.'' Kalani gave her a shrewd look out of the corner of her eye. ''And the kind that grows slowly, I think, is better for a lifetime than the passions of a youthful heart. Parents are able to make wiser choices than a young girl in love.''

Celia did not try to argue as she looked back at the child bride in red underclothing and red stockings on the *k'ang*. She couldn't forget her own impetuous passion for Skye Maarten. If she had had her way, she'd be married to him right now. Her father would have chosen someone more like Ash Claridge—and in the end, she would have been happier.

The music continued, still sounding as if it came from a distance, as the bride was removed from the *k'ang* and seated on a chair, where the women of the household unplaited her hair, combing it for the first time in a matron's knot at the nape of her neck. An expression of pleasure lit up her thin little features as they brought out an exquisitely embroidered red robe, and one of the women held it up so she could look at it for a moment before they eased it over her shoulders. Embroidered red slippers and elaborate hair ornaments completed the costume.

The women had just finished dressing the bride when the penetrating sound of a bamboo flute came from the courtyard.

''Come,'' Kalani whispered, urging Celia toward the door. ''The groom has arrived to drink with the men of the bride's family.''

No sooner had they stepped outside than a wooden horn joined the flute; then cymbals and drums sounded, heralding the appearance of the bridegroom in the doorway. He looked dismayingly old, Celia thought, for the child she had just seen, twenty-seven at least, perhaps more. But he seemed well-to-do, for he was dressed in sumptuous garments, patterned after the robes of a mandarin in the old country.

"Such finery is usual, even at the poorest weddings," explained a man who introduced himself as one of the neighbors. Like China, he had been born in Hawaii, but he was a generation older and not nearly as well-educated, though his English was impeccable. "Twice in their lives, every Chinese man and woman is equal to the highest in the land. When they are married and when they are buried, it is in the garb of nobility."

"A charming custom," Celia admitted, thinking of the wardrobes full of pretty dresses she had always taken for granted. "But isn't it terribly expensive?"

The man laughed. "It is, of course, but not nearly as much as you might imagine. The clothes are hired, you see. Tomorrow they will go back to be cleaned and mended—and brought out for the next great occasion."

The men of the groom's family followed the bride's father and uncle into one of the side rooms. The door was open, and Brandon and Celia watched curiously from the threshold as the *wu-fan* was opened, with much pomp and ceremony. Poor as the family was, they had planned for this moment from the day the girl child was born, setting aside a wine of highest quality dark millet to mellow until it had half-evaporated, leaving a strong, sticky residue.

A pungent aroma drifted through the doorway as the men took appreciative sips from their glasses. Then, judging the wine to be of suitable quality, cups were passed out to the male guests in the yard. The thickened liquid was dark and somewhat gluey in texture, but Celia, sharing a taste of Brandon's, found it sweet and not at all unpleasant.

The music paused briefly as the bride's red sedan chair was moved up to the outer gate, which was too narrow to permit it to be carried into the courtyard, as it would be in a wealthier household. A long wail of horns sounded, and the girl was brought out, kneeling on the arms of an elderly neighbor, a man whose parents and wife were still living. The ornaments in her hair must have been heavy, for her head drooped over his shoulder as he placed her in the chair, taking care that she did not touch the sides.

Matrons whose husbands were alive came forward then to tuck the girl's rented red robe around her before a red curtain was dropped over the opening. A gong sounded one last time, the bearers swung the chair onto their shoulders, and the small procession moved down the street.

Gaily decorated lanterns came first, bright red and dangling on long poles, followed by red banners and tall red boards gaudily inscribed with metallic gold characters. Then came the band, then the groom's green sedan chair and the red chair bearing the bride. The girl's brother walked beside her, a tall cocky youth carrying a length of red fabric which he would hold between her and all the wells they passed, protecting her from the hungry ghosts of those who had drowned themselves and were doomed to remain in the dark waters until they could persuade others to take their places. Last came the cart with the perfect couple, a man and wife whose parents and children were living, and who would act for the bride's family when it came time to give her over to her new home.

Some of the celebrants followed the procession, their raucous shouts adding to the shrill din of the band. Celia and Brandon watched, waving after them until they were out of sight, then returned with China to his house. Old Grandmother had been busy while they were gone, preparing a savory meal, and although she would not join them at the table, she plied them with boiled ginger chicken and cold sliced pork, delicious complements to noodles in hot peppery broth and bowls of sticky white rice. Kalani had walked with them as far as the gate, but Celia noticed she made no move to come inside, nor did China press her.

"My grandmother likes Kalani," he said when the old woman, refusing help from either of the men, had gone out to get more wood for the stove. "But she would never admit it. It worries her to see me with a pretty Hawaiian girl. Some of my cousins have married natives, but she wants me to stay close to our Chinese roots. She has already picked out the perfect wife for me—or so she claims.''

"You wouldn't let her do that, would you?" Celia paused, chopsticks poised over a bowl of spicy chicken. "Arrange a marriage for you?"

China shook his head. "I don't approve of men marrying women they have never met, but I wouldn't say that to my grandmother. She is an old woman. I would not want to hurt her unnecessarily.''

It was late afternoon when they finally said good-bye to China and found the hired coach where it was waiting for them around the corner. The sun had already begun to sink beneath the ridges of the *palis,* leaving a trail of red across the sky, as Celia nestled sleepily in Brandon's arms. They were alone in the carriage except for the driver, who paid no attention from his high seat in front.

It would be so easy, she thought, her head resting on his chest, to forget there was anything else in the world. So easy to pretend that she and Brandon were carefree lovers, with no past to haunt them, no dubious future ahead, no *Moonwind* floating on dark waters with its evil cargo.

"I wish," she murmured softly, "that things could always be like this.''

Brandon shifted his weight so she would be more comfortable, but said nothing as he lowered his lips to touch her hair. Like the bridegroom at the wedding, he was older than this woman he held in his arms, and he knew that their happiness of the moment was fleeting, for life by its very nature meant change.

And change, for them, spelled troubled days ahead.

As it happened, the first awareness of change came even sooner than he had expected. It was a lazy afternoon, and he and Celia were bathing in a cool stream, swollen that year from unusually heavy rainfalls. He had been lying on the bank sunning himself while she frolicked in ripples that splashed teasingly around her breasts. He still could not get her to go into the ocean without the suit he had had made for her, even at dusk, when they could be sure of privacy, but the inland pools had a secluded feel, and she was comfortable here with her nakedness.

It was the sort of dreamy afternoon he loved, and at first he noticed nothing out of the ordinary. He was lying there quietly, enjoying the look of her body, the way the water gave a pink-and-ivory sheen to her skin, the way the sun played on feminine curves, when it occurred to him suddenly that there was something different about her. Her breasts had always been full, tempting him to reach out; now they seemed ripe to the point of bursting. Her hips, slender before, had taken on a new roundness, somehow more womanly.

Slowly he sat up, reality intruding on the dream; yet not intruding truly, for the realization was not an unpleasant one. He should, of course, have considered the possibility before. But if he had, mightn't he have backed off from what he wanted all along?

He held out his hand, certain now, waiting for her to come to him. The words, when he spoke, were merely a formality.

"Are you pregnant?"

22

Celia looked up, too stunned for an instant to speak.

Pregnant? The thought had never even crossed her mind, though she knew now it ought to have. Belatedly she recognized the changes in her body, corresponding to those external signals Brandon had picked up. The way her breasts felt sometimes, that vague sense of lethargy she could not shake, the slight nausea when she first got up, not quite morning sickness . . . not yet.

She dropped her eyes, unable to meet his penetrating gaze. "Yes," she said, feeling suddenly as if her whole world were falling apart. "Yes, I'm sorry, but I think I am."

Brandon studied her in silence for a moment, then reached out with a gentle hand to touch her face. "Look at me, Celia, and tell me the truth. Do you say you're sorry because you don't want a child right now? Or are you sorry because you think I'll be angry?"

"I . . . I don't know." The breeze had turned cold, and Celia picked up a flowing pink robe, slipping it over her naked flesh. "Both, I suppose. Oh, Brandon, only a few days ago, when we came back from the wedding—do you remember?—I said I hoped things would never change. Now it seems they have."

She was embarrassed to feel tears in her eyes, and she moved away from the stream, not wanting him to see. Which *did* she mind most? The change in her own life,

348

which had been so happy, or the fear that she had displeased him? What if he hated the idea she was pregnant? Most men would, wouldn't they? What if he stashed her someplace out of the way and never bothered to see her again?

But to her amazement, Brandon Christopher turned out to be descended from all those puritan forebears after all. With no hesitation that she could see, though a bit stiffly, he insisted they get married, the sooner the better.

"I don't want my son to be a bastard," he said, his jaw set in a stubborn line. "I want him to know who his father is, and to bear my name."

For just a moment, at those words, Celia's heart leapt up, and she dared to hope this was his awkward way of telling her he had been as happy these past weeks as she, that he did truly want to marry her. But then she remembered he had spoken only of the child—the word "love" had never once been uttered, or even, God help her, "fondness"—and she felt more miserable than ever.

"What if it's a daughter?" she said, masking her hurt behind a flippant tone. "These things happen, you know. You'd be sorry then that you'd gone to such drastic extremes."

"No I wouldn't." His voice was quiet but firm. "A girl has as much right to a father as a boy, and believe me, I would rejoice every bit as much to hold a daughter in my arms. But the babe you are carrying is not a girl. I can't tell you how I know—I simply do. This child is my son." Celia was aware of his eyes watching her, waiting for her to say something—hoping, perhaps—but she didn't know what it was. Unable to bear the intensity, she looked away.

She loved this man so much, she thought as she stared at the *palis,* clear and crisp in the distance. She hungered to accept the security he was offering, but, dear heaven, she did not want it this way! If only he had said: I care for you, Celia. I *care*—that was all. If only she could believe he wanted her, at least partly, for herself, not just for the child in her womb. Not for the baby he had already begun to call "my son."

"I don't know," she whispered, her voice barely audible as it drifted back. "It doesn't seem right, marrying like this, for . . . for *expediency*. I don't know if I can do it."

"I do." Brandon took a step toward her, then stopped. "I know things haven't always gone smoothly between us—certainly we have misunderstood each other in the past—but if I've learned one thing, it's that there is great warmth in your heart . . . and generosity. You wouldn't let your son suffer for your sins or mine. And he would suffer, believe me, being born a bastard."

He held back as she faced him, the breezes blowing her hair around her head, the sun turning it into a silvery coronet. If only things were different, he thought fleetingly. If only . . .

But they weren't.

He took hold of her wrist, his fingers a subtle pressure as he drew her toward him.

"I'm sorry, Celia. I realize what I'm asking is difficult. God knows, I'm no prize as a husband—not as things stand now. There's much I have left to do, much that will keep getting in our way. But when it's over, I promise, I'll give you anything you want. Whatever your heart desires, I'll buy it for you. You want a house—a castle!—I'll build it, anywhere in the world." He paused, trying to find something in her reaction that would tell him how she felt. Then, seeing nothing, he forced himself to say the words that came hardest. "We'll live there together if you want—or if you've decided by that time I'm a bad bargain, it can be a marriage in name only. The terms will be yours. All I ask is that you don't deny me the right to give my name to my son."

Celia drew her hand back, conscious, though she tried not to be, of the place where he had touched her. I'll buy you anything, he had said. I'll *buy*, not I'll *love*.

She wandered over to a shallow rise that looked down on the sea. It was funny, the way she was focusing only on herself, all caught up in trivial things, fretting more over the fact that he hadn't said he loved her than the dark secrets that had kept them apart before. Caring more that he was a reluctant suitor than a pirate and an opium smuggler.

Yet it wasn't *she* who counted at all, she reminded herself, forcing things into perspective. It was not herself she should be thinking of now, it was that new little life just beginning inside her. And Brandon was right: son or daughter, her child would be deeply hurt by the taint of bastardy. Any father, even a pirate, was better than no father at all.

"Very well," she said dully, "I will marry you."

Brandon heard the words, but he did not try to reply. Her back looked so rigid as she stood there, turned away from him, staring out at sun-glistening waters—not seeing them at all, he'd warrant. He had half-hoped, when he threw out that clumsy marriage proposal, that she was going to leap into his arms with a female squeal of excitement. Only, of course, she hadn't.

Dammit, what had he expected? He had offered the girl a life of glamour, battles on the open seas, adventures on exotic islands. Now he was taking it all away for the pain of childbirth and a marriage that was precarious at best. How else could she react?

Perhaps later, when motherhood had matured her, when he had done what he had to and come home again, they would be able to come to terms with each other. Perhaps then he could make her understand the depths of his feelings about opium, why he had had to carry on this damnable deception—and he would understand whatever it was she needed. Perhaps then, at last, she would love him with her heart, as she did now with her body.

"We are doing what is right for our son," he said as he went over to stand beside her. "That much, at least, we can share. Our love for him, and the pride with which we will watch him grow."

*   *   *

The wedding took place four days later.

The morning after Celia agreed to marry him, Brandon saddled the powerful chestnut gelding he kept in a local stable for his use whenever he was on the island and rode in to have a talk with the pastor of St. Andrew's on Beretania Street in Honolulu. There, with some difficulty, and having to reveal more of his activities than he liked, he arranged to have the marriage take place without the customary posting of banns. He personally had seen no trace of Teresa Valdes since they arrived in Hawaii, but he had had his men make discreet inquiries, and he knew she was nearby, seething no doubt at the closeness of his liaison with another beautiful young woman. If she found out they were married, her wrath might well come down on Celia instead of the man who had earned it.

He had toyed briefly with the idea of postponing the ceremony until he returned from that last voyage to the West Coast, which he had rashly promised Quarrie he would make. Now, coming out of St. Andrew's and turning west on Beretania, he was glad he had decided against it. The mission he was about to undertake would be dangerous—only a fool would deny that. He might not have a second chance to make things up to Celia, or give his son the name that was his by right. There was one errand yet to run, and he accomplished that quickly, stopping by the offices of a lawyer he could trust. At least, he thought as he headed home again, Celia and the boy would be well provided for if anything happened to him.

He was in an exuberant mood when he dismounted in front of the small grass house and went inside to inform Celia that everything had been arranged. They were, he told her, quite pleased with the way he had handled it, to be married the next day.

To his astonishment, she flatly refused.

"I couldn't possibly be married *tomorrow*. Two days after that maybe, but no sooner. I have to have a dress made."

"Good God," he blustered, trying not to let her see

how pleased he was at the high spirits that just had wreaked havoc with his plans. "Don't tell me you're going to insist on one of those lacy white concoctions? With a veil so I can't see who I'm marrying?"

"I might," Celia replied, laughing. "And if that's what I choose, that's what I'm going to have! Don't forget, you promised this marriage would be on *my* terms."

That those terms did not include formal wedding attire was a decision Celia had already made, though she did not mention it to Brandon at the moment. She would feel more than a little foolish, masquerading as a virgin in a frothy white gown when she was already carrying a child in her belly. Besides, such pallid finery hardly seemed appropriate on the islands.

Kalani, who had come to help with the arrangements, could not have agreed more. "Why would anyone wear *white*," she said, genuinely astonished, "when there are so many pretty colors to choose from?"

In the end, Celia settled on a pale lavender silk, brightened slightly by a subtle pattern of pink and white roses. Much too subtle for Kalani's taste, though Celia did her best to convince the girl that discretion was better suited to the solemnity of the occasion.

Kalani, who saw no reason why weddings should be solemn, was still skeptical. But she had to give in the next day when Celia stepped out of a small cottage next to the church and she saw her in the sunlight.

"How beautiful you look," she said generously. "The dress is very pretty—and so is that wreath of pink and white tea roses in your hair. Your bridegroom will be very proud."

Celia felt as if the air were shimmering as she half-walked, half-floated across a perfectly manicured lawn toward the church. Brandon had chosen the small Anglican cathedral especially for her, assuming a British girl would be more comfortable in that uniquely British setting, but Celia, who had never seen her parents' homeland, felt no particular affinity for classically strong lines and heavy gray stones imported all the way from England. Still, there was something majestic about the place, a spirituality she could feel, if not see, and she was aware of a sense of awe as she stepped into the cool, shadowy interior.

Was this really her wedding? she thought as she spotted small bouquets of white hibiscus at the ends of the front pews. Once before, she had made plans for a day like this—only then she was going to marry Skye Maarten and she had been filled with such expectations, such excitement. There was no excitement in her now, only a kind of trepidation, mixed with deep new longings she could not identify.

Brandon was waiting at a side doorway near the rear of the church, and her heart skipped a beat as he came forward, meeting her halfway down the aisle. If only he would sweep her up in his arms, she thought helplessly, if only he would bend his head to hers, whispering: I love you, my darling . . . what a fool I was not to tell you before . . . I love you and I *want* you to be my wife. . . .

But he said nothing, and she had to be content with slipping her hand wordlessly through his arm. He laid his own hand on top of it, an unexpected gesture, comforting, and they walked together toward the altar where they were to become man and wife.

Later she would remember little of the ceremony that followed. The minister spoke all the appropriate words, intoning them as if by rote, she and Brandon made all the appropriate responses, and a circlet of pearls and sapphires found its way to her finger. Then, somehow, she was in her new husband's arms . . . somehow, his lips were on hers, hard and possessive . . . and for just a moment everything was perfect, the way weddings were supposed to be. For just a moment she *was* the happy young bride she had longed to be, with nothing but love in her heart for the man she had married, and the oh-so-sweet illusion that he loved her.

The aisle was crowded with people the instant the ceremony was over. Brandon was still determined to keep the marriage a secret, but for Celia's sake he had compromised enough to invite a few of their friends. Only a skeleton crew remained on the *Moonwind*; the rest of the men were already enjoying themselves, especially young Freddie, who seemed to have forgotten his crush on Celia as he spotted first the gorgeous Kalani, then one of China Kwan's prettier young cousins. Old Grandmother was there too, and a handful of other relations Celia had met at the Chinese wedding. But most exuberant of all were Luka and Iopeka, who could hardly wait to brush everyone aside and crush the young bride to their ample chests.

Celia's cheeks were pink with pleasure by the time Brandon finally uncorked several bottles of champagne, which the minister, understanding the circumstances, had allowed them to drink in the privacy of the church. She had not realized how many new friends she had made, and she was a little surprised at how good it felt to have them all there. The magic of Brandon's kiss had not yet worn off, and she was feeling quite giddy as he slipped an arm around her waist and guided her toward the door.

"I'm glad you're enjoying yourself," he said, laughing. "I wanted to please you, and it looks like I succeeded. But I didn't have it in mind to spend my first hours of married life in a church."

"Oh . . . and what *did* you have in mind?"

Brandon raised a wicked brow. "It is customary, after the wedding, to enjoy at least a brief honeymoon."

"Is it?" The champagne made her light-headed, and she couldn't resist teasing. "I thought we'd had the honeymoon already."

"So we did." He grinned appreciatively. "And I won't deny that I am looking forward to a repeat of that . . . but later. This evening I have a different sort of honeymoon activity in mind. You are Mrs. Brandon Christopher now, my dear, and as such, I think you're entitled to a taste of elegance."

Before she could ask any questions, he hurried her out to a waiting carriage, drawing thick velvet curtains across the windows as they rode through city streets. Celia protested, laughing, that he was shutting out the cooling breezes, but Brandon only nuzzled her neck with ardent lips, telling her quite pointedly that he didn't want the whole world peeping while he kissed his new bride.

And because he was being so good to her and she was so happy in his arms, Celia did not object.

She had expected the coach to carry them back through the hills to that shore on the windward side, but a short distance from the church, the driver reined in his horses, holding them to a slow walk as they rounded a corner. Peeking curiously through the curtains. Celia saw the elegant facade of the Hawaiian Hotel, which had been built by royalty to entertain their guests and even now was the most fashionable place on the islands to stay. Long-legged planters lounged on the veranda, chatting idly with guests who were leaning against tall pillars, but the carriage jogged past them, heading for one of the cottages in the rear.

"You didn't think I was going to ask you to spend your wedding night in a grass hut, did you?" Brandon laughed as he picked her up, carrying her, with all the romance her heart could hunger for, across the open threshold. "You deserve at least one night in a real room. With a real bed, not a rustic cot lashed together with leather thongs."

Celia was at a loss for words as Brandon set her down. Never had she seen anything quite as pretty or as luxurious as this place he had chosen for their honeymoon. The wide double bed was covered with a heavy satin spread, a deep glowing rose hue that dominated the room, and a mahogany dressing table with a gilt-edged mirror stood next to the tall, ample wardrobe. In an alcove near French windows leading out to a private terrace, a round table had been set with a bowl of lemon-scented white hibiscus, like the bouquets at her wedding.

A half-open doorway on one wall led to a gentleman's dressing room; through another, Celia saw a velvet-upholstered chair and love seat, hinting at a small but superbly appointed parlor. She had only a glimpse of it, however, for Brandon strode over and shut the door.

"I don't think we'll be needing a sitting room tonight," he said with a suggestive grin.

If he had told her they were going to have dinner at that small table in their bedchamber, Celia would not have been surprised, nor would she have objected, for it was pleasure enough just being with him when he was in a mood like this. But his plans for the evening, it seemed, went beyond that.

"I can't offer you a honeymoon in Paris or London or New York, though you shall have that later, if you want. But I can give you a night at the best hotel in Honolulu. And dinner at the finest restaurant."

"Oh, Brandon . . ." Celia clapped her hands, as excited as a little girl at the unexpected treat. Now if he had only been thoughtful enough to have her clothes removed from the hold of the *Moonwind* and brought to the hotel! The blue crepe de chine with its graceful lines might not be *au courant,* but it was flattering, and she knew she looked pretty in it.

But when she ventured to ask, he shook his head— rather wryly, it seemed to her.

"I have no doubt it's exquisite," he said, maddeningly tongue-in-cheek. "And all laced up to a twenty-inch waist!"

"Nineteen!" she started to snap, then caught herself, aghast. "Oh, I had forgotten about *that.*"

"I hadn't," he said somewhat more gently. "So you see, even if you could squeeze into your corset, and even if you were silly enough to try, I could never permit it. I want you to take better care of my son."

His son.

Celia turned away briefly, feeling as if a cloud had dimmed the brightness of the day. His son again—always his son. Couldn't he let her forget, just for a little while, that that was the only reason he had married her?

The sense of sadness lasted barely a second, however, for Brandon had one more surprise up his sleeve. As he threw open the door to the wardrobe, Celia saw why he had been so cavalier about the lost blue crepe de chine and why her disappointment had not touched him. There, glowing against the dark wood of the cabinet, was the loveliest gown she had ever seen.

"The seamstress had more than lavender silk on her mind," he told her, "when she measured you for your wedding dress."

Celia gasped as he took the gown out of the wardrobe and laid it on the bed. Yards of silver lace, woven with metallic thread, sparkled in the last of the afternoon sunlight spilling through open windows. The bodice was fitted, though not too tight, she noticed, with bouffant sleeves almost to the elbows and a daringly low heart-shaped neck. The skirt, pencil-slim in front, flared slightly over a cluster of white silk roses, forming a small bustle in the back.

Brandon retired a few minutes later to his dressing room, and Celia sat in front of the mirror watching as the hotel maid fussed with her hair. It was a relief not to have to worry about it herself—she had never been very good at things like that; Sin-Sin had always been there to do them for her—and she marveled at the way nimble fingers rolled her long hair up into a modish "French twist," topping it with a soft modified pompador. An exquisite diamond comb, which Brandon had left, almost as an afterthought, completed the coiffure, but she wore no other jewels. Nor did she use more than a hint of rouge, sensing that her long, slightly tanned neck and youthful complexion would be all the more appealing without the distraction of artifice.

Brandon appeared in the doorway just as she finished dressing. Celia started toward him, then hesitated, realizing suddenly that she had never seen him in dark, tapered evening pants with a black waistcoat and casual, sophisticated "tuxedo" jacket. Could this handsome, worldly figure really be the same reckless pirate who had abducted her from a ferry in Hong Kong and carried her off on his ship?

"Why, Brandon," she said, "you look positively elegant. I had hoped, in my pretty new dress, that everyone in the restaurant would turn and look when we came in. I think now they will—but not at me."

Brandon laughed, his eyes running appreciatively down the lines of the silver lace gown. As always when he saw her in a new guise, he was struck all over again by her beauty. It occurred to him that he was going to enjoy it immensely when he could finally present her to the world as his bride.

"Heads *will* turn tonight," he said gallantly. "And for exactly the reason your mirror told you."

The restaurant was softly lit as they entered, with candles glowing on each table and sparkling in elaborate crystal chandeliers. Heads did indeed turn, if discreetly, for they made a striking couple, he with his dark red hair and dark evening suit, she a vision of silver in her stunning new outfit.

Brandon was solicitous as he pulled out her chair, helping her politely into her seat, but although he greeted the waiter by name, Celia noticed that he made no attempt to introduce her as his wife. A small point, but disconcerting— another dark cloud to momentarily mar the pleasure of the evening—and it was hard to brush it from her mind.

Dinner, which Celia trusted Brandon to order, was superb. First came a really excellent chowder, with plump oysters floating in a buttery cream, accompanied by a dry white wine. Celia sipped the latter sparingly, all the while marveling, wide-eyed, at the opulence of the setting: immaculate white table coverings, cut from the most expensive damask, and crystal goblets catching and diffusing the candlelight; fresh-cut flowers in silver vases at each place, and flowering plants arranged, as if at random, on stands throughout the room. In one corner, screened by lush green ferns, a small string orchestra provided muted background music.

"I've only been in a real restaurant once," she confessed, "and it was nothing like this. My father took us to

Rangoon on my eighteenth birthday, to a place where all the planters go on holiday. I remember how small and square it was, very smoky, with a smell of beef fat in the air. The linens were white, but they were all spotted—the steak sizzled so much when it was served, you had to hold the tablecloth in front of you to keep from being spattered."

Brandon laughed at the description of a place he knew by type, having dined in similar establishments himself.

"But surely you ate out while you were in Hong Kong," he reminded her.

"No." Celia shook her head. "Not in restaurants, anyway. That would hardly have been suitable for a woman traveling alone. Naturally, I took my meals in the ladies' dining room at the hotel."

"Naturally," Brandon replied, his eyes twinkling at the thought of a young lady who would not go into a restaurant unescorted after she had just defied every other convention to run off and join her lover.

The waiter appeared a few seconds later, clearing away the soup dishes and returning with small plates of pinkish fish smothered in a thick, flavorful sauce.

"Oregon salmon," Brandon told her. "It comes in tins, so it's not nearly as tasty as the local seafood. But anything imported is fashionable no matter what, so it seemed more suited to a festive occasion."

Celia, who secretly thought the fish was delicious—and a welcome change from the "local seafood," which she had had almost every day since her arrival—wisely said nothing as she finished her portion. A meat course followed, thick slices of roast beef with perfectly done Yorkshire pudding, crisp and brown on the outside, slightly doughy within. There were also small Irish potatoes, glistening with butter, and string beans, cut French style in thin strips, and crusty chunks of bread to be smeared with sweet guava jelly.

Celia did not need to be urged to finish everything on her plate, for she could tell herself she was eating for two now and need not watch her figure. A second bottle of wine had been opened with the meat—an extravagance, for neither she nor Brandon had done more than taste the first—and she raised her glass to the candlelight, enjoying the jewellike clarity of burgundy red against delicate cut crystal.

As she did, an unaccustomed flash of color caught her eye, blue sapphires shimmering darkly between small perfectly matched pearls. The ring was so new she couldn't resist looking at it.

Brandon, seated across the table, noted the gesture with a slight twinge of guilt. He had wanted to buy her a heavy gold band, traditionally set with diamonds—surely every young girl's dream—but caution advised against it. For the same reason he had drawn the curtains in the carriage, and failed to mention to the waiter that he was married, so had he settled on safer, less identifiable pearls and sapphires. Even for the few hours they would be in public tonight, he dared not take the chance that someone would see and guess the truth.

He was going to be gone for weeks, perhaps months, on this last mission; he would not be there to protect his wife or his unborn son from whatever dangers they might face. The risks were slight, of course. Careful plans had already been laid to make sure Teresa Valdes followed the *Moonwind* when it sailed out of the cove where it was anchored. But in case she didn't, in case something went wrong, it was better for Celia that the marriage remain a secret.

"I am sorry, my sweet," he said lightly. "I know you would have preferred diamonds, but this was the best I could manage on short notice. I'll buy you a more extravagant ring later."

Celia looked up, sensing something in his voice she longed to hear, yet not quite sure. She couldn't help wishing he were speaking of love now and not of jewels.

And yet, she reminded herself, wasn't it a form of love, that he wanted to marry her because she was carrying his child?

"I don't care about extravagance," she said quietly.

"Nor do I need diamonds. This is a beautiful ring and I am proud to wear it."

They sat in silence for a moment; then, taking refuge in idle conversation, began to chat about trivial things, about the salad—alligator pears dressed with a thick, sweetened oil—and the tasty ice, flavored with tropical fruits and served with a thin biscuit which Brandon persisted in calling a "cookie," a silly term, but one Celia found amusing.

It was almost, she thought, puzzled, as if they were talking, yet not talking at all . . . as if they were using words to shield rather than communicate. As if they both had things they wanted to say but were afraid to utter them aloud.

A thousand questions ran through her mind. What happens next? Where are we going? How will we live? But something in his manner held her back. He had insisted, the day before, that she write to her parents, and even included a note himself—but he said nothing about his own people.

What will they think of me? she longed to ask. Will they like me, your four sisters and the little brother with the red-blond hair? But the subject of his family always seemed to make him draw into himself, and she could not bear the thought of pushing him even farther away.

He did, indeed, seem withdrawn as she looked over at him, staring down at a demitasse of strong black coffee, barely touched on the table in front of him. Then, breaking the mood, he smiled and glanced at the dance floor, beginning to fill with people.

"It occurs to me," he said, scraping back his chair, "that we have shared nearly everything except a dance. I think it's time we remedied the situation."

"I would like that very much."

For the next few minutes, in Brandon's arms, Celia almost recaptured the illusion of love she had felt, however briefly, when he kissed her at the altar. There was in his dancing the kind of masterful perfection that had al-

ways appealed to her. He seemed so strong, so sure in
every graceful movement of his body, she couldn't help
feeling secure . . . couldn't help longing to believe that
everything would be all right.

The orchestra, hidden in their leafy bower, must have
sensed the presence of lovers on the dance floor, for the
music grew softer, sweeter, ebbing and flowing with a
seductive rhythm that seemed to have been created for
them alone.

Celia's eyes drifted shut. The music caught her up, and
she felt as if she were floating like a leaf on the perfumed
tropical wind. Did it really matter that he had not spoken
of love when he was being so kind, so thoughtful . . .
when he made her so happy tonight? What was it Kalani
had said before? *There are many kinds of love. And the
one that grows slowly, with time, is the one that is best for
a marriage.*

Mightn't it be that way for Brandon and her? God
knows, she had enough love for both of them now. Mightn't
his love come too, in the end, if she had the wit and the
patience to earn it?

This marriage will be on your terms, he had told her.

Very well, then, *these* were her terms. Love . . . complete and unqualified. Her love for Brandon Christopher
. . . and his for her.

She was smiling as the music ended, a secret half-smile
she was careful to keep to herself. For the first time since
he had looked into her eyes and said, ''Are you pregnant?'' she knew what she wanted, and she was not afraid
to try to get it. Love was not a gift, after all—it was a
prize to be sought and won. And she was going to win it!

But as they sat down again, facing each other across the
table, reality returned, bringing her to earth with a shock.
One minute she had been wonderfully confident, a pretty,
pampered girl with the world about to fall at her feet—the
next, she was aware of something strange and dark in his
eyes . . . and she felt cold all over.

She could not have said where it came from, but suddenly she knew what he was thinking. And she knew what it meant for her.

"You're leaving, aren't you?" she said dully.

Brandon took a deep breath, hating himself for the words he was about to say. He had seen the look on her face when they finished dancing, and he knew he had given her a moment's happiness, only to snatch it back again. Damn Quarrie and the promise he had exacted! And damn his own compulsive need to stop Teresa Valdes!

"Yes, I'm sorry, I must. Tomorrow morning. But I'll be gone only as long as I have to. And when I come back . . ."

When I come back, he started to say, we'll never be parted again. Only he wasn't sure that was what she wanted to hear. And dammit, could he blame her? After all the secrecy and half-truths?

"When I come back, things will be different. I promise you that."

23

Brandon had planned to leave an hour or two after midnight, timing his arrival on the windward shore to coincide with the first faint rays of dawn. But the bed with its rose satin coverlet was hard to leave, the warmth of Celia beside him a sweet temptation, and he lingered longer than he had intended. They spent those last precious minutes in each other's arms, not speaking, not even making love, just clinging together, conscious of the parting so soon to come.

Hints of grayish light had already begun to seep through the half-drawn draperies by the time he finally rose, dressing swiftly in the semidarkness. As he glanced back at Celia, so little in the wide double bed, childlike with the covers drawn up to her chin, he was bitterly conscious that he might be looking at her for the last time.

Death had never seemed real to him before. Life had always been a plaything, a gamble to be won or lost, a sometimes exciting, sometimes dreary existence that came or went with the toss of a coin. Now, for the first time, he had dreams for the future, a reason to want desperately to live—and the game had changed.

Now, for the first time, he was afraid.

He went over to the bed, masking his feelings behind a noncommittal expression as he sat one last time beside her. "Take care," he said softly. "You are . . . very precious to me."

She was his whole life now, everything he had ever wanted, everything he *needed,* but he could not tell her. Not because he worried any longer about whether she would welcome the words, but because he was more conscious than ever that he might not be coming back, that if he didn't, words of love between them now would make it harder for her.

"Don't forget," he said, "you're the mother of my son. I want you to promise you'll see to all his needs. And yours."

"I promise." Celia no longer questioned his priorities, accepting his concern for their unborn child as a form of caring for her. Nor did she remind him that "his son" might turn out to be his daughter, for that, too, was not important. All she could think was that he was leaving and she had no idea where he was going. "Is it . . . very dangerous? What you are about to do? I wish you'd tell me more—"

"Shhhh." He laid a finger on her lips. "No, it's not dangerous . . ." He broke off, catching himself with a laugh. She had been with him too long; she knew what a pirate's life was like. He couldn't fool her so easily. "At least, no more dangerous than the things I've already done—and you know me. I always land on my feet. No, my dear, I'm not worried about myself in the weeks to come. But I am concerned about you."

"Me?" She looked surprised.

"I'm leaving China Kwan behind. He'll take care of you, and some of my best men will be with him. Still—"

"But that's crazy," Celia interrupted. "I'm not going to need China, not here. And you might! Oh, Brandon, I'd feel so much better if he were with you. I'll be all right in the little house on the beach—"

"You're not going back to the beach." Brandon spoke sharply, then softened his voice as he brushed a wispy curl back from her brow. He didn't want to alarm her, not unnecessarily—no need to mention how open the house was, how vulnerable she would be there. "I don't want you isolated like that, especially when your time comes. You'll be better off in . . . in town.''

Celia looked up, feeling vaguely edgy, though she wasn't sure why. "You think then that I'm going to be in some kind of . . . danger?"

"No, actually I don't. I'm being overcautious, I admit, but as I said before, you are very precious. Humor me, my sweet. Abide by my precautions, even if they do seem 'crazy' to you. I'll rest easier if I know you've promised to listen to China and not take any chances unless he authorizes them first.''

Celia caught hold of his hand, pressing it against her lips. "I've already promised I'd take care of the baby and myself.''

"I want to hear it again. I want you to say it as if you mean it.''

She let go of his hand, hating the empty way she felt when she was no longer touching him. "Very well,'' she said quietly. "I promise.''

He leaned down, kissing her lightly on the lips, an unspoken promise of his own that he would do everything in his power to try to return to her. For just an instant, as he reached the door and looked back, he felt an urge to stop all this madness, to stay with the woman he loved. If only he could forget everything that had happened, he thought bitterly . . . if only he hadn't gotten in too deeply to get out now.

Then, reminding himself it was too late for regrets, he slipped through the door and shut it behind him.

China Kwan was waiting in the shadows of a hibiscus hedge as he emerged from the cottage. "You're late,'' he greeted Brandon in a tense undertone. "I expected you three hours ago. The carriage has been waiting.'' He gestured toward the same small coach, still screened with dark curtains, that had brought Brandon and Celia from the church. "It's already getting light. By the time you reach the *Moonwind*—''

"I know.'' Brandon nodded grimly. A faint pink glow

had begun to color the horizon, and he had a clear view of the grounds surrounding the hotel. A pair of children, a shabbily dressed boy and girl of mixed blood, were playing on the lawn, but the gardener had just come on duty and chased them off. "It *is* a risk, but perhaps it's better this way. We'll have no problems at this end, I think." He looked down the drive, seeing nothing. Even if the hotel were under surveillance, which was unlikely, the watchers would follow his coach. China could take Celia later in another closed carriage to the Kwan house, where he would keep her until dark, then transfer her to the place they had arranged. "As for my arrival at the *Moonwind* . . . well, the timing was always tricky on that. I was afraid we'd get there too soon and have to stall. There's got to be enough light so they can see what's going on."

"Can see, yes," China agreed, frowning. "But not see too clearly. And the light, I'm afraid, is going to be *very* clear."

Brandon glanced back at the hotel, every window visible now, empty, or so they appeared. He did not waste his breath arguing. China was undoubtedly right, but there was no way he could have left Celia earlier, even if those last hours cost him his life. He had needed the extra time to ease the separation, to make the final moment of parting less painful.

His eyes were uncharacteristically clouded as he turned back. "Take care of her, China—I'm leaving my life in your hands."

"I will guard her as if she were my own wife," the other man promised. "You know that. But, Bran . . ." He hesitated, troubled. "Don't be too reckless. Don't take foolish chances, thinking it will end things more quickly. It will mean nothing if I keep her safe and you do not come back."

Brandon shook his head slowly. "No, my friend, you are wrong." For the first time that morning, he felt calm, ready to accept his destiny, whatever it might be. "You are very wrong. It will mean everything."

He swung into the carriage, barely glancing at the slim figure already seated inside. As they rounded the corner, he noted, without paying much attention, that the boy and girl were still there, playing on the street. They looked up curiously at the sound of passing carriage wheels, but Brandon had parted the curtains only a fraction of an inch, and they could not see inside.

Leaning back in the seat, he took a closer look at the other occupant of the coach, satisfied with what he saw. He had considered, briefly, bringing a woman with him, but because there would be no way to get her off the ship when they sailed—and because he did not want the trouble and responsibility of a female on board—he had settled on the youngest member of the crew instead, a Chinese lad.

The boy was an inch or so too tall, but otherwise the illusion was perfect. His slender body was convincingly feminine in a long-sleeved, high-necked *holoku*, generously padded in front; his white-gloved hands looked properly demure folded in his lap. The gauzy pink veil had been drawn back from a broad-brimmed straw hat, exposing disconcertingly masculine Oriental features, but when it was lowered again and he stepped from the carriage into the small boat that would take them to the *Moonwind,* anyone watching would swear they were looking at Celia St. Clair.

And someone would be watching. Brandon was sure of that. He would not be able to see, but he would be aware every second of dark, penetrating eyes on the hillside, and he would know that Teresa was there. Hot-blooded as she was, she would smolder with fury when she saw him escort his mistress on board, especially veiled, for she would assume that was his clumsy attempt to shelter the woman, to keep their relationship a secret.

Nothing on God's earth could keep her from coming after him then. She would follow him onto the open seas, follow, against all sense, to the West Coast—where Quarrie and his men would be waiting.

And Celia, left behind in Hawaii, would be safe.

*   *   *

As it happened, it was not Teresa Valdes who was staring through a spyglass on the hillside when Brandon arrived. It was Schuyler Maarten, who had taken over the lookout duties from her a short time before.

At first, when Teresa had seen the passion simmering openly between the Tiger and his lady, she had been wild with jealousy and insisted on keeping every watch herself, following every movement the lovers made from sunrise to the last dim light of dusk. But of late, the strain had taken its toll; she found herself tired all too often, dozing off when she could least afford it, and she had been forced, reluctantly, to turn the glass over to Maarten for brief intervals each day.

Thus it was he, and not she, who was watching that morning and picked up the little clues she might have missed.

It was a clever ruse, and it almost got past him, for the costume, not the figure in it, was dominant and caught the eye. But Skye had known Celia since she was a little girl—he knew her gestures and her mannerisms, knew the way she walked—and something about that slender figure on the beach struck him as not quite right. Of course, he hadn't seen her in recent months, and people *did* change . . . but that much?

He squinted into the glass, studying her intently, looking for details he had missed before. The woman, whoever she was, was about the right height, and her build was similar. A silver-blond curl peeked out from cream-colored straw, clinging to the back of her collar. Nothing wrong with that—curls did have a way of peeking out from bonnets—but would they have been so careless when the rest of the disguise was meticulously planned?

And she was wearing gloves, odd in that warm climate. To conceal . . . what? The fact that she wasn't white?

Then a foot showed, just briefly beneath a ruffled hem—a rather large foot clad in dark Chinese-style slippers—and

Skye laughed out loud. Celia St. Clair had small feet and
they were always daintily shod.

Not a woman at all, then. A man! And it was a hasty
masquerade. A man could wear a woman's dress, her hat,
her gloves—but shoes required a certain amount of practice.

So . . .

He lowered his glass, mulling over what he had just
discovered, quite pleased, on balance. Two things were
immediately apparent. Brandon Christopher had just divided his forces. And he was going to great lengths to
protect the woman he was leaving behind.

The idea amused him, and Skye was a man who enjoyed
being amused. It occurred to him that the situation might
well be turned to their advantage. He had balked before at
the idea of meeting Brandon's men on the ground in
Hawaii. But now that the Tiger's forces were weakened . . . ?

Which did she hate most? he wondered, his pretty pirate
paramour. The man who did not return her passion, or the
woman he so obviously adored?

If he had had to put money on it, he would have guessed
the woman.

He would have been wrong, for every feeling, every
passion in Teresa's body was directed at the man, and
nothing else—no *one* else—truly entered her range of
vision. But in an odd way, he was right too, for those very
feelings led her to exactly the conclusion he had anticipated.

Her first reaction, when he reached that makeshift camp,
changed every few days so they would not leave themselves too vulnerable, was a childishly feminine burst of
temper. She paced back and forth, from wall to wall in the
small hut where they had been staying, cursing hotly under
her breath, swearing she would raise canvas on the *White
Lotus* and follow Brandon Christopher wherever he went,
whatever the cost.

Her second reaction was slower to come, but it was
more in keeping with the devious shrewdness of her mind.

"The *Lotus* will follow, all right." She turned slowly,
eyes flaring with a sudden brightness that sent chills through

him. "But she'll be carrying just the crew she needs to sail her, no more. See to it, Maarten, that a sufficient number of men are ready to leave when the *Moonwind* takes off. Tell them to show themselves once in a while, but not to get too close, not to take chances. I don't want anyone to guess I'm not on board."

"We're going to stay here, then? With the *Jasmine* and the *Red Peony* and the bulk of the men?"

Teresa's lips twisted coldly, a smile, but one with no pleasure in it. If Brandon had left his heart behind in Hawaii, then that was where she wanted to be. That was where she could hurt him most.

"We're going to stay." For three years they had played a cat-and-mouse game with each other, and she had always lost—until now. "He has played into our hands at last, Maarten. We have the hold we need. If he has gone to such lengths to protect the woman, he'll have her well hidden, of course—but I have my contacts. I'll find her. And when I do . . ."

She walked over to a small sea trunk against the wall and pulled out the same gun she had once brought with her when she went to meet the Tiger. Only then she had been too much of a fool to use it.

"When I do, I'll have Brandon Christopher right where I want him."

24

Celia rested her hand lightly on the window frame as she stared through slatted shutters at the crowded street below. It was midday, a dingy neighborhood just on the edge of Chinatown, and a motley assortment of people could be seen: black-suited Punti women shuffling past on bound feet, with straw baskets balanced on poles on their shoulders; men with long queues hanging down their backs; rough sailors who called the waterfront home whenever their vessels were in Honolulu; young wastrels with black velvet collars and gold watch chains, searching for the seamier pleasures the area had to offer.

It had come as a surprise to Celia, two days earlier, when the closed carriage in which she and China had been riding pulled up in front of a squat two-story building on one of the wider streets near the docks. She had started to get out, albeit tentatively, when he handed her a hopelessly dowdy hat with a long dark veil to hide her face.

One look at it and Celia had been moved to protest. She could not possibly put it on, she told him emphatically. She would feel like a matron in mourning! And anyway, if secrecy was their goal, wouldn't she just make herself conspicuous when everyone else was dressed with a maximum of color and a minimum of modesty?

China remained unmoved. "No one is going to look twice," he said, laughing. "They're used to it by now. In fact, many of the women who come here have their faces veiled."

Celia had little time to ponder that enigmatic comment, for China hustled her out of the carriage and toward an open doorway, from which she could already hear the exuberant rhythm of castanets and violins and twangy Hawaiian guitars. As they entered and mounted a narrow stairway to the upper floor, the music became louder, mingling with an ear-splitting din of shouts and raucous laughter.

The building was larger than it had looked from the outside. To the right of the stairs Celia caught a glimpse of what appeared to be a gaming room, perhaps a hundred feet long and half again as wide, where a rousing game of billiards was in progress. To the left she saw a long, dimly lighted hallway with doors leading off at intervals on either side.

She had just opened her mouth to ask why anyone would want so many small rooms in a gambling establishment when one of the doors opened and a striking-looking Oriental girl started out. Behind her, a man appeared, dressed in the uniform of some navy Celia did not recognize—or partially dressed, for his clothes were in considerable disarray. Before the girl could go anywhere, he grabbed her and pulled her back into the room, tugging her dress off one shoulder to reveal a small but perfectly formed tawny-golden breast.

Celia felt a flood of color rush to her cheeks, and she was grateful for the veiled bonnet she had disdained before. "Why, this is a . . . a . . ."

"A house of ill repute," China filled in obligingly. "The girls in the dance hall bring their men up here, where they're allowed to keep half the money they make. And of course married ladies of somewhat higher social standing have been known to make an occasional assignation. So you see, they really do arrive with their faces veiled."

"But . . ." Celia faltered, feeling puzzled for a moment, then hurt. "Why would Brandon want me to stay in a place like this?"

"Because it's the last place on earth anyone would think of looking. And don't worry, no one expects you to stay in one of those narrow little cubbyholes, where you'd be subjected to noise and embarrassment all night long. I think you'll find the quarters we have arranged surprisingly pleasant. Come, let me show you."

He clapped his hands, and an elderly woman appeared, carrying a candle and a large ring of keys. She fitted one of them into a door at the far end of the hall, then handed China the light and slipped back down the passageway, moving noiselessly on felt-soled shoes.

The room behind the door seemed to be a warehouse of some sort. As Celia stepped inside, she looked around curiously, barely noticing the sound of rusty hinges as China shut them off from the hallway. Shelves were crammed with supplies, but everything looked so dusty in the flickering light, she couldn't imagine it had been touched for years. The impression was heightened as they moved farther back, where rows of shelving still ran to the ceiling, but not one of them had anything on it.

China confirmed her suspicions. "No one comes here anymore. The door is kept locked, and most of the girls think it's a small storeroom, with nothing of any particular interest. It makes the perfect cover for a hideaway—like this."

He threw open a door on the rear wall to reveal a startlingly sumptuous suite of rooms. The decor was simple, almost masculine in feel, but there was a richness about it no one would expect in such a seedy setting. Dark green silk tapestries covered the walls, setting off low cabinets of Chinese lacquerwork, and subtly shaded silk cushions were arranged in piles on the floor. Through a curtained arch on one side Celia spied a sleeping chamber with a large, comfortable-looking bed; a hallway opposite led to niches containing a copper bathtub and a kitchen of sorts, with a small cast-iron stove and deep sink.

"You can prepare snacks if you want," China told her, "but your meals will be brought in three times a day by my cousin, who runs the restaurant next door. Order anything you like, Chinese food, of course, or English or French—even Indian, if you prefer. She is an excellent cook. Your clothes have already been placed in the drawers, and any toiletries you might need. I think you'll find everything to your satisfaction."

"Well, yes, I'm sure I will, but . . ." Celia looked around, bewildered. What was a place like this doing stashed away at the back of a brothel?

China sensed the unspoken question and smiled apologetically. "This is your husband's private apartment," he explained. "Brandon has always had elegant taste."

"Brandon keeps a private apartment *here*?" Celia took an unconscious step backward, hating the opulent green silk that had seemed so tasteful before, hating the fact that the man she had just married kept permanent rooms in a bawdy house.

"It's not quite the way it looks," China said gently. Brandon Christopher was an intensely masculine man; it would be folly to pretend that the girls in the rooms down the hall held no appeal for him, but there was no point making things harder than they were. "He liked to be able to slip in and out of Honolulu without anyone knowing he was here, sometimes even when he was on official business for the Christopher Lines. This was a convenient place for him to hide—as it will be now for you."

Convenient, no doubt, Celia thought dryly, though she realized later, rather to her surprise, she was more amused than hurt. She had already known there were women in Brandon's life, many women before he met her, and she found now that she didn't mind too much. Assuming, of course, she wasn't going to have to come face to face with one of them in the hall!

Not that there was much likelihood of that. She grimaced slightly as she turned back to the window, looking out for perhaps the twentieth time that hour. The rooms in which she was staying were effectively sealed off from the rest of the establishment: no one knew they were there, and no one was likely to venture near. Except for the cousin who delivered her meals, and who spoke only halting English, and China himself, who came whenever he could, she had had no human contact at all.

Sighing, she looked down at the street again. The shutters had been cleverly constructed, with the slats angled so she could look out but no one could see in, even at night when the lamps were lit.

Everything looked drearily the same. Black-haired women in high-heeled shoes were picking their way gingerly through the filth, a familiar sight by now. At the end of the street, a sailor reeled drunkenly against the walls, stopping to vomit in the gutter. A little girl dressed in dirty rags whined shrilly until an older boy—her brother?—came out of a nearby doorway, scolding as he caught her arm and dragged her off.

It was the boredom, Celia thought, as she turned away from the window, that she hated most. The boredom and the loneliness. She had expected to be frightened, staying there alone, especially after the shock wore off and she realized that Brandon *was* worried about her safety. But surprisingly, she had hardly considered that at all. Even fear, it seemed, could not survive in a climate of constant, unending tedium.

She gave up her vigil at the window and went over to contemplate a row of remarkably dry-looking volumes in a bookcase on the bedroom wall. As she did, a knock sounded at the door, and she jumped up eagerly, expecting only the woman who brought her lunch, but grateful even for that diversion.

When she cracked the door, an unexpected face beamed in at her.

"Kalani! Why, what on earth . . .?" She squealed with pleasure as she flung the door wide open. "I never thought I'd see you here—but oh, I am glad you came!"

Kalani laughed as she breezed into the room, throwing

herself down on a comfortable pile of pillows. She was a big woman, but she moved with surprising grace and today looked especially fetching in a long, clingy robe of Indian silk edged with bands of gold.

"It was a slow afternoon, so I declared myself a holiday—and here I am!" She sprawled languidly on the pillows, shifting one of them under her head. "I hope you really *are* glad to see me, because you aren't going to get rid of me now."

"I wouldn't want to." Celia flopped down beside her, sitting cross-legged on the floor. "It's so lonely here, I even look forward to seeing China's cousin—and she speaks hardly a word of English! You're a special treat. I had forgotten that China told me you work in the city. Is it near here? Will you be able to come and see me often?"

"It's very near." Kalani looked at her, black eyes sparkling with mischief. "In fact, I am just down the hall."

"Down . . . the hall?" The words didn't register at first. When they did, Celia felt herself stiffen. Surely Kalani couldn't mean what she was saying. She couldn't work *here*, unless of course . . .

"Oh, you mean in that big room I saw? Bringing drinks on trays to sailors at the gaming tables?"

"No." Kalani's expression changed subtly, taking on an unexpectedly defensive look as she propped herself up on one elbow. "No, I didn't mean that at all. I am paid for something quite different." Then, as quickly as it had come, the wariness vanished and she was her old impish self again. "Are you shocked because I work in one of those cubicles down the hall and bring a different man—sometimes two or three—to my bed each night?"

"Shocked?" Celia heard her voice come out in an odd little squeak. For someone of her sheltered background, "shocked" hardly covered it. "But isn't that . . . isn't it *unpleasant*?" Oh, God! She felt the color rise to her cheeks. What a stupid thing to say! But all she could think of was that room full of raucous men, and the drunken sailor she had seen before, vomiting on the street.

Kalani only laughed. "No, of course it's not unpleasant. I wouldn't do it if it were. In fact, I find it quite pleasant, being with a man. There *are* places where things like that aren't very nice—in little shacks in the alleys, run by men who don't take care of their girls. But here the proprietor is strict. No one is ever beaten or abused. And I am very popular. I choose the men I go with."

There was something so matter-of-fact in her voice, Celia was stunned. Promiscuity in itself was a subject to be discussed only in hushed whispers. But to add payment in cash . . .

"How can you do it, Kalani?" she blurted out. "Sell your body like that—for money?"

The other girl looked amused. "How funny you *haoles* are. You talk about a woman's 'body' as if it were a holy shrine, so sacred it can never be touched. Then you have to feel guilty every time you let it be defiled. We Hawaiians are more sensible. Anyway, I don't do it for the money. I do it because it's fun."

"*Fun?* How can you say something like that?"

Kalani's eyes twinkled. "You've done the same thing yourself—once or twice. That baby in your belly didn't blow in on the windward breezes. Are you telling me, when you were with your lover, it wasn't fun?"

"Well, no . . ." Celia hesitated, confused. "No, of course not. It was . . . fun, but I'm in *love* with Brandon."

Kalani burst out laughing, unable to contain herself any longer. "You truly are a *haole* when you say funny things like that! I'll be in love with someone myself one day, and I'll be faithful too—at least I suppose I will. I haven't thought that far ahead. But come, let's talk of something else. I can stay only a little while. We wouldn't want to spoil our time together quarreling."

Celia agreed, glad to be quit of a conversation that was growing increasingly confusing. Everything had always been so simple before, black and white, right and wrong, especially in matters pertaining to the opposite sex, but now even her basic beliefs were being called into question. She and Kalani passed the next hour pleasantly, chatting about the islands, about feelings and attitudes, customs that had endured and customs that had changed with the coming of the white man, taking care all the while to steer clear of the one subject that was bound to cause contention.

Only when she was leaving did Kalani turn serious just for a moment as she reached out to catch Celia by the hands. "I hope you don't hate me for being different," she said impulsively. "I want us to be friends."

"We are already," Celia replied. "And, no, I could never hate you, Kalani."

Later, after the girl was gone, Celia found herself running through that conversation again and again, not at all sure how she felt anymore, or how she was supposed to feel.

Perhaps, in a way, Kalani had been right. Perhaps Celia *was* being a hypocrite. She hadn't hesitated to give herself to Brandon, without benefit of clergy or commitments, and she would do the same thing all over again if she had a second chance. And yes, though she wouldn't have expressed it quite that way, it had been fun.

She didn't want anyone else, of course, nor would she ever, for she belonged to Brandon now. But if someone different had come first, if a Schuyler Maarten had succeeded in seducing her, would she have been any more content than Kalani to sit around chastely waiting for her one true love to show up? Honesty compelled her to doubt it as she recalled the intensity of her own physical reactions, the way she felt when Brandon's hand so much as brushed her arm . . . the terrible bittersweet yearning that already racked her body only two days after he had gone.

Brandon . . .

Celia leaned back against the cushions, letting her eyes drift shut as she tried to work things out in her mind. Brandon. How did she feel about him? She adored him, yes, that was easy—but for the rest? Sometimes it seemed to her he was a hopeless maze of contradictions. He had never so much as uttered the word "love" to her, yet his actions that last evening had been loving and gentle. He thought nothing of bringing a shipload of opium to men whose lives would be destroyed by it, yet he had not hesitated an instant to accept responsibility for his child. A perfect gentleman and the devil incarnate—kind and cruel, generous and scurrilous, thoughtful . . . and utterly amoral.

So many men in one, she thought helplessly. She did not even know who he was. And did she really care? Loving or merely dutiful, caring or careless, good or evil, she still missed him—and she ached to have him back.

She laid her hand on her belly, trying to feel the new life stirring inside her, not succeeding yet, for it was too soon for Brandon's son—or Brandon's daughter—to make its presence felt. If she lost the man she loved, if he did not come back, by choice or by fate, at least she would have a part of him to keep, and for that she would be eternally grateful.

The weeks passed slowly for Celia in her silk-and-velvet prison. The rooms, however elegant, grew cramped after a while, and sometimes she was so restless she would go out into the storeroom and wander up and down the aisles, searching idly through supplies that had been abandoned years before. China relented enough to allow some of the other "dance-hall girls," the ones he knew and trusted, to visit her from time to time, but there always seemed to be a new ship in port, and often they were so busy, Celia did not see them for days on end. Even the wonderfully romantic novels she had coaxed one of them, a fiery-haired Scotswoman named Georgina, to pick up in the local tourist shops failed to hold her interest.

More and more she found herself thinking of Burma, of the open, airy house where she had been born . . . the placid, muddy waters of the Irrawaddy . . . the temple on the hillside, glowing pink in the first light of dawn. She missed the friends she had left behind, missed her gentle, soft-spoken mother, missed especially Papa, who beneath that gruff exterior must be grieving terribly for the irresponsible daughter who had run off to chase a will-o'-the-wisp.

The last thing in the world she expected was to hear from any of them, for she had no idea that Brandon had given her parents an address where they might reach her, so it came as a pleasant surprise one afternoon when China arrived with an envelope posted in Rangoon. She had known, of course, that she would receive no firsthand news from Brandon—he had warned her that communications between them would be much too dangerous—but a letter from Ian and Serena was the next best thing and went a long way toward raising her spirits.

China tactfully left her alone, and she curled up in the center of the bed, finding it hard to get comfortable, for the baby was growing larger in her belly.

She picked up her father's letter first, chuckling as she read. How typical of Papa, all stiff and polite, with formal phrases instead of the affection she knew he longed to pour out. Would any other man in the world have extended "congratulations and best wishes" to his own daughter? Still, the tone was generally pleased, unexpectedly so, Celia thought, for she had assumed that the news of her impulsive marriage would only worry him more. She couldn't imagine what Brandon had said in his note, but plainly he had won him over.

Mama's letter was eminently more satisfying. After a few brief paragraphs expressing her relief that Celia was well and happy, and chiding her gently for letting them fret so long, she went on with the pages and pages of gossipy news she knew her daughter would be hungry to hear.

Sin-Sin, it seemed, had had another baby. A second boy, which was good because natives valued a son above everything else, and her position would be greatly enhanced by the "blessed event." Otherwise, there was little to report from the servants' quarters, except that one of the Indian gardeners, an exceptionally handsome lad, had run off with a girl of higher caste, causing great talk among the locals, if only a ripple in the foreign community.

Considerably more intriguing was the fact that the Maarten plantation now had a new owner, a widower named Rowley with two lively and marriageable daughters.

"One in particular," Mama wrote—and Celia could almost see her laughing between the lines—"the elder, is quite dazzling. Much to the annoyance of 'Lady Eliza,' I might add, who has lost every one of her beaux to the girl, even Ashton Claridge—if indeed she ever had him. Her parents were forced to ship her back to England, where there are, as her Mama put it, 'suitable young men for her to choose from.' "

As if it would do her any good, Celia thought, feeling vaguely sorry for Elizabeth, but amused all the same. If a beautiful young woman couldn't find a husband in the colonies, where males outnumbered females twenty to one, she was going to be hard-pressed at home.

"It looked for a while as if Ash was going to marry Mistress Rowley," Mama went on, "but he proved a great deal more sensible than anyone suspected. (Not that there's anything wrong with the child, mind you, she's just a little flighty.) Two or three months ago, he began courting, of all people, Delilah, and just last weekend, at an extravagant gala, they announced their engagement.

"Really, Celia, you should see her! Ash has taken a hand in her dress, and she looks quite charming. (Of course a girl in love has a special glow that always makes her a beauty for a while.) He has even taught her to dance, which she does tolerably well. I think there are more than a few young men in the vicinity who wish now that they had not been so quick to pass her by."

The letter ended all too soon, and Celia reread it several times before folding it up and tucking it under her pillow. She was surprised at the unexpected glitter of tears on her lashes as feelings and memories she had half-forgotten came flooding back.

She loved Kalani dearly, heaven knows, and she was

grateful for the friendship that had sustained her through this long lonely period, but she couldn't help remembering how kind and thoughtful Delilah had been. If there was one person she longed to talk to, one person she was sure would understand, it was that gentle girl who had never judged or looked down on anyone in her life.

Her eyes were still misty a short time later when Kalani came in, followed after a brief interval by Georgina and a fragile dark-haired girl named Shanti, who had been born in Ceylon.

They all spread out on the bed as she read sections of the letter aloud, laughing when she came to the part about Delilah.

"She is the dearest, sweetest, kindest person in the world," she told them. "But she's not pretty, and no one thought she would ever catch a husband—much less Ash Claridge, who is very, *very* handsome."

"I don't see why not," Georgina said, stifling a yawn as she got up to wander about the room. "Some of the ugliest women in the world are married—especially if they're rich."

"Even if they're not," soft-voiced Shanti put in. Her name was Indian, but she had pale, almost milky skin and jade-green eyes. "Looks don't matter that much. Boys make fools of themselves over pretty faces, but men usually outgrow it. They choose good-looking women for their flings—and one with character for a wife."

"And regret it ever after." Georgina plopped down at the vanity table and began rummaging through Celia's scant supply of cosmetics. "A man may think he wants 'character,' but believe me, he doesn't. No matter how old they are, they never lose their eye for beauty—thank God! Where would we be if it weren't for all those frustrated husbands? Forced to make do with sex-starved sailors just off the ship, no doubt. God, Celia, don't you have *any* makeup? I can only find a spot of rouge, and no kohl at all for the eyes."

"Celia doesn't need makeup," Shanti drawled. "Her eyes are big enough without it. And she doesn't require rouge to make plump cheeks fashionably hollow."

Georgina stuck out her tongue, making her round cheeks even rounder, but she was too good-natured to stay angry for long. "Everyone needs makeup, Shanti—even languid young beauties like you. At my age, I can either pile on the paint or give it all up and look for a husband."

"A husband?" Kalani laughed. "You? I can't imagine your throwing away all the bright lights and music to keep house for some middle-age man just because he has a few coins jingling in his pockets."

Celia looked up, curious at the sudden hardness in her tone.

"You sound so cynical—as if marriage were a punishment. Aren't you interested in settling down yourself? Surely you must have had plenty of offers. I know you're popular—you've told me often enough yourself. Besides, I've heard Georgina say it too."

Shanti gave a soft laugh. "And Georgina never says anything kind about the other girls unless it's undeniable."

"True, darling," Georgina agreed. "True."

"Then you *could* get married," Celia persisted. "Even if some of the men are put off by your . . . well, your *background*, there are plenty of others. China would have you in a minute, I'm sure, if only he thought you were interested. And he'd make an excellent husband."

"China?" Shanti looked puzzled. "Ah, you mean that slender young man who's been hanging around lately, with an exceedingly wistful look in his eye. What about it, Kalani? Are you sweet on him?"

"Don't be ridiculous, Shanti." Georgina leaned forward to peer into the mirror. "Kalani would never marry a Chinese. Would you, darling?" She dabbed a generous smattering of rouge on full lips, liking the way they looked when she pouted. "Kalani has her sights set on something much better than that."

"Better?" Celia glanced over at Kalani, who was laughing as if she agreed. "Why, what a thing to say! Who could be better than China?"

"Nobody," Kalani admitted. "He's a wonderfully good

person, and I am truly very fond of him. But his people would make me miserable if I lured him away from the little Chinese girl his grandmother has picked out. Anyway, I don't intend to spend the rest of my life in crowded streets on the waterfront, setting aside every penny so 'the family' can buy more land and more open-fronted restaurants. I *am* going to get married, but I want a man who will give me the kind of life I enjoy."

"She's planning on marrying a rich *haole*," Georgina explained with a toss of her bright red curls.

"Why not?" Kalani agreed. "I am part royal Hawaiian, so that makes me different. You know, more snobbish and acceptable. Not that there are many rich *haole* families on the islands without a few drops of Hawaiian blood in their veins. And of course standards for 'natives' are much easier. No one expects us to be pure when we wed. I'm sure I can find *someone*."

"But what if you don't love him?" Celia asked, horrified.

To her consternation, the remark was greeted with laughter. Then, seeing her expression, Shanti smiled. "You still have much to learn of the world, little Celia. Perhaps if you're lucky, you won't have to. It's easy for you to sit there and talk of love and romance. You've already found your man. And he's richer than anyone Kalani is likely to get—and though I've seen him only once, very handsome."

"And very sexy," Georgina added, her eyelids dropping suggestively. "Any girl here would adore to go to bed with Brandon Christopher . . . and not for just a night."

Something in her voice caught Celia's ear, and though she hated herself for it, she could not help being a little jealous. Hadn't China told her that Brandon had had these rooms for quite a while? Surely he was acquainted with the ladies who paraded up and down the hall in their high-heeled slippers and gaudy gowns. And red-headed, high-spirited Georgina was just the sort a virile man would enjoy.

"Come on," Kalani broke in, laughing. "We'd better get out of here before we upset this poor child any more. You mustn't mind us too much, Celia. We always joke like this when we're together. And don't worry about me—I swear I won't marry any rich *haole* I don't love."

They were still laughing as they paraded through the door, promising to come back the next day if they could. Celia laughed with them, but later she found herself thinking back on what they said, and even hours after they were gone, she could not shake a feeling of uneasiness. Wandering over to the window, she stared down unseeing at the dusk-dimmed street.

Kalani had said they were joking, but were they? She glanced back at the bedroom, with the wide double bed a none-too-subtle invitation behind its curtained arch. She could almost see Brandon stretched out there, his lean muscular body naked against the quilted-silk coverlet. Or lounging in the deep copper bathtub while a scantily clad woman leaned over him, pouring warm water down his back . . . climbing in beside him.

Georgina—with her red lips parted to pleasure him? Or Shanti, for all that she said she had seen him only once?

Celia stepped back from the window, knowing she was being unreasonable but unable to help herself. China had handpicked the girls who were allowed to visit her—surely he wouldn't have chosen one of Brandon's former favorites. Her imagination was beginning to run away with her. It wasn't good, being alone like this.

If only Brandon were there.

She went over to the bed and sank down on the soft mattress. If only she could feel his arms around her, hear the deep, rich baritone of his laughter in her ears. He was so far away from her now; she did not know what dangers he might encounter—or what was in his heart. She did not even know if she would see him again.

If only she could be sure he was coming back, she thought, picking up a pillow and crushing it to her breast. If only she did not have to wonder whether her child would ever know its father.

25

As her pregnancy advanced, Celia grew increasingly restless, and China was reluctantly forced to allow her out, though only after nightfall, and then only to the Kwan-family compound, where he was sure she would be safe. On such occasions, rather to her amusement, he insisted she wear a long cloak with a voluminous hood that kept her face in shadow.

Thus it was that she stepped, all bundled up, out of the darkened side doorway of the bawdy house that first night of the Chinese New Year. A sense of holiday was in the air, even as the carriage wheels began to roll, and she peered, fascinated, through the curtains at dazzling flashes of color that seared across the sky, giving a fairytale prettiness to the daytime-dingy streets of Chinatown.

"To scare away the Skin Tiger," China explained as a new burst of fireworks exploded through the darkness. "This is the night he comes out to prowl. If you're not careful, he'll steal all the cakes from the poor—and give them to the rich."

Celia laughed. "Are you serious?"

"Of course. We Chinese are practical. Not like you Westerners. You would have a pretty legend with someone stealing from the rich to give to the poor—but we know better. We have the Skin Tiger, and the poor had better watch out!"

"Don't tell me you believe all that?"

"No one who was educated by the missionaries *believes* in the Skin Tiger," he said, then added, smiling: "Of course, we set off fireworks anyway—just in case."

They arrived to find the Kwan house lavishly decorated, with dozens of candlelit lanterns strung out on lines, lending a burst of color to the night. A crimson banner had been draped above the door, with glittering gold characters spelling out an invitation for lucky spirits to come in and grace the house.

Old Grandmother herself greeted them at the gate, an unusual gesture, but one which Celia took as a tribute to her special fondness for Brandon. It surprised her a little to see how small she looked in the flickering light, and it occurred to her that she had never noticed her standing still before. The bindings on her feet had been loosened frequently of late, for they had been giving her trouble, but tonight they were tight, and as she moved slowly toward the kitchen, it was apparent she was having difficulty walking.

This was the last night of the old year, before it would be swallowed up by the first dawn of the first moon, and the entire Kwan family had gathered for the occasion. Everything was done in accordance with the time-honored rituals. No meat was served at dinner, nor had any been prepared throughout the day, for the use of a knife, however careful, might mean the cutting of a cherished friendship. And of course the rooms had not been cleaned, for a broom might sweep away good fortune.

Celia was amused, though she was careful to keep it to herself, as she watched Old Grandmother set a lamp before the empty niche of the Kitchen God, lighting his way back from the long journey to the heavens, where even now he would be making his yearly report on the family's conduct to the Jade Emperor. Not that the contents of that report were in doubt, as China assured her. Good recommendations had already been guaranteed by burning a small amount of paper money as a bribe, and in case that failed, smearing the effigy's lips with enough rice wine to fuddle his thinking.

Once the festive dinner was finished, the family retired to the courtyard, which had been decorated with fragrant branches of evergreen, gathered from the nearby *palis*. Everyone vied with each other now, seeing who could tear down the most boughs and trample them underfoot. Everyone except Old Grandmother, who stood to one side watching the others.

Perhaps because her feet hurt so much, Celia thought sadly. What a barbaric custom, binding a woman's feet in the odd conceit that those "golden lilies" would make her more attractive to a potential marriage partner.

Renewed flashes of fireworks lit the sky as China's eldest uncle touched a match to the boughs, sending them up in flames as a symbol of the departing year. Red envelopes were handed out to the delighted children, who clapped in glee when they looked inside to find the "lucky money" that would ensure their safe passage through the coming year.

China turned to Celia with a grin. *"Kung hei fat choy!* That means, 'I wish you a prosperous new year!' Though I think"—his eyes dropped playfully to her belly—"that you have already found *your* good fortune."

Celia smiled as her hand rested on the rounded bulge that used to be her waist. The way the baby had begun to kick, Brandon was probably right—he was certainly athletic enough to be a boy! She could still remember how excited she had been, not long before, when she felt him move inside her for the first time. It had been for her a private miracle, so wonderful and unique she couldn't believe any other woman had ever felt like that before.

She looked up to see the grandmother's eyes on her, asking a question that could be understood without words.

"Yes," she replied. "Here." Taking a gnarled hand in hers, she laid it on the new little life in her belly.

Light glinted briefly in her dark eyes, a flash of feeling Celia could not quite grasp, and she was reminded once again how old and frail the woman had looked standing in the gateway. Then the weariness vanished, and a quiet peace came into that aged face as she spoke a few words in her own tongue.

"She is saying that it is good," China translated, smiling rather vaguely, Celia thought. "She is saying that life—the cycle of life—goes on. Some die, some are born . . . and the world continues, as it was meant to."

He was still smiling, but something in his voice tugged at Celia's heart, and suddenly, for no reason at all, she was afraid. Life goes on—surely that was a comforting thought. Why then did the night feel so cold?

"Yes," she said softly, trying to shake off the mood. "Brandon's son will be born soon, and that *is* good."

"My son will be born too," China added with a twinkle in his eye. "At least that's what Old Grandmother says. Nine months and a day after I marry the nice Chinese girl she has picked out for me."

"But you wouldn't . . ." Celia broke off as China gave a warning shake of his head.

"Perhaps not," he agreed, glancing at his grandmother, who had hobbled over to the other side of the court. "But there is no need to speak of that tonight."

The last fireworks had faded from the sky by the time the family was ready to retire, and China went around the corner to call the carriage, which had been waiting in one of the side streets. Celia felt a little sad leaving, for she would have liked to be there at dawn when they threw open the doors to greet the new year, and the incense was lighted and the ancestors were honored—and the Kitchen God was once again ensconced in his shrine above the stove. But she sensed China's instincts were sound. Now that her condition was noticeable, she would be much too obvious slipping in and out of that house where married "ladies of quality" kept their rendezvous. It had been unwise enough, insisting on coming out at night. To return by light of day would be folly.

Her last glimpse through half-drawn curtains was of Old

Grandmother standing in the gateway, not moving at all, just looking out—as if she were trying to say something. But what it could be, Celia had no idea, and once again she found herself shivering.

The feeling persisted as she sat alone in her room with the lamp turned so low the furnishings were barely shadows looming out of the darkness. She kept seeing that last look on the old woman's face, kept hearing her words over and over again. *Life goes on,* she had said. *Life goes on. Some are born . . . and some die.*

Brandon?

Oh God. Suddenly Celia understood, and she knew what it was that had made her afraid before. The cycle of life, moving and changing . . . Brandon's child growing inside her, and Brandon himself . . . where?

Facing what?

Was that what Old Grandmother had been trying to tell her? Old people were like that sometimes, more attuned to things beyond the senses, perhaps because they themselves were so close to eternity. Was her lover's life forfeit then? Was she to hold Brandon's child in her arms only to know she had lost Brandon forever?

The days and weeks that followed brought little respite. China did not invite her to his home again, and Celia, understanding the reasons for his caution, or thinking she did, was disinclined to press him. But too much time alone led to too much brooding, and she found herself dwelling on that vague, unpleasant premonition Old Grandmother's words had stirred in her. And because she had been so wrapped up in herself lately, because she had had so little else to think about, she couldn't help feeling that whatever it was, it had to do with her.

And she was certain it spelled an end to her happiness with the man she loved.

As it happened, however, it was not Brandon Christopher's death the old woman had been predicting. Had Celia been less self-absorbed, she would have realized sooner. It was her own. Old Grandmother died quite easily in her sleep two weeks before the baby was due to be born. Her last evening had been spent, as usual, fussing over records and scolding everyone in sight for spending too much money on too many foolish things. The next morning, when her granddaughter had gone to wake her, she did not respond.

"You must not grieve so much," China said when he came to fetch Celia for the funerary rites. It was the first and only time she had been allowed to leave her small suite of rooms in the daylight. "Chinese do not look upon death as you Westerners do. To us it is not an end, but a transition. Oh, we might weep for the death of a precious child or a young man or woman who has barely begun to live. But there is only gratefulness in our hearts when we say good-bye to an old person whose life has been rich and full and who has died, as she would have wished, in peace."

And who would be buried, Celia knew, with all the rituals and traditions that were so important in the Chinese village where she had been born.

When they arrived at the house, the large pine coffin was in its place in the center of the courtyard, and Old Grandmother had already been laid inside, with a little red bag attached to her buttonhole, containing a pinch of tea and a piece of candy, a bit of salt to add savor to her food, and a silver coin to buy whatever she might need in the land to which she was going. A small bundle of food was in one hand, so she would be able to feed the dogs as she crossed the Great Dog Mountain, and her feet had been bound together so her body would not be tempted to get up again.

The entire family had kept her company the night before, dressed in unbleached, unhemmed garments as they sat beside the coffin in the yard. Musicians had been hired to help her on her way, for it was only natural that the spirit would want to linger by the body and find it hard to begin that long voyage into the unknown.

The coffin was loaded onto a gaily painted wagon, and

Celia, who had changed into a white robe like the others, with a white cap covering her blond curls, was helped onto the back, where she would ride with the little children who were too young yet to walk. As they moved slowly through the wide gateway, they were followed by the band, and then the mourners, forming a long procession, for the Kwans were a powerful clan and the old woman had been well-respected.

A brief stop was made at the small neighborhood temple where Old Grandmother had often paused to light a stick of incense as she returned home with a brace of chickens or an armful of leafy yellow-green *bok choy*. Her eldest son, serving as the chief mourner, knelt on the ground pounding three times with a wooden pin to knock at the gates of Hades, then raising it three times to appeal to the gates of heaven. That accomplished, they moved on to the crowded Chinese cemetery, where a gravesite had already been prepared.

Sadly Celia watched as an earthen bowl was set out and all the paper money and clothes were burned, the houses and carriages and servants that Old Grandmother had never allowed herself to enjoy in life because they always seemed too frivolous.

The flames burned slowly to a pale gray ash, and the bowl was broken, severing the old woman's ties to the earth at last.

Celia returned with the mourners to the house in Chinatown, but sensing the need of the family to retreat into itself, she left them almost at once to go back to her own rooms. There she sat alone for a long time, thinking of Old Grandmother and the mystery of death . . . and wondering what it was, if anything, that lay beyond the darkness of the grave.

It would be so easy, she thought, if she could believe, like the others, in the paper houses and the paper servants—an exact extension of the world she had always known. Too easy perhaps, for she sensed an essential wrongness in simple answers to such difficult questions.

Where were they now? All the people she had ever
cared about and lost? Where was Old Grandmother with
her red bag hooked on her buttonhole and food for the
dogs in her hand? Where would Brandon be if one day
they came and told her that he too was gone? What
comfort would there be for her then in the paper images
that solaced the others today?

She was still sitting up, sometime around midnight,
when she was aware of a sudden strange sensation. Not a
pain exactly, but a *something*, a little twinge strong enough
to catch her attention. Tensing, she waited, wondering if
she was about to go into labor earlier than the doctor had
predicted.

When the feeling did not come back, she relaxed enough
to laugh at herself. If she was going to be alarmed every
time she felt something out of the ordinary, she was going
to have a long two weeks ahead.

She finally went to sleep an hour later. When she woke
the next morning, the sun was already streaming through
the shutters, casting long, distorted shadows on the floor
and walls. China arrived as usual, shortly before noon, and
she considered telling him about that moment's queasiness, but dismissed the thought, embarrassed at mentioning such a delicate subject in front of a man.

"I think I'm getting a little nervous," she said instead.
"It's almost . . . well, almost *time*, you know."

China gave her a sharp look. "I thought the doctor said
you had two weeks yet."

"He did, and I'm sure he's right. I don't have any
reason to suspect the baby's coming earlier, not really. It's
just that . . ." She let her voice drift off, finding it hard to
express her feelings. She was not afraid of childbirth,
though she was naturally a little apprehensive, even with
the "twilight sleep" the doctor had promised. But she was
eager to have it over and done with, to feel the child in her
arms and know it was whole and healthy.

"But you can't help being overanxious, is that it? Well,
I can't say I blame you. We're all on pins and needles

these days. Don't forget, this is my first time being a stand-in father. And good practice, too—in case I repeat the process one day for real.''

Celia smiled, as she knew he had intended. "But what about later?" she asked. "After the child is born? Am I going to have to stay in these cramped little rooms until Brandon comes back, whenever that might be? I can't think it's a healthy environment for a baby, and I don't mean the brothel either. I mean the rats and the roaches.''

"Lucky for you my grandmother is no longer with us.'' China laughed a little as he shook his head. "I could never have considered moving you if she were. Chinese ladies are very particular about things like that. She'd have had my head if I risked the baby's life by exposing it to the open air before it was three months old.''

"Does that mean''—Celia looked up hopefully—"that you're considering it now?''

China hesitated. He had, in fact, been considering just that, especially after yesterday, when he had taken Celia out in broad daylight and nothing had happened. There had been no sign of Teresa Valdes or any of her men since the day Brandon sailed—and rats *were* a menace to newborns, to say nothing of lice and fleas, which carried the plague.

"Very well. I don't see what harm it would do. But not until after the baby is born and you have regained your strength.''

"Oh, China!" Celia felt as if something heavy had been lifted from her shoulders. So all this hiding *was* just a precaution. If she were really in danger, China would never give in to her pleas. "You don't know how good that sounds. I can hardly wait to go back to the house on the beach and—''

"No, not there. I don't want you to return to that house—ever again.'' The words came out sharper than he had intended. True, he had had the house watched for several weeks and no one had spotted anything except a few children playing around, but still, it was too dangerous. "I've found a place in the *palis* that's more suitable,

a little above the beach at Diamond Head. It's small, but
there's a room that would be perfect for you and the baby,
and another for the *amah*, who will stay with you all the
time. If you like, I can make the arrangements.''

If she liked? Celia was so excited at the thought, she
could think of nothing else for the rest of the day, not even
the impending birth of the baby, which after all was still
two weeks away.

Everything had already been attended to, and in fact
there was little left to worry about. Kalani had moved her
things into a room at the end of the long hallway, where
Celia could reach her by rapping on the warehouse wall,
and in a day or so Shanti would begin sleeping on the
cushions in the small sitting room just outside the curtained arch. Not that there was any hurry. First babies
were always late. Georgina had said so often enough, and
Celia felt confident, for Georgina seemed to know a great
deal about babies and the process of giving birth.

She was relaxed, if a little uncomfortable, when she
went to bed that night, dozing off occasionally, though
never quite falling into a deep sleep. Then suddenly, out of
nowhere, a wrenching pain jolted her body, so sharp it
took her breath away, leaving her gasping for air even
after it was gone.

The room was pitch dark, and for a moment she could
not get her bearings or figure out what had happened.
Then she realized.

It had started. That was the first pain, the one they had
told her to expect. The child was ready to be born.

Her first instinct was to throw on her robe and run into
the warehouse, pounding wildly on the wall to tell Kalani
to go for the doctor. Then, realizing how late it must be,
and not wanting to disturb anyone at that ungodly hour,
she decided to wait, at least for a while. The pains would
be spaced evenly, with a long time between them at first—
Georgina had told her that too—growing closer and closer
as labor advanced. Probably the baby would not be born
before dinnertime the next day. Wouldn't she feel like a

fool, dragging everyone out of bed, only to have them sit and wait for hours?

The next pain came almost before the thought was completed, much sooner than she had expected, though she did not have a clock and couldn't be sure how long it had been. She was tempted again to rouse Kalani, but again she opted against it, certain it was not necessary. By the time she realized she was wrong, it was already too late. The pains were so close together they were almost constant, and she couldn't have gotten out of bed and dragged herself across the floor of the storeroom even had she had the strength to try.

She was in a state of near-panic, not knowing what to do, when suddenly the door opened and Georgina, who had been unusually restless all night, peeked in to make sure everything was all right. One look at Celia's face was enough to tell her it wasn't.

She set the lamp she had been carrying down on a table beside the bed and laid a light hand on Celia's brow, speaking a few soft, reassuring words before hurrying off again. When she returned five minutes later, she told Celia that Shanti had gone to call the doctor, while Kalani was fetching an excellent Hawaiian midwife who lived nearby.

In only a few minutes, however, it became apparent that neither doctor nor midwife was going to make it in time. Georgina, assessing the situation with a cool glance, rolled up her sleeves and got to work. First she stripped the top covers from the bed, then eased Celia gently onto her back, tugging off the sheer nightdress that would only have been in the way.

"It's too damn hot in here," she said gruffly. "You're already drenched with sweat. No point getting tangled in your nightclothes too."

The pains had grown more intense, tearing at Celia's body, leaving no room for embarrassment as she lay naked on the bed. Georgina tore off a length of sheeting and twisted it into a rope, which she wrapped around the bedpost and placed in her hands. Celia wanted desperately to say something, wanted to ask what was happening—if she was going to be all right—but the pains kept coming and coming, and she could not find the breath.

Georgina seemed to sense what she was thinking. "It's just fine, love," she reassured her. "You've an impatient little rascal here—much too quick for a first baby—but otherwise everything's normal. Don't worry about a thing. I know exactly what to do."

She didn't, of course. She had witnessed childbirth several times and had a vague idea—as long as everything went well. But she had already sensed it would go easier on Celia if the girl were confident and unafraid.

Celia had neither the time nor the will to question Georgina's words. Letting instinct take over, she closed her eyes and tugged at the twisted cord, following a natural urge to bear down. She could feel the baby moving inside her, feel it struggling to get out, and she struggled with it, lost to everything but her need to give life to her child.

Only once did she look up. Georgina was standing over her, moist red hair plastered, like Celia's own, against her brow. Thick black mascara ran in streaks down her cheeks. To anyone else she would have looked comical, but Celia thought she had never seen anything so beautiful in her life.

"I'm sorry," she whispered, trying to smile. "You don't even have someone to boil the water for you."

Georgina chuckled, glad to see that the girl had not lost her humor. "Don't you fret about that. I've always said it's only for the fathers anyway. Makes the poor dears feel as if they were of use—which, Lord knows, at a time like this, they're anything but."

A new wave of pain swept over Celia, worse than anything that had gone before, and it was all she could do to cling to the cord, concentrating on the need to remain quiet, not to scream out, even though Georgina had told her it would be all right. Childbirth was hardly uncommon in a brothel—no one would think anything of a woman's cries.

Then, even that was too much and she let go, not screaming, as she had expected, but grunting, pushing, forcing the child through the last stages of birth. There was one final moment of resistance, one moment she was terrified it was never going to happen, and then, incredibly, she felt something between her legs.

"I can see the head," Georgina called out excitedly. "There you are, love, keep pushing—that's a good girl. Just a little longer, just a minute now . . . we're almost there."

Are we? Celia thought, praying that Georgina was right, that the birth really was as simple as it appeared, that she hadn't hurt her baby by foolishly neglecting to call for help in time. Then there was one last burst of pain, almost but not quite unbearable, and suddenly it was over. Suddenly the baby was there in Georgina's hands, wriggling, squirming—alive!—and she heard it begin to howl. Great lusty cries, announcing to the world that it had arrived and was healthy.

"It's a boy," Georgina shouted with a laugh. She hadn't even had to turn him upside down and clap him on the back to get him breathing. "A fine strapping boy! And the image of his father, I declare."

A boy! Celia smiled as she looked up at that tiny form, kicking and crying already with a will of its own. Brandon had been so sure the child was going to be a son, and he had been right.

By the time the midwife arrived, all that was left was to apply freshly gathered herbs to coax out the afterbirth, though even that was not necessary, for as Georgina had declared, it was a normal delivery in every sense, except, of course, for the speed. When the doctor came in a short time later, there was nothing for him to do but look her over, nod his head gravely from time to time, and think how he was going to brag to his wife that he had just earned the largest—and easiest—fee of his life.

Celia listened politely to the instructions he gave her, though she was much too exhausted to take them in, and it was with a vague sense of relief that she finally saw him leave. She had eyes now only for the tiny newborn who had been wrenched so recently from her body, and she reached out as Georgina came to lay him, swathed in a soft white blanket, beside her on the bed.

He fitted perfectly into the crook of her arm, nestling instinctively against her breast, seeming even more a miracle now than he had when she first felt him stir within her. She bent her head, brushing her lips against surprisingly thick golden hair, touched with red in the lamplight. Was Georgina right? she wondered. Was he going to look like Brandon?

Certainly he didn't look like Brandon at the moment. He didn't look like anyone except his own tiny self, which was fine with her, because as far as she was concerned, he was perfect in every way. Celia glowed with pride as she stared down at that amazing little face, red and crinkly to anyone else, but utterly beautiful to her—at a little hand peeking out from the edge of the blanket, tiny baby fingers so small they hardly seemed real.

At last she understood the instincts that had driven Brandon from the first, compelling him to protect his unborn son at any cost. Understood and felt them a hundredfold, for she was a woman, and those months of pregnancy and hours of birth had given her a bond with her child no man could ever share.

She leaned back against the pillow, tired but feeling no urge to sleep. She had thought, until that moment, that there were things in her life she would change if she could. Now she knew that was not so. Whatever had happened in the past, whatever she had or hadn't done—whatever the future might bring—there was one accomplishment no one could take away from her.

She had given birth to a fine, strong son.

26

MOONWIND

If there was one thing that clouded Celia's happiness in the weeks following the birth of the baby, it was that Brandon was not there to share it with her.

The boy was wonderfully healthy, growing by leaps and bounds, and in no time at all he had lost his newborn redness and begun to take on a round, quite satisfied look. No doubt about it, Celia thought, secretly proud, he was the greediest little creature in the world, gobbling up an amazing amount of her milk with each feeding and gaining precious ounces every day. Sometimes, when she held him in her arms and looked down at him, it made her heart ache. He was going to be so big the first time his father saw him—Brandon was missing so much.

She no longer worried about Brandon, at least not the way she had before, for the frightening premonitions were gone now and she sensed that he was safe and well. But it still grieved her to think he had not seen his son, and in all likelihood didn't even know he had one. The first thing she had wanted, when Georgina took the baby out of her arms and laid him in his cradle, was to send a telegram, but China had been adamant, insisting that word be passed through the channels Brandon had set up.

And since those channels entailed sending messages only on steamers that flew the flag of the Christopher Lines—and then only with a handful of selected captains—she had no confidence he would ever find out.

The birth had been an easy one, and Celia recovered her strength quickly, feeling almost like herself again after the first two weeks, as long as she remembered not to overdo. With renewed strength, however, came a return of the high spirits that had always made her unpredictable and hard to manage, and China was more than a bit apprehensive when he had to tell her that the house he had found was unacceptable after all and it would be three or four weeks before they could move to the hills.

To his surprise, she took the news calmly, almost as if it didn't matter. Any other time he would have felt prickles of alarm at that abrupt about-face; now he was relieved enough to accept it without question, attributing her change of heart to the gentling influence of motherhood, a phenomenon about which most males managed to be thoroughly informed. At any rate, it had plainly worked in this case, for here was Celia, docile and sweetly obedient, who had never been either before.

He would not have been whistling quite so cheerfully as he headed down the stairway and out onto the street had he known that she was giving in only because a new plan had begun to take shape in her mind. A plan that required being close to the telegraph office.

China had told her most emphatically that she couldn't send a message to Brandon, but on thinking it over, it had occurred to her that China was hardly in a position to give orders. He wasn't her father or her husband. He was a dear and cherished friend, and she would listen to whatever advice he offered, but she didn't have to take it if she thought he was wrong.

From that conclusion it was just a step to the realization that she had, after all, an alternative. Just before Brandon left, he had written out an address for her, a place on the West Coast where he could be reached "in case of dire emergency." All she had to do now was wait until no one was looking, duck out, and send the message . . . and who would be the wiser?

This was not an *emergency* perhaps, dire or otherwise—

not in the accepted sense of the word—but surely a man had the right to know he was a father. And honestly, she thought, mulling it over, what harm would it do? Even if someone found out about the telegram after the fact, it wouldn't make any difference. As long as she didn't put her address on it, no one could use it to track her down.

Slipping away proved harder than she had expected, and she didn't find an opportunity until two days before their scheduled move to the hills to a small one-room house China had located. It was shortly before noon, and the baby was sleeping in his crib, with the *amah*, a stern-looking middle-aged Chinese woman, dozing beside him. The telegraph office was only a few blocks away—Celia had seen it once as they rode through town—and she was sure she could be there and back before anyone even knew she was gone.

Outside, the air was hot and steamy, and Celia found herself strolling more slowly than she had expected, looking over her shoulder every few seconds, and feeling foolish as she did, for no one was paying the least bit of attention. Still, she was conscious that she was disobeying China's orders, and it was a relief when she finally reached the office.

There was only one clerk on duty, a youngish man of eighteen or nineteen, who did not seem the least bit pleased to see her.

"If you'd come a minute later," he said rudely, "you'd have had a wait, that's for sure. I take my time over lunch. An hour at least, maybe more on a day like this when no one's around."

"Lucky for me then," Celia said evenly, "that I didn't walk slower." Lucky indeed! Her knees were shaking just at the thought of it! She would never have dared wait an hour—and who knew when she'd have a chance like this again?

The clerk's sleepy eyes narrowed as Celia handed him Brandon's name and address, and for just an instant she felt a twinge of apprehension. Then, laughing it off, she reached for the pen and pad of paper he shoved across the counter. Of course he had recognized the name Brandon Christopher! Wasn't Christopher Lines the most important shipping firm on the island?

She forgot all about the clerk as she began to compose the message, scribbling down a phrase or two, then scratching them out, not even bothering to count the words. This was hardly an occasion for thrift. She had already gone through several sheets of paper by the time she was finally satisfied and leaned back to read the result: "You were right, my love. You have a son, and he is very beautiful. He has red hair, not dark like yours, but strawberry blond, and his eyes are a lighter green. He does not have a name yet, for I could not choose one without consulting you."

There, that was what she wanted to say. It was not much, of course, but it would have to do until they saw each other. Picking up the pen again, she jotted a hasty P.S.: "I will try to come back in case you can send a reply. You may reach me care of the telegraph office."

The clerk didn't say anything when he took the paper, but his eyes were greedy as he scanned it, ostensibly to tally up the words so he would know what to charge. Celia *Christopher*, she had signed it. Now, that was interesting. And Brandon Christopher had a son. Interesting again.

His eyes flitted toward the window, but the street outside was empty. Too bad the boy wasn't there, tending to his little sister. He turned to the paper again, counting the words for real this time. Well, no matter. She *had* said she was coming back.

And when she did, there would to be money in it for him.

Brandon Christopher scowled faintly at the paper in his hand. A telegram? What the devil had possessed them, sending a message like that? It was much too dangerous.

Still . . . China Kwan must have authorized it. He glanced up for a moment, seeing nothing unusual on the lazy Monterey street where he had been staying. Yes, certainly China had agreed. Celia was a willful minx, but she would never have done anything like this on her own. And if China believed it was safe, then it was.

He relaxed a little as he read the words again. A son. *His* son. It was hard to fathom somehow, as if the term did not apply to him, and yet he knew it did. There were so many times, these past long months, he almost believed it was a dream, almost believed he had fantasized Celia and the child conceived of their love. Now for the first time he was beginning to understand it was real.

You were right, my love. You have a son. The words leapt out at him, making him smile. Her way of reminding him that he had been sure all along . . . and she had doubted. A kind of teasing mock surrender.

Only nothing Celia ever did was a surrender. She was not the kind of woman for that. She was the kind to challenge, to demand—to make a man give more of himself than he ever dreamed possible. God, how he missed her! How he longed to be with her again, to catch her up in his embrace, to rejoice with her in the son she had given him, to make love until they were exhausted and fell asleep in each other's arms.

He has red hair, not dark like yours, but strawberry blond . . .

Brandon looked down at the telegram again, not seeing it at all, seeing only the smoky outlines of an opium den in Shanghai, a still figure lying on a wooden pallet, red-gold hair dull as dirty straw. Damn! Why did his thoughts keep drifting back to that godforsaken hole? That grotesque face, a death's-head—only the eyes staring out of it alive? Was the vision to haunt his dreams for the rest of his life?

Michael, the boy who had started this insane obsession . . . Michael, to whom there were debts still unpaid, promises to be fulfilled.

His eyes came back into focus, picking out the words, reading them again. *My love . . . you have a son.* There was a certain rightness about it, a sense of compensation

. . . as if in some strange way part of the promise had been kept. Perhaps the only part that ever truly could be.

He turned the paper over on impulse, scratching out three words on the back. Then, wrapping it around a dollar bill, he handed it to a passing lad, the son of a friend he trusted.

"Here, boy, take this into town. See that it's sent to Mrs. Celia Christopher, care of the telegraph office in Honolulu."

She would have her answer now, he thought, smiling to himself as he glanced down the empty street again. Perhaps one day he would be able to tell her what it meant.

Celia received the telegram a few hours before she was due to move into the new house on the hillside. She had barely managed to sneak out, and all the way over to the office, she had had her fingers crossed that she would find it open. Now, as she looked down at the slip of paper with those three terse words, she could not keep from laughing.

How exactly like Brandon! Not a word of concern about her, though he would know, of course, from the tone of her message that she was all right. And not a word about his own feelings either, though he must be fairly bursting with pride to know he was a father. Just that one simple, concise, utterly practical phrase: "Name him Michael."

It was a little past noon and the same clerk was on duty. Celia noticed that he made no move to go to lunch, though he did wander over to the window, scratching curiously at the glass, as if one of the many spots of dirt on that filthy pane offended him.

What was there about Brandon that made him so endearing and so frustrating all at the same time? Obviously he cared deeply for the boy—he had made a point of participating in the choice of a name, all that he could share at that distance. And he would never have broken his own rule about communication if he didn't care for her too.

But, oh, sometimes he did have a funny way of showing it! She folded the cable up into a tidy little square and tucked it in her pocket. Why couldn't she have fallen in love with someone nice and sensible, someone like Ash Claridge, who always said and did the right thing? Why did she have to set her heart on a man like Brandon Christopher?

The street outside was nearly deserted as she stepped through the door. A carriage rumbled past, moving slowly— then there was no one but a small thin boy huddled in a doorway with a girl who might have been his sister. Dark eyes stared at Celia, haunting her. As if he were hungry, she thought, and she pulled out a coin, tossing it to him. A strange look came over his face as he caught it, almost reluctant, as if he didn't want it, but she was in such a hurry, she barely noticed.

She did not look back as she continued down the street. If she had, she would have seen him thrust the girl deeper into the shadows and follow in the same direction.

Storm Winds Rising

27

Celia paused for a moment on the gently sloping trail and stared down at the waves as they broke, foamy white against glittering golden sands on the beach at Diamond Head. It was the first time she had been out by herself since they had moved into the little house three days before, and the feeling of freedom was so exhilarating she laughed out loud.

The horse beneath her snorted impatiently, throwing his mane into the wind, and she reached out to lay a hand on his neck. The chestnut gelding had come as a surprise, for though she had seen Brandon ride him often enough, it hadn't occurred to her to wonder where he was now that his master was gone. She couldn't have been more delighted, earlier that morning, when China showed up with the horse tied to the rear of the cart.

"He needs exercise, and so do you," he had said, then added, with the caution that was so typical of him: "I want you to stay close to the house. No riding into town or down on the beach, where you'd be too visible. And cover your hair with a riding hat. There aren't many platinum blonds in Hawaii."

Celia laughed again as she tossed her head, shaking the gauzy veil over her shoulders. She had obeyed China's instructions to the letter, though, heaven knows, she must look a sight! She had no proper riding outfit, only a pair of Levi's from the ship and a light blue shirtwaist blouse,

tucked in at the belt. From the neck down, she looked just
like a tomboy; from the neck up, she was a perfect lady,
with that dainty blue silk chapeau and long floating veil.

The beach stretched out below her, empty as far as the
eye could see, and for just an instant she was tempted to
defy China and ride boldly across the sand. How she
would have loved to gallop along the water's edge, listening to the *clop-clop, clop-clop* of the horse's hooves,
feeling the wind against her face, the taste of salt on her
lips. But she had already asserted her independence once
that week, and now that the escapade at the telegraph
office was over and nothing had come of it, she was
beginning to feel a little guilty.

Not that she wouldn't do it again. She would, of course,
but China *was* her friend. It didn't seem right, going
behind his back like that, not even telling him afterward
what she had done.

She tightened her hold on the reins, easing the horse
into a slow walk as she turned his head toward home. The
day was beautiful, the breezes wonderfully cooling, and
there was a lazy sense of contentment in the air. Perhaps,
after all, she thought, she would confess the truth. No
harm had been done. China would be angry for a while,
but he'd get over it, and then there'd be honesty between
them again.

She had just rounded the last turn and had the house in
sight when she was startled to see a slender figure racing
toward her down the path. Frowning, she reined in the
horse as she recognized the young Chinese girl who had
been hired to help with the baby.

Her first reaction was not apprehension, but anger. The
amah had gone into town that morning with China to pick
up supplies, and the girl had been given strict orders not to
leave Michael alone. She couldn't have been out of the
house for more than a minute or two, but still . . . Babies
need constant care.

Celia slid to the ground, fully intending to give the girl a piece of her mind, when she caught sight of the look on her face.

Something was wrong! Every mother's instinct in her body told her that, even without the girl's garbled cries, which made no sense, for they were only half in English. Something was desperately wrong, and it concerned her child.

Dropping the reins, she began to run, not even aware of the frightened girl who was scurrying unsuccessfully to keep up. Every sense was alert now: her eyes scanned the front of the house, her ears strained for the cries that would tell her Michael was sick or hurt. But she heard nothing, nothing at all, and she she was more afraid than ever.

The door was open when she reached it. Inside everything was strangely silent, and she faltered for a moment on the threshold, expecting to find Michael pale and still in his crib, expecting perhaps a pool of blood around him . . . expecting anything but what she saw.

The crib was empty.

For a moment she only stood there, too numb to react or even to think. Then instinct took over, and whirling around, she caught the girl by the shoulders, shaking her so violently she could hear her teeth rattle.

"He's gone," she cried, half-hysterical by now. "My baby's not in his crib! In God's name, what happened? Where is he?"

The girl's face was ashen, and Celia loosened her hold, realizing she had frightened her too much to speak. Tense and trembling, she waited as the terrified servant struggled to get out the story.

It was several minutes before Celia could piece things together, and then only sketchily. Apparently the girl had heard a strange noise—just what, Celia was never sure—and had gone out to investigate. Seeing nothing in the vicinity of the cottage, she had followed the sound for some distance before she gave up and came back.

When she got to the house, the baby was gone.

"Oh, my God . . ."

Celia barely whispered the words as she stared, dazed, at that empty crib. Her eyes kept wanting to drift away, to search the room, as if somehow, by trying hard enough, she could find him, as if he had just crawled off and gone to sleep in the corner. But all the time, she knew.

Michael could not have crawled out of the crib by himself, and no one had carried him off to croon sweet lullabies in his ears. Michael had been kidnapped.

She leaned wearily against the door frame, trying not to give in to the faintness that swept over her. China had been right. It *was* dangerous here in Hawaii—and she hadn't listened! She had insisted on sneaking out to send that telegram to Brandon. It had seemed a prank at the time, a harmless lighthearted prank that could never hurt anyone.

Only it hadn't been harmless at all. Someone must have seen her at the telegraph office, perhaps had even been waiting the second time she went . . . and had followed when she left.

Now her son had been kidnapped.

She spun around, brushing past the startled girl as she went to find the horse where he had wandered off to graze in an adjacent field. The reality of what she had done was hideously clear, but she didn't let herself dwell on it. If all this was her fault, then she couldn't waste time feeling sorry for herself. She had to do something, and she had to do it quickly. One thing at least was on her side. Whoever had taken Michael wanted him alive—for now.

She had to find him before they could change their minds.

Sick with fear, she touched her heels to the horse's flanks, urging him into a dangerously hasty gait down that steep, twisting path. Why, *why* had she been such a fool? She had known all along that Brandon was a smuggler and a pirate. She had known that danger followed wherever he went, that he had many enemies. Why hadn't she listened when China tried to warn her? Why hadn't she done what he said?

A low-hanging branch brushed her cheek, and she had to duck to keep from being unseated as she pressed the horse on. The heat was brutal, and she could feel him tiring by the time they reached the outskirts of Honolulu, but she dared not let up. The sturdy mount did not fail her. Sensing her desperation, he maintained a steady gallop even as they plunged into Beretania Street, kicking up a film of yellow-ocher dust to linger in the air behind them.

Only when they pulled up in front of the Kwan house did he falter at last, and Celia panicked, certain she had killed him with the wildness of that frantic ride. But as she dismounted, he seemed to steady himself, and she sensed he would be all right, though he was clammy with sweat and a faint white froth showed at his nostrils.

A slender dark-haired girl, the pretty cousin who had caught Freddie's eye at the wedding, Mary they called her in English, came running through the gate. Celia thrust the reins abruptly into her hands, not even listening to her greeting as she asked urgently where China was.

Startled, the girl gestured toward the far end of the street, and Celia recalled suddenly that one of the Kwan family businesses, a market selling groceries and other supplies, was just around the corner. Naturally that was where he would have gone with the *amah*.

Turning, she began to run in that direction.

China had just carried a heavy sack of rice flour out of the store and was in the process of loading it on the wagon when he glanced up to see Celia racing distraught down the center of the crowded street. Alarmed, he shoved the sack under the seat and jumped down a second before she reached him.

"Oh, China . . ." Celia gasped out the words, half-choking on them as she threw up her hands. "He's gone— Michael's gone."

Gone? China stared at her dumbfounded, wondering for

an instant if some terrible accident had occurred and she was trying to tell him the boy was dead. But that feverish expression on her face was not a look of grief—it was fear.

"What do you mean, gone? What about the girl who was supposed to be taking care of him? Don't tell me she's gone too?"

"No." Celia shook her head so violently the riding hat fell unnoticed into the dust. "She says she just left for a minute to check on a noise outside. It must have been intentional—someone wanted to get her out of the house. I'm sure she's telling the truth. She was terrified when she got back and found Michael gone."

China nodded grimly as he took her arm and guided her into the back of the store, settling her on a stout wooden barrel before she could collapse. He had no doubt she was right. From the looks of things, the operation had been carefully planned . . . and there was only one person who would have gone to all that trouble. So Teresa Valdes was still on the island, despite all evidence to the contrary. She and her men must have been watching the house since the day Celia moved in, biding their time, waiting until everyone but the serving girl was out.

"Still I don't understand." He pulled up a packing crate and sat opposite her. "I was so sure you'd be safe in that house. I had it under surveillance for weeks, and there was nobody around. If someone found it, they must have followed you from Honolulu. Only how did they know where you were?"

Celia's eyes brimmed with tears as she was reminded once again how foolish she had been. "I made it easy for them," she said miserably.

"You made it *easy*?" He looked at her quizzically. "What do you mean?"

"I know you told me not to get in touch with Brandon, but I couldn't help it! It seemed so unfair. He didn't even know he had a son. So I . . . well, I sneaked out while the *amah* was asleep, and I . . . I sent a telegram!"

"You sent a *what*?" China lept to his feet. "After I expressly forbade it? Why on earth—"

"I told you why! I'm sorry. I know I shouldn't have done it—or at least I should have told you later so you could be on guard. But I didn't . . . and I can't go back and change things now."

"No, I suppose you can't." He went over to the open doorway and stared out. The telegraph office! If Teresa *was* in Hawaii—which seemed more than a possibility now—that was the first place she would have put a watch. Maybe she even had someone inside. He seemed to recall a young clerk, a shifty sort, who was rumored to be unhappy with his job. It would be easy to get at someone like that.

He turned slowly to Celia. "I want you to think carefully. Did you say anything in that telegram—anything at all—except that the child had been born?"

"No, not really . . . just that the baby was a boy and that he had red hair."

"Do you remember how you signed it?"

She looked confused. "With my name, of course. Celia Christopher."

China groaned softly as he turned back to the doorway, not wanting her to see his concern. The sun was almost directly overhead, and the half-loaded wagon stood out starkly, casting hardly any shadow at all. So Teresa knew everything now. She knew that Celia had borne Brandon a son . . . and that he had married her.

He could almost see the look on her face when they brought her the news. Disbelief first, then anger, dissolving slowly into hatred. Not only had the man she wanted thrown her over for another woman, he had married her besides! There was nothing she wouldn't do to destroy him now.

China looked back at Celia, sitting forlornly on the rice barrel in the midst of all those chaotically stored supplies, and it was all he could do to keep from blurting out the truth. If they had been honest with her from the beginning, if she had understood the reasons why she had to hide, none of this would have happened. But he owed Brandon too much—he had been loyal too long to go against his wishes now.

"Well, there's no point worrying about what's done," he said gruffly. "All that matters is finding the boy and getting him back."

"But *why*, China?" Celia asked dully. "Why would anyone want to steal my child?"

"I don't know," he replied, acutely conscious that he was lying. He *did* know why someone would want the child—and he knew that Michael was in mortal danger. "It could be anything. You know the kind of business Brandon's involved in. Maybe they're looking for ransom. If so, we don't have to worry. Brandon has a great deal of money at his disposal, and he'd release any of his assets to free the boy."

"Brandon?" Celia's head snapped up, her expression turning almost hopeful. "Oh, China, why didn't we think of that before? We have to tell Brandon. We have to get in touch with him at once."

"No!" The word slipped out, a little too fast, but she didn't seem to notice. "No, we can't do that. It . . . it wouldn't be wise."

"Wise?" She started to laugh, an empty, brittle sound. "What does wisdom have to do with any of this? It's total insanity, all of it. Oh God, I wish Brandon were here. I wish he were here right now. I need him so much."

"I know you do." China went over, squatting on the ground beside her. "I know the pain you're feeling, believe me I do. But we *can't* send another cable to Brandon."

"Why not?" Her voice was bitter as she got up and went over to the door, unable to look him in the eye, knowing that the blame for everything was hers. "The damage has already been done. Whoever kidnapped my son knows I'm here and knows I got in touch with Brandon before."

"Yes, but you mustn't do it again. Don't you see? It wouldn't be . . . it wouldn't be fair." The words sounded lame even to his own ears, but he couldn't risk the truth. Not if it meant betraying Brandon—and frightening her even more. "He couldn't get here for two weeks at least, maybe three or four. He'd be out of his mind with worry until then. It wouldn't be right, telling him, when there's nothing he can do."

"It wouldn't be *right*?" Celia gaped at him, incredulous. "What isn't right is keeping this from him! Brandon is Michael's father, China. He has to be told—even if he *can't* do anything! If our positions were reversed, I'd want to know."

Reasonable, China thought, so reasonable—but for the boy's sake, he had to stop her.

"Trust me, Celia." He kept his voice steady as he took a step forward, ready to reach out and grab her if he had to. "I told you once before not to send a telegram . . . remember? You should have listened. I can't let you make the same mistake again."

Celia backed away, sensing what he was up to, determined not to let him get too close. Brandon might not be able to *do* anything, but he could cable instructions to her. And he had a right to know!

"You can't stop me. I'm sorry, China. You *were* right last time, but you're not right about this. I have to tell Brandon. He'd never forgive me if I didn't."

Without giving him a chance to react, she whirled around and began to race wildly down the street, almost knocking over an old man with a vegetable cart in her haste to get away. She could hear China's voice calling after her, but fear lent wings to her feet and she knew he could never catch her. She had to get to the telegraph office, she thought, blocking everything else from her mind—she had to send that message! Brandon would know what to do.

If she could just get word to him, if she could just hold out until she received his reply, surely everything would be all right.

28

The nightmare continued as she reached the telegraph office.

Out to lunch.

Celia stood there dismayed, staring at the sign she knew she should have expected on that tightly latched door. Judging by the sun, it had to be well past noon, and the clerk had told her he always took an hour for lunch, sometimes more when no one was around.

She turned back to the street, so discouraged she could have burst into tears. Certainly no one was around today, no one except the same ragged little urchin who had been there before, playing once again in a doorway with his sister. Now he broke off, staring at her quite strangely—almost, she thought with a shiver, as if he knew why she was there. Or perhaps it was just that he had never seen a lady in Levi's before, with a mannish shirtwaist blouse.

What if the clerk didn't come back until late afternoon?

Celia leaned wearily against the wall, longing for a spot of shade, but afraid to go away even for a few minutes. She didn't know if China could find a way to stop her, but she knew he was going to try, and she had to get to the clerk before he did.

She could not have said herself how long she'd been standing there, perhaps half an hour, perhaps more, when she became aware of a man approaching from the end of the street. At first she barely noticed him, for he was so nondescript he seemed to blend into the buildings in the background. But as he drew near, she realized he was heading directly for her.

Looking up, she was surprised to see dark eyes focused on her face. Not the casual eyes of a stranger, but curious and intent, as if he were waiting for something—a word from her perhaps, a gesture. When it did not come, he spoke.

"You don't remember me, Mrs. Christopher?"

Celia stared at him numbly, aware of a vague sense of alarm, though his voice was soft and well-modulated. "No . . . no, I don't think I do."

"Well, no matter. I remember you." He gave a curt nod. "Colonel Robert Quarrie, U.S. Army, retired. We were never introduced, though we saw each other briefly on a stretch of beach on the windward side of the island. Apparently I didn't make much of an impression. But then, your eyes were—how shall I put it?—occupied elsewhere."

Celia started to shake her head, then slowly things began to come back. That first night with Brandon . . . a dark figure standing incongruously at the water's edge. She hadn't noticed him then either. Not at first.

"Yes, I . . . I do remember. But . . ." She hesitated, eyeing him cautiously. Brandon had had "business" with the man, and she knew what that meant. "What are you doing here? Did you come to send a telegram? I'm afraid the office is closed."

"No. Actually, I have no interest in the telegraph, except indirectly. I came here to see you."

"To see *me*?"

Celia's mind began to work, fastening on details, sorting them out. If this man was an associate of Brandon's, then he had to know how much money he could raise. And if he had come to see her . . .

"You have my son, don't you?" Her voice rose to a shrill pitch. "You took him! You took him, and you're holding him for ransom!"

The man laid a hand on her arm, just enough to quiet her. "No, Mrs. Christopher, I'm sorry. I don't have the boy, and I don't know where he is. I only came to help . . . as best I can."

"You don't have Michael?" Strangely, the words brought no comfort. She had been terrified at the thought of her baby in this man's clutches, but then at least she would have known what she was dealing with. "You're sure? You don't know where he is?"

Quarrie's eyes softened slightly. "No, I'm afraid I don't. As I said before, I'm sorry. I wish, for your sake, it could be as easy as that."

"But . . . what am I supposed to do?" Celia began to shake so badly even the boy in the doorway was visibly frightened. She knew she was being irrational; she had barely seen this man before, but she had to talk to someone. "How am I supposed to find him when I don't even know where to look? Oh, if only that clerk would come back! At least then I could cable Brandon."

"You could," Quarrie agreed. "But you'd live to regret it." He caught hold of her elbow, taking advantage of her confusion to steer her toward a restaurant a short distance away. "There's no point staying here—the clerk is notorious for his long lunches. He won't be back for half an hour at least. You really should have listened to China Kwan, you know, when he tried to tell you what to do. He's a good man, and he understands the situation."

"China Kwan?" Celia jerked free as she stopped to look up at him. "You know China? You've spoken to him? Today?"

"Of course." Quarrie's voice was composed as he took her arm again. "He came to me right away—as soon as he realized he couldn't reason with you. How do you think I knew where you were? Ah, here's the restaurant. Come along now, you and I are going to have a little talk."

The place was crowded when they entered, a small, unappealing lunchroom with dirty dishes everywhere and a steady hum of conversation. Miraculously, a table was empty at the rear, a bit apart from the others, and Quarrie guided her toward it, turning as he did to wave the waiter away.

He waited courteously until Celia was seated, then sat down himself and leaned forward, pitching his voice so only her ears would pick it up. "There are some thing about the man you married I think you ought to know."

For the next hour Celia listened stunned as Colonel Robert Quarrie told her everything about her husband's activities for the past three and a half years. He made no effort to sugar-coat the story for her, leaving in all the seamy details, all the breathcatching elements of danger that had become so much a part of Brandon's life. The target of the operation, he told her bluntly, was opium trading, but the specific goal, in Brandon Christopher's case, was to break up the organization of a man called Lin. That organization was now run by Teresa Valdes.

Celia stared at him dully, unable, even after he had finished, to grasp the implications of what he was saying. All she could think was: What does this mean to *me*? How does it affect my relationship with Brandon?

All those times she had wanted to believe in him, she thought unhappily . . . all those times she had been so sure there was something else, something deeper, beneath the reckless facade he presented to the world. Why hadn't she listened to the instincts of her heart instead of assuming the worst?

"I should have known," she said softly. "I should have *known*."

"How could you?" Quarrie replied reasonably. "Brandon didn't tell you what he was doing. As a matter of fact, as I understand it, he went to great pains to make sure you didn't know."

"But why?" Celia's eyes widened as she tried to puzzle it out. "Why would Brandon keep me in the dark like that? Does it mean he doesn't trust me?"

"I can't answer that. Only you and your husband know if there is trust between you. As to why he might want to keep you in the dark . . . well, I can make a good guess. There are many reasons, of course, but primarily, I think he was trying to protect you.''

"To *protect* me?"

"A mistaken belief perhaps. But Brandon thought the less you knew about this, the better off you'd be. Your safety and the welfare of the child were paramount in his mind. Surely you can't blame the man for that.''

No, Celia thought, beginning to see things clearly at last, "blame" was hardly the word. More and more now, she was coming to realize that Brandon did truly love her, even if he hadn't felt free, with all this hanging over him, to put his feelings into words. But, oh, he had made a tragic miscalculation when he thought he was protecting her. Ignorance hadn't made her safer at all. It made her blunder into the worst kind of trap.

"You were right,'' she said, feeling her fear grow with each passing minute. "What you said before. I should have listened to China. If I had, none of this—''

"You can't do anything about that now," Quarrie interrupted, laying a hand over hers on the tabletop, a reminder to keep her voice down. "All we can do is wait for them to get in contact with us, which incidentally they'll have to if we don't make the first move. If they're after a ransom, of course—''

"*If* they're after a ransom?'' Celia felt something knot in her stomach, a fear she did not want to acknowledge. "What else could it be? Brandon is a wealthy man, and from what you've told me, a very powerful one. Whoever has done this wants something from him; if not money, then *something*, perhaps leverage to keep him from comig after them—perhaps the opium in the hold on the *Moonwind*.''

"Perhaps. . . . There *are* practical matters that must be taken into consideration, of course. But the most likely motive is . . . revenge.''

"Revenge? Then you mean . . . Teresa Valdes?''

Celia leaned back, staring down at small scratches in the

scarred wooden tabletop. A picture kept flashing into her mind, the way Teresa had looked that one time they came face to face. There had been hatred in those dark eyes then, a hatred so intense it was easy to believe she might be capable of anything.

"But I thought you said she was in California. Isn't that why Brandon went there? To lure her to the West Coast, where she'd be subject to American laws?"

"Yes, and for a while it looked as if he had succeeded. I was there myself as a matter of fact, arranging a dragnet to pick her up, and I'd have made book on it that we were going to have her in a month at most. Unfortunately, it didn't work out that way. The *White Lotus* was spotted several times, but no matter how clever we were, we could never draw closer—hardly the kind of pattern we'd expected from Teresa. Finally I began to get suspicious. That's why I came back to Honolulu two days ago. And damn lucky I did, too."

"Then she *is* here?" Celia shivered. "But that's all the more reason to cable Brandon! If anyone can stop Teresa Valdes, he can. I've only seen her once, but I think she really does love him, in a twisted way perhaps, but still she *does* care. Maybe he can talk to her, appeal to her sensitivities—"

"Which would be like appealing to the sensitivities of a cobra," Quarrie interjected coldly. "No, my dear, I'm afraid you're not thinking things through. If you did, you'd realize this is all the more reason *not* to send that cable."

"But . . ." Celia hesitated, confused. "That doesn't make sense."

"Doesn't it? You know what kind of relationship Brandon had with Teresa. I wasn't able to be tactful about it, though judging from your lack of surprise, I suspect you already knew. In light of that, you have to realize she has a personal score to settle with him."

"Yes, yes, I know. And a score to settle with me too. After all, I am the woman who took Brandon away from her, at least that's how she has to see it. And the best way to hurt us both would be through the baby."

Quarrie shook his head grimly. "I think you're overestimating your importance to the lady, and in a way, the child's too. You see, for her, neither of you exists except in terms of Brandon Christopher. She's perfectly capable of using you and the boy to get back at him. But I can't imagine her being satisfied with the vague thought of Brandon off in California grieving over the loss of his wife and son. No, she wants him here, where she can see his pain."

"She wants him . . . here?" Celia felt her blood run cold as she began finally to understand. "Then that's what this is all about—following me from the telegraph office, kidnapping Michael, everything. It was to force Brandon to come back to Hawaii."

"Precisely. She has to have the child to get the father where she wants him. After that, of course, she won't need him anymore."

"You mean—"

"I mean she'd kill him without a second thought. Life doesn't mean a thing to a woman like that."

Oh God . . . The world seemed to be spinning. Celia clutched at the table to steady herself. She knew Quarrie was telling the truth—all the pieces fit together. But there was one thing that didn't make sense.

"Then why . . .?" She groped for the words, trying to put her thoughts in order. "Why doesn't Teresa send the cable herself? If she has someone inside the telegraph office, the way you think, then she already knows the address where I reached Brandon before."

"Yes, but she can't be sure he's still there. He might have moved since then, or he might have given you several addresses, telling you to use a different one each time so he couldn't be traced. He might even have supplied a code word or phrase to prove the communication was genuine."

"But he didn't," Celia protested, bewildered. "He could

hardly have gone throught that kind of rigmarole without
telling me what was going on."

"I know that," Quarrie reminded her gently, "and you
know it, but Teresa doesn't. And she doesn't dare take the
chance. She has to wait for you to get in touch with him."

"And if I do, if I send that cable . . ."

"Then you know what will happen." Quarrie paused,
letting the effect of his words sink in. "But you aren't
going to do that, are you? You're going to be a wise young
lady and let us handle the situation. After all, we're professionals. We know what we're doing."

Celia looked up, nodding slowly, as if to say yes.

"Good." Quarrie's voice was crisp. "We're in agreement then."

He got up, passing a crumpled bill to the waiter, who
seemed to understand, as if the whole thing had been
prearranged. Then, almost as an afterthought, he put his
hands on the back of his chair and leaned forward. "I
can't stop you from sending that telegram if you really
want to. But you and I both know it would be very . . .
foolish."

He let go of the chair and turned to weave his way
between the tables, littered with the remnants of half-eaten
chicken sandwiches, wilted Chinese vegetables, and bowls
of drying purple *poi*, an eclectic assortment that made his
stomach churn. Outside, the sun was hotter than he had
remembered, and he moved slowly, nursing the dull ache
in his knees. A natural sign of aging, the doctors had said,
nothing much to do about it. But then, they were the same
ones who had told him it wouldn't hurt so much in a warm
climate.

Taking a handkerchief out of his pocket, he mopped
ineffectually at his brow. Damn, she was a pretty little
thing to be so frightened. He didn't think he'd ever seen
eyes quite so soft before. They'd do what they could for
her, of course, but the situation being what it was—the
interim government, no police at all to speak of—they
didn't have a prayer. He only hoped he wasn't going to be

the one to break it to her. He could see the look in those soft eyes then.

He tucked the handkerchief back in his pocket and started down the street again, conscious of the pain with every step. Maybe the doctors were right after all. Maybe he *was* getting old.

Behind him, in the crowded restaurant, Celia sat alone for several minutes, staring numbly at the door as strangers came and went. *I can't stop you from sending that telegram*, Quarrie had said. *I can't stop you . . . but you and I both know it would be very foolish.*

And it would be, she thought bitterly. Damn him, he was right—about one thing at least. She wouldn't send the telegram. She didn't dare. But he was wrong if he thought she was going to leave everything to him.

He and his men might be professionals, but they had botched things badly so far. Where were they when Brandon's son had been kidnapped? Off on a wild-goose chase in California! Besides, she'd be a fool to trust her baby's life to people who thought of him only as a pawn in some greater game.

She pushed her chair back from the table, her legs wobbling a little as she stood. She had never felt so frightened—or so vulnerable—in her life. Always before when she had been troubled or hurt, there was someone to turn to, someone to trust. Now, for the first time, she was completely alone. No one but Brandon had the same terrible stake in what was happening here. And Brandon was on the other side of the ocean.

If Michael was going to be rescued, if she was going to hold her baby in her arms again, she had to see to it herself.

29

"Why didn't you tell me the truth?"

Celia's voice was steady as she faced China in the Kwan-family courtyard. Now that she had decided what to do—now that she had set herself on a course of action, however tentative—there was a new authority in her manner. She was in charge, and they both knew it.

"I couldn't" he said, avoiding her eyes. "I wanted to, but I couldn't. Brandon had given strict orders that no one was to say anything to you."

"And you, of course, do everything Brandon says."

Her tone was edged with sarcasm. China shifted his weight uncomfortably, sensing no reasonable answer, but he had to try. "Brandon is my friend . . ." he began clumsily.

"I'm your friend too. At least I thought I was. Oh, China, I understand why Brandon kept everything to himself. He's so stubborn sometimes, so inflexible, it would take a volcano to move him. But you . . .? Couldn't you have trusted me?"

"Trust had nothing to do with it," China said, then hesitated. Trust had had *everything* to do with it, at least in the beginning, but how could he tell her what it looked like when she came to Hong Kong inquiring after Skye Maarten? He was almost positive she didn't know about the blond stranger who had been glimpsed with Teresa those early weeks in Hawaii, much less that he might be her former suitor.

"You don't understand," he said unhappily. "I owe Brandon Christopher my life. More than my life! I cannot go against his wishes, even if I think he's wrong."

Celia brushed his protests aside with an impatient wave of her hand as she wandered back into the kitchen, dim and cool despite the kettle of water boiling on the stove. It didn't matter what China had done or why he and Brandon had been so secretive. All she cared about was finding Michael and getting him back unharmed.

"He's so little," she said, struggling to hide her tears as China appeared in the doorway. "I'm so afraid for him."

"He'll be all right. Don't forget, it's in their best interests to take care of him." At least for a while, he thought grimly. "Right now they need Michael. Until they're sure Brandon is on his way back to Honolulu, they can't let anything happen to him."

"But he's just a baby, a few weeks old—he'll be so frightened." Oh God, she couldn't bear to think of him alone someplace, hungry, wondering where his mama was when she had never failed him before.

"He's old enough to live on cow's milk and *poi*, if that's what you're worried about," China reassured her. "And wherever he is, I doubt very much he's anywhere near as frightened as his mother."

Celia tried to smile as she went over to the stove where the kettle was bubbling. Certainly there was something in that gentle gibe. Even if Michael was howling his head off right now, he couldn't be as close to hysteria as she had been a moment before. She found a glazed pot and filled it with jasmine-scented tea leaves, the way she had seen Old Grandmother do, then poured in boiling water. The sweet, flowery fragrance gave a momentary illusion of normalcy, as if somehow, with those familiar gestures, she could make everything all right again.

"I've been trying to sort things out in my mind," she said, picking up the pot and bringing it to the table. "All the way over here, I was so afraid—I was running and running—but I kept asking myself: If Teresa Valdes *is* on the island, would she have cut herself off like this? With no means of escape? It doesn't seem likely. I can't believe the *White Lotus* is her only vessel.''

"Nor can I." China brought over a pair of chipped blue-and-white cups, filling them with steaming tea. "That's been bothering me too. I was discussing it with my cousin before you came—the one who spent two years on the *Lotus*. He says Teresa was very mysterious with her crew, telling them nothing, but he sometimes got the feeling there was another ship just beyond the horizon . . . perhaps more than one."

"More than one?" Celia's mind leapt ahead, catching the possibilities in that rather startling statement. "Then I could be right."

"I'm sure you are. I recall hearing rumors myself, something about two ships—the *Black Jasmine* and the *Red Crescent*—that used to belong to Lin. That's where my cousin is now, over at the harbor checking to see if anyone has spotted them recently."

Celia's eyes narrowed as she took a sip of tea. "You think that's wise? Sending him on a mission like that?"

"Why not?" He looked surprised.

"You did say he was with Teresa for two years. You don't think he might have developed a certain . . . well, loyalty in that time?"

"He did," China admitted. "In fact, he had many conflicting feelings when he first joined us. Teresa paid him well, and she was always fair with her men. That's why Brandon left him behind when he went to the West Coast. He didn't want him involved in what was going to happen there."

"And now?" Celia lowered her cup to the table.

"Now that loyalty is gone. The last of it died this morning when he learned she had stolen an innocent baby from its mother. My cousin is a decent man: he would not stand by and let such a thing happen." He did not add that his cousin had gone on to say, with a grim look on his face, that he feared for what might already have happened to the boy. Teresa's notorious fondness for children would hardly extend to the baby Brandon Christopher had fathered by another woman. "But he should be here any minute now. Then we'll find out what's going on at the waterfront."

"If they are there, either of those two ships . . ." Celia looked up, daring to hope. "If they're in the harbor, then that's where the kidnappers must have brought Michael. All we have to do is locate the ships and—"

"Not so fast." China was quick to break into her train of thought. "It sounds promising, I admit. But I don't think that's where Teresa would have had him taken."

"Why not? It's the logical place."

"That's just it, it's too logical. The thought has already occurred to both of us—and if you'd sent a telegram to Brandon, that's the first thing he'd have cabled back. Teresa probably assumes we don't know about the *Jasmine* and the *Crescent*. But we were bound to figure out that there's at least one other ship involved and start asking around the harbor. What if someone remembered a crying baby being rowed out to a particular vessel?"

Celia slumped in her seat, sensing even before he finished that China was right. Teresa Valdes was no fool. She wouldn't hide the baby in the one place they'd be sure to look.

"I wish I knew how they'd gotten to me in the first place." She stared moodily into her cup, then finished the tea in a gulp. "It was one thing to intercept that message in the telegraph office. But how could they follow me on the streets in broad daylight? Without my knowing anyone was there?"

"I'd give a lot to have the answer to that one." China picked up the pot and poured out a fresh cup of tea. "Think back on it, Celia. When you went to collect the telegram from Brandon, did you see anything unusual?

Someone loitering around perhaps . . . anything that shouldn't have been there?''

Celia sighed as she shook her head. "I wasn't paying much attention," she admitted. "I was so excited, just hearing from Brandon. But, no, I didn't see anything out of the ordinary. I wasn't looking, of course, but I'm sure I would have noticed if someone was around. All I saw were a couple of children . ."

She broke off suddenly, remembering the strange look on the little boy's face as he watched her from the shadows. She had thought then he was hungry, but that wasn't it at all! And he hadn't seemed to want the coin she threw at him.

"That's it, China! The children! That's why I didn't notice anything—and I wouldn't have, even if I'd been looking. You don't pay any attention to kids . . . they're just there, playing . . . perfectly harmless. You don't give them a second glance."

"I think you're right."

China leapt up from his seat, pacing back and forth across the floor as he recalled the few times he had gone back to that little house on the beach. There had been children playing there too—he remembered them particularly, a boy and a girl.

And Teresa had a way with children. It was perhaps her only redeeming quality.

"Those children at the telegraph office," he said, swinging around abruptly. "Was one of them a little mixed-blood boy, more Oriental than Polynesian, about eight or nine years old? And the other a younger girl, probably his sister?"

Celia stared at him. "Why, yes. How did you know?"

"Because I've seen them myself. At the beach house for a few weeks, then later here in town. The boy's an eager little worker, quite devoted to the girl—he'd do anything to earn an extra coin or two. Only he's had a few too many of them lately!"

He was already at the door before she had a chance to

digest his words, calling out to the pretty girl who had been there when Celia rushed in that morning. She heard him say something, but his voice was so low she couldn't even make out whether it was English or Chinese.

When he came back a few seconds later, there was a new light in his eyes, a kind of excitement that communicated itself to her.

"I sent Mary to find the boy," he explained, still pacing, but less tensely this time. "Unless I miss my guess, he'll be at the telegraph office. Teresa is going to want someone to bring back a message if you show up. I doubt she has the baby with her, but that lad's wily enough for a dozen street urchins. I'd bet everything I own he knows where Michael is."

"And you think Mary can get the information out of him? Oh, I don't know—it doesn't seem right, sending a girl, and such a young one at that." Mary couldn't have been older than fifteen, and belonged to the new generation of Kwans, more Western than Chinese. "What if she isn't able to persuade him? Maybe you should have gone yourself."

China shook his head. "Mary will make a better job of it. A girl is less frightening, I think, especially to a child. The boy may be more willing to talk and to take the very generous bribe I sent along. And if you're afraid he's going to get away—don't worry. I told her to find her two brothers and have them waiting around the corner, well within earshot."

Celia was aware of an agonizing sense of suspense as they settled down at the table again, not trying to speak any more, both caught up in thoughts that were half hopeful, half too troubling to utter. The only sound was the dull *tick-tock*, *tick-tock* of a small clock in its niche beside the Kitchen God, now dingy with grease and dust, for a good part of the year was already gone. Every time Celia looked up, it seemed to her that the hands had not moved at all.

If only she could start to work things out, if she could form some plan in her mind—but everything depended on the information she was waiting to receive. Oh God, what if China had been wrong before? What if Teresa wasn't the least bit worried about taking care of the child? What if it was only the kidnapping that had mattered to her, the act itself, designed to make Celia desperate enough to send a telegram? What if she didn't see any use for him beyond that?

The sun had already turned to a reddish gold and the courtyard outside the kitchen door was deep in shadow when China's cousin finally returned with news from the harbor. It was exactly what they had been waiting to hear. The *Black Jasmine* had been sighted, he told them, and another ship that matched the description of the *Red Crescent*, though it was known as the *Red Peony* now. Ordinarily they kept up a good cover, sailing on a fairly regular schedule between Oahu and Lahaina, on Maui, but tonight both were anchored somewhere in the vicinity of Honolulu.

Celia listened without comment until China had nearly finished translating his cousin's words, then broke in abruptly. "Which ship is the fastest?" she asked.

China looked startled, but said nothing as he turned back to his cousin, repeating the question and waiting for a reply.

"The *Black Jasmine*," he said when the cousin had finished. "The *Red Peony* is larger and sturdier, but the *Jasmine* has all the speed. Why do you ask?"

"Because we're going to need a ship of our own after we rescue Michael. Teresa isn't likely to just stand there and watch us walk away. She's going to come after us with everything she's got—and God help us if we don't have an escape ready and waiting."

China nodded approvingly. He had wondered if she was thinking that far ahead, or if her plans only extended to the sweet moment when she could hold her baby in her arms again.

"My thoughts exactly," he agreed. "Though I must admit I hadn't considered taking one of Teresa's ships. I would have preferred commandeering a steamer from Chris-

topher Lines, but you're right. There's no time for that.
We need a ship tonight—now. Only I think we ought to
take both of them, not just one. We don't want to leave
her the means to come after us."

"No." Celia stood in the gateway, looking out at the
street. "We barely have enough men to handle one ship.
We'd be spreading our forces too thin. Let's go for the
Black Jasmine—and put the *Red Peony* out of commission
if we can. But the *Jasmine* has to be our top priority."

China didn't waste time debating the merits of a plan
that was at least as good as anything he could have come
up with. Taking his cousin over to a corner of the courtyard, he began to speak rapidly, conferring with him on a
hastily thrown-together course of action. They were just
finishing when the girl Mary came back, her cheeks pink,
her eyes sparkling with suppressed laughter.

Even before she could say anything, Celia knew she had
succeeded. Her first words confirmed it. The boy, it seemed,
had been more than willing to talk—in fact, he hardly
needed the bribe China had sent.

"He's not a bad child," Mary Kwan explained. "He
only took the money that woman gave him because he
needed it so badly—for the little girl, he said, his sister,
who has never been very strong. But he became frightened
when he realized what was happening." She turned to
Celia with a sympathetic look. "Especially today, at the
telegraph office, when he saw how devastated you were.
He said you were kind to him once. You gave money
without being asked. He was glad, I think, to have a
chance to make amends."

"Then . . ."—Celia's heart began to flutter, much too
wildly, but she couldn't help it—"he told you where
they're keeping Michael?"

"Yes. They brought him inland, to a place called . . ."
She broke off, realizing that the small interior valley she
was about to name would mean nothing to someone who
didn't know the island. Snatching up a ladle from the

counter in the kitchen, she returned to the courtyard and used the handle to scratch out a rough map in the dirt.

Celia almost shouted with excitement at the picture that began to take shape. The valley, as Mary described it, was just beyond the outskirts of Honolulu—they could reach it in an hour on horseback. And the couple who were keeping the baby for the night were Hawaiians, good people who almost certainly didn't know what they were doing. There would be guards around the hut, of course, but not too many, two or three at most, for Teresa wouldn't want to arouse suspicion.

"Still, we're going to have to hurry." Her brain was spinning as she tried to take in everything at once. If Teresa had made such casual plans, it might mean she didn't intend to keep the baby longer than one night. "We've got to get to him before—"

"Not *we*." China took a step forward, positioning himself between her and the street. "I'm going to handle this myself—with the men Brandon left behind. I don't want you anywhere around."

There was enough authority in his tone to stop her for a moment, making her revert to the sheltered female, a role for which she had had all too much practice these past months! Then, remembering herself, she tilted her chin up. "Michael is my son, China! I'm going to be the one to get him back!" She gave her head a defiant toss, as much to spur her own spirits as to assert herself to him. "I'm in command now. I thought you understood that when I came back this afternoon."

"I did," he said quietly, "and I'm not disputing it. But even a commander has to know when to stand back and allow his forces to do the fighting. You can't put yourself in the line of fire—it would be too risky. Teresa has young Michael now. If she loses him, she's going to look for another hostage to lure Brandon back to Hawaii. You, I'm afraid, would do just as well."

Celia gulped, realizing, even though she hated it, that he was right. Brandon *did* love her, she knew that now—no

matter that the words had never been spoken between
them. He would be frantic if he heard she had been
captured: all that arrogant male protectiveness would surge
to bursting in his heart. She could just see him, coming
after her like a madman, raging across wind-whipped seas,
vowing to rescue her at all costs, to trade his life for hers if
he had to.

"Then . . . I can't go with you? But, China, I can't
bear to be left behind! Not while my baby's in danger!"

"I know." His hand was gentle as he laid it on her
waist, easing her away from the gate, out of sight of the
street. "But believe me, there's no other way. I can't even
allow you to wait for us here. As long as the telegraph
office is open, nothing will happen. But as soon as it
closes, Teresa is going to get nervous—and then she'll try
to find you."

Celia shuddered. "But do you have someplace for me to
hide?"

"Yes. It's not exactly elegant, but you'll be safe. For a
while at least . . . and that's all we need. We're going to
make our move as soon as it gets dark. With any luck, I'll
be back for you shortly after that."

The hours that followed were the longest of Celia's life.
The place China had taken her to was a small cluttered
shack wedged between two slightly taller buildings in a
tangled maze of dingy alleys half a block from the harbor.
Waterfront sounds came from far away, random shouts
and tinny music, the occasional hoarse cry of a drunk, but
close at hand all she could hear was a faint rustling, as if
rats were scurrying through the straw on the floor.

Celia stood slightly back from the only window, taking
care not to expose her features in the almost day-bright
moonlight that filtered through dirty panes of glass. Outside she could detect no sign of life, no movement at all in
the darkness—not even the glow of a lantern at the far end
of the street. It was like being shut up in a packing crate,
she thought, shivering. Like being shut in a dark, empty
place with no way to see or hear what was going on.

Even at that moment, in the harbor, China and his men must be making their desperate attempt to seize one of Teresa's vessels. And in a small interior valley, someone—oh God, she didn't even know who!—was trying to rescue her child.

At least Brandon wasn't with them. She turned away from the window, moving carefully, for it was too dark to see anything in that small enclosed space. She had been so miserable before, she had wanted him with her so badly—now she was glad he wasn't here. Whatever happened tonight, whatever the outcome, at least she wouldn't be donning widow's weeds in the morning. Wherever Brandon was, he was safe.

Wherever he was. . . .

The shadows in the back of the shed were too deep to penetrate. She had not seen a lamp when she entered, nor would she have dared light it even if she had. Dear heaven, it made her feel so empty, realizing she didn't know where he was at that moment.

They had funny houses in California, someone had told her once, Indian-style structures with mud-brick walls and slick earthen floors and only the crudest of furnishings. Was Brandon in a place like that now, staring moodily at the flames in the fireplace, brooding about her perhaps, sensing dangers he could only guess at? Or was the picture all wrong? Was he attending a gaslit gala in some Victorian mansion in San Francisco, garbed as he had been that last night she saw him, handsome and sophisticated, sipping wine out of a crystal goblet . . . not thinking of her at all?

Was it even night there?

She sat down on a wooden crate, tucking her feet up around her, not wanting to touch the straw-covered floor. She knew so little about changes in time, only that it grew later the farther one traveled east. Was it past midnight already? Was Brandon asleep in his bed, not dreaming, not thinking at all? Or was it morning? Was he going to breakfast, steak and eggs perhaps? Americans ate barbaric breakfasts—with greasy potatoes and heavy flapjacks that sank to the bottom of one's stomach.

Oh God, her mind was rambling. She started to get up, then sat back again, hating the way her thoughts were going, those oddly disturbing images of Brandon, off someplace by himself. It was almost as if some instinct were warning her that she wasn't going to come out of this, that she wasn't going to see him again.

The darkness had begun to close in; the shadows almost seemed to move, looming up, threatening, all around her. China had been gone so long. So long! Surely it was past time for him to come back. She wished now he had left her in the Kwan-family kitchen, no matter what the risk. If she could only look up at the clock in its cubbyhole beside the Kitchen God, at least she would know if there was any reason for the fear that kept growing inside her.

What if they *had* been gone too long? What if they weren't coming back? What if the cold light of dawn began to seep through the windows and still they weren't here? What was she going to do then?

Don't think about it, she told herself tensely, *don't think about it*!—yet thinking was the one thing it was impossible not to do, there in that terrible empty darkness. Thinking about Brandon, longing to be with him again, thinking of the way her baby had felt the last time she clasped him to her breast.

Her baby?

Celia caught her breath, trying desperately to steady her nerves. What if they had already hurt him? What if rescue came too late?

"Oh, Michael . . . be safe." She whispered the words out loud, not to reassure herself, but because she couldn't stand the silence any longer. "Be safe, my baby . . . don't be afraid . . . Mama will come soon. Mama will take care of you."

Memories came flooding back, images and feelings she could not resist. Michael . . . so tiny and dependent, a warm, wriggling miracle when they laid him for the first

time in her arms. Michael . . . pudgy cheeks puffed out,
lips puckered into a little round O, greedily smacking as he
finished his meal. "Piglet," she would call him then, and,
oh, how Kalani would laugh—but Georgina would pretend
to be indignant, for she had grown quite attached to the
boy she had delivered. Michael . . . a little baby hand
catching at her finger as she held it out, holding on so
tight, clinging, as if he couldn't bear to let go.

She got up again, restless, even more frightened than
ever as she moved back to the window, standing much too
close. If only she could be out there with the others, if she
could be doing something, *daring* something. It was the
waiting that was hardest. The waiting, and not knowing if
her child was still alive.

She had just turned away from the window when a
sound came from somewhere outside. Whirling around,
she caught a flash of movement out of the corner of her
eye. Her heart gave one wild thump against her chest; then
the door swung open and she recognized China Kwan
standing on the threshold. There was just enough moonlight to see that his eyes were burning with excitement.

"Michael . . . ?"

She took a step forward, daring in spite of herself to
hope. But then she saw that his hands were empty, and she
stopped again. He hadn't brought Michael with him! Did
that mean . . . ?

China saw the look of fear in her eyes and hastened
forward, holding out a reassuring hand. "I sent others to
get the child. They're not back yet, but they had farther to
go. There's no reason to think they haven't been successful."

"Then you don't have *any* news?" Celia sank back on
the packing case, discouraged.

"Ah, but I do." He glanced out at the street, silent,
with nothing to be seen. "Very good news. We have the
Black Jasmine, and it was even easier than we hoped.
Teresa had only a minimal crew on board—it looks as
though she might be short of manpower. Even the weather
was with us. A cloud passed over the moon at just the

right moment, and we were able to slip on board without being seen. We didn't suffer a single casualty.''

"That *is* good news!" Celia found herself catching his excitement. "What about the *Red Crescent*—the *Red Peony*, I mean? Were you able to put it out of commission?"

China hesitated a fraction of a second. "No, we couldn't manage that. Apparently it came in from Lahaina yesterday, and it's still anchored beyond the coral reefs. There was no way we could get to it without being seen. I think Teresa herself is on board . . . unfortunately."

Celia did not miss that slight catch in his voice, and little beads of sweat stood out on her forehead. "Unfortunately?"

"We got the *Jasmine* all right, but there were . . . complications." China took a deep breath, not wanting to describe for her the bloody slaughter that had taken place, for he had been determined not to let anyone get away. But in the darkness: "I'm afraid some of the men may have slipped past us. They could be with Teresa right now."

"And if they are, if they're on the *Peony* . . ." Celia felt herself shiver.

"Then she knows we're coming, and we're going to have a devil of a time getting by her without being seen. If we're lucky, the clouds may hold . . . but they've had a way of drifting in and out all evening. If the moon is bright . . . ? Well, the entrance to the harbor is too narrow for comfort, and Teresa may already be in position."

Celia glanced at the open doorway, sensing that China was right. The worst dangers still lay ahead of them. She tried to force herself to concentrate, tried to work out the details of a rough plan just beginning to take shape in her mind, but it was hard to think of anything but the rescue mission that had been sent to that small interior valley. A mission that must by now already have succeeded or failed.

She and China left the shanty, following a twisted path through the web of darkened alleyways, fouled by a stench of urine and rotting garbage. It was the long way around,

but Celia dared not protest, for she knew that if Teresa
Valdes wasn't on the *Peony*, if China had been wrong
about that, her men might already be closing in on the
waterfront.

Buildings seemed to rush past her, a blur of sensations,
rough wooden walls, red-shaded lanterns flickering out of
open doorways. Faces stared at them as they passed, gaunt
and haunting, the painted pallor of young girls, barely
more than children, imported from brothels in Macao and
the Philippines to cater to the more perverse needs of
rough sailors and spoiled young sons of well-to-do planters.

Oh, please, let him be there when we get to the ship,
she thought over and over again, her words echoing the
frantic rhythm of her feet. Please, *please* let him be there.

But the ship, as they pulled up in a small boat, which
had been waiting for them at one of the docks, was
ominously silent. No baby sounds could be heard as China
grabbed the base of a fraying rope ladder and held it
steady. No faces were visible except a pair of crew members leaning anxiously over the rail to help her up.

The deck on which she found herself was smaller than
she had expected, with warped boards and rusty fittings,
and she had the sudden fleeting thought: Is this vessel
seaworthy? A cloud drifted across the moon, and China's
face was barely visible as he emerged over the railing.
Below him, Celia caught a glimpse of something black and
shadowy in the water—a second boat closing in on the
first!

She had just opened her mouth to cry out, alarmed,
when the moon reappeared and she saw a massive figure
pulling on the oars with long, even strokes. Iopeka! She
could have wept with relief at that welcome sight. Beside
him, a startling burst of flame-red hair was only slightly
overshadowed by a vivid red dress with bangles sparkling
like scarlet stars. Wonderful, flamboyant Georgina! Even a
mission of stealth couldn't tone down her exuberance.

China started down the ladder, but Georgina waved him
back, insisting on climbing up unaided, a little blanket-

wrapped bundle clasped against her breast. She refused to
let go until she was so close Célia could reach out herself
and take the sleeping baby in her arms.

Michael whimpered a little at that awkward transfer, but
settled down quickly, trusting, as he always had, that
everything would be all right. Tears streamed down Celia's face, and she sank onto the deck, laughing and crying
both, not at all sure how she felt. Relieved, yes, of course
she was relieved, and excited too . . . and utterly terrified
now that it was over and she dared to let herself think how
close she had come to losing him.

It was a miracle all over again, looking down at little
red-gold lashes, so soft in the moonlight, fluttering against
plump cheeks, as if he were dreaming pleasant baby dreams.
Celia laughed again, softly this time, as she saw how
peaceful he was. All that worrying, all those agonizing
questions—Did he feel alone? Was he afraid?—and he had
been asleep all the time!

Well, not *all* the time. She noticed a small spot at the
side of his lips, dark, faintly purplish, as she dabbed at it
with her finger. *Poi*! China had been right—Michael *was*
old enough to live on cow's milk and *poi*. And he, Mama's
little piglet, had loved every bit of it! It seemed he was a
child of the islands after all.

Only slowly did she become aware of sounds around
her: the creaking and groaning of ropes . . . the cries of
the men, "All ready forward!" "All ready the cross-yard
jacks?" "Aye, aye, sir!" "All ready the main!" . . . the
heavy metallic clanking of the anchor chain. So China had
decided to put out under full sail. It would be risky through
the coral reefs, but they were going to need all the speed
they could get when they hit open water.

Reluctantly she surrendered the baby, giving that sweet
little forehead one last tender kiss as she told Georgina to
take him below and settle him in the captain's quarters.
She ached to hold him just a few minutes more, but there
were things that had to be discussed, decisions that had to
be made now, before the *Jasmine* had gone too far.

She found China in the bow, squinting at moon-brightened waters with a worried expression on his face.

"The clouds are dispersing," he said, glancing over his shoulder at her approach. "Not a good sign. I had hoped to head for Molokai. There's a cove there where we would have been safe, for a while at least—on the other side of the island from the leper colony. But with the *Red Peony* close on our heels . . ."

"It doesn't matter." Celia was surprised at how calm her voice was, now that everything was settled, in her own mind at least. "We aren't going to Molokai."

"Where then?" He looked thoughtful. "Lanai?"

"Not to Lanai either . . . or anywhere on the islands. We're going to California."

30

The moonlight seemed to intensify, an eerie blue glow reflecting off mirror-dark waves as the *Black Jasmine* glided out of Honolulu harbor, easing a careful path between the treacherous coral reefs. When they reached the open water, Celia was surprised at the number of ships that had chosen that far anchorage, and she found herself studying them warily, wondering which, if any, was the *Red Peony*, carrying the notorious Teresa Valdes.

They all looked so alike, lying there silent, great sheets of canvas furled, tall masts stretching, naked, to the skies.

Then a flicker of movement caught her eye, and turning her head to the right, she saw a ship coming toward them from the west end of the harbor entrance, a smallish barkentine, like the *Jasmine* under full sail. Teresa! There was no doubt in her mind that that was who it was. She might not have been warned in time to cut off their escape, but she was already close enough to see them clearly—and she could hardly fail to recognize the ship she herself owned! With sinking heart Celia realized that whatever few options she had had were gone now. There was no way they could turn around and hide in the islands, even if they wanted to.

The wind continued steady through the night, strong gusts that swelled the sails, proving that China's cousin had not judged wrong when he said the *Jasmine* was swift. By morning they had pulled out of sight of the pursuing vessel, but even then Celia could still sense its presence, hovering somewhere in the dawn mists behind them.

That close call the night before had at least had one positive effect, for China no longer questioned Celia's decision to head for California. He too now realized they would never be safe in Hawaii. They might elude Teresa for an hour, a day, a week if they were lucky, but she would keep on searching: she would never let up. As long as they stayed, their lives would be in danger.

A more conventional move perhaps would have been to set sail for Hong Kong, a route both she and China had traveled and knew fairly well. But even there, authorities could be bought, might *already* have been bought by Teresa and her men. Better to count on the American police to protect them—and American justice to put an end to that evil crew once and for all.

And perhaps, Celia thought, leaning against the railing their second night at sea, it was for the best. There was something in the salty wind whipping against her face, a briskness, a spirit of adventure that was hard to deny, and she could almost feel the excitement that must have come over Brandon whenever he closed in on the *White Lotus*. She did not understand the obsession that drove him— maybe she never would—but she was ready to do her part by luring Teresa to the California coast.

Perhaps then, when it was over, he would finally be able to let go. Perhaps then she would have him all to herself—at last.

"You look like you're a million miles away," China said a few minutes later, pausing in his duties to stand beside her at the rail. "Where are your thoughts now— with Brandon in California?"

Celia shook her head, smiling faintly. In reality, she *had* been thinking of Brandon, but her feelings were too private to share, even with China.

"No, actually I was back in Hawaii, wondering about that 'bold rescue' of my son." She laughed as she recalled the way China had described the scene. Good-hearted

Luka and Iopeka gathering all their giant friends together, marching on foot into the valley—and nearly causing a riot as they added new recruits along the way. But when they had reached that small shack, they had been met only by a bewildered Hawaiian couple, who handed the child over willingly, if a bit sadly, for they had been told they were to raise the little "orphan boy" as their own.

"Bold indeed," China said ruefully. "But hardly necessary. It seems I misjudged the situation."

"Still, it is strange." Celia brushed a loose curl back from her forehead, tucking it under the sailor's cap that covered her hair. "It's almost as if . . . well, as if Teresa intended to go off and just leave him there. As if she never meant to hurt him at all."

"Maybe she didn't," he ventured. "Teresa is a complex young woman. I can't even begin to understand her. She never seems to care about anyone, and yet she's always had a special fondness for children. I wouldn't have thought, with Brandon's child, that would make a difference. Apparently I was wrong."

Celia stared back at the water, feeling strangely moody as she tried to reconcile that unexpected core of softness with everything she had heard about Teresa Valdes.

The thought was disconcerting, nagging at her conscience in ways she had not anticipated. As long as Teresa had been "the enemy," a monster without redemption, it was easy, even exciting, to play the game, to lure her to the California coast—and the hangman. It wasn't quite the same, thinking of her as a woman who had once held Michael's life in her hands . . . and been gentle enough to spare it.

The days that followed seemed to race by with the swiftness of a sudden gust of wind at sea. Even inexperienced as she was, especially at navigation, Celia nonetheless assumed command, enlisting China and his cousin to serve as first and second mates. It was a decision that proved wise, for as men, they were in a better position to give direct orders to the crew and expect to be obeyed.

The *Black Jasmine* was a small ship, quite different from the *Moonwind*, and Celia had all she could do to try to master it. It too had three masts, but it was bark-rigged, carrying square sails only on the two forward masts, with fore-and-aft rigging on the mizzen. Sometimes it seemed to her the vessel was as skittish as a wild horse, and equally difficult to handle. But for all its lack of sturdiness and history of poor maintenance, she had to admit it was fast, as long as the winds blew strong, and she couldn't help being thankful that it had been the *Jasmine* and not the *Red Peony* in port that night.

If only it held together, she thought more than once as she stared down at rotting boards in the deck or listened to the ominous groaning of the masts when the wind picked up, they wouldn't have to worry about being overtaken by Teresa.

The crew was small, numbering fourteen, with the only able seamen among them the two Kwans, for Brandon had chosen the men he left behind with an eye toward valor and trustworthiness, not a knowledge of ships. Fortunately, most of the others, with the exception of three who had been recruited at the last minute to participate in the raid on the *Jasmine*, had been to sea at least once, and all were hard workers, willing to do double and triple duty. Even Freddie, the cabin boy, who had torn himself away from the waterfront brothels to serve as cook, cleaned up his pots and trenchers with good cheer and then went out to help on deck.

Most surprising of all was Iopeka. Celia had offered to send him ashore, together with Georgina and any of the men who cared to leave, but like the others, he had refused. At first, his decision worried her, for she remembered how kind Luka had been, and she was sure the woman would be angry.

But when she expressed her fears, he only laughed. "Luka, she good woman. Got plenty men, no problem, Luka. Pretty soon, she tire Iopeka—then Iopeka *pau*. Mo' bettah he *pau* now. Go see the world." By which Celia gathered he meant that Luka's notoriously roving eye had begun to rove again, and seeing the handwriting on the wall, he was ready to move on.

The giant Hawaiian proved a tireless worker, plunging into tasks at sea with the same single-mindedness he had once used to avoid them on shore. Everywhere she went, Celia seemed to see him—holystoning the deck with his huge brown arms; tying taut, surprisingly expert sailor's knots; tossing barrels and crates around as if they were chips of balsa; entertaining the men with his stories and songs. Did he ever sleep? she wondered, bemused. It hardly seemed so, for he was always there.

Georgina, too, had opted to remain on board, and after those first few days, Celia could not imagine how she had ever thought of getting along without her. It was Georgina who took care of the baby while Celia was on deck working with the crew or recording noon-to-noon sightings in the logbook. It was Georgina who rocked him back and forth on a hard wooden bench in the cramped, poorly ventilated saloon while Celia pored over maps and charts, trying to pick out the best course. And when Celia was so exhausted she fell asleep, still holding the baby after he had finished nursing, it was Georgina who eased him out of her arms, laying him in the little hammock they had rigged up beside Celia's bunk in the captain's cabin.

"You're so good with children," Celia said, smiling as she came into the cabin one afternoon to discover Georgina on the floor romping with Michael on an old cotton sheet. "Looking at you like that, one would almost think you had a baby of your own."

Georgina glanced up, a closed look coming into her eyes for just a moment. "I do," she said softly. "It's no secret, but I guess you didn't know. I don't talk about it much. I have a little boy too. Well, not a little boy anymore, of course. He was almost two when I gave him up. He'd be twenty-one now."

"You . . . gave him up?" The remark was so unexpected it caught Celia off guard. "But how could you do

that?" she blurted out. "*Why* would you do it? If anyone
tried to take my baby from me, I'd . . . I'd kill them!"

"Would you?" Georgina's features relaxed, reverting to
their usual good humor. "I think you might at that, but
you can't say our positions are exactly the same."

"N-no, of course not, but surely you could have changed
all that! Oh, Georgina, if you really wanted your baby, if
you *loved* him, you could have made yourself into . . .
into anything you wanted!"

Georgina grinned. "I only know how to do one thing—
though I do that quite well. But it hardly qualifies me as a
good mother."

Her voice was flippant, as usual, but something in her
manner warned Celia not to persist, and she threw herself
down exhausted on the bench. "Oh, Georgina, I'm sorry.
I should never have said that. I'm so tired nowadays, I
don't know what I'm doing. I'm sure you only did what
you had to . . . and I know it must have broken your
heart."

"Well, you're right there—it did." Georgina lost a little
of her buoyancy as she handed the baby to Celia and went
over to the other side of the room, fidgeting needlessly
with the light in the sconce. "It was the hardest thing I
ever did, but it was for the best. They're a good couple,
the people I gave him to. He has a good home now, a
good life—in California, they say. That's part of why I
wanted to come with you. I thought I might be able to see
him."

"Oh, but that's wonderful!" Celia gave Michael an
extra kiss as she smiled at Georgina, trying to make up for
her tactlessness. "You'll be able to tell your son who you
are . . . and why you had to give him up. Once he sees
you, once he talks to you, I know he'll love you and—"

"Oh, no." Georgina looked shocked and a little embarrassed. "I would never do anything like that. I wouldn't
want him to look at me and . . . well, *know* what his
mother is. Anyway, what would that change? It couldn't

bring back the memories I never had. No, it will be enough just to see him all grown up, a fine young man.''

It would *not* be enough, and they both knew it, but it was all she would ever have, and Celia found herself marveling in the following days at the quiet resignation that gave even gaudy Georgina a measure of dignity. Thery were so different, she thought, she and this woman who had come to be her closest friend—yet in many ways, they were alike too. What if her own fate had been different? What if Brandon had been less than eager to make an honest woman of her? Mightn't she have been faced with that same cruel decision? Cling to the child she loved so desperately—or give him up so he could have a better life.

Clear skies followed them nearly all the way from Hawaii. The weather was so balmy that the men worked most of the time shirtless, a boon to them, but Celia found herself constantly worried about the belts of calm they passed through with disturbing regularity. Night after night she sat up late, her brow puckered as she pored over the charts, trying to figure out where she had gone wrong. At least she could be thankful Teresa had left a full supply of navigational aids in the captain's saloon; otherwise they would have had to steer into the rising sun and hope for the best. Still, she couldn't help wishing she had more skill when it came to interpreting those wriggly lines on the maps.

It was just past eight bells, an uneventful Friday evening, and the last leg of the dogwatch was coming in when a cry of ''Sail ho!'' went up. Celia, who had been resting in the cabin, pulled on a lightweight jacket and rushed up on the deck, peering through her glass at a ship on the dusky horizon.

The *Red Peony*? Every muscle in her body went taut. It could have been, for clearly it was a barkentine, but she could see nothing else that set it apart. In any event, it was flying no flag, an ominous sign, and dark shadows showed on the side of the hull. Places where cannons were mounted?

The wind had begun to pick up, favoring them, for the

Black Jasmine moved well under the right conditions, and Celia had every available inch of canvas run up, even ordering the men to fashion lifeboat oars into makeshift spars for more studding sails. Night fell quickly, with almost no preliminary grayness, and she saw to her relief that the moon was barely a sliver in the darkness, offering no illumination at all.

They sailed without lights throughout the long night, and Celia knew that every man on board was holding his breath, wondering where the other ship was, whether it was closing in. When morning dawned, the horizon was empty, blue as far as the eye could make out, with only the faintest wisp of white cloud showing in the southern sky.

Whether the ship actually was the *Peony*, Celia would never know, but the mere fact that it could have been was enough to unnerve her. They had made good time those first days out of Honolulu, but the calms had slowed them down, and Teresa, with more experience at reading maps, could well have narrowed the gap between them.

They lost more precious time a few days later when they ran into a storm and were forced to reef the sails for a full twenty-four hours. Celia could have wept as she felt the last of their advantage slipping away, for while the *Jasmine* was swifter, the *Red Peony* was the sturdier of the two ships and better able to ride out the storm without pulling in canvas. As they approached the California coast, she was bitterly aware that Teresa might have caught up with them by now—or even spurted on ahead to lie somewhere in ambush!

For all her trepidations, however, she couldn't help being curious, and as they covered those last few miles, she found herself leaning over the railing, fascinated by the land that was getting closer and closer every minute. She had expected California to be all golden sand and sunlight, like Hawaii, with gracefully swaying palm trees visible on the shore. But all she could see was a thick wall of fog, heavy and drifting, as if storm clouds had settled over the earth.

She had never experienced anything like it before. Huge rolls of silver-gray billowed toward them from the unseen land, ebbing until they almost seemed to vanish, then surging up again like great primitive waves. Everything was strangely mystic, frightening in a way, yet beautiful too, deep and compelling . . . hypnotic. The air grew subtly cooler, and little tendrils of fog began to swirl around the ship, touching Celia's cheek with icy fingers. Within minutes the vessel was so deeply enveloped she could not see the nearest mast.

China materialized suddenly in the fog beside her. "We can't bring the ship in," he said tensely. "Not in something like this. But we don't dare stay where we are. The *Red Peony* might be almost anyplace. The only way out is to take the *Jasmine* down the coast. Santa Barbara, I think—but I'll leave that to your discretion when you get there."

"To *my* discretion? But . . ." Celia turned her head, trying to make out his features in the fog. "Where are you going to be?"

"I'm going to take a few of the men and try to land in one of the lifeboats. It'll be tricky, but a small boat is more maneuverable—it won't be like bringing in the *Jasmine*. Brandon is still in the Monterey area. I have to get word to him that Teresa is here—before she has a chance to get away."

"You think she's going to do that? Try to get away?"

China nodded. "She's angry, but she's no fool. If she can't find us in this fog—and I'm not sure she'll even try—she's not going to risk hanging around on U. S. soil. She came after us on impulse, but she's had time to think things through, to calculate her risks. Unless I miss my guess, she's looking for the *White Lotus* right now. And when she finds it . . ."

Celia didn't need the rest of the words to know what was going on in his mind. *When she finds it, she's going to cut her losses and head for home.* And then they'd be right back where they started!

"I'm going to go with you," she said impetuously. She had promised herself she would help Brandon, and she was going to see it through.

China tried to dissuade her, but time was short, and once he saw that her mind was made up, he gave in reluctantly. Celia hurried below to get a pea jacket and cap, pausing only for one heart-wrenching moment when she caught sight of Michael, asleep in his little hammock, round cheeks puffed out with contentment.

He was his father's son, all right. She tried to smile, but her lips were trembling. He had slept through everything, calms and storms alike, even when poor Georgina was so seasick she could hardly tend to him. A little sailor already, with the love of the sea in his blood. She had not realized it would be so hard, saying good-bye, perhaps for several days, though she knew he would be all right. Hadn't he managed without her before?

"We're going to be together soon, baby," she whispered as she bent down to kiss that downy brow. "We're going to be together as a family—not just you and me, but you and me and your daddy . . . who loves us both very much."

Back on deck, she discovered that China had already lowered the boat, setting it in the water before they climbed in, a needless precaution, for the wind was almost unnaturally still, the sea as calm as glass. Was it always like this when the fog rolled in? she wondered as she scrambled down the rope ladder. A moment of eerie calm with nothing stirring?

The mist clung to her skin, damp and chilling, and she found, as she turned her head, that she could not even see China, though she knew he was seated beside her. Her hand groped for the edge of the boat, clutching at it, holding on for dear life as she felt it begin to move. The only audible sound was the rhythmic splashing of the oars dipping into the water.

Although she could not see them, she knew there were four rowers. Four men besides China and herself in the boat, a little party of six setting out against . . . what? Suddenly the whole thing seemed hopelessly rash, and she was tempted to call out, telling them to turn back, to put her off before this madness went further. But even as the thought crossed her mind, she knew it was too late, for the *Black Jasmine* had already disappeared into the fog. They could not find her again if they tried.

She was only dimly aware of the moment they finally reached the shore, sensing rather than seeing it. There was something different in the air, a coldness that seemed deeper than before, a strange sandy scent in her nostrils. Then suddenly she could hear it too, and she felt China tense in his seat. Was that the sound of waves crashing on the shore? Had the wind picked up, then? She hadn't noticed, but she had been so caught up in her own feelings. Yes, there it was, cold and biting, dashing the waves against . . .

Against what? Her body went rigid as she listened. The sand? But that didn't sound like sand. It sounded like the roaring of water against rocks.

China reacted instantly, reaching toward the rowers—at least that's what it seemed like, though she still couldn't see. He gave a sharp cry, words Celia could not make out, but the men seemed to catch them, for they began to row backward almost at once, working feverishly against the current.

They held that tenuous position for one long, frightening moment; then they were easing sideways, and Celia heard a grating sound against the bottom of the boat. Jarring, but not the awful crash she had expected, and she knew they were safe on land.

It wasn't until the next morning, when the fog had eased slightly and she could see something of the cove where they had come in, that she realized how truly precarious their situation had been. Dark jagged rocks seemed to be everywhere, whitecapped waves crashing like thunder against them, with only one shallow ledge of sand, which some-how, miraculously, they had managed to find.

"How did you know what to tell the men?" she said as she stood beside China, staring down at that rocky beach in awe. "A few seconds more—*one* second more—and we'd have been swept onto the rocks. If it weren't for you, we might have been killed."

"It isn't as impressive as it seems," he replied, smiling almost apologetically, as if her praise embarrassed him. "A sailor learns to use all his senses, not just his eyes. I could hear by the sound of the surf that we were headed for rocks, and I knew we were in trouble."

"And that ledge we landed on?"

"Mostly a lucky guess—though I was following the sound in that case too. I told you, a sailor uses all five senses, and the sixth one too."

Not unreasonable, Celia had to admit—China had been at sea for many years, and she supposed he had landed in foggy coves before this—but she couldn't help wondering how many other sailors would have done as well. They had paused for a moment on a natural path, just above the beach; now they started forward again. There were just the two of them, for one man had been sent off the night before with instructions to make his way into town and find Brandon, and the others were setting up camp.

The mists had turned unpredictable, lifting at times to expose the stark wildness of the wooded terrain around them, then closing in again, so dense Celia could hardly see where she was going. China had moved on ahead, but he paused occasionally, glancing over his shoulder to make sure she wasn't lagging behind.

The forest seemed strangely silent, not the silence of houses at night, or open rice fields shimmering in the sunlight, but a deep, brooding silence that etched itself cold into her bones. Even the smells were different, the scent of pine and cypress, pungent, mingling with the salt moisture of sea and fog, and a mantle of decaying needles felt soft beneath her feet.

They had been walking for perhaps an hour, with the fog clearing perceptibly, when they came to a distinctly marked path leading downward. China hesitated, scowling at the faint traces of a footprint in the mud, then began to follow it, turning back just long enough to hold out a cautionary hand, warning Celia to be quiet.

Here the trees were thicker, with gnarled cypress roots twisting across the path to catch at Celia's toes. Looking up, she saw a tangle of branches, dark green with foliage, stretching so high they seemed to dissolve into the fog. Dead trees rose, bleached and barren, their barkless limbs covered with red algae, as if in that humid climate even the moss had turned rust.

The path ended, and Celia almost ran into China, who had stopped abruptly and was staring straight ahead with an intent look on his face. At the sea? she wondered as she turned to follow his gaze. At another cove like the one in which they had landed? But the wind was howling again, and the fog was a swirling veil around her.

Then, just as she was about to ask what was wrong, the wind eased and the mist drifted out, revealing the hazy outline of a full-rigged vessel lying at anchor a short distance from the shore.

"The *Moonwind*?" It was more a wish than a question, dashed quickly by China, who was already shaking his head.

"No such luck." He had taken out a captain's glass and was focusing on the ship as he spoke. "The *Moonwind* carries five sails to a mast. This one has six. See, you can pick out a moonraker there on the mainmast."

Celia felt her heart sink as she studied the ship and realized China was right. But if it wasn't the *Moonwind*—then what? Once again she started to ask; and again the wind answered, drawing the fog away from a pale expanse of hull.

"The *White Lotus*?"

"So it seems." China lowered the glass, frowning slightly

as the fog oozed back, still dense, but not as enveloping as before. "And Teresa is already on board."

"But how can you tell? Especially in this fog? Even if you saw a woman with dark hair, you couldn't be sure it was her."

China started to hand her the glass, then changed his mind, tucking it back in his belt. "I don't have to see her. Teresa's crew is Oriental, except for one man—a blond." He glanced over at her to see if the words had registered, but nothing showed on her face. "He's on board now. And if he's there, she is too. I'd stake my life on it."

Celia stared at the ship, fascinated in spite of herself. It looked so elegant in the cove, so innocently pretty.

"If that's true, if she *is* there . . ."

"That means she's already abandoned the *Peony* and is getting ready to sail. Damn!" He cursed softly under his breath. "I had hoped my man would reach Brandon in time. But the way the fog looks, it could lift anytime. And the minute it's safe to leave, she's going to slip through our fingers."

And when she did, Celia thought helplessly, when she sailed the *White Lotus* out of that cove, the whole thing was going to begin all over again! Because even if Brandon could abandon the obsession that had consumed him for nearly four years, Teresa Valdes could not. Until this thing was settled once and for all, they would never be free of her.

She whirled around, eyes flashing blue-gray in the fog. "We can't let her get away. We have to stop her."

31

The water lapped up around Celia's ankles as she waded out into the cove, inching her way carefully, for the rocky bottom was slippery with moss. She was dressed simply, in snugly fitting denim pants and a man's tailored shirt, with the sleeves torn out so her arms would be free.

"Are you ready?"

She looked back at the two men on the shore behind her, barely visible in the haze. The plan was a bold one, hastily thrown together, and she would not have been surprised if one or both wanted to back out, but they showed no signs of it, giving only a curt nod in reply. She would have liked to call for volunteers, but only two of the men besides herself were strong swimmers: China, who had practically grown up in the surf of Hawaii, and young Freddie, who, surprisingly for a sailor, was as comfortable in the water as on it.

"We'd better get going." China's voice was sharp as he threw a quick look at the white clipper, rising ghostlike out of the mist. "The fog is getting thinner every minute. More visibility means more danger for us."

"You're right." Celia patted the thick leather scabbard on her belt, then grinned impulsively. "I still think I should have swum out to the ship with the knife between my teeth."

China grinned back. "You have too much imagination. You've been looking at pictures of swarthy pirates with gold rings in their ears and daggers in snarling teeth. A knife that sharp is better off in a case. Besides, how could you hold on with your teeth chattering from the cold?''

Celia turned back to the ocean and began to move again. The water was well above her knees now, and she felt a moment's tension, not fear exactly, more like a heightened awareness of the dangers she was about to face. Glancing over her shoulder, she saw a reflection of the same emotion in China's grim features, but Freddie's eyes were glowing with excitement.

This is an adventure for him! she thought with a pang. She wished there were someone older she could take, someone who understood the risks. To a boy like that, a brush with death was a glorious adventure, and he could hardly wait to get going.

The water was icy as she slid into it, a bitter shock against her skin. The Irrawaddy had always been tepid, almost unpleasantly so, the sea in Hawaii tempered by tropical currents. Now she felt the coldness keenly as she plunged beneath the surface, gliding underwater.

She swam with ease, for the cove was protected, and as exertion warmed her body, making her feel almost normal again, she sensed that she was making good time. Surfacing for air, she gave herself a moment to look around and saw with a surge of exhilaration that she was nearly halfway to the ship.

It was a daring gambit, but if it worked—and there was no reason why it shouldn't—they would buy the time they needed. As soon as they got on board, they were going to split up, Celia going aft, China to the midsection, Freddie taking the foremast and flying gibs. Once there, their knives would make short work of the shrouds and halyards, disabling the vessel so it couldn't pull out when the fog lifted. A good crew could make repairs in a few hours, of course—but a few hours would be more than enough. The messenger that had been sent to Brandon must have reached him by dawn at the latest. With swift horses he and his men could be back . . . when? By noon surely. And noon could not be more than two hours away.

Celia was aware of the cold again as she reached the anchor chain and stopped swimming. Breaking the water cautiously with her head, she was relieved to see that the fog was still relatively dense. The wind had a sharp edge to it, and as China had predicted, her teeth were beginning to chatter. Almost enough, she thought, trying to hold on to her sense of humor, to make her drop the knife if she had been carrying it that way.

China reached the anchor a second later, holding on with one hand while they waited together for Freddie to catch up. They did not try to speak, even in a low whisper, for their plans were already made. They knew what they had to do.

When Freddie reached them, China pulled out of the water first, climbing with a nimble athletic grace up the anchor chain. Celia waited until he had had time to get to the top and look around; then, when he gave the signal, she started after him.

The wind rose as she climbed, howling around her, and her drenched clothes felt as if they were turning to ice. The links were broad, and she had thought it would be easy to get a grip on them, but the fog made the metal slimy, and so cold she could hardly touch it. It seemed to take forever, but somehow she found the strength to work her way inch by inch to the railing.

Her teeth were chattering audibly by the time she reached it, and she clenched her jaws together, terrified, irrationally, that someone would hear. The deck seemed deserted, with only the usual coils of rope and odd pieces of equipment visible through the fog.

No one but the watch about, she thought, relieved but not surprised. Everyone else would be below, enjoying a last cup of tea or a mug of warming grog before it was time to set sail.

Staying as close to the center as she could, away from the railings where the men on watch would be stationed, she made her way cautiously aft. The fog seemed lighter around the mizzenmast, but she tried not to think about that as she wasted precious seconds struggling to free the knife from its scabbard. Her fingers were so numb she could barely make them move. Even when she got it out, it was hard to get a hold on the handle.

The ropes proved tougher than she had thought, and she was scowling as she sliced through first one, than another, grunting with satisfaction when she heard them snap.

She did not even recognize the point at which the fog finally began to lift. She had been concentrating so hard, she couldn't see anything but the knife in her hands, the stout, stubborn cords as she hacked them apart. She knew only that suddenly she looked up and everything on deck was standing out with frightening clarity, the mainmast, with ropes dangling from it, telling her that China had worked with exceptional skill—even the foremast, also disabled.

She was keenly aware of her danger now, scenting it as an animal might scent the hounds behind him, and she slipped the blade hastily into her scabbard. Thank heaven the two men, at least, had completed their tasks. It was too late to do anything more to the mizzenmast. If she didn't get away now, she was never going to.

She had just started toward the rail, planning to slip over the side and dive neatly into the water, when she heard a sound in the bow, not so much a shout as a howl, full of rage and surprise. Even before she turned, she sensed that Freddie had been the first to be be spotted. She was not wrong. He had crawled out on the jibboom, a fortunate position, for as one of the crewmen lunged toward him, he let go and splashed into the sea.

Celia had taken a step forward, so caught up in the scene she was witnessing she didn't realize that her own position had become equally precarious. Sensing her mistake a second too late, she swung around just in time to see a large sallow-skinned man advancing toward her. Large enough to be a Mongol, she thought, shuddering as much at the glint of excitement in those dark slanting eyes as at the large double-edge sword raised above his head. Rigid with fear, she realized there would be no softness in a man like that, no mercy for her because she was a woman.

All she could do was throw her hands up, an ineffectual gesture, no use against that broad, heavy sword, but she did it all the same, cowering as she waited for the blow to fall. Almost at the same instant, a bloodcurdling cry rent the air, startling the man enough to make him falter. Looking up, Celia realized what had happened. China, seeing her plight, had leapt onto one of the lifeboats and was doing everything he could to attract attention.

She did not hesitate. Before the man could recover, she grabbed up a heavy metal pin that had been lying on the ground and hurled it toward him with all her strength. He seemed to sense his danger, for he turned, but not in time. There was a moment of recognition in his eyes—one brief second of shock and fear—then the makeshift weapon smashed into his face, knocking him over the rail.

With a cry of exhilaration, Celia spun around, intending to wave at China, to tell him she was all right before she too leapt over the side. But as she did, she saw to her horror that the same scene was being enacted there, only in reverse. Even as she watched, a sturdy wooden object—a capstan bar?—flew through the air, catching her friend from behind, throwing him off balance. A second later, he plummeted downward, striking his head with brutal force against the rail before toppling into the sea.

"China?"

For a second she was so stunned she could only stand there staring numbly at the spot she had last seen him, longing to do something, though instinct warned her it was too late. *I owe my life to Brandon Christopher,* he had told her once. Oh God, why did she have to hear those words ringing in her ears? *I owe him my life—more than my life.* A heavy debt that had now been paid.

Her heart was aching as she turned back, only to see

that that one split second of hesitation had cost her dearly. The deck, which had been so empty before, was now swarming with men. They seemed to be everywhere at once, rushing about as if they were bewildered, as if they had poured out of the forecastle and hold too quickly to get their bearings. Some were still pulling on their jackets; others, eyes shifting this way and that, clutched at empty scabbards for the swords they had forgotten below. Sick with fear, Celia realized she could not possibly get to the railing without being seen. She was trapped on the ship, with only a knife to defend herself!

Could the crew really be that large? Momentarily dazed, she searched in vain for a shadowy corner to hide in. The light was clear now, the fog almost completely dispersed. China had been right, then: the men from the other ship *were* on board, though even with that, she was surprised to see so many. Was that why it had been easy to take the *Black Jasmine*? Because most of the crew was already with Teresa on the *Peony*?

Frightened, Celia pressed her back against a nearby wall, feeling somehow safer with that hard, impenetrable mass behind her. Her breath was coming in gasps now, catching in her throat as she stood there, tense, waiting for one of the men to turn around and see her. Yet when it finally happened, when she finally saw dark eyes aimed in her direction, they simply flitted over her—as if she weren't there!

Only slowly did she realize that everyone's attention was focused on the windward side of the ship. Something seemed to draw them all that way, their concentration so fierce the deck had begun to slant.

Inching her way to the end of the wall, Celia peered around the corner just as a second tall-masted clipper glided into sight, pulling even with the *White Lotus*. A heavy ramming sound followed a few seconds later, so jolting it almost knocked her off her feet.

The *Moonwind*! Celia could have wept with relief as she recognized gleaming brasswork and billowing white sails.

Of course, the *Moonwind*! What a fool she had been, counting the hours it would take Brandon and his men to reach the cove with swift horses. Brandon Christopher would never arrive on horseback! Not when he had a fleet ship of his own.

The two great clippers held abreast for several minutes, time enough for man after man to leap over the rail, swords flashing in a sudden spurt of sunlight, pistols raised to explode in short staccato bursts.

Celia's heart began to beat wildly as her eyes swept over the deck, searching those dark heads for a welcome flare of fiery red. Brandon's men, all right, she thought with a surge of excitement. There was Jorge, the swarthy Filipino whose lewdness had frightened her so much before—now his eyes were ablaze with a different kind of light. Try as she would, however, she could not catch even a glimpse of the lithe, athletic figure she hungered to see. The action was so intense, the jungle of flailing arms and careening bodies so dizzyingly thick, everything was barely a blur in her vision.

Perhaps it was for the best. Taking comfort where she could, she sidled along the wall, trying to get out of the way. She wouldn't be able to go to Brandon anyway; he wouldn't be able to come to her. Wouldn't it only make things harder if he had to look up and see her cowering, frightened, across the deck? He needed his head clear now, needed all his thoughts and instincts to deal with the battle raging on every side.

Something brushed against her, startling enough to make her jump back, and she glanced down, horrified to see a thin red line forming on her arm, blood oozing out where a sword tip had grazed her. With a cold sense of fear she realized that rescue was not yet hers. Brandon and his men might be on board, but she was in as much danger as ever. No one was looking for her, true—none of the bullets flying around were aimed in her direction—but that would be cold comfort if she got caught in the line of fire.

Spying a half-open doorway, she headed toward it, not

knowing where it led, not even caring, knowing only that somehow she had to get out of that wild, unpredictable chaos.

Beyond the door, a flight of stairs led downward, short and steep, ending in an unexpected flood of almost glaring sunlight. Celia faltered at the base, surprised to see a line of small square windows in what was obviously the captain's saloon.

Odd, she thought, pausing for a moment to stare at them. It didn't make sense, putting windows low in a ship's wall where they could be washed out in an ocean gale. She could not know that the cabin had been designed for Teresa Valdes, and Teresa had always had a horror of enclosed spaces.

Even without knowing, however, she could sense a woman's presence in that small, cramped chamber. Perhaps it was the smell, she thought, tilting her head unconsciously to take in a deep breath. There was something light and flowery in the air, mingling with the more masculine odors of wood and whale oil and the salty tang of the sea. It occurred to her vaguely that she hadn't seen Teresa on deck. But then, she hadn't seen Brandon either, and she had been looking for him.

The noise from above seemed to have subsided somewhat, and Celia found herself glancing apprehensively at the windows, as if somehow, in that broad expanse of sea and sky, she could catch a hint of what was happening on deck. What if the fight was not going well for Brandon? Fear flooded her heart as she recalled how frighteningly even the battle had seemed. An element of surprise on Brandon's side perhaps, a slight edge in manpower on Teresa's. What if, even now, the tide was turning against him?

Frantically she looked around the room, searching for a weapon, something, *anything*, she could use to protect herself. A small chest had been built into one wall, and she started there, tugging open a drawer in the middle first, for no better reason than that it had been left ajar. To her surprise, she spotted exactly what she wanted.

There, lying on a soft flannel rag, was a small pistol, the barrel slender and silver, the teak handle custom-carved in an ornate dragon pattern.

She had just pulled it out of the drawer and was gripping it tensely when a sudden unexpected darkness fell over the room. As she looked up, she saw that the *Moonwind* had closed in on the side of the ship again, blocking the light from the windows. The sight held her attention for a moment, engrossing her so completely she did not hear the sound of footsteps on the stairway behind her.

When at last it registered, all she could think was: I forgot to close the door!

The gun still in her hand, she whirled around, expecting to see dark features lowering at her, a vile beast like the man who had nearly cornered her before. Instead she found herself staring into a familiar face.

"Skye?"

She was so stunned, all she could do was stand there and gape at him. Skye Maarten? Here? It seemed incredible, yet plainly it was he. The shadows had deepened fair hair to honey gold and his tanned skin was now etched with faint lines, but there was no mistaking those blue-violet eyes.

Those same eyes widened slightly, a mirror of her own shock as they ran down her figure, taking in the man-style denim pants, too tight for dainty modesty, the sleeveless shirt clinging, ocean-wet, to every curve of her breast. Then, regaining his composure, he swept her a low, half-mocking bow.

"Your servant, madam." Hints of amusement tugged at the corners of his mouth. "I must say this is a pleasant . . . surprise. You do have a way of showing up in the most unexpected places."

"But . . ." Celia hesitated, not quite catching those enigmatic words. Half of her longed to throw herself into his arms, sobbing with relief because he was a friend and she was safe; yet the other half held back. "I don't understand. What . . . what are you doing here?"

He began to laugh, a soft, not at all pleasant sound.

"Come now, you're a smart little girl. Surely you can answer that one yourself. Or do I have to spell it out for you?"

"Nooo . . ." Celia felt something cold and quivering run down her spine as she gazed into the handsome, decadent features of this man she had once loved so much she risked everything to be with him. "No, you don't have to spell it out. You're one of *them*, aren't you? One of the men—the pirates—on this ship?"

"Obviously." Skye leaned against the door frame, casual, yet taut, and Celia felt every muscle in her body go tense.

"That's all you have to say? Just 'obviously'? What is this, a game to you? Another high stake to be thrown on the poker table?" She felt sick inside as the pieces started to fall into place. "You've been with them all along, haven't you? You were there in Hawaii, spying on us. And that's what you were doing on Lantao! No wonder people looked at me so strangely when I asked about you. And even"—she paused, everything becoming frighteningly clear—"even before that!"

"Ah, I see you're beginning to get the picture."

"Oh, my God!" Celia half-closed her eyes, bitterly conscious of the irony of it all. She had doubted Brandon so many times; she had loved and not believed; she had sensed the deep, abiding decency in his nature and not dared to trust her heart. But it had never once occurred to her to suspect Schuyler Maarten! "I should have figured it out a long time ago, right from the beginning. You came back to Burma too quickly after that card game when your father lost everything. And you had too much money. If only I'd been thinking clearly, if I'd just had the sense to ask a few questions . . ."

"If you had, you would have gotten the same answers as everyone else." Skye pushed away from the door, suddenly impatient. He had forgotten how annoying it could be, that girlish naiveté of hers. "I had a good story all worked up, I assure you—daring exploits in the ivory trade, that sort of thing. Even your father had to buy it. He didn't want to, but he did."

"And all that time . . ." Memories came flooding back, unwanted . . . feelings . . . the shameful way she had let him touch her. "All the time you were courting me . . ."

"And kissing those ruby-red lips? Yes, my dear, all that time I was a hardened criminal, with blood on my hands and evil thoughts in my heart. Not that that diminished your pleasure, which, as I recall, was quite intense. You seem to have a propensity for picking men of—how can I put it delicately?—vigorous action." A slow grin came over his face, amusement returning as he watched a flood of crimson rise to her cheeks. "I think perhaps I made a mistake, turning down your very generous offer that morning by the riverside. It would have made a most enjoyable . . . memory."

His eyes began to slide down her body again, more mocking than lewd, but all the same, they made her feel dirty inside. How could she have let him use her like that, hold her, whisper sweet promises in ears that tingled with the warmth of his breath? Suddenly she was glad she had the gun. With it she would be safe, no matter what he intended.

"Stay away from me," she said, leveling it pointedly at his chest. She was trembling so badly she had to hold on with both hands. "If you come any closer I . . . I'll use this. I swear I will!"

Skye only laughed. "What, my pretty? You think I have designs on that lovely body? Any other time, I admit, you might be right." It really was quite titillating, the way that absurd outfit had begun to dry, as if the fabric were painted onto her flesh. As for the fact that she was unwilling? Well, sometimes that made things more intriguing. "But right now, alas, time is too short for that sort of dalliance."

"Then what . . .?" Celia watched him warily, sensing something she didn't like in his tone. "What *do* you have in mind?"

Skye saw the fear in her eyes a second before she recognized it herself. "You should trust your instincts—they're right, you know. I have it in mind to get to that row of windows behind you. I had planned to leave gracefully, sliding down on a rope like a cat burglar from the second story. Now I'm afraid my exit is going to be somewhat more hurried." He started forward as he spoke, easily, not threatening—not yet. The smile on his face was almost winsome as he held out his hand.

For the gun? Celia thought, panicking, though she knew that was foolish. He couldn't get it away from her, not if she didn't let him.

She was only dimly aware of the rest of the ship now; the noises above had faded until they were barely noticeable. Was Brandon winning then? He must be, for why else would Skye Maarten be here? No one would try to escape through the windows if there was a better way out.

"It's no good, Skye," she said quietly. "You told me to trust my instincts—and instinct tells me it would be suicide to hand over this gun. You aren't going to leave someone behind to set up a cry when you start down that rope."

"You think not? . . . Ah, but perhaps I would. I'm a gambling man, after all. I might give you a sporting chance—if you give me one now." He stretched his hand a little farther, enticing the sparrow to take a crumb from his fingers. The lulling smoothness in his voice sent a chill down her spine.

"I told you before . . ." She raised the gun, aiming it with cool precision. "Don't get too close. I don't want to shoot, but I will if I have to."

"Oh?" He drew his hand back, still smiling. "I don't think so. Remember, I knew you very well before . . . too well. You're all spit and spark—and very little flame. I don't think you have it in you to kill a man."

He took a step toward her, than another, not rushing things, but closing the gap between them. Instinctively Celia began to back away, all her concentration riveted on those intense eyes boring into her face. What was it she saw there? A gambler's love of daring? Yes, surely, but something else too. An extra thrill that seemed to come from sensing that slight edge of danger.

And he would think the danger was slight! Skye Maarten, with all that cool arrogance, would be supremely sure of himself now. Sure of his hold on her.

Then suddenly the wall was there, against her back, and she realized with a cold certainty that the moment of choice had come. Listen to this man's lies one more time and pay for it dearly—or defend her life the only way she could.

"I'm sorry," she said softly.

And, oh God, she was. Desperately sorry. All the hatred was gone now, all the bitterness, the anger, and she was aware of only one thing, a terrible, overwhelming sense that it was his life or hers—and she was not ready to die for such a shabby cause. Drawing in a last quick breath, she squeezed her finger.

The trigger caught for a fraction of a second, then released—with a dull click.

Stunned, Celia looked down, aware of laughter in her ears as she did. When she looked up again, the expression on Skye's face was smug and satisfied.

"It isn't loaded," he informed her. "I should have told you, but it was much more fun trying to figure out what you would do. I was in the process of cleaning it when that god-awful commotion broke out on deck." He paused to watch her, enjoying the confusion that was just beginning to turn to fear. "It isn't loaded—but *this* one is."

He slid his hand into his breast pocket, pulling out a small pistol. The mate to the one she had found? Celia tried not to look at it, but she couldn't tear her eyes away. The same compact barrel glinted silver in the dim light as he pointed it at her; the same carved handle almost disappeared into his palm.

It was funny, the tricks her mind was playing, focusing on all the wrong things. She should have been clinging to the memory of Brandon now, the look on his face the last time she saw him, the feel of his mouth as he kissed her good-bye. She should have been frightened, dwelling on the pain, wondering how much the bullet was going to hurt as it shattered her breast. Instead, all she could think was how very blue Skye Maarten's eyes were—and how little that mattered to her now.

"I don't suppose you would have brought the gun out," she said, "if you didn't plan to use it."

Skye acknowledged her words with a slight nod, giving grudging credit for the coolness he had not expected. Who would have thought such a flighty little thing would manage a show of dignity in the end? In a vague way, he was disappointed. He would have preferred tears, a trembling woman on her knees pleading for her life. It would have made him feel more masculine, more in control.

"As you said yourself, I *am* sorry. But I'm afraid it has to be done."

There was a quiet finality in his voice, but Celia barely heard it, for a sudden coldness had spread through her body, making her numb to everything, even fear. He was *not* sorry, she thought. For all the pretty politeness of his words, he would not feel an instant's regret when he pulled the trigger. It would mean nothing that she had once loved him to distraction, that he had held her trembling in his arms, that he had kissed her . . . and she had kissed him back. If anything, it would add a touch of macabre excitement to the moment.

Then he raised the gun, pointing it not at her breast, as she had expected, but at her face—and at last she was afraid.

32

The gun moved slowly upward.

Celia pressed back against the unyielding hardness of the wall. She could feel the fear now, great incapacitating waves that flooded over her, robbing her of the last measure of her self-control, and she realized bitterly that he had seen it too. Something in her expression must have given her away, a narrowing of her eyes, an involuntary twitching of the muscles of her mouth, for his hand hesitated just briefly, then began to rise again, until the gun was level with her eyes.

So she was not as brave as she had seemed.

One corner of Skye Maarten's mouth angled upward as he recognized the fear she herself had acknowledged only an instant before. Rather to his surprise, he found himself enjoying the sensation. He had killed before, and there had always been, in that act, a certain grim satisfaction, like the thrill that ran through the hunter when one clean shot plummeted a wild goose to earth. But he had never killed a woman, and he sensed now a subtle, almost exhilarating difference.

If there was any sadism in the feeling, he did not recognize it, for his thoughts, as always, were centered not on the woman in front of him, but on himself. It was not her pain that counted, but his own pleasure, and he was conscious of nothing so much as the keen, almost sexual excitement it gave him to hold a pistol on her and comtemplate pulling the trigger.

Tilting the gun slightly to one side, he watched fascinated as her eyes followed it, now an inch off center, now harmlessly pointed at the wall. One moment of respite, he thought—one moment in which she would let herself hope. The idea tantalized, and he held the gun away a second longer, anticipating the look that would come into her eyes when he aimed it back again.

It was that one brief second that proved his undoing, for it gave the man who had slipped up behind him in the shadowy stairwell the opportunity he had been looking for. As long as the gun had been pointed at Celia's brow, he had not dared make a move, knowing that even in death a finger could contract around the trigger. But now that it was pointed away . . .

He wasted no time pressing his advantage. The knife was already in his hands, a long slim-bladed dagger he had drawn out of his belt. Now he raised it, and with one deft motion buried it in the side of Skye Maarten's neck.

The gun exploded instantaneously, but the shot went wild, breaking the colored glass of a lantern on the far wall. The recoil threw Skye off balance, his shoulders jerking upward as he staggered back against his assailant. Still alive? the man thought, eyeing the gun in his hand as he shoved him away in disgust. Or the last compulsive twitching of muscles already dead?

Celia, unable to see anything in the dark shadows behind Skye, knew only that she had heard the shot she was waiting for, and for just an instant her own muscles contracted, half-feeling the pain that was not even there. Only slowly did she become aware of things around her. The sound that followed that burst of gunfire—glass shattering somewhere behind her—the uncharacteristic awkwardness of Skye's body as he took a stumbling step toward her . . . the way his eyes widened suddenly, as if he were surprised, as if somehow, unaccountably, he had been betrayed. Then, as she watched, horrified, he crumpled up like a rag doll with all the stuffing pulled out of it, and slid to the ground.

It was a moment before she noticed the jeweled hilt of a dagger protruding out of his neck. The edges of the wound were surprisingly clean, as if the blade had been inserted with great force; only one slender trail of red seeped down to mar the immaculate white of his collar.

Looking up, she saw a man standing in the doorway, his broad shoulders extending almost from frame to frame. The windows had cleared suddenly, and bright sunlight splashed the room, catching in dark red hair that was already shimmering from the sudden spate of tears in her eyes.

Brandon. The word was a cry in her heart, but she was so stunned, nothing came out of her lips. She just stood there staring at him, thinking idiotically that she had forgotten how handsome he was. Preposterous, but there it was. She would have died if he hadn't arrived in time; she hadn't even been sure until that very second that he himself was not dead somewhere on deck; and all she could think was: *I forgot how handsome he was.*

Then suddenly—later she would not even recall how—he had vaulted over the body between them, she had taken that one step toward him, and they were in each other's arms. Suddenly he was pulling her down against the long captain's table and she was half in his lap, half on the bench beside him. His jacket was off, and he was wrapping it around her; his lips had found her hair, her temples, the soft round arc of her neck and shoulders.

They remained like that for a long time, clinging to each other in the sweetness of a reunion that was all the more precious because it had seemed forever in coming. Then all at once they were both talking, the words spilling out in an unintelligible torrent.

They stopped as they had begun, together. "You first—" Brandon started to say, but Celia interrupted with a laugh.

"No, you first." The tears were streaming down her cheeks, but she made no effort to check them, sensing at last that it was truly over. For the first time since she had looked down into the cradle and seen her baby gone, she dared to let herself cry. "There's so much I want to know. I was so afraid when those men caught us on deck—and then I looked up and saw the *Moonwind*. How did you find us so quickly? When I sent a man to you last night, we didn't even know the *White Lotus* was here."

"You may not have, but I did. We found out several days ago where the ship was anchored, but we held back, knowing by that time Teresa wasn't on board. When word came that she was headed for the coast on the *Red Peony*, we assumed she'd try for a rendezvous with the *Lotus*, though we did expect to have more time. We hadn't realized it would be so soon."

Celia shivered as she nestled closer into his arms. "There was no time for anything at all. When we got here, she had already ditched the *Peony* somewhere and transferred her men to the larger vessel."

"So I discovered when I approached and found the ship with double its usual crew. Then when I learned you were there too . . ."

He broke off, not even wanting to think about it. Later, when he could trust his voice, he would tell her how he had felt when he came down that blasted stairway in search of Schuyler Maarten—and found the bastard with a gun pointed at Celia's forehead. Later he would talk of the helplessness, the anguish that swept over him when he realized he might lose her, and there wasn't a damn thing he could do about it!

"You little fool—what made you do it? It was insane, going on board like that, with only two men to back you up. Don't you know you could have ruined everything?"

The words came out harsher than he had intended, and Celia pulled back, a little hurt. "I had to, Brandon." she protested softly. "Please don't scold me. It *was* insane—I know that—but I didn't know what else to do."

"Ah, sweet, I'm sorry." Her lower lip had begun to tremble like a little girl's, and Brandon felt his heart melt.

"Was I scolding? I didn't mean to. I know you were only trying to help. If anyone else had done it, I would have said, 'By God, what a courageous act!' But don't you see, my dearest, it wasn't anyone else—it was *you*. And nothing on earth is worth your life to me."

"But she was going to get away, Brandon! I couldn't let that happen. Not after you'd risked so much to get her here."

"I don't give a damn what I'd risked or what happened to Teresa Valdes! She could have taken to the seas, and welcome, as long as I knew you were safe. Don't you think . . . ? Ah, but I'm doing it again, scolding when I promised I wouldn't." His voice softened as he shifted her weight gently, settling her on the bench beside him. "We'll talk of all this later, and much more. What matters now is that we love each other and that we're together."

Celia sighed as she sensed the strength of his arms, still tight around her. At last the words she had longed to hear: now that they had finally been spoken, they seemed so easy and natural, she wondered she could ever have doubted.

"But I am curious," she said, drawing just far enough away to look up at him. "Didn't you tell me a minute ago that you knew I was on board the *White Lotus*?"

"I did," he conceded, "and a lucky thing, too. Teresa and her men weren't the only dangers you faced today."

She wrinkled her brow. "I don't understand."

"I had planned to come broadside on the *Lotus* and open fire with my cannons. Fortunately, we found young Freddie floundering in the water, pulled well off course by the undertow and drifting out to sea. When he told us you were on board, I made a few hasty changes in my plans."

"Well, then . . ." Celia shuddered at the thought of the violent cannonade that had nearly caught her on deck. "All I can say is, thank heaven for Freddie. I'll have to give him a big hug when I see him."

Brandon's expression changed, flashing a warning, it seemed to Celia, as though he were trying to tell her something. But before it could register, he had composed his features again. "Don't think about that now—just come to my arms and let me hold you. I've been such a damn fool about so many things. It's going to take the rest of my life to try to explain, to justify what I've done. Even then, I wonder . . . will you be able to forgive me?"

Celia snuggled back into his arms, smiling to herself as her head found his chest. Would she be able to forgive him? How silly men could be sometimes. Didn't he know he had the whole thing all twisted around?

"I thought you just wanted to hold me, my love. Isn't that enough for now?"

"More than enough," he agreed.

He lowered his cheek, letting it linger against her long loose hair. She was right. It was enough to feel, to touch—to love. Always before, he had clung, fiercely protective, to a sense of his own masculine independence. There had been women in his life, many of them, and he had cared for some more than others, but he had never loved, nor truly wanted to. It came as a surprise now to realize how little that independence really meant.

They remained in the small, stuffy cabin for well over an hour, and Brandon Christopher, the man who never let anyone do anything for him—the captain who always had to be in command—meekly stood aside while his men took over the unpleasant task of cleaning up on deck. He left Celia only once, briefly, to give a few hurried instructions to the crew, not the least of which was the removal of Skye Maarten's body, which still lay where it had fallen on the floor.

Celia watched dry-eyed as a pair of men wrapped Skye in an old blanket, stained with grease and tar, and carried him up the stairs. There was no horror in her for what had happened to him, no pity . . . no feelings at all. She knew that she had loved him once, but she knew it only with her head. Her heart did not recognize him anymore.

Brandon was sitting across the table from her now, still holding her hands, but chatting only carelessly, as if he sensed her need for some semblance of normalcy. They talked a little of Hawaii, of his love for the islands and the beautiful, spacious villa he would build for her when they returned. But mostly the conversation drifted back to Michael, Brandon asking hungrily for details about the baby he had never seen—and puffing up with as much pride as Celia when she told him, with a mother's usual objectivity, that he was perfect in every way.

"Is he talking yet?" Brandon demanded to know. "Of course he is—he's my son, after all. And has he taken his first steps?"

"You'll have to wait a few months for that, I'm afraid," Celia retorted. Then, seeing the sparkle in his eyes, she realized he had been trying to make her laugh. And he had succeeded. "What a fraud you are, Brandon Christopher. You strut around like the cock of the walk, trying to make everyone believe you're strong and invincible—and inside, you're as tender and as vulnerable as a woman."

"Caught," he admitted, smiling as he pulled her toward him again. "But don't tell any of the crew, or they'll never listen to me again."

The fog had completely lifted by the time they ventured outside, and the clear September air was crisp with a promise of coming autumn. Most of the deck had been cleared by that time, but blood still made the boards slick in places, and the smell was so foul Celia was afraid for a minute she would faint. The *Moonwind* was already gone; not a trace of skysail showed beyond the rocky cliffs that edged the cove, and a new ship was anchored next to the railing, a squat gray steamer flying the red-white-and-blue flag of the United States.

"A military ship," Brandon explained as a group of uniformed men tossed what appeared to be long sackloads of grain from one vessel to the other. "Out of San Francisco. She arrived five minutes too late to see any action."

"But what are those . . .?" Celia started to ask, then stopped, sensing she didn't want to know what the men were doing.

Brandon picked up on the unspoken question. "The

bodies of some of Teresa's men," he explained grimly. "They're being taken to the city, where an attempt will be made at identification. After that, I daresay they'll find a common grave in some pauper's cemetery."

Celia watched, fascinated in spite of herself, as the men swung the last of the bundles over the rail. It seemed smaller than the others, as if it held a slight, exceptionally slender form. Slender enough for a girl?

"Was she among them?" she asked. "Teresa Valdes?"

"No." Brandon spoke slowly, dreading the words he had known he would have to say. "We didn't find her among the dead—or the wounded either. In fact, no one's seen her since the beginning of the battle. I suspect she realized early on that it was hopeless and leapt overboard."

Celia felt her heart sink. "Then . . . she got away."

"I doubt it." Brandon set his jaw in a hard line. "She isn't much of a swimmer—I don't think she's been in the water three times since she was a child. There's a nasty undertow here, especially on the sea side of the *Lotus*, which is the only way she could have escaped without being seen. Even . . ." Celia was conscious of a faint break in his voice, though it lasted only a second. "Even young Freddie was caught up in it. He would have drowned if we hadn't spotted him when we did."

"Then perhaps we'll hear soon that her body has washed ashore somewhere down the beach."

"Perhaps." Brandon didn't add that he had already sent a man to check on that; it was one of the first things he had done. "But I wouldn't count on it. With these tides, she could end up almost anywhere. We may never know for sure."

A young man in a police uniform appeared, and Brandon turned to confer with him, leaving Celia alone to look around the deck. One glance was enough to tell her that the cost of that brief but savage struggle had been appallingly high on both sides. The last of the enemy casualties had been removed, but everywhere she looked, she seemed to see another body she had not noticed before, one of

Brandon's men. Some had already been tended to by their
shipmates and were wrapped in clean canvas cut from
spare sails and tied with a stout length of cord. Others still
lay where they had fallen, and although she tried not to,
she couldn't keep her eyes from passing over them, picking out the faces that she recognized.

So many of the men she had known, she thought
sadly—so many of the men she had worked with those
long stormy nights at sea. There by the rail, propped up as
if he were just resting, she spotted an older man who was
said to have been with Brandon from the beginning, although he spoke only sailor's English and she had never
talked to him. She had not even bothered to learn his
name; now she never would. And young Freddie Brown.
Her eyes stung with tears as she looked at his still body,
facedown on the deck. So that was why Brandon had been
reticent whenever his name came up. He seemed to have
been hit from behind, and she took comfort in that, hoping
at least that he had not seen death coming, that he had not
felt more than one swift second of pain.

A short distance away, near the mainmast, she caught
sight of the swarthy features and unruly mop of black hair
that belonged to Jorge, the one man among all Brandon's
crew she had truly disliked. The feeling seemed shabby
now, totally unjustified, for he had never done anything to
her, and she was about to shed the same bitter tears for
him that she had for Freddie when suddenly, to her amazement, he sat up, raising his hand to his head with what
sounded like a string of very potent curses.

One of the passing men, another crusty old salt who had
served Brandon for years, saw the startled expression on
Celia's face and broke into a grin. "Don't you worry
about Jorge, ma'am. He's the meanest man ever sailed the
Moonwind. God don't take 'em when they's mean like
that. He don't want 'em neither."

Celia tried to smile back, but she didn't quite manage.
She was beginning to shiver as she went over to the railing
and stared out at the ocean, cool and glassy in the dis-

tance. It did seem to her that the man was right: the tough had a way of surviving. It was the young, like Freddie, who couldn't hold on. And the gentle, sensitive China Kwans.

It occurred to her that she was standing almost at the place she had seen her friend go over the side, and she pulled her hands back from the rail, recoiling as she stared hypnotically into the water, half-expecting to see a face in those murky blue-green depths, dark hair floating out around it. Death . . . it seemed so real at moments like that, and yet so intangible. She couldn't help remembering the funeral she had attended with him once, the little paper figures burned in their earthenware bowl, bringing comfort to them all, China included.

She hadn't understood then, but she did now. It was not the ritual itself that counted, not the paper houses and the paper servants, but the fact that there *was* a ritual, a way of saying good-bye, however inadequate, instead of the terrible empty feeling inside her now.

Her eyes were misty with tears when Brandon finally finished talking to the young policeman and came over to stand beside her. Knowing nothing of what she had been thinking, he assumed she was upset by the bloodshed and brutality around her; then he saw the prone body of Freddie Brown lying on the deck. Damn! He had hoped he wouldn't have to tell her about that until later, when the first of the horror had begun to wear off.

"The lad told me once that he came from farmland in Canada," he said quietly. "He hated it there. The poverty, the flatness of the place, the drudgery that was the same day after day, with no way to get ahead of the debts and the drought. That's why he ran away—to see the world."

"Well, he didn't see much of it," Celia said, unable to choke back the bitterness any longer.

"He saw a great deal actually. And he saw what he wanted. He could have stayed in Canada if he chose, and farmed the land like his father, and grown to a ripe old age—and never known a minute of excitement in his life."

He slipped a hand around her waist, guiding her gently toward the other side of the ship. "We all have to die someday, you know, like it or not—and most of us hate it like hell! The point is, what's more important? Living a long time or doing what you want to with your life?"

Celia yielded to the pressure of his hand. "I think you're trying to confuse me," she said, grateful for the distraction she sensed he was throwing out deliberately. And perhaps, in a way, he was right. She had never seen anyone as happy as young Freddie when he discovered the charms of the pretty Hawaiian girls, or as excited as Freddie that morning when they set off on what seemed to him a great adventure.

Brandon guided Celia into the small lifeboat that was to take them ashore. As they settled themselves on the seats, men in uniform began to work the pulleys, lowering the boat slowly to the accompaniment of rusty creaks and groaning ropes. The long white hull, which had seemed so gleaming and ghostly from a distance, was in reality in poor repair, and as they descended, Celia could see old layers of green and brown and black showing through the blistered and peeling paint.

They had ventured forth alone. Now Brandon took up the oars himself, rowing the boat expertly around a sharp promontory and into the cove with the small sandy beach where Celia had landed the night before. She kept her face resolutely turned toward the land, letting cool breezes cleanse the stench of blood from her nostrils. Everything seemed so natural here, so wildly beautiful—nothing but waves and rocks, and tall cypresses bent into primitive shapes by the ocean wind—it was hard to remember that a battle had been fought on the decks of a ship just behind her, and men were dead and dying.

"What's being done with the wounded?" she asked softly. "Where are they?"

Brandon paused, drawing the oars back for a moment. "My crew was my top priority," he said, "especially the wounded. They're on the *Moonwind* now. The government steamer brought a doctor, fortunately, and a hospital ship is scheduled to meet them in the harbor. They'll have the best of care."

"I had assumed that," Celia said. "What I meant was, where are Teresa's wounded?" She shivered as she recalled how brutal the fight had been. "Or wasn't anyone taken alive?"

"No quarter given, you mean? Don't worry, the civilities were all observed. The doctors will do what they can for Teresa's men too, even the ones who are seriously hurt—though Lord knows they won't be doing the bastards a favor. Those who survive will only face the hangman."

Celia looked down at the water glittering in the sunlight. "I know they're only pirates," she said thoughtfully, "but somehow it seems wrong. Putting them through all that pain only to die in the end."

"I daresay you're right," Brandon agreed. "But try to tell that to the doctors. They're there to save lives, not to pass judgment. And maybe that's the way it should be. It's a strong instinct, you know, the urge to hold on to life—even when there's no point to it."

He had begun to pull on the oars again, and Celia resisted the impulse to look back as they left the promontory behind and glided into the cove. The wind was rising slightly, but it barely penetrated that sheltered area, and she knew they would have no trouble beaching the boat.

"What about the men who are still on the *Lotus*?" she asked. "Freddie and the others. Is the government steamer going to take them away too?"

"No." Brandon had stopped rowing and was using the oars as rudders to guide the boat. "I don't give a damn what happens to Teresa's crew, but my men are sailors—I'm not going to leave them to rot in alien soil. The *Moonwind* has orders to come back as soon as she finishes in the harbor. They stood by me when I needed them, God knows. The least I can do now is see that they have an honorable burial at sea."

Celia remained in the boat while Brandon dragged it

onto the sand, then leapt out and scrambled up the bank with the aid of his hand. Even without the wind, the air had a distinct bite to it, and she did not protest when he insisted that she keep his jacket, though she knew she must look a sight, with the sleeves rolled up so her fingers could peek out and the hem hanging almost to her knees. There were horses waiting to take them into Monterey, Brandon told her, but they would have half an hour's walk or more before they reached them.

This was the same terrain she had covered that morning, but now, with the sun shining and Brandon beside her, everything looked different. The cypresses were green and graceful, not the twisted black shapes that had loomed out of the fog earlier, and long shafts of light streamed golden through the shadows. They reached a wide meadow and began to cut through knee-high grasses with splashes of autumn wildflowers showing on every side.

Only at one point, about halfway to the place where the horses were tethered, did Celia catch a glimpse of the bay where the battle had just been fought. Almost against her will, she paused to look back.

The government boat was gone now, and the *White Lotus* stood by herself, looking strangely solitary in that sun-drenched expanse of water. Her sails had been drawn up and furled; her tall masts rose naked against the stark blue backdrop of the sky. For all that any passing eye could note, she might have been a pleasure craft or a fisherman's boat waiting for favorable winds to blow.

"What's going to happen to her?"

"*Her*?" Brandon looked puzzled. "Ah, you mean the *Lotus*. She was a proud vessel once, one of the finest ever built. In another era, she would have carried tea from China—and raced the *Moonwind* right down to that last hour into port. It's not her fault, the way she's been used. She doesn't deserve to be chained to a pier in San Francisco so the curious can climb aboard at a nickel apiece and gape at the 'pirate ship'—or dismantled and turned

into scrap, for that matter. I've arranged to have her towed
out beyond the breakers this evening and set afire at sea."

Celia stared at the ship a moment longer. She could still
remember the way the *Lotus* had looked the first time she
saw her, frightening yet beautiful, with that spectacular
white hull half-dissolved into the shimmering brightness
of the water. There was so much about her that had been
evil, but Brandon was right: it was not an evil of the
clipper, but of those who had sailed her.

"I'm glad," she said softly. "I know I should hate
her—heaven knows she's struck enough terror into my
heart—but I can't. I don't want to see her mocked either.
Or cut up and sold in pieces."

She felt a light touch on her arm, and smiling, she
realized what he was telling her. Time to leave the past
behind. They had a short walk yet to the horses, a long
ride after that to the house he had told her about on the
outskirts of Monterey. There was so much still unspoken
between them, misunderstandings to be cleared up, plans
to be made for the future, and she was as eager as he to
begin.

33

Firelight bathed the small room in a flickering reddish glow, warming drab adobe walls and catching in the highlights of Celia's silver-blond hair as it spilled across the pillows. Brandon, sitting on the edge of the bed, looking down at her, was struck not merely by her beauty as she lay there half-asleep, long lashes fluttering against her cheeks, but by how very precious she was to him—and how close he had come to losing her.

He had intended, when they came back to the house, to sit her in a chair beside the fire and tell her all the things he should have said long ago. But the sweet softness of her body close to him, the inviting half-smile on her lips as he closed the door and turned to see her watching, had proved too much, and he had carried her over to the bed, making love again and again with a tempestuous hunger fed by months of abstinence. When at last he had drawn back, lingering one final moment to kiss her again, he had expected her to reproach him, gently perhaps, but a reproach nonetheless, reminding him that there was still much to be explained. But she had said nothing, accepting him, as she had so often in the past, without question, even when he hurt her most.

He reached out, fingers aching to brush back the tousled hair that half-hid a soft white shoulder. "I don't deserve your sweetness, love," he whispered softly. She gave a murmured response, only half-hearing as she nestled closer, her cheek sliding down instinctively to rest against his hand.

He had left her only once that afternoon, and then only long enough to speak with some of his men, who had gathered in a nearby tavern to discuss the aftermath of the battle and wait for their final orders from him. She was still sleeping when he returned, and he woke her with a kiss to tell her that a message had just been received. The *Black Jasmine* had not gone to Santa Barbara after all, but had made instead for San Francisco harbor, and even as they spoke, Michael and Georgina were safely ensconced in the finest hotel in town.

She had been relieved at the news; he could see it in her face, hear it in the soft sigh that slipped out of her lips, and he berated himself guiltily for not having realized before how worried she was about the baby. He had thought then that he would let her rest again, but it had been a long time since they had been together, and he had found, as his hand lingered temptingly against her thigh, that she was no more interested in sleep than he.

He was aware now of a strangely restive feeling as he got up and went over to the fire, poking at it even though the flames were still glowing brightly. It was late afternoon, almost dusk, and only the scantest light filtered through small glass-paned windows set high on the two end walls.

Celia, sensing the change in his mood, opened her eyes to see him standing immobile before the fire. He had changed into a deep burgundy dressing gown, and the color seemed to soak up the flames, reflecting one more time in the dark auburn of his hair. After a moment she sat up, wrapping the smooth cotton sheet around her, for it had grown noticeably colder in the room.

The movement caught Brandon's eye, and he came to sit beside her again. "We have so much to say to each other, my love. Or rather, I have so much to say to you. It's a long story—I wonder, do you have the patience to listen?"

Celia smiled. "Only if you're very nice to me, Brandon, and tell me how beautiful I am and that you love me very much."

The gentle tact of that teasing remark did not escape him, and leaning closer, Brandon touched his lips to the corner of her mouth. "You are very, very beautiful, and I love you more than I can say—but that doesn't make this any easier. The things I have to tell you now, I've never told anyone before . . . and they are very painful to me."

He got up again, finding it easier not to face her as he talked. The light was almost gone now, and the fire caught his eye, holding him with an almost hypnotic power.

"God, I don't even know where to begin."

"It seems to me," he could hear her soft voice coming from behind him, "the most sensible thing would be to begin at the beginning."

The beginning? Brandon's mouth twisted wryly as he watched the flames flare up, spitting sparks onto the hearth. Where the devil was the beginning anyway? That damned opium den in Shanghai? The day he took the *Moonwind* out of port for her last extended voyage? Or before that—long, long before—when he used to go back to Boston and tease his sisters in the carriage and watch a wildly whooping little boy play Red Indian on the lawn?

"I suppose," he said, turning at last, "that I had better begin by telling you what kind of man I was then. It isn't easy for me—I daresay it wouldn't be for anyone, but I seem to be less adept than most at admitting my flaws in front of others. Perhaps I could best describe myself as restless. No . . ." He thrust out a hand, forestalling the protest he could already see on her lips. "Not the way I am now. There was no pent-up anger in me then. I had not yet become the Tiger—my men hadn't taken to saying I was a jungle animal trapped in a cage. My restlessness was more the restlessness of a bright lad at school, capable enough, but bored by the lessons he is given."

He went over to the window, looking out to see that dusk had already fallen. The narrow dirt street that ran toward the ocean was silent and empty. "You must remember I had been spoiled all my life. Other men have to work for what they get. I had everything handed to me. I don't mean I sat around on my duff doing nothing. My grandfather, the old rascal, would have been proud of my industry. The Christopher family owned a shipping line when I took over; five years later we had diamond mines in Africa, hotels on three continents, sugar plantations in Hawaii—you see, my sweet, you didn't marry a pauper. But the thrill of trading in inherited wealth, even trading upward, began to pall after a while. I needed—or thought I needed—new challenges. New horizons to conquer."

Turning away from the window, he picked up a lamp that had been sitting on the table and carried it to the fire. "Perhaps that's why I was so attracted to the Orient. Everything was different there, the crowded *hutungs* that passed for city streets, the exotic food, the sailing conditions, even the languages. I had learned French and Spanish easily enough, but Chinese is a tonal language. A challenge, you see—something I had never tried before. I remained for several years, wandering aimlessly, as one of my maiden aunts put it, though I kept enough of a rein on the family businesses to ensure that she and the others lived in comfort. Then I stumbled onto Hawaii—I had originally come to check on some investments—and ironically, I found what I was looking for.

"Fate does have a way of playing tricks, doesn't it? Everything I wanted, well within reach—and I thought for a moment it was going to be mine." His voice had taken on a new tone, a quiet self-mocking Celia did not recognize as she watched him turn up the wick on the lamp and light it with a long stick from the fire. "I made one final trip to Hong Kong, or so I thought at the time, and arranged to sell the *Moonwind*, the last of the Christopher clippers, to the Portuguese Navy as a training vessel. I decided to deliver her myself, a last sentimental voyage of youth, I suppose—past Hawaii, then on to California and around the Horn, into the Atlantic. I had just stopped in

Canton to pick up a load of porcelain for the East Coast market when I received a letter telling me that . . . someone I knew—a friend—was in Shanghai.''

He put the lamp back on the table where he had found it and stood for a moment staring into space, almost as if he had forgotten Celia was there. Golden light shimmered upward, not gentle, but harsh, casting long, unnatural shadows on his face.

"The story really begins there. The letter was several months late—it had been following me from port to port— and when I arrived in Shanghai, the person I sought was no longer at his hotel. I checked in anyway, though it was hardly the kind of place I prefer. It had just been modernized, no expense spared, all that sort of thing, with electric lights in little sockets on the ceiling and no damn charm at all.

"Ah, but I'm digressing—perhaps on purpose. The next part of the story, I'm afraid, is not very pretty. You see, the hotel may not have pleased *me*, but it attracted Western tourists in droves, and with them, a number of unsavory opportunists—one man in particular. He was a British citizen, I was told, but he had affected an international air, and he used his cosmopolitan charm to make money from some of the more gullible visitors to the city.

"The desk clerk told me how his operation worked. He was a little hesitant to discuss it at first—the shadier details are not the sort one readily admits to knowing—but there was a certain weakness for liquor, and the bottle of rum I produced from my suitcase loosened his tongue.

"The whole thing was simple really, brilliantly so, for simplicity is harder to see through. The man in question would pick a young fellow traveling alone, introduce himself, and offer—from the depths of his heart, of course, no monetary gain involved—to show him the sights of the city. If those sights were on the seamy side, though cloaked in the exotic trappings that make vice more palatable, the man was so charming, the boy he had chosen so invariably naive, he was eager to go along, if only to please. The brothels he was taken to had the most beautiful girls in Shanghai, the opium dens were private rooms with carved rosewood couches and silk hangings on the walls—how could he be expected to guess that they cost only a fraction of the money he had just given his new friend?''

The lamp sputtered suddenly, flickering with a low hissing sound. Brandon paused to adjust the wick, then moved back to the fire, much to Celia's relief, for that eerie play of light and shadow had given his face a hollow look.

"I saw him once—in the reading room at the hotel, where I had stopped to glance through the Hong Kong papers. To say that you can see evil in a man by looking at him sounds presumptuous; yet in this case, it was true. I didn't merely sense it because I knew it was there, I *saw* it—and I found myself repulsed and fascinated at the same time. Like Lucifer, there was an almost too-perfect beauty in his face, a grace even to the arrogant tilt of his head: the spell he cast would be a powerful one. Women, I thought, would fall easy prey to that self-conscious charm—and a certain type of man as well, one who was young, as yet unformed.''

His voice drifted off for a moment as he leaned against the mantel, staring broodingly into the fire. "It was all petty stuff at first, nickels and dimes, you might say, barely enough to cover the rent. Then he had the fortune, or misfortune, as it may be, to meet up with a man named Lin. I won't go into who he was: you know a little already, and that's enough. Suffice it to say, he was looking for a way to pick up some ready cash in China—transferring funds back and forth was getting to be dangerous—and young Lucifer, with his looks and charm, was exactly what he had in mind.

"Forget about the whores, Lin told him—except as a sideline. Concentrate on opium. Get a man hooked, and he'll give everything he owns for another pipe.''

Celia crouched forward on the edge of the bed, feeling sick inside as she realized what she was hearing. She longed to say something, longed to reach out and remind him she was there, but she dared not break the mood, sensing it would be harder for him to go on. And she knew he had to finish.

"One of the young men who fell into his trap was staying at the hotel," Brandon continued after a short pause. "His name was Michael, and everyone assumed he was very rich. In fact, he *was* rich, but most of his money was tied up in trust, and Lucifer got damned little for his pains. The desk clerk, who was well-lubricated by this time, told me all about it, chuckling under his breath, as if he thought I'd be amused. I encouraged him. I had to—I wanted to hear the rest.

"Lucifer, it seems, had gone his master one better, finding a way to bring on the addiction even sooner by adding a certain . . . titillation to the process, and satisfying his own whims at the same time. He had always been inclined to favor slim boys over pretty young ladies, and this one was exceptionally well-favored, with red-gold hair and eyes that were an unusual pale shade of green. It was apparently a simple matter to take advantage of the breakdown of inhibitions caused by the drug—he had catered to it before with prostitutes—and teach the boy a few things he wouldn't otherwise have learned."

Brandon's nostrils flared with distaste as he took a deep breath, forcing himself to go on. "He robbed that boy of everything, not merely his dignity, but his masculinity as well, his self-image—his very humanity. When I saw him, he was close to death, a mere shell of what had once been a living spirit. There was no money left for the incense-scented paradise where he had acquired his habit, and he was now in a foul cellar, kept there only, as I later learned, by the charity of the proprietor. Charity, God! What a word to use!

"I won't describe that filthy hole to you. Imagine your worst nightmares—and put them all together. It was, in some grotesque way, almost medieval, a vision of purgatory, with emaciated men stretched out on wooden pallets and smoke rising like steam all around them. I just stood there looking down at him, feeling so goddamn helpless—and all I wanted was to go back and shoot that bastard in the hotel!''

"What stopped you?"

Brandon jerked his head back, startled by the sound of her voice. "Fate, I suppose. There was a man there in the den. He approached me with a proposition—a better way to get even. I took it.''

A better way? Celia stared down at the sheets, still rumpled from their passionate lovemaking, and wondered if it wouldn't have been easier, for her as well as him, if he had just taken a gun the way he wanted and shot the man dead. Would anyone have blamed him? Would any authority even care if one foreigner killed another in lawless Shanghai?

"So that was what it was about, pretending to be a pirate, then lying to your own wife because you were afraid to tell the truth.''

"Pretending, yes—though once committed, I had no choice. But lying to you was a mistake, and I plead guilty, my love. I can only say that I was already caught in a web of intrigue and lies, and hope you understand.''

"Yes, I think I do, in a way.'' She had felt the horror herself, when he stood there and told her what that man, the one he called Lucifer, had done; yet strangely, it seemed anticlimactic. Indignation, yes, she could believe that, and disgust—but the driving obsession that had consumed him to the exclusion of everything else? What a deep impression he must have made, young Michael on his pallet, so close to an unnatural death.

Young Michael?

For the first time the coincidence struck her, and she wondered that she had not noticed before, however wrapped up she had been in the story, and in his need to tell it.

"How your heart must have ached,'' she said softly, "to name your son after a stranger.''

"A stranger?'' Brandon turned away from the fire, crossing over to the window again, where a soft orange glow was beginning to touch the western sky. Sunset, he thought—then he realized it was too late for that. "Hardly a stranger, my love."

His eyes were deep in shadow as he turned.

"He was my brother."

34

The room was silent after Brandon had finished. Only the crackling of the fire could be heard, its fading glow a faint reflection of the muted red that filled the window-panes. He stood for a moment, caught up in thoughts of his own; then his face changed, softening as he looked down at Celia.

"You see now why it was so important for me to bring the last remnants of Lin's organization to justice. Do you have any idea how it haunted me, remembering the way Michael used to follow me around when he was a little boy, looking up to me as if I were some kind of hero? It was because of me that he went to the Orient in the first place. He wanted to be like me, to do what I had done. God, how many times these past four years I've said to myself: if only I had been a better brother . . . if I had gone home a few times, gotten to know him better . . . if I had learned the needs of his heart . . ."

His voice broke, and he turned back to the window, unable to go on. Celia wrapped the sheet around her and went over to stand beside him, feeling his pain and aching to share it.

"You must not blame yourself so much, darling. It does no good, these terrible reproaches."

"I know." He relaxed enough to smile as he put an arm around her. "I was aware of it even then, but I couldn't help myself. I had to do something, however inadequate. There was no way I could help Michael—he was beyond saving by the time I got to him—but I could keep some other boy, someone else's baby brother, from coming to the same end. It became the consuming passion of my life, God help me. I almost destroyed your love for me in the process, and cost my son his life.''

"But you didn't," she reminded him. "Michael's life was never truly in danger—it seems Teresa meant him no harm—and nothing could ever change the way I feel about you. Oh, dearest, what a terrible burden to carry all by yourself. If only I had known from the beginning, if you had just been able to trust me . . ."

"I should have, I daresay. Hindsight is so clear, isn't it?" He paused, his lips twisting almost painfully. "But be fair—you did create a rather dubious impression, you know. The first time I heard about you, you were wandering up and down the streets of Hong Kong asking for Schuyler Maarten.''

"Oh!" Celia was startled by the thought that had not occurred to her. Naturally, he had been suspicious. "You knew all along that Skye was with Teresa and her gang.''

Brandon hesitated, his expression darkening. "I knew more than that, I'm afraid. I didn't want to tell you this, but you're going to find out anyway, and I'd rather you heard it from me. Do you remember the man at the hotel—Lucifer, whose evil was cloaked behind such fair features? That was not his real name, of course. His name was—''

"Skye Maarten?" The words slipped out of Celia's mouth with a little gasp of horror. Belatedly she remembered things that had happened in Burma, the servants' gossip about men who preferred to go with boys, the look on Sin-Sin's face when she said, *There are reasons why the Lady Elizabeth refused him.* "Oh, no wonder you didn't trust me! Why, you must have hated me! You must have thought, because I came after him, that I knew what he was doing, that I approved.''

"I did at first," he admitted. "But even then I didn't *hate* you. I just thought you were caught up in passions you couldn't control. Ah, sweet, I wish I could have spared you this. I know how it must hurt, finding out that the man you loved was a blackguard, and worse."

"No . . . not really." Celia shook her head, a little surprised to find that it was true. It didn't hurt at all; it didn't even embarrass her to realize what a fool she'd made of herself. "I never *loved* Skye. I was enchanted by him, but it was a childish feeling, a daydream more in my heart than in reality. And it was over long ago." She caught his face in her hands, feeling the rough stubble of his whiskers beneath her fingertips. "I didn't know what love was until I met you."

Brandon drew her into his arms, holding her so close it hurt, though she would not have protested for the world. The shimmering redness at the window seemed to grow brighter; she could see it echoed in the deeper wine hues of his dressing gown. It was funny, she thought, the way everything had worked out, coming together at the end with almost perfect timing. Fate might be cruel sometimes, but it could be kind too.

"The man who approached you in Shanghai," she said, curious as she pulled back a little to look at him. "Was that Quarrie?"

He looked startled, then laughed. "None other. I'd forgotten that you had run into him. Poor devil, he must be pacing the floor now, stuck in Honolulu while the action is here. The best he could do was send a detailed cable telling me everything that had happened. I was half-frantic when I learned the risks you had run. Then, when I found out you were on the *White Lotus* . . ."

His voice caught, choking on thoughts too terrible to consider.

"My God, Celia, why did you do it? *Why*? You could have been killed. Surely you knew that it didn't matter. I'd have given up a dozen pirates—a thousand—before I'd risk losing you!"

Celia had *not* known, of course—how could she, without his telling her?—but she was tactful enough not to bring the subject up, though she made a mental note to mention it later, when the words could be said with teasing, not hurt. "But it *did* matter," she reminded him instead. "You were obsessed with the idea of stopping Teresa. I didn't know why, but I knew the obsession was there, and I was afraid to let her get away."

"Because you thought I'd go after her?" With a harsh laugh Brandon turned to the window, staring at distant cypresses, black against that red-orange background. "No, my love, I am not such a fool as all that. I had already told Quarrie he had one more month—that's why he went back to Hawaii in such a hurry—then I was going to call it quits. It's taken me a damnably long time, but I've finally got my priorities straight. What's important is not vengeance, not assuaging the guilt of the past. It's you and that little boy I haven't even seen yet."

Celia followed his gaze, realizing for the first time what it was, the deceptively pretty glow in the western sky: the *White Lotus* had been set afire, as Brandon had promised. All her evil, all her beauty, would soon be gone forever. "*You* might have been able to let go," she said softly, "but Teresa would not. If you didn't go after her, I knew she'd come after you. There was only one way to keep that from happening."

Brandon was silent for a moment, sensing the truth in what she said. Her bravery might have been foolish, but it was not misplaced. Then, slipping his arms around her waist, he drew her back against him as they both looked out the window.

"It's all right," he said. "It's all over."

"Is it?" The light from outside was softer now, that one swift blaze of intensity dying away. "I know you mean to reassure me, but I can't help wondering if she's still alive somewhere out there."

"I don't think so." His voice was thoughtful, as if considering. "It wouldn't matter if she were. The organization is broken now—there's nothing left, neither ships nor men . . . but no, I don't think so. The undertow was too strong. She couldn't have come to shore in the immediate area or she'd have been spotted . . . and she didn't have the strength to fight the tide for miles along the coast.''

"You think she was carried out to sea? Even so, if she knows how to float, she might still be alive.''

"Perhaps, but not for long. I sometimes had the feeling there was a bond between Teresa and her ship, so strong their identities seemed to merge. Fanciful perhaps, but I think she sensed it too. The *White Lotus* was Teresa, and she was the *Lotus*. I cannot imagine one existing without the other.''

"If she is alive then, floating somewhere at sea, she must see the fire. I wonder, does she know what it is?''

It was not truly a question, for even as she spoke, Celia sensed that the other woman would indeed have noted the flames and know what they signified. She could almost see her, alone in a vast expanse of water, feeling the last of her strength ebbing as she watched the destruction of her ship. It seemed a sad, lonely death, and she hoped, somehow, that Teresa had been spared . . . that it was she who had died first and not the *White Lotus*.

"You know, I can't help feeling sorry for her. I only saw her once, but I'll never forget the look in her eyes, all anger and jealousy . . . and pain.'' Teresa had loved Brandon too—a selfish, devouring passion perhaps, but love nonetheless—and it was hard to hate her for that. "I wish things could have been different.''

"As do I, my dearest. She had a gallant spirit sometimes— God knows, her life was hard enough. She never really had a chance. But her heart had turned to evil, and it's better that she is gone.''

Celia was conscious of the comfort of Brandon's arms, the feel of his chest, solid against her back as she looked one last time through the window. The fire was almost out now, she could barely see the last traces of it in the darkness, and she sensed that wherever Teresa had been before, she was there no longer. They were free of her at last.

But at what cost?

Tears shimmered on her lashes as images leapt unbidden into her heart. Young Freddie, lying so still on the deck . . . China Kwan, the wind whipping through his hair as he gave the cry that had saved her life. She knew, as she turned back, that Brandon would be distressed by her pain, but the hurt was too heavy to conceal.

"Oh, my love," she said softly, "I do wish China could be with us now."

Brandon looked surprised for a second, then lifted one brow. "What, *here*?" He looked down, taking in first his dressing gown, then the sheet that barely concealed her voluptuous form. "Right now?"

In spite of herself, Celia had to laugh. "No, not *now*—later, of course. Tomorrow at breakfast perhaps, over a pot of that vile coffee you both love so much."

"I do not think, my darling"—his fingers ran along the edge of the sheet, easing it down so her breasts were almost exposed—"that I will be ready to share you, even in the morning. Time enough to talk when we're all back in Hawaii. Then we can sit around and reminisce like old folks in their rockers on the porch of the royal hotel."

Reminisce? Celia looked into his face, strangely placid, with no signs of grief that she could see. What was he thinking? she wondered. Then suddenly she realized. He didn't know China was dead! How could he? The *Moonwind* had arrived some minutes later. He probably didn't even know the other man had been on board.

Her heart ached at the thought of having to tell him, and for just a second, cowardlike, she considered putting it off, waiting until later, when it would not mar the joy of their reunion. But there had been so many secrets between them already, so much that should have been said and wasn't, she could not bear to add to it now.

"Oh, Brandon," she murmured unhappily, "I was there.

I saw him go down. It was awful. He struck his head—so hard—against the railing.''

"Yes, I know," he said quite calmly. "He got a nasty gash, too.''

"A gash?" Celia stared at him, trying to grasp what he was saying. Had China's body been found, then? But, no—Brandon would hardly be so cool if it had.

"You mean he's . . . alive?''

"Of course he's alive. What did you think? Oh, my God . . ." He broke off, stunned. "You didn't think he'd been killed? Ah, sweet, it didn't occur to me . . . I never realized . . . No, no, of course that didn't happen. He got a bump on the head, that's all. It stunned him for a second, but he came to in time to board the *Lotus* with the rest of us. You know China. He insisted on taking part in the fight—even though the blood was streaming into his eyes—and a damned good thing, too! We needed every man we could get. I put him in charge of the *Moonwind* when they took the wounded to port, but instead of staying in the hospital with the others, he came back to report to me. It was he more than anyone I went to meet when I left you this afternoon.''

"Then he's all right?" Celia's knees felt so weak she could hardly stand.

"Fit as a fiddle." He grinned. "However fit a fiddle might be. He'll have a bit of a scar, but he says he doesn't mind. It'll give him a rakish look—like the ex-pirate he is.''

"Oh! Then we really *are* going to see him tomorrow. Not for breakfast maybe—''

"Or for lunch," Brandon broke in. "He should be halfway to San Francisco by this time. Christopher Lines has a steamer leaving for the islands tomorrow, and he'll be on it. He's already given us enough of his time, and damned unselfishly, too. He didn't want to tell you—you had enough on your mind as it was—but he had to put off his wedding to help you get to the Coast.''

"His wedding?" Celia gaped at him, then started to

giggle, feeling suddenly light-headed. Not only was China all right, but one of her fondest dreams was about to come true. "He's going to marry Kalani, then? Oh, Brandon, I always knew he would."

"Kalani?" Brandon shook his head teasingly. "What an incurable romantic you are. You want the perfect happy ending for everything—and perfect to you means matching up the people you love. No, my dear little girl, he is not going to marry Kalani. In fact, she's already promised to someone else, a planter's son, I hear, who is not only handsome and rich but also adores her to distraction. Can't you just see her sitting at a long banquet table with all those stuffy descendants of missionaries? Every man there is going to know about her past—and not a one of the women!"

Celia couldn't help laughing at the picture he had painted. "But if China isn't going to marry Kalani, then who?"

"Do you remember the Chinese girl Old Grandmother had picked out, the one she said was just right for him?" Brandon saw the look of shock on her face and was quick to cut her off. "No, he didn't agree to marry a woman he'd never seen just to honor his dead grandmother. They had a chance to speak first, and from what I understand, it was love at first sight. She's very beautiful, he told me—and quite smitten he sounded, too—and exactly what he's been looking for. As a matter of fact, he said she reminded him of you."

"Me?" Celia looked surprised.

"It seems she's a spirited little hussy. Refused to have her feet bound when she was young, and she wouldn't even consider a betrothal unless she could meet the man first. Now, does that or does it not sound like you? Poor devil—I told him so, but he wouldn't listen. If it's true, he's going to have his hands full." He leaned closer, whispering suggestively in her ear, "I think the wedding was consummated a bit in advance of the ceremony, so it's no wonder he's in a hurry to get back."

His voice had dropped low in his throat, offering a

husky invitation that was echoed in deep green eyes smoldering once again with longing. A slow, responsive warmth spread through Celia's body, and she was tempted to give in. But there were still questions unanswered, things she was curious to know.

"We've spoken so much of the past, and not at all about the future. What's going to happen now? You described the house you're going to build for me in Honolulu, but you didn't say a word about yourself. Are you going to be there with me? Or will you be off all the time on the *Moonwind*?"

"Not a chance." He put his arms around her, easing her away from the window. "I told you before—weren't you listening?—the *Moonwind* was sold to the Portuguese a long time ago. They've been patient enough, waiting for delivery. Now, don't protest—it belongs to them and I couldn't tie it up at some dock in Honolulu as a plaything for you even if I wanted to. Nor would that be any fitting end for a proud vessel. I like to fancy that the men who learn their craft on her will remember her past glories and boast in the taverns of Europe—as I once boasted myself—that they are crew to the finest ship in the world."

They had paused briefly beside the table. The lamplight, so stark before, now felt rich and warm as it caressed Celia's skin.

"Then you won't be sailing anymore?" she said.

"No, my days at sea are over, at least as captain, and I leave them without regret. Commanding a steamer requires skill, I admit, but the excitement, the challenge, is gone. I shall devote myself to the more mundane task of making Christopher Lines into the largest, most influential shipping firm in the world."

"Well, then, I'll have you to myself—for the nights at least." She glanced up, unable to resist adding impishly, "But I doubt I'll see much of you during the day, knowing the capacity you have for throwing yourself into your work."

"Not anymore." Brandon laughed easily. "I've learned

two lessons these past four years. First, that carefully chosen, well-paid managers can run the business with a minimum of supervision from me. And second . . .'' He paused, his eyes only half-teasing as he took hold of her hands, drawing them gently away from the sheet. ''Second, that life is precious only if you take time to share it with someone you love.''

The red glow had faded from the window; embers barely flickered now on the great stone hearth. Only the golden rays of the lamp softened the darkening shadows.

''In that case,'' she said, barely feeling the sheet as it slipped to the floor, ''I can think of a way to begin.''

35

The mists had cleared the harbor. The air was cool, the wind rising as the steamer *Aurelia Ann* chugged slowly out to sea, decks vibrating with the force of her engines. Celia stood beside Brandon at the rail, enjoying the feel of ocean breezes as they teased her hair, daring tidily arranged curls to try to stay in place. She had been a little surprised when he insisted that they go home by conventional means, for she had thought he would want to take the *Moonwind* to Portugal himself, continuing from there to Burma, where they were planning on visiting her parents. But he had proved unexpectedly protective.

"The *Aurelia Ann* is the sturdiest of the Christopher steamers," he had told her. "She's named after one of my maiden aunts—so you know she wouldn't dare founder!" He had gone on to remind her, with some validity, that a long sailing voyage would be hard on young Michael; adding, more fancifully, that since he was sure she was already carrying his second child, a girl this time—hadn't he been right before?—it would be hard on her too.

Celia, who did not feel the least bit pregnant, nonetheless humored him, sensing the loss he had felt at being left out, not only of Michael's birth, but of the long months of anticipation as well. It was, after all, a harmless pretense. If she wasn't pregnant now, she soon would be, for she and Brandon had both agreed that they wanted a little brother or sister for Michael as soon as possible.

Besides, she could hardly deny that the steamer was better for the boy. He had proved a good sailor on the *Moonwind*, but it wouldn't be fair, keeping him cooped up in a stuffy cabin for days or perhaps weeks on end. Nor could she carry him topside except in the calmest weather, for clipper decks had a way of swaying wildly when you least expected it.

"Maybe I ought to check on him," she said, eyeing the open stairway that led down to the owner's private suite. "I don't like the idea of leaving him this long. I want to make sure he's all right."

"You've left him exactly five minutes—and he's fine." Brandon laughed as he tightened his hold on her waist. "He's survived kidnapping and storms at sea and a diet of *poi*, for God's sake. Now, if he can only survive an overprotective mother . . ."

Celia tried to frown, but it was hard—his laughter was contagious. "I'm just not sure of that nurse we hired," she protested. "I'd feel better if Georgina were here." She had tried halfheartedly to persuade the woman to come with them, though hardly with any expectation of success. Not only had Georgina finally seen her son, she had actually met him—his adoptive parents had proved surprisingly sympathetic—and while he still didn't know who she was, he accepted her readily, seeming quite fond of this "old friend of his mother's."

"Georgina has her own life to live, sweet," Brandon reminded her. "The nurse is extremely competent—we must have interviewed a hundred applicants in the month we were in San Francisco. She's worked with babies all her life and comes highly recommended."

Celia surrendered to that irrefutable logic, sighing a little as she leaned against him, her head resting on his shoulder. Brandon was right: she should get pregnant again as soon as she could. With only one child to dote on, especially after what had happened, she was bound to be overprotective. She needed several children running around, getting underfoot all the time, so she couldn't hold on too tight and they'd have the freedom they needed to develop and grow.

They were still at the railing a short time later when the *Moonwind* glided past, making her last voyage under the blue-and-white flag of the Christopher Lines. She had never looked more stately. Her prow skimmed lightly out of the water; her tall masts soared to the skies, dwarfing the squat steamer that was already losing ground to her graceful speed. Word must have spread around the ship, for suddenly people seemed to be everywhere, emptying out of doorways and spilling onto the deck to watch as one of the last of the great clippers sailed by.

There was an almost holiday mood among the watchers. Murmurs of expectation rose on all sides as strangers turned to their neighbors, betting on the outcome of the impromptu race that had sprung up between the two vessels. A little boy pushed his way to the rail just beside Celia, and she looked down to see eyes as wide as saucers. His grandmother, who had spent her honeymoon on a tea clipper bound for China, knelt beside him, telling him, in the gentle tones one sometimes uses with a child, to look carefully at the ship. He would not see her likes again. She belonged to another era, a time that was passing and would be gone before he was a man.

Another era? Celia heard only a little of what the woman was saying, but those words caught her ear, and she sensed, sadly, that they were true. Another era, when the world had been larger, when travel time was measured in years and months, not weeks and days, and there had been seas left to explore, lands that civilized men still had not seen. The steamer was more practical; its graceless lines and steady pace were a stepping-stone to the future; but the clipper was romance, excitement, glamour—it was adventure—and she was glad she had had a chance to experience it, however briefly.

If the old ship sensed its era was over, nothing showed in the proud, almost haughty bearing that had been a hallmark of the clippers from the day they first took to the seas. The wind seemed to grow stronger, swelling canvas sails into great billowing clouds, and the flying jibs stretched taut—Celia could almost hear them straining as the *Moonwind* picked up speed, leaving the stodgy steamer in her wake. Tears misted her eyes, blurring the outlines for a moment, and in that shimmering light she almost thought she could see them, the men who had captained and sailed her through the decades. Old Levi Christopher, ranting like a tyrant on the quarterdeck . . . Brandon, his favorite grandson . . . China Kwan . . . Freddie, the cabin boy . . . all the men who had climbed her mainmast and swabbed her decks, who had repaired her spars and untangled her lines, seen her through the storms and the calms.

Only one of all those elusive figures was real. Celia smiled, brushing the tears back from her eyes as she caught a glimpse of Jorge, the "meanest man who ever sailed on the *Moonwind*"—and one of the bravest. He had earned the right to captain the ship on her last great voyage, and Brandon had given it with a will.

"It's all over, isn't it?" she said, not even aware that she had spoken the words aloud until she saw Brandon look down at her. His eyes were damp too, and she knew the moment was even more poignant for him, sweet as well as bitter. But for her sake he put his own feelings aside.

"The *Moonwind* is the past, my love," he told her gently. "Let it go."

Celia pretended to frown, deliberately teasing. "Only if you promise me one thing," she said.

"And what's that?"

"That you'll make the future even more exciting."

"Exciting?" He gave her a skeptical look. "Are you sure, after everything that's happened, it's really *excitement* you want?"

Celia smiled, nestling closer in his arms. "There's more than one kind of excitement, you know."

He bent his head, kissing her, and she let him, oblivious of the people who had begun to smile and whisper around them. The *Moonwind* drifted slowly into the distant horizon; they did not see her go, nor did they feel the need to say good-bye again. She was a part of them now, of their past, their memories—their love. They would carry her always in their hearts.

The ocean was empty, the winds had eased slightly when they turned away from the rail, and hand in hand, like new lovers, made their way to their stateroom.

ABOUT THE AUTHOR

Susannah Leigh was born in Minneapolis and raised in St. Paul, Minnesota. After graduating from the University of Minnesota she moved on to New York City, where she worked at a variety of jobs and appeared in many off-Broadway productions. She stayed in New York for twelve years and then left for a year of traveling to such spots as Morocco, Nepal, and Afghanistan.

Ms. Leigh is currently living in the San Bernardino Mountains of Southern California, where she spends her nonwriting time indulging her interests in reading, travel, history, and hiking in the woods.